What Reviewers Say About

≈

KIM BALDWIN

"*A riveting novel of suspense* seems to be a very overworked phrase. However, it is extremely apt when discussing Kim Baldwin's [*Hunter's Pursuit*]. An exciting page turner [features] Katarzyna Demetrious, a bounty hunter…with a million dollar price on her head. Look for this excellent novel of suspense…" – **R. Lynne Watson**, *MegaScene*

"*Force of Nature* is an exciting and substantial reading experience which will long remain with the reader. Likeable characters with plausible problems and concerns, imaginative settings, engrossing events, and a well-tailored writing style all contribute to an exceptional novel. Baldwin's characterization is acutely and meticulously circumscribed and expansive. It is indeed gratifying to see a new author attempt and succeed in expanding her literary technique and writing style. Kim Baldwin is an author who has achieved both." – **Arlene Germain**, reviewer for the *Lambda Book Report* and the *Midwest Book Review*

≈

ROSE BEECHAM

"…her characters seem fully capable of walking away from the particulars of whodunit and engaging the reader in other aspects of their lives." – *Lambda Book Report*

"When Jennifer Fulton writes mysteries, she writes them as Rose Beecham. And since Jennifer Fulton is a very fine writer, you might expect that Rose Beecham is a fine writer too. You're right…On the way to a remarkable, and thoroughly convincing climax, Beecham creates believable characters in compelling situations, with enough humor to provide effective counterpoint to the work of detecting." – *Bay Area Reporter*

❧

Ronica Black

"Black juggles the assorted elements of her first book with assured pacing and estimable panache…[including]…the relative depth—for genre fiction—of the central characters: Erin, the married-but-separated detective who comes to her lesbian senses; loner Patricia, the policewoman-mentor who finds herself falling for Erin; and sultry club owner Elizabeth, the sexually predatory suspect who discards women like Kleenex…until she meets Erin." – **Richard Labonte**, Book Marks, Q Syndicate, 2005

"Black's characterization is skillful, and the sexual chemistry surrounding the three major characters is palpable and definitely hot-hot-hot. If you're looking for a more traditional murder mystery, *In Too Deep* might not be entirely your cup of Earl. On the other hand, if you're looking for a solid read with ample amounts of eroticism and a red herring or two, you're sure to find *In Too Deep* a satisfying read." **Lynne Jamneck**, L-Word.com Literature

❧

Gun Brooke

"*Course of Action* is a romance…populated with a host of captivating and amiable characters. The glimpses into the lifestyles of the rich and beautiful people are rather like guilty pleasures.…[A] most satisfying and entertaining reading experience." – **Arlene Germain**, reviewer for the *Lambda Book Report* and the *Midwest Book Review*

"*Protector of the Realm* has it all; sabotage, corruption, erotic love and exhilarating space fights. Gun Brooke's second novel is forceful with a winning combination of solid characters and a brilliant plot." – **Kathi Isserman**, *JustAboutWrite*

❧

Jane Fletcher

"*The Walls of Westernfort* is not only a highly engaging and fast-paced adventure novel, it provides the reader with an interesting framework for examining the same questions of loyalty, faith, family and love that [the characters] must face." – **M. J. Lowe**, *Midwest Book Review*

Lee Lynch

"There's a heady sense of '60s back-to-the-land communal idealism and '70s woman-power feminism (with hints of lesbian separatism) to this spirited novel—even though it's set in contemporary rural Oregon. Partners Donny (she's black and blue-collar) and Chick (she's plus-sized and motherly) are both in their 50s, owners of the dyke-centric Natural Woman Foods store, a homey nexus for *Sweet Creek*'s expansive cast of characters....Lynch, with a dozen novels to her credit dating back to the early days of Naiad Press, has earned her stripes as a writerly elder; she was contributing stories to the lesbian magazine *The Ladder* four decades ago. But this latest is sublimely in tune with the times. "
– Richard Labonte, Book Marks, Q Syndicate, 2005

Radcly*f*fe

"...well-honed storytelling skills...solid prose and sure-handedness of the narrative..." – **Elizabeth Flynn**, *Lambda Book Report*

"...well-plotted...lovely romance...I couldn't turn the pages fast enough!" – **Ann Bannon**, author of *The Beebo Brinker Chronicles*

Ali Vali

"Rich in character portrayal, *The Devil Inside* by Ali Vali is an unusual, unpredictable, and thought-provoking love story that will have the reader questioning the definition of right and wrong long after she finishes the book....*The Devil Inside*'s strength is that it is unlike most romance novels. Nothing about the story and its characters is conventional. We do not know what the future holds for Emma and Cain, but Vali tempts us with every word so we want to find out. I am very much looking forward to the sequel *The Devil Unleashed*."
– **Kathi Isserman**, JustAboutWrite

Visit us at www.boldstrokesbooks.com

Lessons in Love:

Erotic Interludes 3

edited by

RADCLY*f*FE and
STACIA SEAMAN

2006

LESSONS IN LOVE: EROTIC INTERLUDES 3

ISBN 1-933110-39-2

This Trade Paperback Original Is Published By
Bold Strokes Books, Inc.,
New York, USA

First Printing May 2006

Credits
Editors: Radclyffe and Stacia Seaman
Production Design: Stacia Seaman
Cover Design By Sheri (GRAPHICARTIST2020@HOTMAIL.COM)

Contents

INTRODUCTION

Bold Strokes Books is pleased to offer another volume in the Erotic Interlude Series with selections that reflect the passion that is uniquely ours. The depth and diversity of our sexuality is as limitless as the creativity of the authors who write of it and the lesbians who celebrate it.

Expect to be surprised, amused, aroused, and most definitely satisfied!

Stacia Seaman and Radcly*f*fe 2006

TALKING DIRTY
MEGHAN O'BRIEN

"Teach me."

The voice was feminine, sweet as honey, with just a tinge of the throaty, early-morning purr that always made Kate weak in the knees. This, she knew, could be a worthy student. She looked up to where the cute brunette from her afternoon seminar waited in the doorway, a shy smile on her face.

"Rachael, right?" Kate zipped up the bag she'd just packed, eyeing the clock on the wall. "Actually, I was just getting ready to head home."

"Ten minutes," Rachael said. "Or give me five. Please." She took a step into the room, then folded her arms over her stomach. She looked adorably nervous. "It's taken all my nerve to even ask, but I thought what you were saying this morning was fascinating. I want to learn how to…you know…but I just—"

"Come in and close the door." Kate recognized the sheepish expression on Rachael's face, and it melted her resolve. Maybe getting home early wasn't *that* important. "But you're shy?"

"Not usually." Lifting a shoulder, Rachael conceded, "About this, maybe. A little." Another step closer. "I've just never done it before."

That voice sent a shiver through Kate's body, to the tips of her toes. "I find that hard to believe."

"Really?"

"Really," Kate murmured. Rachael's pleased little grin hit her right between the legs. "You've got the voice for it."

"I do?"

"Oh, yeah." Kate dropped her own voice an octave, letting every bit of the attraction she felt for the other woman color her words. *Lesson one.* "What is it you want to learn, exactly?"

Rachael closed the distance between them, but she kept her arms folded in front of her. It was as if she were protecting herself from the blatant heat Kate was sending her way. "Well, earlier you were saying…you know, about being able to get a woman almost all the way…there…just by talking."

"Yes."

"Teach me," Rachael said. "I'm sure I've never done that before. And to be honest, I can't imagine how that's even possible."

"Oh, it's possible." Kate curled a finger under the strap of Rachael's tank top, detecting just a subtle flinch when she made contact with the bare flesh. With a half smile, she tugged Rachael to a chair near the front of the room. "Why don't you sit down?"

Rachael gave her a dazed nod, then dropped into the empty seat. Her green eyes glittered, riveted to Kate's throat.

"Comfortable?" Kate suspected that this would be a rather easy lesson to teach.

"Very."

Kate sat in a chair close to Rachael's, and after a pause, placed a hand on each of Rachael's thighs. "Is this okay?" she asked as she gently parted Rachael's legs.

"Uh—"

"I noticed you the moment you walked into my seminar earlier, you know." Kate eased her own thighs between Rachael's spread ones, so that her knees nearly touched the denim-covered crotch. The jeans were soft, nicely worn, obviously loved. "These jeans look good on you, Rachael. I'm guessing you get noticed everywhere you go."

Lips parted soundlessly for a long moment. Rachael finally whispered, "Thank you."

"Is this the part where you're going to get shy?" Kate gave her a reassuring smile but kept both hands on her thighs. She stroked up and down, from knee to hip, and stared into her eyes. "There's no reason to be shy. We're just talking here, right?"

Rachael swallowed. "Right."

"Have you ever tried to talk dirty to your lover before?"

Rachael's face went pink. "I mean, you know…"

"Mmm, no, I don't. Why don't you tell me?"

"Well, I don't actually have a lover right now."

Oh, yes. This might be more fun than I thought. Kate grinned mischievously. "In the past. Tell me how you've talked to your lovers in the past."

"I might, uh… well, you know…tell her that her…pussy feels good or something."

"When you've got your fingers inside of her?" Kate slid one hand down to Rachael's inner thigh, feeling her tense. At Rachael's nod, she asked softly, "How about when you're licking her? What do you say then?"

"I don't really say anything," Rachael said, looking confused. "My mouth is, uh…busy."

Kate clicked her tongue, continuing her slow caresses on Rachael's thighs. "Missed opportunity. But what you really want to know right now is how to get a woman ready to come, ready to do just about anything, simply by talking to her. Am I correct?"

Rachael's nostrils flared as she exhaled raggedly, clearly fascinated by Kate's busy hands on her thighs. Her voice strained, she whispered, "Seems to me that you're doing a lot more than just talking."

"Point taken." Kate removed her hands and stood up.

Rachael's mouth dropped open. "But…I—"

Kate walked behind Rachael's chair, then bent down low so she could talk directly into her ear. Careful not to touch her again, she murmured, "The most important thing is to try and tap into what is going to turn your lover on. What gets her wet? What is it that she wants to hear?"

Rachael nodded, her fine, wispy hair brushing Kate's nose. Kate inhaled deeply, savoring her subtle fragrance, then exhaled with a quiet moan. "You smell good."

Rachael's throat worked at the compliment. "Thank you."

"Answer a question for me?"

Breathless silence, then a quiet, "Okay."

"Is this what you were thinking about when you were sitting in my seminar earlier? Coming back this evening and finding me alone in the room, asking me for a private lesson?" Kate moved her mouth from the right ear to the left, then inhaled again. "For a shy girl, this seems awfully calculated."

Rachael shook her head. "I just want to learn. I never know what to say, and I always feel so silly, and you seemed so confident about it all. I—"

"You like that. The confidence," Kate guessed. "You want to be able to make a woman wet like I can make you wet, don't you?"

Rachael said nothing.

"Your pussy *is* wet, isn't it, Rachael?" Kate moved her lips so close to Rachael's ear that they just barely skimmed over the lobe. "Sitting there on that chair facing away from me, it's killing you not to squirm around right now, isn't it? You're so fucking wet you can hardly stand it, but you aren't quite ready to let me know how dirty you are. Not yet, at least. Are you?"

"No."

Rachael's voice was so quiet, the denial was hardly convincing. The back of her neck was flushed a deep red, evidence of her embarrassment and arousal. Kate grinned triumphantly, flush with the power. *Almost too easy.* She'd barely even had to open her mouth, and Rachael was hers. Now it was a matter of waiting for her to admit it.

"You *will* tell me when your pussy is wet, won't you?" Kate breathed. She leaned in and, cheating a bit, kissed Rachael's earlobe. "You'll tell me when you're almost there, almost ready to beg for it, and all because I stood behind you and told you that I know exactly how badly you want to get fucked right now. Won't you, Rachael?"

"I—"

"So shy," Kate continued, thoroughly enjoying the tease, almost as much as she sensed her pupil was. "I'll bet you're not so shy when you're bent over a table, or the couch, panties around your ankles, your lover's fingers buried deep inside that wet pussy. Are you? Because that's how you like it, isn't it? You like someone to take control of you, don't you? You like being taken."

Rachael's chest heaved now, so hard that Kate could see it over her narrow shoulder. She could practically smell her arousal.

"Is that what you're hoping will happen right now?" Kate moved to the other ear again, brushing brunette hair aside so that she had an unobstructed view of its delicate shape. "Somewhere deep down inside, you're hoping that I'll just pull you out of this chair and lay you down on that table over there. You want my mouth on your pussy, don't you? You want my tongue inside of you. You want to come all over my face, because you've been dying all day, thinking about talking dirty. Talking dirty with me like a bad girl."

Rachael's hands were on her own knees, a white-knuckled death grip. She seemed almost beyond speech now, her whole body trembling.

Kate knew she was hers for the taking. Any way she wanted. *Shy girls are so much fun.*

"What do you say, Rachael? Would you like it if I took you over to that table right now? Would you resist? Or would you let me take off your panties and feel just how wet you are?"

Looking dazed, Rachael was silent.

"Rachael," Kate whispered. "Would you let me?"

Rachael jerked as if aware for the first time that an answer was required. That either the lesson was over, or it had just begun.

"I wouldn't resist." Rachael's voice was a bare whisper. She sounded scared to death, and thrilled beyond measure.

Triumphant, Kate pulled back. "So…learn anything?"

"What?" Rachael sounded as if she could barely breathe. "Huh?"

Kate walked around the chair and offered Rachael a hand. "Did I get you nice and ready to come?" She pulled Rachael to her feet, then caught her as she stumbled forward a few clumsy steps. Easing an arm around her shapely waist, Kate kissed the side of her neck. "Are you wet?"

When Rachael moaned low in her throat, Kate felt the vibration against her lips. "Why don't you find out for yourself?"

Kate smiled in satisfaction. "Very good. You're a fast learner."

"Good teacher," Rachael said, obviously having a little trouble forming complete sentences.

Despite the fact that she was doing a reasonable job keeping her cool, Kate could sympathize. Her knees felt like they were made of jelly. She couldn't remember the last time she'd been so turned on. Taking Rachael by the hand, she led her to the table at the front of the room. "All right. Now it's your turn."

Blinking rapidly, Rachael leaned against the table as if she might fall over were it not for its support. "My turn?"

"Talk to me."

"About…?"

"What do you want me to do to you?" Kate grinned wolfishly and closed the distance between them. "Don't be shy, Rachael. I already know that you want me to fuck you. Now I just want to hear it. You wanted to learn; I'm teaching you."

Raising determined eyes to Kate's face, Rachael took in a deep breath, then whispered, "I want you to fuck me, Kate. Please."

"How?"

Biting her lip, Rachael broke their eye contact to stare at the floor. "I want you to…uh…you know, like you said—"

"Tell me. Whatever you want, I'll do it. But I need to hear it from you."

Rachael looked as though she was gathering every bit of her courage before she finally spoke. "I want you to bend me over the table."

"Yes? Then what?"

"Then…take off my jeans."

Kate allowed her gaze to travel down the length of Rachael's thighs, admiring. "I can do that. Is that all?"

"And then I want you to push my panties to the side, and…"

"And?"

"Put two fingers inside of me."

Pleased that Rachael had asked for what she wanted, Kate wrapped both arms around her. "I'm going to make you feel so good," she murmured into Rachael's ear. "Now turn around."

Rachael hesitated. "Kiss me first."

There was more than a hint of vulnerability in that sweet voice. Kate looked into Rachael's face, so open. Then she captured her full, ripe lips in a soft, sensuous kiss. When she finally broke away, it was only because she simply couldn't breathe anymore. "Your mouth is perfection."

Rachael turned around without a word.

Kate took a deep, measured breath, struggling not to throw Rachael down across the table right then, tear down her jeans, jerk her panties aside, and fuck her hard and fast. Her clit hurt, she wanted her so bad. But this was too good, too exciting. She wanted to make it last. Most of all, she wanted to make it good for Rachael.

Easing her arms around Rachael's waist, Kate whispered, "You're a good kisser."

"So are you."

Kate found the button on Rachael's jeans and had them unzipped within seconds. "I want you."

"Then take me."

"You seem a little less shy all of a sudden." Grinning, Kate worked the jeans down Rachael's shapely legs.

"In this position, I think I have to be." Rachael stepped out of her jeans, then kicked them aside.

Kate ran admiring fingers over light yellow panties. "Pretty." She dipped a finger inside, tracing a path over the crease of Rachael's inner thigh, tickling the soft hairs beneath. "I like these."

"I was hoping you would."

Kate grasped Rachael's tank top. "Lift your arms." When Rachael obeyed, Kate pulled it over her head, leaving her in a bra that matched her panties. "Oh, very nice."

"The door locks automatically, right?"

"Don't worry. Nobody's coming in here."

"Then hurry up and fuck me already. I'm so horny I can hardly stand it."

"That's what I like to hear." Kate pressed down on Rachael's shoulder blades until she was bent over the edge of the table. Completely at her mercy. Then she yanked those yellow panties to the side, exposing dark, kinky hair and wet, pink flesh. Exhaling, she played her fingers over her slick pussy.

Rachael shuddered and thrust her pussy higher into the air.

"You're beautiful," Kate breathed. She ran her finger up and down over Rachael's labia, her hard clit, then circled her entrance. She drew it out, teasing her as long as she possibly could, until Rachael was shaking and gasping and grinding her pussy against Kate's hand.

"Please," Rachael choked. "Please, fuck me. I need you. Now."

Kate pushed two fingers inside, torturously slow, savoring every inch of the tight heat that enveloped her. She moaned out loud as she reached the first knuckle, the second, until she could get no deeper.

"How does that feel?" Kate whispered. She wasn't going to let Rachael stop talking now, just when it was getting really interesting. Pulling out slowly, then thrusting in again, she wrenched a loud groan from her companion. "Does that feel good?"

"Oh my God." Rachael's words were muffled against her arm, where she rested her head. She was the picture of perfect surrender, bent over the table in only her bra and panties, Kate's fingers buried deep. "So good. Fuck me harder."

Kate complied, driving into Rachael with powerful strokes, nostrils flaring with arousal. She needed to make Rachael come, needed to feel it on her hand. She couldn't remember ever needing anything so badly.

"Yes," Rachael moaned. "Fuck it, baby. Fuck that tight pussy."

Far from thinking that stopping was even an option, Kate reached around and shoved her other hand down the front of Rachael's panties. She found her swollen clit with her fingers, rubbing fast circles.

To hell with drawing it out. She wanted to see if she could make Rachael scream.

For the next few minutes, neither of them spoke. The only sounds in the room were Rachael's soft grunts and the wet, rhythmic pumping of Kate's fingers in her pussy.

"You're going to make me come," Rachael suddenly cried out. Her whole body stiffened beneath Kate's hands. "Oh God, I'm gonna—"

She may have been shy about talking, but Rachael came without inhibition. She threw her head back and moaned loudly, so loudly that Kate was slightly concerned that someone else in the building might hear. Her concern wasn't strong enough to convince her to try and silence that beautiful sound.

"That's right, baby," Kate encouraged as Rachael continued to mewl in pleasure, a string of incoherent words. "Come on my hand. You feel so fucking good on my fingers, Rachael. You're so tight, so hot." She never stopped thrusting, determined to get every last bit of pleasure from her partner. "I've never fucked a pussy that felt so good before."

Rachael got louder, if that were even possible, until finally her cries cut off with a sudden, sharp gasp. She went completely still, then collapsed, boneless, onto the table.

"Stop," Rachael whispered. "You're gonna kill me. Stop, please."

With a grin, Kate withdrew her hand from the front of Rachael's panties. Loath to leave her so soon, she kept her other fingers inside.

"That was incredible," Kate said. "You felt incredible."

Rachael pushed up from the table and looked back over her shoulder. Her eyes were glazed, full of lazy pleasure. "*You're* incredible."

Withdrawing, Kate helped Rachael straighten, then turned her around.

"So did you learn anything?" Kate asked again, holding her in a surprisingly comfortable embrace.

With a grin full of newfound confidence, Rachael reversed their positions. She pinned Kate against the table and dropped her hands to the front of Kate's pants. "This lesson isn't over. Not by a long shot."

PUBLIC PET
CYNTHIA RAYNE

"Come on, pretty. It's time to go out," Lisa purred. "You've been such a good pet by putting all of our things away. Your reward is a walk." She unfurled the leather leash she used to lead me. It snapped open easily. "Come here."

I felt a rush of illicit pleasure at her words. She was actually going to take me outside the comfortable confines of our hotel room and show me off. Lisa and I had played bondage games in the privacy of our own apartment plenty of times, but this was the first time we'd do so in public. I kept my head bowed, my mouth shut, and my legs apart as instructed. When doing a scene, Mistress Lisa was very strict. Deliciously so.

I still couldn't believe I was doing this. I'd had fevered fantasies for ages about being put on display, but I was really going to do it. I trusted Lisa completely and I'd confessed this to her when we first got together. We both worked at a law firm in Chicago and she was my boss. We'd fallen into a relationship quite by accident. She told me she could see my desire to submit to her in my eyes. When I was late for a meeting once, she'd taken me in my office and berated me for my negligence. I was rushing to explain myself when she smacked my ass with a file folder. The anger had quickly elevated to sexual arousal. Lisa had watched with a knowing expression as my nipples peaked under my silk shirt and my breathing grew a bit shallow. We've been together ever since.

She fisted a hand in the short dark curls that framed my face. "Where is your head tonight, pet? Take off your shirt. I want to see my property."

I immediately complied. I stripped off the black tank top and neatly folded it before I placed it on the bed. I was left in my black bra and the leather miniskirt that my Mistress favored. She slowly walked a circle around me. It was a game we played often. She liked to make me nervous, but tonight I was in awe of her.

She was dressed in a pair of black leather pants and a red silk shirt. Mistress Lisa was over six feet tall and very thin with long golden blond hair that she kept in a ponytail. Her breasts were barely a mouthful, and I loved to suck them. The hair between her legs was bushy. She smelled musky and sweet at the same time. Mistress reached over and undid the catch on my bra. I knew better than to try to stop it. It fell to the floor.

She pinched my left nipple, which was already stiff and upright. "Did you know that it's legal for women to go topless in public in Canada?" She grabbed a breast in each hand, roughly squeezing them.

I shivered. "No, Mistress Lisa." I only spoke when asked a direct question.

"It is. And tonight, I'm going to take you out, just like this. I want everyone to see these ripe breasts. But first," she said, slapping my right breast just slightly, "I need to get them ready." She grinned as she shoved a hand in her pocket and pulled out a long silver nipple chain with alligator clips. Mistress Lisa had gotten me accustomed to them. She always liked my nipples clamped and she'd stretched them daily. She pulled my right nipple out and clamped it, then did the same with the left.

I let out a small yelp. There was some pain involved, but not enough to really hurt. It was exciting more than anything else. I liked how sensitive the clamps made my breasts.

"There you go, pet." She smacked both breasts slightly, enjoying the pretty shade of crimson they turned as they bounced. She slid her hand down my side and over my hips. "And we can't let your pretty pussy go outside all covered up." She pulled my panties down my legs and reached up between them to smack my pussy lips. "Pets should always be accessible. Don't you agree?"

"Yes, Mistress."

"Good girl. What are pets for?"

"Fucking, Mistress." The instant I said it, I knew it was true. It's what I had always dreamed of, and Mistress Lisa was the best there was.

"That's right. You are such a good girl." She pulled me close to her and claimed my mouth. She kissed voraciously, as if she were trying to fuck me with her tongue and lips. When I was breathless, she pulled away. "Now, let's put your collar on." She took it out of her back pocket and affixed it tightly to my neck. It had a large O-ring in the front that she snapped the leash on. "Remember the rules, pet. Others may look, but no one touches you without my permission. You may only speak when I ask you a question. Pets are for fucking. Not talking. Understand?"

"Yes, Mistress."

"Bend over and show me that sweet ass of yours."

I obeyed, bracing my hands on my legs and thrusting my behind in the air. She lovingly caressed the smooth white flesh before she brought her hand down sharply. "How does that feel?"

"Good," I moaned.

She smiled with satisfaction as she tugged the leash and I followed behind her. I was nervous and so excited about being seen by others like this. She pulled me down the hallway and into the elevator. It was empty. I wasn't sure if I was relieved or disappointed. Then she dragged me past the front desk of the hotel. The night manager was on duty and his eyes nearly bugged out of his head.

Mistress Lisa decided to have a little fun at his expense. She pulled me along with her to the desk. "My pet and I need more towels in our room." Lisa played with my right breast, making it jiggle in her palm. "We shower after I fuck her," she explained. " So we shower a lot." Her smile was wolfish.

"Yes, miss," the manager said, eyes straying to my breast as Lisa's talented hand manipulated it, enhancing the pleasure. It was so taut because of the tightly clamped nipple. I was having trouble not making a sound.

"Thank you," Mistress Lisa said, pulling me along behind her. "Come on, pet." She'd found a club near where we were staying called the Velvet Dog. It wasn't quite a fetish club, but it was fetish friendly. It catered to those people who'd had vanilla sex all of their lives and were too afraid to try something really different. Those who were in the lifestyle were welcome to scene in the club, as long as they let people watch.

Mistress Lisa had to give a password to the doorman but we were let in without a hassle. Inside, the lights were lowered; the windows were draped with long black velvet curtains. There were candelabras on every table. The music was low and throbbing, the melodies of sex. There were several people scening throughout the room. It smelled of sex. Middle-aged couples sat on long comfortable benches, waiting for someone exciting to join them. Lisa thrived in an environment like this. She was a sleek, predatory cat in a room filled with dozy mice.

She picked a couple in their late thirties to sit with. The man had been avidly watching us as we entered the room. What is it with men and lesbians? The woman looked nervous, but her eyes kept darting toward us with a hint of excitement.

"Mind if we join you?" Mistress asked.

They both nodded and made room for us. "You needn't scoot over so far. My pet won't be sitting with us." She turned her attention to me. "Why is that?"

"Because I should be on the floor at Mistress's feet."

"And why is that?"

"Because pets don't have furniture privileges, Mistress."

Lisa sat down and pushed the table away from everyone so they could view me between her legs. "My name is Mistress Lisa and this is my little pet. What are your names?"

"Jane and Scott," the man answered. It was so obvious that they were fake names. "How long...how long has she been your pet?" He had a big boner in his pants. Disgusting.

She pulled at the chain on my breasts and I cried out. "A few weeks now. She's a good little pet pussy that knows her place. In fact," Mistress said, eyeing the prim and proper wife's white skirt and matching sweater set, "why don't you ask this nice lady if she'd like a little head from you, pet?"

Jane's eyes widened. "Oh, uh, thank you, but that won't be necessary."

I was turned on by the idea of servicing a stranger. It was another first. I was already dripping wet, just feeling the couple's eyes on me was so terribly exciting. I hoped I could get through my performance without embarrassing myself. I crawled to Jane on all fours and rested my head in her lap. "May I please pleasure you?"

"You should let her, Jane. My little pet licks pussy three times a day, sometimes more. She'll give you the best head you've ever got." There were other folks in the club licking and sucking each other. Nudity wasn't something that was prohibited. "Come on, Jane. What do you say?"

Her husband nudged her. "It's okay, honey."

Jane blushed. "Well, I guess it would be all right."

I smiled and very deliberately licked my lips. I heard Mistress snort with laughter behind me. If I'd done it to her, she would have smacked my ass. I pulled up Jane's virginal white skirt and parted her thighs. She wore plain cotton underwear.

"Let me see," Scott said, pushing the skirt back, exposing his wife further.

I pulled the panties down and put my hands on her thighs to push them apart. Then I gently pulled her ass forward so that she was wide open to me. She was beautiful, angelic blond hair and white cream cheese thighs. With a sigh, I bent my mouth to her. I lapped at her like it was my job. The small little berry of a clit, I took in my mouth and sucked. She tasted so sweet, almost innocent. She shouted and writhed against me like a wild thing. I bet her husband did a few obligatory tongue strokes and shoved his dick in her. Not me. I was all tongue, all the time. I couldn't get enough. I licked her to completion, savoring the sweetness of her juices on my mouth and cheeks. I made a big show of wiping her juices from my face and licking my hands clean, like a cat.

Jane was undone. Her thighs were open, her face was flushed, and she looked a little dazed. "So good," she whispered quietly. She patted my head.

"Make her do me," the husband ordered, going for the zipper on his pants. "Tell her to suck my cock."

"Sorry, my pet doesn't do pricks. She's strictly for pussy."

Scott looked like he was about to get angry, but Mistress Lisa glared at him. "Can I watch you fuck her?"

"Now, that, I'll happily do." Mistress Lisa snapped her fingers. "Take off your skirt and get on the table, pet. Spread yourself like a good girl."

I stood up, feeling the couple's eyes on me as well as some onlookers on the bar. This was my moment. I made a big show of stripping off my skirt and running my hands over the exposed skin. Then I scrambled up on the table, eager for her attention. I lay down on the table with my legs spread. Mistress Lisa took the candelabra from the tabletop and blew out the candles. The wisps of smoke blew over me. She tipped her hand and the heated wax streaked against my tits and my belly. "Oh, how careless of me."

I let out a little scream. The wax burned at first, but then it soothed me, forming a warm wall around my flesh. Mistress Lisa began to peel the wax away from my belly, taking the fine little hairs with it. "Do you want one of those candles inside that hungry little pussy of yours?"

"Yes, Mistress."

"What did you say?"

"Yes, Mistress!" She shoved a long, white candle up inside of me. It was warm and thick, but what I really wanted was Lisa's fingers inside of me. I knew that it wouldn't happen until I begged for it at home. "Oh! Yes!"

She found my clit with her expert finger. "Tell me who you worship, pet."

"Mistress Lisa!"

"Whose pussy do you crave?"

"Yours, Mistress!"

"Come now!"

Later when we walked home, Mistress Lisa yanked my chain. "Did you enjoy yourself?"

"Yes, Mistress." I was sleepy and sated. I never knew my fantasy would be so satifisying.

"Such a good pet." She slapped my ass. "I like this exhibitionist side of you. We may have to move to Canada. I like the idea that others can see you but can't touch."

"Me, too."

"We'd have to lobby for complete nudity, though. Your pussy is the best part."

"Thank you, Mistress."

"You will. As soon as we get home. I'm going to make you lick me until you beg me to stop."

"I never will, Mistress. I never will."

TRANSFORMING STONE
KAREN PERRY

Damn it!" Tanner Stone cursed as her right bicep bulged. Her knuckles were white. Beads of sweat rolled into her eyes and she blinked rapidly to ease the burning sting, never losing concentration on the barbell clutched in her grip.

Biting her lip in pain, she felt a wave of disgust at how difficult it was to manage the small, eight-pound weight. She should have been happy that she could move her arm at all; the damn thing had practically been severed.

She had been going sixty-two miles an hour, ecstatic with 1200cc's of raw power between her thighs. Her Ninja 2X-10R sport bike felt as if it were an extension of her body, but she had no control over either when suddenly, without warning, a hulking piece of construction machinery careened into her path. The last thing she remembered was screaming for mercy as both she and the bike slid under the biting tread of the machine.

Life as Tanner knew it, as she had carefully built and arranged it, disappeared in one brutal, life-shattering moment. It was only because of the talented hands of a gifted surgeon that she still had her trembling arm at all. Surgery had saved her limb, but healing had been excruciating. She had lain in the hospital for months on end, just cognizant enough to realize that she should not have survived at all.

Now, the problem—the thing that had crawled into her gut and gnawed at her—was that her new limitations conflicted horribly with the streak of butch ego that ran deeply through her core. Weakness had no place in her former life. Before the accident, she had been tough, almost invincible. Her body had been honed to perfection. No one messed with her, and the ladies were hers to do with as she pleased. Now there were still times she thought that death would find her.

The only person who stood in the Grim Reaper's path, defiantly telling him to fuck off, was Robbie Marks. As rebelliously butch as Tanner, Robbie had initially been Tanner's competition. Like two snarling dogs, they had traded threats and jibes, defending what they felt were rightfully theirs—the city's finest femmes. Their mutual love of motorcycles finally inspired a truce.

Robbie had been there the night of the accident, a few paces back on her own Kawasaki crotch rocket. She had watched helplessly as Tanner almost died, unable to do a damn thing but make a phone call. In the hospital, other friends disappeared, but Robbie stayed. She was the one who fed Tanner tiny ice chips and held a straw to her parched, cracked lips. Robbie was the one who knew that she got cold easily and kept the blankets pulled warmly around her.

Even when closest to death, Tanner had wanted to reject her help. It had been the pain—mind-boggling, soul-shredding pain—that forced her to cling to Robbie instead, but the helplessness was just as excruciating as her injuries.

As a fellow butch, Robbie had understood that internal conflict. Still, one week before Tanner's hospital discharge, Robbie announced, "I'm moving in with you. You're going to need me."

"Fuck you! I don't need anybody," Tanner snapped. Her right arm and both legs were in casts but she'd be damned before she let anyone play nursemaid.

"And just who in the hell is going to take care of you? Are you going to let them send you to one of those old geezer places, a nursing home where all the chicks' tits hang below their belt lines? You can't go home by yourself."

Tanner had been living with the steady drip of morphine in her veins and the fear of death in the pit of her stomach ever since she regained consciousness. She had learned the hard way that no one was indestructible; not even a strong, butch dyke. Robbie was the only person whom she had ever allowed to get close, and she knew she needed her. If it made her look like a "weak-kneed femme," so be it. She had relented. "I'd like for you to move in. I'll pay you, of course, with the money from the insurance settlement."

Refocusing on the dumbbell in her hand, Tanner forced her arm to obey her command one final time before allowing the barbell to drop to the floor. It clanged loudly against another weight, but she didn't care. All that mattered was letting go of the heavy burden.

Standing slowly, she peeled off her damp T-shirt, grateful for the rush of cool air on her moist skin. Catching a glimpse of herself in the bedroom mirror, she stared as she often did, bewildered by the changes. Her black hair, formerly cut to the point of bristly spikes, had not been trimmed in well over a year and now hung softly onto her shoulders. She had also gained weight, inertia and Robbie's cooking replacing hard-packed muscles with softer flesh. She could easily fool herself into believing that the person in the mirror was a stranger, but the ugly, vicious scar that ran across her stomach and chest was her reality check. Although the wound was healed, it was still angry and vividly red. Its path slithered across her body, wrapping up and around a breast that she had nearly lost. Robbie suggested having a snake tattooed along its path, and the idea did have a certain appeal.

She glanced at the clock with trepidation. In her former life, she had practically lived in bars. Now that she was stronger, Robbie was convinced that she needed to "get back in the saddle." Tonight would be their third outing in as many weeks, but she simply could not get excited. With a sigh, she looked at the outfit Robbie had laid out for her—motorcycle boots, ragged jeans, and a black tee. It was the uniform of her prior life, but after spending months in nothing but hospital gowns and sweats, she dreaded wearing them.

The worst part was what lay in the center—a brand new soft leather harness that sported an impressive nine-inch cock. A year ago she could not have imagined leaving the house without a dick between her thighs, but that had changed. Ignoring the harness, Tanner dressed.

At the bar, she sat with one foot tucked upon the railing of her bar stool, doing her best to look comfortable in a place that no longer held her interest. By one a.m., her only wish was to go home. She was tired of ignoring the unabashed, hungry stares of women she didn't want.

Wanting to rush Robbie along, she said, "You should pick out what you want to play with tonight, so we can go home."

Robbie brushed a lock of blond hair from her eyes. "Don't you mean *whom*, not *what*? Damn, Tanner! You're talking about these lovely women like they're objects, not people."

Laughing uncomfortably, Tanner punched Robbie's arm. "Yeah, right! Since you're so concerned about these women's individuality, what was the name of the woman who spent last Friday night in your bed? Our walls are thin. I heard you call her three different names."

Wide-eyed in disbelief, Robbie said, "No, I didn't!"

Tanner grinned triumphantly. "Yes, you did. So tell me, was it Becky, Joan, or Gretchen?"

Robbie cocked her head, deep in concentration before her nose crinkled. "Oh, hell! I can't remember, but at least I was with someone. You act like you don't care if you go home alone or not."

Tanner leaned back against the bar, feeling the sharp edge of the counter cut into the tender flesh of her back. She didn't bother pulling away to ease the pinch. She had become accustomed to pain. It reminded her that she was alive. So much of her adult life had been about sex. She had used it to feel powerful and in control, never letting a woman linger in her bed for too long. It surprised her, but now she realized that it had all been hollow, an empty shell in comparison to the life she had unexpectedly built with Robbie. She liked being with her, hanging out at home watching television or doing nothing at all. It was enough.

"I know you think you know best, and I hate to disappoint you," Tanner said, "but the fact is, I really don't care."

"How can you live without sex? I like it too much to give it up."

"That bulldozer must have crushed my libido, too. I don't feel a thing. Just pick somebody and let's go home."

Robbie eyed her suspiciously, but indicated a woman leaning against the wall by the dance floor. "What do you think about her?"

Tanner scowled. "I'll bet you ten bucks that your girl is an M to F. I think *she* is actually a *he*."

"You're out of your mind! Look at her hands. They're too small to be a man's. Besides, she doesn't have an Adam's apple!"

Pulling out a ten-dollar bill, Tanner waved it in front of Robbie's nose. "That, my friend, is a chick with a dick. Go start a conversation and look for signs of razor stubble. Check out the voice, too. A man can hide his weenie. He can duct tape it down, but the voice never lies."

Perplexed, Robbie stared at the woman.

Tanner laughed. The look on Robbie's face was priceless, marred with self-doubt.

Waving the bill at Robbie again, she said, "Check her out. If I'm wrong, you get the money and the woman." Pausing as if a new thought had struck her, she softly added, "If I'm right, you go home with me."

"With you? I'm afraid that you can't give me what I need, buddy."

Tanner drew in a deep breath. She really didn't want anyone else to go home with them. Lowering her head, her gaze on the floor, she spoke, feeling as if the words were coming from a foreign place deep inside herself. "And just what exactly would that be?"

Robbie cast a leering stare up and down Tanner's body. "Are you flirting with me?"

As Robbie's appraising eyes scanned her body, Tanner felt her pulse increase. She flushed with embarrassment as she realized that she was feeling desire for the first time since her crash. It was almost overwhelming.

"No, I'm not...flirting, that is. I wasn't meaning that." Her denial was weak, the words so poorly spoken that she didn't even convince herself.

Robbie cocked her head sideways and moved to fill the gap between them. Pushing soft strands of Tanner's hair behind her ear, she said in a slow drawl, "I think you are, and I'll willingly admit that it turns me on. If I had to pick between you and any other woman in this bar, it would be no contest."

Tanner swayed as Robbie bit her earlobe.

Robbie whispered, "If you don't want this, tell me right now. We'll forget that it ever happened."

Stunned, Tanner couldn't speak. Her knees buckled when Robbie spoke into her ear, filling it with hot, moist air. Her skin felt warm, her breath shallow. She knew that Robbie was a demanding lover, that she would not go to bed with any woman who refused to let her use her equipment, but would she expect it with her? Granted, Tanner could admit that she was not the hard butch that she used to be, but that didn't mean she was ready to be a femme bottom either. Still, the idea of sleeping with Robbie took her breath away. She couldn't say no.

Robbie took Tanner's hand. Leading her out of the bar, she murmured, "Don't think so hard, Tanner. I would never do anything that you don't want."

Once home, Tanner mumbled, "I can't stop shaking," as Robbie reached for the fly of her jeans.

Robbie directed Tanner's hand to the bedpost. "Here, hold this." She hugged Tanner and whispered, "You'll be okay. I promise. It's just been too long. You've needed this for so long."

Robbie's hands, sure and soft, roamed under the loose band of Tanner's pants until the jeans fell to the floor. She covered Tanner's face with nibbling kisses, avoiding her lips. With one hand clinging to the post, Tanner placed her other on Robbie's hips, riveted by the delicate touches. This softness was not what she expected, but it was exactly what she needed. Robbie had taken care of her for so long. It took this act, dropping her last vestige of withholding from Robbie, for Tanner to realize that she loved her.

The trembling began anew. She groaned loudly as Robbie cupped her ass and pulled her close. Their hips melded and Tanner felt the nudging of Robbie's dildo between her thighs. A strong, deep pulse beat in the wetness between her legs. Letting go of the bedpost, she took Robbie's face in her hands. Clutching at her, she demanded, "Kiss me, Rob. I need you to kiss me."

When Robbie's tongue filled her mouth, Tanner tried to suck it deeper into herself. She was starving. She would have gone on kissing her forever but Robbie pulled away and laid her gently upon the bed, as tenderly as when she brought Tanner home from the hospital.

Tanner nearly cried out when Robbie took her in her strong, protective arms. It had been an extremely long time since she had felt safe, and at that moment, she did not give a damn what anyone might think of her. When Robbie began stroking her nipples through her shirt, she gasped loudly and gripped the sheet into her fists. She could not stop the slow, gyrating motions that propelled her hips into Robbie's thigh, but her breath froze in her throat when Robbie's hand slid under the hem of her shirt. Robbie had bandaged her wounds for months, but this was different. Tanner felt vulnerable and weak.

Holding Tanner's cheek in her palm, Robbie looked into her eyes. "Trust me, baby. Your scar is beautiful to me. I wouldn't be here with you, like this, if you didn't have it. It's as much a part of me now as it is you."

Robbie kissed her again, so piercingly that Tanner felt safe once more. She guided Robbie's hand under her shirt, her back arching in pleasure as bare fingers settled on her breast. When she could stand it no longer, she pulled her shirt free and tugged it off.

Robbie's eyes soaked her in, a look of awe on her face as she began tracing the jagged scar with her fingertips. Her lips soon followed. She drew them slowly along the line from Tanner's hip, over her stomach, her chest, and around her breast. Tanner could only clasp the back of Robbie's head, threading her fingers into the soft blond hair as Robbie completed this ritual over and over. It was so loving that Tanner felt as if her bones, once crushed, had now melted. When Robbie latched onto her nipple and began twirling it with her tongue, Tanner felt the telltale quiverings of a pending orgasm and wetness oozed from her. Wanting to feel skin, she grasped Robbie's shirt. "Take this off!"

Sliding off the bed, Robbie quickly pulled her shirt free and dropped it to the floor. Her fingers were clumsy as she tried to unhook her big silver belt buckle. When it finally came free, she pushed her jeans off her hips, along with her boxers. She paused, and they both stared down at eight inches of hot pink latex that protruded from Robbie's hips like a steel rod.

"I'll take it off," Robbie said quietly.

Humbled by Robbie's willingness to lay aside the thing that represented her most sexual self, Tanner knew that she could never ask that of her. She felt naked, hungry, because of Robbie's absence. She lifted a hand, beckoning her. "Leave it on."

Robbie crawled to Tanner's side, capturing her mouth in a kiss as she ran a hand down her body. When she reached the band of boxer shorts, she pushed them down as Tanner lifted. Once they were free, she traced her fingers up inner thighs that opened for her. With a deep moan, she slid her fingers into the wet depths. Tanner called out her name and sank fingernails into the flesh of her back.

Robbie circled Tanner's hard clit over and over, causing bright bursts of light to appear behind Tanner's eyelids every time contact was made. Lifting her hips, she arched against those hands, trying to bury them deeply inside herself. Robbie shifted to kneel between her legs but didn't attempt to penetrate her. She claimed Tanner's nipple with her hot mouth before slipping her hand back between their bodies.

Tanner had feared that her body's ability to feel passion had been crushed by her death-defying crash into unbending steel, but it burst back to life under Robbie's hands. As her orgasm claimed her, she heaved upward, her body frozen until spasms, deep tremors that seemed to originate within her heart, wracked her body.

Gasping for breath, she pulled Robbie up, needing to kiss her again. She felt a new shock wave surge through her as Robbie's cock rubbed against her cunt. Her orgasm had not even fully subsided but she wanted Robbie inside of her. She wanted to give herself to Robbie, to hold nothing back. When she felt the tip of the cock slide inside her folds, she frantically clutched her lover's shoulders. She knew that Robbie was waiting for her to take only what she wanted, so she wrapped her legs around Robbie's hips, curling her calf muscles to propel Robbie forward. The movement forced Robbie into her depths. They both moaned and shuddered at the joining.

Slowly, sensually, Robbie began to rock and the pace built as Tanner lifted to meet her stroke for stroke. As Tanner's orgasm approached, she sank her heels tighter into Robbie's ass, impaling herself even farther onto the shaft as she screamed, "Oh God, Robbie! I love you so fucking much!"

Robbie whirled over onto her back, bringing Tanner upon her. In the dim light of the room, she once again took Tanner's face in her hands and softly kissed Tanner's trembling lips. "I love you too, baby."

Tanner could not stop a ragged sob when Robbie slid out from under her, separating them, leaving her feeling empty. Instead of pulling away, Robbie gripped Tanner's hand.

"I'm not going anywhere. Help me," Robbie said as she stood by the bed, unbuckling her harness. When it came free, she held it out to Tanner. "Put it on."

Amazed, Tanner stared at Robbie. fresh tears flowing, as she comprehended that Robbie was making herself as vulnerable and open as was humanly possible. She was offering to give Tanner everything, just as Tanner had done. Mutely, Tanner did as she was told while Robbie helped buckle the harness onto her hips. She felt like an invalid child instead of an experienced dyke who used to wear a strap-on to the 7-Eleven just because she felt naked without it. Once it was in place, Robbie lay back on the bed with her knees raised. When Tanner came between them, it was Robbie who was quivering with nervousness.

Tanner felt as if she were kneeling in front of an altar. This woman, this tough but sensitive dyke, had brought her back to life. Robbie had loved her the way no one else had, and she was everything Tanner wanted. Reverently, Tanner caressed Robbie's legs, allowing only her fingertips to glide along the path from toes up to the softer flesh of inner thighs. Robbie's eyes were glazed with lust as she began dancing against Tanner's moving hands. Tanner knelt even more prayerfully and sank her mouth onto the wetness of Robbie's sex. Robbie guided her with her hands as Tanner explored, drinking the rich nectar until Robbie came, contracting and pulsating around her tongue.

Not willing to relinquish the pleasure, Tanner stayed away from Robbie's sharply sensitive clit but continued to lick her, tasting her. While Robbie softly stroked her hair, Tanner slid her hands under

Robbie's hips and lifted her tighter against her mouth. She slowly brought her passion forth, letting the next wave of desire build. Rising, she lay upon Robbie, capturing her mouth in a fevered kiss. Then, taking Robbie's hands in her own, she interlaced their fingers. She whispered softly, "I want to fuck you."

Robbie tensed but, her eyes locked on Tanner, reached between them and guided the head of cock to the mouth of her cunt. "Go slow. I've never let this happen before."

Tanner already knew that. They had talked about the need to be in control many, many times. As she slowly pushed forward, she prayed that Robbie would feel the same sense of rightness that she had felt when Robbie filled her. Clinging to Robbie's hands while she sank inside, she said, "Feel me loving you, Rob. Feel me inside you. I didn't even know that that's where I wanted to be, but it feels so right. So perfect."

As she continued her loving litany of words, Tanner thrust slowly in and out, her body moving with a graceful ease that belied her weak, damaged muscles. She watched Robbie's face closely as the tense anxiety slowly gave way to fiery passion. As Robbie's tender, strong hands clung to her, guiding her deeper, faster, with each stroke, Tanner's love for her burgeoned.

Tanner's accident had left her wounded, savagely bent, twisted and broken. The hospital staff had saved her life, but it had been Robbie who had healed her, Robbie who had somehow transformed stone.

QUIET, PLEASE
RACHEL KRAMER BUSSEL

I was in the middle of telling Jackie all about my day at work, the words tripping over themselves as I rushed to get them out quickly, my hair falling sloppily across my forehead as I took another breath, when she reached her fingers up and put two of them to my lips. "Shh," she said. "No talking."

At first, I was upset; wasn't I in the middle of telling her an important story, trying to get her to understand how rough my day had been? But then I took another look at her pretty face, the light dusting of freckles across her pale skin, the shock of red spiky hair sticking up from her head, her natural red color enhanced with day-glo chemicals she seemed to apply every other week. Her pale, lightly frosted lips were pursed, as if about to blow on a cup of cocoa, but she was simply telling me she wanted my full attention. Then Jackie leaned forward, letting her fingertips trail down my cheek, along my neck until they'd reached my bra strap. She fiddled with it while bringing her own lips forward, until their glossy, sticky surface met my bare ones, brushing against mine slowly, lightly. My body, starting with my shoulder blades, relaxed, the pent-up story slowly leaking out as I sank into the chair, into the kiss. I tilted my head back slightly and she angled forward, pouncing on me as she moved to straddle me, her body edging over mine as her fingers snaked down lower toward my breast. Her other hand easily slipped the ponytail holder from my hair, letting it fall in a wave down my back. Jackie's smaller than me, thin and lithe, but I never underestimate her. She's like a snake, careful to bide her time, slithering her tongue out just so when she wants something, like she did just then, her tongue darting between my lips for a brief instant, long enough to connect with my tongue and ignite a fire that began in my mouth and coiled all the way down my throat, into my belly, and settled in my groin. I could feel its rumblings stirring my pussy and felt the very last vestiges of the day's stress leave me as I succumbed to Jackie, my Jackie, the girl of my dreams for the last decade.

Jackie stayed home painting her masterpieces, for local galleries, occasional magazine work, or commissions, and I often returned to find her covered in paint, her eyes so focused on the canvas in front of her she hardly took notice of the smear of blue or yellow across her cheek. I'd sometimes find errant streaks along her hands, and we'd made washing her off a very sexual ritual. But today she'd been scrubbed totally clean, as if ready to attack, which is exactly what she did, pinning me to the chair as her fingers tangled in the roots of my hair, pulling it just the way she knows makes me gasp, makes my pussy contort with pure need. I started to moan, to say "Yes," but once again, she shut me up, this time with a kiss. "No talking," she insisted, and when she moved on to my chest, her lips leaving mini-kisses along my dewy skin until she reached the gap between my breasts, I clamped my lips together and let her show me what she had in mind. She burrowed her head in the expanse of my cleavage, reaching her arms behind me to undo my bra. I wasn't used to being so passive, to taking and taking without giving anything back, but from Jackie's fevered panting, she was apparently getting off on our silent adventure just as much as I was. She lifted her head from my skin to remove my shirt, then pulled my bra forward, over my arms, but instead of dropping it on the ground she moved behind me, tying my wrists behind my back with the slightly clumsy but effective bow of my bra.

I'm usually the one to take charge, so this must have been something she'd been saving up for a while, and from the hungry look on her face when she was once again before me, Jackie was totally enjoying her newfound power. And, a bit surprisingly to me, so was I. Having no choice but to surrender to her, I reveled in the way she danced around me, bent over so I could see her tight jeans strain against her ass, which she thrust up in my face before grinding herself against my lap. Normally, it's Jackie who's lying across my lap while I spank her ass until it's bright red, but watching her from this position made me see my little nymph in a whole new light. She knelt down in front of me, looking up at me as she prepared to lick my pussy through the fabric of my jeans, her blue eyes gleaming. She began with her fingers, pressing her folded knuckles against the tightness where my jeans stuck to my sex, pushing against the damp fabric while I melted further into my seat, my cunt spasming already as she glided her fingers along my slit and then focused on my clit, kneading me in such a way that made me desperate for her. She pinched my clit through the layers, then brought her fingers to my nipples, which were poking forward into the air. She twisted them between her fingers while I spread my legs as best I could, giving her room to smash her face against my pussy, making her mouth felt against the thickness of the denim. Her licks traveled slowly, teasing me as she tapped her tongue against my cunt, the muffled response causing me to twitch in the chair, feeling the bra straps scrape against my wrists as I moved. I wanted to cover her head with my hands, to press her deeper to me, to clasp her tight, but instead, I alternated thrusting my thighs far apart so they butted against the edges of the chair and then closing them, trapping her head between my legs while she burrowed as deeply as she could until finally, Jackie had mercy on me and lifted her head slowly, inching her tongue along the metallic tang of my zipper before taking it between her teeth and sliding it down, her fingers leaving my nipples to undo the button. I was grateful I'd chosen my most comfortable pair, because she easily slid them down my legs, leaving me sitting there in only my black cotton panties. Once again, Jackie breathed against my pussy, pressing her tongue against the musky wet cotton before finally moving it aside to taste the real thing.

Her tongue slipped easily inside my hole, and my whole body seemed to twist and tense like a pretzel, contorting as my breath caught in my throat, my pussy clamping down around her wet, slippery tongue. But Jackie wouldn't let me hold her, and she pulled my panties down roughly, the elastic clawing against my calf until they were off and she had me, her prey, spread out in front of her. I had no time to be nervous or embarrassed, to worry about what this role reversal might signal, because there was Jackie fishing something out of her pocket, a small, tiny vibrator I hadn't noticed before. It must have been new, and I looked down to see the bright blue buzzing toy about to connect with my cunt. I could hear it whirring, and my body braced for the onslaught. Jackie slipped two fingers into my pussy, pushing deep inside me as she rubbed the toy against my clit, making me tense up once again. Her eyes sought out mine once again, willing me to relax, and I let go of that final edge of control I'd been unknowingly clutching, that last barrier between my independence and my orgasm, and gave myself, all of myself, to my lover. Her fingers edged along my insides, seeking, stroking, healing, as she easily pushed another finger inside, filling me as she spread them apart and turned them for maximum impact. I lifted my ass slightly, feeling her fingers curl and caress in the most powerful of strokes while her other hand kept the vibe trained directly on my clit, and suddenly, I didn't want to pull away at all.

I was no longer afraid of what might happen, only curious, desirous, as I looked down and watched my body accept that of my true love. She eased the toy away, leaving my clit pulsating, the air a revelation as my engorged skin continued to contract with need. And then her mouth was on me, her lips wrapped around my clit as her fingers probed me everywhere I needed her to be. I shut my eyes as her tongue gently brushed my nub, a softer, gentler pressure that seemed to radiate inward and outward at once, leaving me light-headed. Tears of pleasure welled up in my eyes as her fingers pressed quietly and deeply as far as they could go, touching that part of me that only Jackie has ever been able to access, that special place where my cervix meets my soul. I felt a tear fall as her tongue wandered along the contours of my clit, as if she were tasting me, meeting me, pleasing me, for the first time. And in some ways, it felt like that long-ago moment, except now we were giving and taking so much more, and when Jackie flattened her tongue against my clit, and I felt the pressure not just of her tongue and fingers but her entire heaving body, every breath and beat of her heart thudding against me, I came, making the chair teeter as my liquid trickled down onto her fingers.

Jackie kept her head pressed against my lap, kissing my inner thighs, stroking me with her wet fingers, until our breathing faded back to normal, the silence moving from one of frantic arousal to soothing calm. She finally rose, her breasts hovering near my lips as she reached behind me to unclasp my arms before sitting sideways across my lap, her legs dangling over the chair's edge. Her face was streaked with sweat, that same sweet, intense smile lurking across her features. "See what happens when you sit still and quiet down, baby?" she whispered before resting her head against my shoulder. We stayed curled like that in the chair for over an hour, neither of us daring to break the stillness.

Erotica 101
Radclyffe

The really good thing about having a best friend you've known since grade school is that you don't have to lie about anything—she's already seen you puke in the gutter, treat nice girls badly, fall for the bad girls who always break your heart, and generally act like an asshole. Even more important, maybe, is that you don't have to clean the house or get dressed up when she comes by unannounced to "just hang."

So when Angie knocked on my door at a little after seven on Friday night, I was ensconced on the battered leather sofa in front of the fireplace in my living room, wearing baggy sweats with the cord missing from the waistband and a faded T-shirt that was once blue, reading sex stories from my favorite dyke publisher.

"Hey," I said as I held the door open for her. "Come on in. Want a beer or something?"

"That'd be cool," Angie said as she breezed by, bringing a cold rush of winter night air along with her. She draped her faux leopard jacket on the newel post and disappeared down the hall in the direction of warmth.

I watched her go, wondering why, if she was going to wear a skirt that barely covered her buns, she didn't wear a coat that reached a little lower. I was willing to bet that the calf-high, black leather boots with the three-inch, needle-thin heels didn't do much to keep anything else warm either. In between the top of the black leather boots and the bottom of the teeny black skirt was a long, *long* expanse of creamy skin and toned muscle.

Five minutes later, I handed her a pilsner with a perfect head, set a bowl of mixed nuts on the coffee table in front of us, and sat opposite her on the sofa. She was curled up in the corner, her feet drawn up beneath her butt, her boots abandoned on the floor. Her normally vibrant brown eyes were sulky, her pretty pink Cupid's bow lips tightened into a thin pale line, and her heart-shaped face a study in discontent beneath a riot of black curls. It wasn't like Angie to be moody. Unlike me, she wasn't given to dark thoughts and a desire for long stretches of solitude. On Angie, quiet was bad.

"Give," I said, patting my lap. Wordlessly, she stretched out her bare feet and planted them solidly in my crotch. I covered her toes with my palms and rubbed my fingers over the cool balls of her feet. "What's the matter?"

She shrugged and swiped her tongue over the foam that hung on the rim of her glass. "I got stood up."

Rapidly, I ran down the list of her latest conquests. A face came into focus. One not unlike mine, really. Short dirty blond hair, pale blue eyes, broad expressive features no one would ever call delicate. Sturdy body, kind of like mine too. "The cop, right?"

"Umm." The pout got poutier.

"So what happened?"

"We were supposed to go to a movie and then out clubbing."

"She canceled?" My voice reflected my surprise. Angie was a looker and always had studs standing in line. She was not the kind of girl you kept dangling.

"Work." She said it as if it were a dirty word. "Somebody called in sick and she had to take their shift."

"Doesn't sound like she stood you up," I ventured carefully. "You know, just one of those things that happens."

Angie shook her shoulders dismissively and burrowed her feet a little tighter between my thighs before announcing, "I was looking forward to it all week. And now I'm horny."

I laughed. "Oh, now I get it."

She glared at me.

"So, did you make another date?"

"Tomorrow," she said as if it were a decade away.

"Well, you'll probably survive until then." I wiggled her big toe between my fingers. "You could always, you know, take matters into your own hands in the meantime."

Her pout turned to disdain. "Hardly. It's boring."

I felt my eyebrows lift. Now, I enjoy a night with a hot sexy woman as much as the next dyke, but whether I'm getting it regular or not, I've never found a do-it-yourselfer boring. In fact, a lot of the time, it's faster, easier, and hotter to get exactly what you want exactly the way you want it. "Boring? You're kidding, right?"

"It just…oh, I don't know…it never really works for me."

The little bit of sadness in her tone wiped the grin off my face. I sat up straighter, unconsciously stroking her ankles and calves. "You mean you don't think jerking off is fun?"

"Most of the time I can't do it. I just get more frustrated."

In the firelight, her color seemed to deepen, and I wondered if she was blushing. How could I not know this about her? We'd been trading sex stories since we were old enough to think about sex, let alone have any. And she'd never once told me that she didn't like to masturbate.

"Maybe you need more practice."

"Please."

I laughed. "Okay. Let's analyze this rationally."

"There's nothing to analyze. I don't get that excited when I do myself. I just get tired and my mind wanders." She snorted. "Before I know it, I'm running through my grocery list."

"Well maybe you need better fantasies," I suggested helpfully.

"That's just it. I can't seem to find anything that…well…gets me turned on enough to get me off."

"Instant replays?" For some reason, enhancing Angie's solo career had become my mission.

"Been there, done that." She dropped her head back on the arem of the couch and studied the ceiling. Her hair shimmered in the red glow of the firelight, a reflection of the hot coals dancing. "Once I've done it for real, I'm not interested in fantasizing about it anymore."

"Okaay." I cradled her feet against my stomach and leaned forward to snag the book that I had dropped on the coffee table when Angie arrived. I held it up to show the cover image of two naked women, arms and legs entwined. "Maybe you should try this. It always works for me."

Again she gave a dismissive sniff. "That stuff is just crap. It's either totally unbelievable or it sounds like it's been written by some high school boy."

"Then you haven't been reading the right erotica," I said defensively. "I guarantee there's something in here that would make you hot."

Even in the dim light I could see her eyes glitter. Angie loved to gamble.

"Oh yeah?" She nudged my thigh with her heel.

"Yeah."

"Whatcha wanna bet?"

There was something more than playful about the way she worked her foot back and forth on my leg. Intrigued, I decided to take her on. "I bet you dinner at the restaurant of your choice that I can find a story that makes you hot enough to come."

"And just how are you going to tell?"

Her voice was husky and her eyes huge. I'd been just about to get down to some serious self-pleasure while reading earlier, and now the way she slowly slid the tip of her tongue over her lips zinged straight down to my crotch. Zap. Twitch. Clench. Uh-oh. I was wet, and if it weren't for the thick sweatpants, Angie would be getting a sample of my excitement on her skin. I eased my hips back, away from her slowly rocking foot. In a voice that I hoped sounded steady and cool, I said, "We'll use the honor system."

She grinned and scrunched a little lower into the sofa. The movement caused her skirt to ride up her thighs, and I caught a glimmer of blue satin panties framed by pale velvety skin. My stomach tightened into a hard, hot ball as I casually flipped through the pages of the book, trying to find the one I'd been about to jerk off to. Then, when my brain cleared for a second, I remembered the object of my search and zeroed in instead on what I thought would turn *Angie* on.

"Here you go." I held out the book and she took it with an expression that said, *You've already lost.*

Confident, I shifted one leg up onto the couch so that Angie's feet were between my thighs and settled back for the show. I could see her face above the top of the book, her expression one of polite disinterest.

"I can feel you watching me," she said, without looking up from the pages.

"Uh-huh."

She smiled, pleased, I thought.

A minute went by, then two. She shifted her hips. Sighed.

"Think it's sexy?" I asked.

"Mmm. Sort of. Be quiet."

Her face had tightened, her eyes narrowed just a little. Interested now. The foot resting on my inner thigh twitched.

"What part are you reading?" I couldn't help myself. I wanted to know what was getting her hot. I palmed her foot, caressed her arch. My clit jumped every time her toes dug into my leg.

"She just saw the outline of the blonde's cock in her leather pants," Angie said idly and flipped the page. "She's feeling her up."

Angie slid the foot I wasn't touching higher up between my legs until it was snugged against my crotch, then kind of rolled it back and forth in short, jerky little movements. The vibrations tingled the length of my clit and I ground my teeth. My thighs hurt from clenching them so tightly, trying to keep still. I knew the scene, I'd read it more than once, and I never failed to come with the base of the cock riding over my clit as some dark beauty jerked me off in the shadows of a nameless bar.

"Hot," I croaked.

"Mmm, yeah."

I traced my fingers up her leg from her ankle to her knee and back down again. On the next trip up, my gaze kept traveling north until I reached her crotch. Angie made a sound like purring and shifted again, her thighs parting further. A wet patch glistened in the island of blue. I tugged the heel of her foot hard against my clit. I was so stiff it hurt, but perversely, I welcomed the pain. It always took a hard workout to get me off.

"Where are you now?" I was breathing fast, and from the way the book rose and fell on the crest of Angie's breasts, so was she.

"She's sucking her off," Angie murmured. "Jesus, right there in the bar."

The pale blue covering her sex had darkened, soaked through, and the round prominence of her clit pushed out against the fabric. I imagined I could see it twitching in time to my own.

"She's gonna make her lose it," I whispered, "if she keeps that up. Make her come right there."

"Oh, that's nice," Angie crooned plaintively, dropping one hand to her thigh. Her legs trembled as she fitfully brushed her fingers up and down the silvery skin high inside one leg. The backs of her fingers swept over the blue satin. Her hips lifted. Fell. Lifted again. She pressed her fingertips to the swelling beneath the shiny triangle.

"Oh!" Angie blurted. "She's getting her off." She gripped her clit between fingers and thumb and twisted in quick, spastic little jerks. The book shook in her grasp and her splayed legs stiffened along the inside of mine.

"Touch inside," I urged, rubbing my pounding clit against Angie's heel.

"I'll come," Angie whined, cupping herself and squeezing until the tendons stood out on her hand, tight bands of desperate desire.

"Don't you want to?"

"Oh yes." Her voice was high, strained.

"Do it." I ground into her foot, riding her high.

She shoved the swatch of wet fabric aside, her fingers swirling madly over gleaming ruby flesh.

"So good," she moaned. The book fell to the floor. She skimmed her free hand under her sweater and palmed her breast. My breath fled.

"Unh. Unh." Angie's wrist was a blur of motion, her belly tense, body writhing. "Good. Good. Coming so hard." She jerked upright, her eyes blind, then tumbled back with a wail.

I clutched her foot and clamped my legs tight. The room spun as I chanted, "Oh yeah. Oh yeah. Oh yeah."

"Ooh, jeez," Angie panted after a minute, languorously caressing between her thighs, petting her clit tenderly. She opened her eyes, raised her head enough to see me. Her face was soft, dreamy. Her smile sated. "That was amazing."

The muscles in my thighs trembled at the speed of hummingbird wings. My clit jumped against the sole of her foot as if struggling to escape. I took a deep breath, the first one in what felt like an hour. The muscles in my stomach were so tight with frustrated arousal I could hardly talk. But I grinned. "Outrageous."

"That was a really hot story," Angie sighed.

"Told you," I murmured, eyes glued to her fingers as she continued to play with herself, lazy and content. Her juices glistened on her fingers. Unconsciously, I palmed her foot and rubbed my aching sex against it.

"It was even better with you watching me read it."

I twitched all over.

"We didn't talk about what would happen if you won," she murmured.

I tore my gaze away from her fingers working in her crotch long enough to glance at her face. She was looking down between my legs. I wanted to come so bad. She pulled her foot back, and I whimpered.

"I think," she said musingly, milking her clit a little faster now, "I think I want another story."

"Angie," I groaned.

"But," she tilted her foot forward and nuzzled her toes against my clit, "this time I want you to read it to me."

Smiling wickedly, she scooped up the book and held it out to me. Her toes danced and teased unmercifully. "And no reading ahead."

A Good Butch Is Hard to Find
Crin Claxton

Standing up at Alexandra Palace with all of London falling away before me, I could breathe again. The tall, blinking silhouettes at Canary Wharf, the red lights of the Post Office Tower and the dotted lights of buildings stretched away in white and gold lines. The sky was purple with light spilling upward, and high above were sparklingly clear stars. I fixed on an intensely bright one and thought maybe I should wish on it. There's a song about that. There's also one about catching a falling star and putting it in your pocket but that's just dangerous. I decided to wish for a femme to love me: instantly I thought of my ex, currently lying on a beach in Cuba with the double-glazing sales butch she'd run off with.

I said to the star: Send me someone I can laugh with, someone I can talk to. That was the thing with my ex. She was so easy to talk to in the beginning. The star twinkled at me, shining and fading and shining, and seemed to move…nearer…getting bigger and brighter until I had to screw my eyes up against the intense white hum of its light.

I opened my eyes to find myself standing on the steps of a spaceship. Ahead of me in a huge doorway there was a silhouette of something with a human body and a huge head. As I stared, an eerie and not unflattering pale pink light faded up on the woman, who actually had a normal human-sized head but the biggest beehive I'd ever seen. Behind her three other women were singing and dancing, all doing the same movement, like a '60s Motown backup group. All three women also had enormous hair.

"Wouldn't you like to come in?"

The woman in the doorway had a very persuasive voice; she curled her index finger, beckoning me in. I took a step up and then hesitated.

"Oh, don't be scared," the doorway woman said in a voice of honey. She reminded me of a panther. "You can't stay there all night." She said, "Come on." She beckoned and I felt my body start to move forward. I looked behind me. I quickly turned back. The Earth was a long, long way down, and there weren't any steps beneath me.

"Come inside now, you'll get cold," Panther-Woman suggested firmly, linking my arm and gracefully ushering me into the ship.

Inside was a huge, light, white room. There were seating areas with sofas built into the environment on different levels. There were swathes of material falling from the ceiling and draped here and there. The lighting was soft and diffused in the seating areas and brighter in the central area where the Motown women were still singing.

I heard a shooosh and noticed lift doors opening two levels up. Three women got out, all in shiny, tight-fitting space suits. One of the women was using some kind of machine—a kind of wheelchair, I suppose, but much lighter than anything I'd seen before. It glided along. She looked stunning; in fact, she was gorgeous. I realized I was staring and went to turn away, but she held my gaze.

Panther-Woman had walked me to the center and the room was starting to fill up. I turned around, surveying the room, feeling the stares from all directions. I was obviously a curiosity. Maybe they'd never seen a human before. It was a weird feeling. I couldn't see any guys. They all looked like women. In fact, I couldn't see any butches. I couldn't even see any andro-dykes. All the women, and there must have been over a hundred, all of them looked like femmes. My knees went weak. Panther-Woman grabbed my arm. "Are you all right, honey?" she asked.

I managed to nod.

I tentatively looked around the room again. This time I felt the stares more intensely. Sweat was breaking out all over my body. I know a femme when I see one, and I was looking at over a hundred. I must have died and gone to heaven. I felt a moment of sadness for my former life, but it really didn't seem to matter very much.

Panther-Woman raised her hands and the music stopped.

"Sisters, we have a guest from planet Earth. Please say hello to our new friend Joe."

There was a general murmur, which I think was approximately a hundred femmes saying, "Hi, Joe."

"How d'you know my name?" I asked Panther-Woman, but she just smiled an enigmatic and highly irritating smile.

"Now, I know many of my Sisters would like to meet you personally, and they will," she told me. "But first, I'd like you to come with me to the science quarters."

I didn't like the sound of that. I suddenly remembered I was on a spaceship with, well, they must be aliens. I stopped dead as I realized they were...FEMMES FROM ANOTHER PLANET.

"Oh baby, you're such a worrier." Panther-Woman told me, stroking my face. "Come on, follow me."

She started walking in front of me. Something about the way her buttocks moved in her skintight trousers made my feet start moving, and soon they were following along behind her like an obedient puppy. I would have slowed my feet, for my pride's sake, but I was working really hard on stopping my tongue hanging out. I thought perhaps these alien femmes might have special powers, and were in fact slowly turning me into a dog. Panther-Woman giggled to herself in front of me. These girls sure were strange ones.

We walked down long corridors. After a while, even though her bottom was very exciting, I tore my eyes away to look at my surroundings. There were screens at intervals, computers maybe, or moving art. Every door we passed was closed. Occasionally a woman walked with or past us. They mostly had a good stare at me. Like Panther-Woman and the Motown performers, like all the women in the reception room and the corridors, they all had huge hair. It didn't matter whether the women were black, brown, or white, whether their hair was long or short. It was all enormous. I wondered if the butches, who must be working somewhere in the background, had no hair, as a contrast. Or maybe they had big hair too, huge DAs or something. That was a frightening thought. I briefly considered the possibility that there were men around somewhere, but I dismissed it quite quickly. The femme energy on the ship was rife. I wondered where the butches were.

"Are there any other people on the ship?" I asked Panther-Woman's bottom.

She stopped and turned, and I lifted my eyes to her face.

"Yes, a few Sisters are working elsewhere on the essential functions. Unfortunately they couldn't come and meet you. They'll get their chance later," she promised me.

"Sisters?" I asked. "Are they…like you?"

She looked confused.

"Are they feminine?"

"Oh yes," she confirmed, looking at me intensely. "Every Sister is feminine."

"Are there any…Brothers?"

She paused before answering. "There will be."

Well, thanks for clearing that up, I thought sarcastically. She smiled a secret smile to herself as we walked along. I might have tried to get more out of her but we reached a door. It opened when we stood in front of it and I followed Panther-Woman into a lounge area.

"This is Carmilla." PW gestured with her arm.

This certainly is Carmilla, I said inside my head, staring at the brown, raven-haired beauty before me. She was the woman who had held my gaze from the balcony.

"Hello, Joe." Wind chimes went off when she spoke; wind chimes blowing in the softest, sweetest breeze.

"Carmilla is our science officer," PW told me.

"How wonderful." Who knew what I was saying? I didn't. They didn't seem to care much. PW looked highly amused. Carmilla was smiling sweetly and patting the edge of a couch near her.

"Why don't you have a lie-down and let me have a little look at you?"

I couldn't think of any reason why not to. Soon I was flat out and staring into her intensely brown eyes. She winked.

"Now relax. I just want to find out a few things about you. If you feel uncomfortable at any time, just say."

How sweet, I thought. I felt like giggling. It was all so bizarre. I was convinced they must have drugged me. I felt light-headed and weird. Maybe it had been in the water they gave me, or their fingertips. Some of the women had touched me, Panther-Woman for one.

"Unfortunately, I have to return," she told Carmilla. "I think you'll be safe."

What did she mean? She obviously meant Carmilla. Well, of course Carmilla would be safe. What about me?

"You'll be fine, sweet…butch." Panther-Woman bent and kissed me. The way she said *butch* sounded like a purr. I liked it.

I thought if they did have a drug you could pass in your fingertips, and it felt this good, I could make an awful lot of money selling it to lesbians.

I felt Carmilla touch my arm. "I just want to get some initial measurements. I'm going to run this instrument over your body."

I knew she was aware of how that sounded, but she looked very professional as she swept a little computer pad over me.

"Hmm," she said, sounding like all doctor-type people sound when they say *hmm*. It's supposed to sound noncommittal, but it always makes you worry.

"Why don't you put this on, Joe." She was holding out a visor. Cool, computer games. I took it and put it on.

Suddenly I was lying on a beach. I heard the waves. I smelt the sea. I took the visor off. I was back in the room, and Carmilla was still there beside me.

"It's okay."

"Is it a virtual reality thing?" I asked.

"Um…sort of. I promise it won't hurt you."

I considered that. I didn't feel she would harm me. Sometimes a butch just has to go on instinct. I put the visor back on.

Creamy foaming waves rolled along a long, white, sandy beach. It was very hot. There was a slight breeze flowing over me. I felt good, relaxed. The sky was pure blue, completely cloudless, and it went on for ever. I turned toward the sun, which was a reddy-purple. I looked away, thinking that was strange. When I looked back it was its normal white-gold colour. I felt a shadow over me and turned to look up at a beautiful, tantalizing femme.

"I was wondering if you could help me."

I sat up slightly, noticing I was wearing swimming trunks and nothing else. Funny, I hadn't noticed that before. *It's okay,* I told myself. *It's okay you're topless. And a strange woman's looking at you.*

"How can I help you?" I blurted out.

"I need to put some sun cream on," she said. "And there are several places I can't reach."

"Oh." I saw the sun cream in her hand for the first time. "Of course." I got up and gestured to her to lie down on my large and attractive beach towel. *I've got good taste,* I thought.

She handed me the cream and lay down on her front. She was wearing a bikini. I put cream on my hands and started rubbing them along her back. I rubbed it into the back of her neck where her short, big blond hair stopped, leaving it exposed. I rubbed it over her shoulders, smoothing the skin and starting to massage her a little. She sighed out loud. The cream smelt good, hot in the sun, and the spicy, musky scent of her body smelt good too. I also sighed.

"You'd better put it everywhere," she suggested, reaching behind and undoing her bikini top.

"It's best to be careful, the way the sun is nowadays. And you *are* very light," I said. She was too. I looked for the factor on the sun cream but couldn't see any.

"Don't worry, I won't burn in the sun," the beach babe told me. "You just carry on rubbing that in."

I didn't need to be told twice. I rubbed cream the length of her back, down the back of her legs to her feet and back up along the inside of her legs. When I reached the top of her thighs she turned over and I saw her breasts for the first time. I gasped. She had a beautiful body; all curves.

"Well go on, then, handsome. Rub me some more."

I did as I was told, rubbing cream into her breasts, feeling her nipples stiffen, rubbing cream over her chest and stomach until she was well and truly creamed.

"You haven't quite finished, have you?" she said, taking off her bikini bottoms.

I stared. "Are you sure you want me to rub sun cream…there?"

"Oh yes."

"But you don't know what's in it. It might irritate you." I was genuinely concerned. She looked like I was irritating *her*.

Suddenly I was lying back on the beach towel. I felt a shadow go over me.

"Would you be a darling and rub a little sun cream into my back."

"Of course." I said, getting a deja vu kind of feeling. This was where I came in, wasn't it?

She lay down in front of me and I saw she'd changed. She was deep brown, well toned, and her hair was short, big, black and weaved. I courteously covered her in cream, putting it exactly where she asked me to. Before I knew it we were getting intimately acquainted, her moans falling rhythmically with the crash of the waves. We were making good waves ourselves—she was open and wet, expanding around my hand.

I felt good, deep inside her, and I felt my body stretch, enjoying the moment. I felt soft kisses along my back.

"Um-mm," I said aloud, turning my head to the side and seeing my blond friend from before.

"I wanted to join the party," she said. "Do you mind?"

"I don't mind at all," I said. In the blink of an eye I was on my back and the blond woman was moving on top of me. I felt a harness around my waist and pushed up so she could take more of me inside her. She watched me watching her open her mouth and gasp as she moved around. She was taking little breaths, her eyes half closing now and then. My other lover was kissing her breasts, I could see her nipples were erect, I could see all four of their nipples were erect, and I felt my own leap to attention. Six nipples on a dyke parade ground. My beautiful dark lover fixed her deep brown eyes on me and kissed me, opening my mouth and exploring me with her tongue. I ran my hand along her body, remembering we had something to finish off. Both women were moving on and over me and I moaned along with them… the hot sun, the crashing waves, two gorgeous women and…something made me think of Carmilla.

No sooner did I think of her then I was lying on top of her, her legs spread out either side of me and my tongue in close contact with her vulva. This seemed a bit forward. Weren't we supposed to play around with sun cream a little? I heard her moaning and sighing and felt her upper body moving, her fingers playing with my hair. After a while it seemed perfectly natural. She tasted wonderful: milky, slightly salty. I licked her like an ice cream cone. When I had nearly nibbled her down I felt a surge of energy run across my tongue and through my mouth, shoot through my chest, and explode somewhere around my clitoris. Somehow, like an intergalactic translator or something, I knew this meant she'd come.

I felt the visor being lifted off my face and opened my eyes, blinking in the interior light. Carmilla was sitting beside me like before. All her clothes looked intact. I looked down at mine. They were unchanged, unopened, undiscarded also. *Okay,* I told myself, *that didn't happen. It was just a test, so they could gauge my sexual responses. They gave me some kind of stimuli and I made up the rest in my head, like a fantasy. Carmilla can't know what I was thinking. The scenario must be in the virtual reality program and I just put Carmilla in there. But she doesn't know that. She was just observing me. Shit. She was observing me.*

What if I was moaning or breathing heavy? Or worse, what if I was feeling myself up in front of her? I looked again carefully at my flies. *No, they're done up. Thank God.*

"Are you okay?" Carmilla was looking at me, concerned. "Your blood pressure's shooting up."

"Oh yes, I'm fine," I muttered. "Just fine. How about you?"

"Oh I'm very well, thank you." Carmilla was smiling. "That was really very useful. I'd love to continue but I've had a message from the central console room. There's a lot of excitement that you're on board the ship, and Sisters are dying to meet you. It would be unfair of me to keep you here any longer."

Flattery has always been my weakness. Completely pushing out any worries I'd had about my little fantasy, I nodded.

She took me to a meeting room. On the way I asked her, "What is it you want from me?"

"Oh, we just wanted to meet you."

"Why?"

"We like you."

"But you don't know me."

"Well, we like your type. We'd like to get to know you better."

Ignoring the little sweetener, I went on. "What d'you mean my type? Human?"

"No."

"Lesbian?"

"Of course." She said like there was any doubt.

"So any lesbian. You just wanted to meet an Earth lesbian."

"No. We wanted to meet a butch."

"Oh, that is a bit harder."

We were at a lift. Carmilla lifted her hand and the call button pad slid down so she could press it.

"So have you met—"

The lift doors opened and two women got out. *The* two women: the two women in the virtual reality program. Only they weren't virtual, because here they were in front of me. Waving. I broke out in a cold sweat.

"Joe, I think you've already met Neela and Sindan. Neela, Sindan, this is Joe." Carmilla made the introductions.

"Hi," I said in a pitch only dogs could hear.

"Such a high voice," Neela commented, tall and dark and even more beautiful in the flesh.

"Oh she doesn't normally talk like that," Carmilla told her. "Strange reaction. It must mean something, Maybe they talk like that to women they've had sexual relations with." She considered that. "But then, she didn't speak in that high voice to me."

Oh no. Not you too. I'd hoped at least that part of it really was a fantasy. I looked at them all looking at me for a while. Then Carmilla broke the freeze-frame.

"Well, we'd better be going. You two aren't coming?"

"No, we're working in the kitchens tonight," Sindan, blond and curvy in a very tight spacesuit, said.

Carmilla gestured to me to get in the lift. When the lift doors closed I blurted out, "I thought they were a program. I mean, I thought it was a program and they weren't real."

"Oh. Did you?" Carmilla nodded as if a piece of the puzzle had fallen into place. "I see. How strange. Don't you have sex like that, then?"

"No, not at all. We have it…you know, for real."

Carmilla raised her eyebrows, looking very interested indeed. "Oh, you mean you don't all hook up to the mainframe?"

I shook my head. "Well…there's the Internet, I suppose, but it's not as….vivid."

"Interesting…I'd like to try that," Carmilla muttered to herself as the lift stopped and the doors opened straight into the meeting room. Carmilla took me to a seating area and set herself beside me. I thought that might be because of her role as science officer, but I hoped it was because she liked me. Panther-Woman came over from the drinks area with a group of other women, and they settled around us.

"Joe, I thought you might like to meet some more Sisters." Panther-Woman told me. "This is Nelax, she's our chief engineer."

I looked with interest at the woman PW pointed to. She was chief engineer. Damn! She was the most feminine woman I'd ever seen. Immaculate. She had one of their space suits on but it was tapered in to show every curve, every fold of her body. Chief engineer! She didn't have a smudge on her. Couldn't imagine her getting her hands dirty. I was getting my head around this concept when I heard another woman laughing. PW introduced me.

"And this is Shira, she's our chief advisor and telepath."

Right. Telepath. Should have known they'd be telepathic. They even knew what I was thinking. I suddenly felt very alone.

"Oh, you don't need to be scared of us," Shira said. "We wouldn't, couldn't harm you."

She had a very compelling voice.

"And I'm Robaki." Another woman cut in. She had obviously got fed up waiting to be introduced. "I'm head of leisure services."

"Would you mind if we ask you some questions?" Carmilla asked.

I shook my head and shrugged.

"Are there many like you on your world?" PW asked me.

"What d'you mean like me?"

"Butch," PW confirmed.

"In the whole world?"

They nodded. I thought about it. "Well, I can't be sure. I mean, who knows really? I don't think there's millions, maybe there's thousands— in the whole world. Do you include straight women who are butch?"

They looked confused.

"Yeah, I know. It confuses me too. But then not, I suppose, not if you count butch as a gender."

I could see I'd lost them.

"Anyway, masculine women—into women, into feminine women I suppose, looking at you lot—I don't know. How many are you looking for?"

A row of raised eyebrows greeted me.

"Thousands," Nelax volunteered.

"Really," I said. "Thousands, huh?"

"Do you think you could help us?" Robaki asked.

"Hmm…" I thought about this. Did I really want any other butches in on this?

"Tut tut." Shira mock-frowned at me.

"Can I ask you something?" They nodded. "Where do you come from?" I was thinking this could all be an elaborate hoax and they'd say, "San Francisco."

"Femedom."

"I beg your pardon?" I spluttered.

"Femedom," Carmilla repeated.

I decided it wasn't polite, and definitely not in the interests of galactic relations to tell them what the name of their planet meant in English.

"It means some kind of female contraception," Shira explained.

Damn! I'd forgotten about her.

"How…quaint." PW dismissed it as an absurdity.

"It took me a while to work out the image in her head." Shira was saying. I stared at her in horror. "All I could see was cunt and this funny, rubbery-plastic thing wrapped sort of up and inside." I still stared at her in horror. They all looked at me, completely lost for words.

"We've got a lot to learn," Shira said.

"So how come you don't have any butches with you?" I changed the subject.

"Honey, if we had butches we wouldn't be here," Robaki informed me.

"Really." It was my turn to look at them. "You mean you don't have any," I emphasized the word, "*any* butches at home. Not even one."

They all laughed. And laughed.

"Can you imagine it?" Shira was crying with laughter. "One poor butch."

"On that whole big planet," Nelax shrieked. "All the Sisters." Laugh, laugh, laugh. "And one butch. What a thought!"

I sort of laughed with them. But I didn't really get the joke. Sounded like heaven to me.

"Darling…" Shira smiled at me and patted my hand. She might as well have patted my head. She looked at the others. "It's just how they said it would be. They completely overestimate themselves."

Who were the *they* who said this? I thought they had a damn cheek.

"The Crones, darling butch," Shira told me.

"Joe." Carmilla reminded her I had a name.

"Darling Joe." Shira corrected herself. "The Crones sent us, they said we'd find butches here."

"And we need you to help us," Carmilla explained.

"Well, I'll do what I can." I was thinking there was a limit to what I could do. *I could round up a few, I suppose.* I started going through all the butches I knew. What about the ones who didn't identify as butch but obviously were? Did they count? I looked a little doubtful. Well, I could advertise on the Internet, I supposed.

"And maybe some of you will come back with us," Robaki suggested.

"To Femedom?" I managed to say without smirking. But the image got into my head anyway. "Sounds like home to me, baby!" came out of my mouth before I could stop it.

There was a polite silence. I carried on regardless. "I suppose you need some butches"—I was going with the thought—"to sort things out."

They looked at me. I couldn't imagine a planet completely of femmes. Their houses must be falling down, man. Crying out for DIY. And cars, boats, planes, all waiting for some butch mechanic. I pictured femmes in huge traffic jams waiting for someone to open the car door for them.

I felt a wall of annoyance building up around me, and came out of my reverie. The femmes were stony faced.

"Ladies, I didn't mean any offense. It's just on my world these are usually butch things." I turned to Nelax. "Of course, not always. There are plenty of femmes who do these things, after all we had a huge women's movement once, and that kind of changed things." I could see I was losing them again, but they seemed more relaxed. Carmilla was smiling at me anyway. "After all, what did you think butches do? You didn't just think we were good at sex, did you?"

From their embarrassed smiles I realized they did.

"Tell me, aren't there femmes on your world who like each other, you know, femme on femme? It's quite popular here." I thought about that. "Well, at least it is in the personal ads."

"She means Sisters doing it to ourselves," Shira explained, her telepathy obviously giving her the edge on intergalactic translation.

"Of course!" they chorused.

"It's the norm on our world." Shira revealed.

"Really?" I said, a little disappointed.

"Oh yes." Nelax was obviously amused at my reaction. "We, the ones who want to meet a butch, are thought to be quite peculiar by some of the Sisters. A little queer, in fact."

Well that was a turn-up for the books. "Have you never had any butches?" I couldn't imagine a world without us.

"The Crones' legends tell of a group of butches who existed long,

long ago, but they disappeared." Robaki told me. "Some legends say they disappeared up the Great Femme Vulva."

"That's a possibility," I admitted.

"The other theory is they came to Earth," Carmilla said.

"Really?" I said.

"Yes. There's another planet near us, CloneZone, and they have a similar legend about their Drag Queens. They say a group of them disappeared to Earth about the same time," Carmilla explained.

My mind boggled. Butches and Drag Queens were really aliens. Well, that put a different slant on the gay gene theory.

"Joe, you look a little worn out. Perhaps you want to go back down to Earth?" PW suggested.

Earth. My life. What time was it, anyway? Was I late for work?

I got up and Camilla rode with me to the entrance doors.

"I hope you've enjoyed your visit," she said playfully as we passed along the corridors.

"I would have liked more time with you," I told her, shyly.

She smiled. A lot. "We'll be in touch," she promised.

In the big foyer, I kissed her, hoping I'd get the chance to do it again. Then I felt a pull to be gone. The doors opened, cool air rushed in and I was spinning through misty light until the ground rushed toward me.

I shook my head, blinking like I'd just woken up. As my head cleared I heard birdsong. The sky was streaked with pink; dawn was coming up. London was before me: sleepy, vibrant, alive. A few hours ago I'd been just an ordinary Joe standing on a hillside. Now I was a butch with a mission. I turned and strode purposefully back to my car.

TOY WITH ME
VK POWELL

Night air swept under my silk skirt and cooled the hot center at the apex of my thighs. The swirling fabric tormented flesh too sensitive for a thong. As I walked toward the bar, the fall breeze licked my body, leaving chill bumps that I prayed would chase away the heat.

Another case solved in another lonely town where I didn't know a soul. Sometimes being the top private investigator in the state was more of a burden than a blessing. Thank God for the Gay and Lesbian Hotline, my lifeline to civilization, sanity, and physical sustenance.

"Looking for anything special?" the blond attendant asked, shifting her eyes over my erect nipples and returning the change from a five-dollar admission.

"Just came to dance," I replied, meeting her inquisitive gaze. But the words tasted bitter in my mouth. I could probably come from dancing at this point. It seemed like years since another human being had touched my body with the sole purpose of providing mind-numbing sex.

"That's too bad."

I decided not to launch into just how bad. She probably couldn't care less that my life was a series of domestic assignments in which observations of people having sex far outweighed any opportunities to actually have it. Tonight, my body took offense and insisted on more active participation.

Alternating dark and brilliantly white light temporarily blinded me as I stood by the entrance and allowed my vision to adjust. Music bellowed from huge speakers mounted above the doorway and pulsed my insides with rhythm. I enjoyed the animalistic urges created by the deep, insistent pounding. My breasts grazed against someone's arm at the crowded bar and I purposely lingered before squeezing into a spot.

"Help you, honey?" the redheaded bartender yelled as she placed a cocktail napkin in front of me.

"Vodka tonic with a twist, please."

I watched couples on the small dance floor cling and gyrate against each other in increasingly provocative stages of vertical lovemaking. Their breasts lightly grazed each other, then blended together. Their hips swung from side to side and ground against one another in time with the feverish music. My pulse quickened and I took a gulp of the cocktail, hoping the alcohol would calm my quivering insides. Instead it gathered at that burning place between my legs.

My job required a certain amount of voyeurism and it never affected me—that was work. But tonight, seeing women's bodies in such intimate contact filled me with yearning. I wondered how many of them were with their partners and how many were here for the same reason I was—a hard fuck from an equally hard-up stranger.

Flashing light from the dance floor played an appearing/disappearing act on a dark-haired butch draped over the opposite end of the bar. Her full lips parted slightly and eyes sparkled as she surveyed each new arrival. We locked stares, and a sharp intake of breath caught in my throat. My mouth dried as all moisture rushed to my engorged privates. I recited opposites in time to the pulsing black light—night and day, black and white, good and bad, you and me. Retrieving my drink, I shuffled weak-kneed to the nearest stool.

I reviewed all the times anonymous sex had proven dangerous, superficial, and ultimately unsatisfying. But in spite of any good or pure intentions, my offending eyes wandered back to the butch. Raw passion twisted its way through my body as I looked at what I wanted but knew I would never be bold enough to ask for.

Her dark, close-cropped hair spiked about an inch on top. Her stocky frame appeared to be solid muscle under black jeans and a starched cotton shirt. I detected the bulges and curves of a real woman's body—full and vibrant. She carried herself with an air of total control and reckless abandon as she strolled across the floor. There was something taboo in her gait, almost haunting in its challenge. With each step she took, my clit jerked painfully as if her legs were rubbing against it.

As I returned to awareness, the stranger walked across the floor toward my table. When she strolled past, relief mingled with a sharp stab of disappointment. Momentarily, relief faded and panic seized my body as two hands rested lightly on my shoulders from behind.

"Don't look up." A firm command. Hot breath touched my ear and shot waves of current down my spine. "Just listen."

How could she possibly know that more than anything, I wanted to be relieved of all responsibility? How could she know that the mere thought of relinquishing control melted my insides faster than physical touch? She couldn't know any of that, yet here she was.

Her fingers kneaded the tense flesh of my shoulders. I would've done anything she said.

"Imagine my hands all over your body, stroking your breasts, teasing your nipples into erection. I'm going to slide my fingers up the inside of your thighs into the wetness I can smell there already. Nod if you want me to continue."

The only part of my body that moved was my head. I nodded eagerly. Common sense screamed for me to run, but my legs refused.

A soft chuckle sounded from the woman behind me as she pressed her body against my back. Her pelvis found my spine and came to rest in a position of maximum contact.

"I knew you wanted it the second our eyes met." She whispered, "I'm going to make you beg for things you never knew you wanted."

This was not my first stranger sex, but it was the first time I'd given myself over completely, without question. I'd often masturbated to such a scenario without a prayer that it would ever come true. My body responded to this woman in a way that could only be described as immediate and frightening. The power she wielded magnified the forbidden side of my fantasies and held me paralyzed in their clutches. She knew this from one look. My nipples hardened and pushed against the fabric of my blouse as cold chills consumed me.

She cupped my elbows in her hands and guided me from the stool toward the front door. Nerve endings long dormant flared to life as the abduction played out. She walked a step behind and directed me to a van parked at the darkest end of the lot. The back door of the vehicle swung open as we approached and she pointed.

"Sit here, facing the front of the van." A small mattress on the floor was the only thing visible in the darkness. A heavy material covered the inside walls of the van, creating a barrier against prying eyes. I touched it as I climbed inside—neoprene, soft and slick.

"It helps muffle the screams," she offered.

She positioned herself at my back with her legs around mine. "Tonight you're mine. Do nothing except what you're told."

The authority in her voice left no room for question. Not that I would've—I wanted to give in, to be taken by someone with no expectations or standing to judge. I responded as she commanded.

My crotch throbbed and dripped from wanting her, more from anticipation than anything she'd done. I wanted her mouth all over me and her fingers inside me, and I wanted it now!

Sensing my eagerness, she undressed me with slow deliberation. The tight blouse seemed fiery against my overly sensitive skin. It bound and restricted circulation in a body that screamed to be free. When she released the bondage, my nipples stood erect and ready for her.

She lightly blew her hot breath on my breasts, refusing to allow the instant gratification of touch. I writhed against the fabric of my skirt to ease the pressure building in my middle. My hand automatically reached for the fiery mound of flesh.

She grabbed my hand and repeated, "Do nothing except what you're told. You wouldn't deny me the pleasure of the first touch, would you? I won't make you wait much longer."

My desire to give in to her wishes intensified because I couldn't touch her.

With one hand she unbuttoned my skirt and tossed it aside. When my naked skin contacted the mattress I realized the sheets were satin—cool, sensual satin. A light musky fragrance from the sheets mingled with the scent of my sex, releasing the urge to devour this woman. I clawed my fingernails into the material to contain my craving.

She reached for my clenched fists and released their grip, kissing each of my fingers as she uncurled it. With the speed that foretold lust, she undressed herself and straddled my buttocks. I squirmed feverishly against the silky covers, desperate for contact. She brought my hands back, placed them firmly on her strong thighs, and urged me to hold on tightly.

I knew if she didn't touch me soon that I would come where I sat.

Finally the delicate softness of skin against skin rippled my body with waves of pleasure. She gyrated back and forth on my buttocks—first slowly, then faster—until the warmth of her juices trickled down my backside and between the trembling cheeks of my ass.

This was the only indication that my captor experienced any

sensation at all. I wanted to gloat, to challenge her to fuck me without feeling anything. Just as I started to speak, her hand slid between us. She stroked herself and transferred the ample lubrication across my butt. Shifting to a kneeling position, she guided me to all fours in front of her and slid her hand between my legs. When she grabbed a fistful of bush and lips and squeezed, my surprised yell was suffocated by moans of joy. She pulled and massaged the sore lips, capturing my pulsing clitoris between them.

"Tell me you love this," she commanded and gave another yank. I tried to speak, but my mouth opened and closed in soundless, spasmodic gapes.

She finally plunged a finger inside my soaking cunt. Her roughened fingers stroked in and out of my receptive body. I pumped backward against her hand to increase the tempo, but she wrapped her other arm around my waist and controlled the pace.

She slowly inserted another finger into my eager orifice and dug deep inside me. I bucked and humped to meet her thrusts. She pumped harder and the tension inside my body neared explosion. Just as I felt myself preparing to let go, she withdrew, leaving me a frustrated heap of raw emotion.

"Please," I begged, "I want more, please don't stop!"

"Would it be all right if I use my toy on you?" she asked sheepishly.

"Anything, just don't leave me like this!" I pleaded again.

"You have to promise you won't look until I say it's okay. Promise."

Further speech was interrupted by the rustling of a paper bag. I was tempted to satisfy my curiosity by stealing a quick peek but was instructed to roll over on my back.

"You can look now."

My throat tightened as I opened my eyes. "Don't be afraid. It won't hurt—much."

Two narrow strips of leather around her hips secured a wide piece of black leather between her legs. A large, flesh-colored dildo jutted from a hole in the front panel directly over her pubic mound. She knelt before me, legs parted, beckoning me to touch it. I'd never seen a woman wearing a strap-on so proudly.

I tentatively extended a hand to examine it. The soft, pliable texture was a contrast to the hard rubber rod I expected. It closely resembled a real penis in appearance and touch. Seeing it extended from a body so obviously female was a major turn-on.

"You'll enjoy this," she assured me as she removed a tube of K-Y Jelly from the bag.

She positioned herself between my legs and gently touched the dildo to my aching clitoris. At this point I didn't really care what she probed me with, as long as it was fast and continuous. She squeezed some of the lubricant onto her hands and rubbed them together. With an obvious reverence, she massaged the K-Y onto the pink protrusion with delicate, loving strokes. The care and diligence with which she conducted this ritual couldn't have been more authentic had the attachment been her own flesh.

My body pounded its urgent need as I watched her. The respect with which she admired this thing made me feel jealous and a little helpless. For the first time I realized that I not only wanted to play this game, I craved it. I hungered for the domination and control this stranger held over me. She seemed to know everything about my sexual tastes without allowing me to say a word.

Obviously pleased with her efforts, she guided the greased toy to the mouth of my vagina. A look of utter joy mixed with dark mischief crept across her face as she savored the sight before her. She lovingly cradled her projectile, ready to thrust it into my body.

As she stared into my eyes, I felt the force of penetration as she introduced her adopted extremity into my apprehensive insides. An initial moment of discomfort gave way to a feeling of acceptance as I was alternately filled and emptied by the expertly methodical motions. The friction created by the leather harness against my clit left me breathless with every stroke. My mouth dried as I screamed and clawed at her back.

I opened my eyes to memorize the face of the person who caused such conflict between my mind and body. Looming over me in the dim light was someone I'd never seen before. A glassy-eyed stare emitted a look of absolute power and control. This woman was on the verge of orgasm, and it had nothing to do with making love. She responded to her dominance over me and her control of the situation.

Her eyes darkened as the thrusts of her pelvis intensified. She wanted, needed to bring me to orgasm. I wanted to deny her but I didn't want to deny myself. Passion grew with each frantic movement. Her unspoken desire magnified my own cravings, and I clung to her.

I mentally resisted her attempts to bring me to climax, but my body betrayed me with every breath.

I felt myself floating in the euphoria of absolute resignation. It didn't matter now if she was a complete stranger, if I'd ever see her again or if she was a mass murderer. I only knew I couldn't stop her or myself. I was too near the edge.

Faster and harder she drove her fake phallus into my body, and I took her. She prodded me toward the edge. Her body suddenly stiffened. She grabbed my arms in an unyielding grip. My body quivered and jerked. Waves of pleasure tingled through my toes, up through the core of my body, leaving me dizzy and satisfied. The release of months of pent-up frustration and anxiety poured from my body onto hers. She collapsed on top of me and I lay there, astonished by my response.

"I knew you'd be into it." She smiled from atop my body. "If you're game for another round, I'd love to demonstrate my rear-entry technique."

"What're you asking me for? You're in charge." I heard myself say.

Sometime before daybreak, she kissed me awake and pointed to my clothes in a neat stack beside the back door of the van. "I've had a great time, but you need to get going. Security comes through around six for their morning check."

I slowly replaced clothes onto my overly sensitive body and climbed from the back of the van. "Will I see you again?"

"Not likely, I don't like to strike twice in the same spot." She grinned, licked her fingers, and closed the van door.

When I reached my car, I turned to wave good-bye, but the vehicle and its wild rider had vanished.

ATROPINE
NELL STARK

Everyone assumed they would get married. Including her. But I knew better—or at least, I thought I did. Even from a distance, through a crowd, there was…something. I like to call it a vibe. It has many names. But it was definitely there, and not just because she was beautiful.

She was, of course—long red hair highlighted by a few streaks of gold framing a tanned, freckled face, her smile bursting all over the room as she laughed out loud at a joke. Toned quads and calves leading to bare feet with no toenail polish. Just a bit shorter than me, and slightly thinner. Definitely a few years younger. She caught my eye immediately, and I was rarely wrong.

Still, I thought I'd misjudged when I first saw her with him. They were a striking couple. Only a few months ago, they'd taken first in one of the regattas, moving in perfect synchrony as they roll-tacked their small boat back and forth across the eye of the wind. Watching them, I'd felt at first like I was intruding on something private.

And yet, after the shock wore off at seeing them so fluid, so *together*…well, that nagging feeling was back. They were the best sailors our club had to offer the competition. But that's all they were. I was sure of it.

She realized it too when he called things off just a few weeks into the summer season. She'd been planning to follow him, come the fall— to help him through medical school. Probably to have his 2.5 children. When I heard the news—through another sailing instructor who lived in the same apartment complex—my first reaction was gratitude. But when I saw her a few hours later, trying hard to teach a lesson without looking at him (and failing) as he rigged up a scow nearby, I got angry. When your heart's been broken repeatedly, you forget how hard it is, that first time. Until something reminds you. And she reminded me, with her rigid stance and clenched jaw and fierce, too-bright eyes.

She stopped coming to the weekly meetings and social events. Despite it being summer, she grew paler and paler as the weeks went by. And she started drinking. Heavily. Never before teaching, of course—she was too responsible for that. But immediately after her lesson finished, I'd watch her walk slowly—lethargically—toward the outdoor bar on the edge of the beach and order up a tall paper cup of beer. She'd sip it while looking out at the water, the boats, their sails. And if she saw him, she'd down the whole thing in a few sharp swallows before spinning on one heel and leaving.

One day, I followed her. This day, it's not quite as hot as it has been—around seventy-five degrees, with a steady north breeze and wisps of cirrus clouds salting the sky. Perfect sailing conditions, but he's out on the water in a Laser, and she still can't be anywhere near him. I don't know where she's going, but she's only wearing a white, slightly wrinkled oxford shirt over khaki shorts, and I'm pretty confident that my black tank top and washed-out jeans will fit in. So I shadow her, south a few blocks and then west, to a hole-in-the-wall bar on Spring Street. As far as I can tell, the bouncer doesn't make her pay cover, but I don't even hesitate to shove a crumpled five into his hand. I take the stairs down slowly, to be sure she doesn't see me. For now, anyway.

Once inside, I loiter near the door, watching as she makes her way over to the bar and orders up another beer before commandeering a pool table in the back corner. The felt is stained and its frame marked up with glass-rings and etched graffiti, but she doesn't seem to care. Just reaches into her front left pocket, slips a few quarters into the slot, and racks.

She's good at pool, which surprises me. I sidle over to the bar as she makes her way methodically around the table, punching in stripes and solids with short, sharp shots. At one point, she has to rest her left hip up on the raised ledge in order to lean forward and sink the five ball. From my vantage point, I can see down her shirt to the top edge of the gray sports bra that hugs her breasts. My body stirs, warmth pulsing low and deep. I take a long swallow off my beer and close my eyes, exulting in the sensation, realizing that this is what *she* needs, so much more than I. To feel alive.

But when I open my eyes, she's staring at me. So I go to her. Slowly.

"Who sent you?" she asks. Her voice is quiet and flat, but the hand that clutches the pool cue is visibly shaking. And I realize she's angry. Naive enough, still, to believe her friends would intervene. Her friends are his friends—all caught in the crossfire.

"No one sent me," I reply. Voice even. "I came on my own."

"Why?"

I ignore the question, because she isn't ready for the answer. Instead, I close the few feet that remain between us, fish in one pocket for some change, and deposit more quarters into the table. I rack up efficiently, feeling her eyes on my back; or maybe she's watching the ripple of my tanned shoulders against the tank top. Maybe.

"Break," I tell her, reaching for my own cue.

There's the ghost of a bitter smile on her lips as she sets up and shoots. And then we're moving around each other, circling the table in tandem. I hold my own, but she still wins quickly. And frowns. Thinking I let her.

"You're good," I say, returning my cue to its slot on the wall. "Want another beer?"

She's still watching me, her expression wary. Once upon a time, she was cheerful and gregarious and talkative, but now—now she's curled in on herself. Fetal position. Protect the head, protect the heart. Everyone's out to get you.

"What are you drinking?" I ask again, steadily.

She names her beer, and I head for the bar. When I return, she's found us a table for two in the dimly lit corner. My knees brush hers as I sit, and I feel the brief contact arc through me like a small electrical shock. I wonder what she feels.

"Where'd you learn to shoot pool like that?" I ask, my eyes never leaving the delicate column of her throat as she takes a swallow.

"Older brother." Almost immediately, her fingers begin to peel back the label on the bottle. They're long fingers, and slender, but rough with calluses. I can't help but wonder what they'd feel like, tying me in knots as surely as she ties a bowline. I look away and take a quick sip, then another.

"Your older brother's better than mine," I reply, when I'm sure

I can speak again. For just a moment, the trace of another faint smile plays across her lips before she raises her beer once more.

There's a minute or two of silence, then, as we drink and pretend to watch the two couples who have taken over at billiards. "What's grad school like?" she asks suddenly, settling her empty bottle back down with a dull clink. She's leaning forward on her elbows now, eyes flicking over my face. It feels good, and also intense. Like being out on the ocean at noon without sunscreen.

"Complicated," I answer, rocking my chair back on two legs. "Lots to do...classes, reading, research, teaching." I lift the bottle to my lips again, let the beer swirl around my mouth before swallowing. She's frowning, a little—focused. "Are you thinking of going?"

Her left shoulder lifts in a shrug. "Maybe."

"For what?"

"I don't know." The label is almost entirely gone, now—curling up under her fingers in one smooth piece. She works the rest of it off before raising her eyes back to mine. "Why did you come here tonight?"

I glance away before I even realize it, because something about the way she asks makes me want to answer, this time. Honestly. So I take a breath and force myself to meet her curious gaze.

"I've been worried about you," I say. She frowns and sighs and looks down, but I'm not finished—so I reach out with two fingers and gently press up on the base of her chin. "And I want you," I add, softly.

Her gaze, so slippery a moment before, freezes. I let my hand drop away, reluctantly. *Moment of truth.*

"Why?" she asks, yet again. It's almost a whisper. She doesn't believe me—*can't* believe me—and it's his fault. I have never been angrier with him than at this moment.

I stand up, suddenly, and drain the rest of my beer. "Let's walk on the beach." I don't look back as I thread my way through the tables, out the door, and up the stairs, but as I turn east down the nearest side street, I can feel her beside me. We walk silently until the pavement gives way to sand. I bend down to remove my sandals, transferring them both to my right hand, and find her right with my left.

I'm sailing without telltales here—purely on instinct—knowing the wind could die any second. When she startles a little at the contact, I can't help holding my breath...but as the seconds pass without a reaction, I exhale softly. Her grip is light, but firm. We begin to walk again, my thumb tracing circles around her palm as we move.

"I like your hands," I tell her. "They're beautiful, and strong." I let my fingertips brush against the calluses just above her knuckle line. "Working hands."

My peripheral vision catches the slight movement as she turns her head to look at me, but I keep my eyes facing forward. The sand is cool under my feet. In the patchy light of the half-moon, I watch small crabs scuttle periodically out of our way. My thumb shifts to brush across her wrist, and our pulses blend for just an instant.

"What's your favorite movie?" I ask after a few quiet minutes. She laughs at the random question, and for a moment, I see her old smile resurface. We talk about film for a while, then music, as the constellations gradually shift overhead, pinwheeling slowly around the North Star. Our progress is leisurely. The bells of sailboats moored in the bay come to us intermittently on a warm breeze. I like the way it ruffles her hair.

"Where are we going?" she asks, finally. Her tone is mildly curious—relaxed. Our linked hands swing in gentle arcs between us.

"My apartment." I keep my voice light, like hers.

"Ah." The faint half smile doesn't leave her face.

"I like the way your hair looks in the moonlight," I tell her as we reach the outer door. I slip my key into the lock and watch her while I turn it. "It shimmers."

She laughs and leans into me a little, one shoulder and hipbone pressing against mine. Another jolt. I smile back before leading her up the stairs to the door across from the second-floor landing. Once inside my apartment, she doesn't wait for a tour but moves around herself, taking in the bedroom, the small office, the den. Traces the base of one of my old swimming trophies with an errant index finger. I smile at the sight of her, head turning back and forth as she absorbs the reality of my living space. She feels right here. Like the room has been waiting for her to fill it. Somehow.

I turn on the television and move toward the fridge. "Another beer?"

"Sure."

I hand off the bottle and sit down first, so she can choose. Next to me, on the futon? Or in the armchair a few feet away?

She hesitates for a moment before picking the space to my left. Sliding her right ankle under the opposite knee, she takes a long pull from the bottle. Not touching me, but close. Eyes focused on the television. CNN isn't exactly romantic, or even fun, so I hand her the remote. She grins, clicks a few buttons, and finally settles on an old black-and-white sci-fi film that's so bad, it has us both laughing hard within a few seconds.

She sets down the remote on the coffee table, and when she leans back, she's closer to me. Our shoulders touch. I spend the next twenty minutes absorbed not in the movie but in how warm she is, how the wrinkled material of her shirt feels against the bare skin of my upper arm. It's hard to remember to laugh at the funny moments when she leans even closer. Her entire right side is pressed up against me now, and I swear I can feel the slight curve of her breast against mine.

It's impossible for me to stay still—to not move my palm so it's resting, very lightly, just above her knee. So I do. Her powerful quad muscles ripple under my hand, but when I look at her face, she's still smiling at the television. So I squeeze—gently—and watch as the smile disappears. Her eyes close slowly, then open again. She turns toward me, her face backlit by the intermittent flashes of the screen.

I can feel myself sliding forward, inch by inch. Allowing her to move, if she doesn't want this. But I think she does. And then I know it, as her eyelids flutter closed again just before I'm too close to see anything at all.

Her lips are soft, so soft. Her breath hitches right in the middle of our kiss, and I know what she's feeling. The first time is always a revelation. *How can it be like this? Why did no one tell me?* I slide my hand up her thigh, brush across her hip, and squeeze again. She sighs into my mouth. I suck on her lower lip, and the sigh becomes a moan. I'm dizzy with lack of oxygen, but I don't want to stop kissing her. If I do, she might—

She pulls away, gasping. "God," she murmurs, looking at me. Touching her lips—now swollen—with two fingers. Her eyes wide and dark. "That...God."

"Okay?" I ask softly, willing my voice to be steady. I will not lean forward and take her mouth again, like I want to. I will wait. I find the remote with my right hand and fumble with it until the television goes black. No distractions—not now.

"Okay," she breathes. Her slight laugh is edgy, her eyes focused on my lips. "Definitely okay."

This time, I let my left hand caress the back of her head. My fingers curl in long, thick strands of crimson as my tongue glides over her teeth. She jumps a little and presses closer. My thigh slides against hers as I dip deep into her mouth, swirl, and return. The fingers of her right hand dig into my shoulder as I kiss her, over and over and over. Alternating depth, pressure, teeth, lips. Her hands pull me closer, so that I'm nearly lying on top of her.

Slowly, so slowly, I walk my fingers across the hem of her shirt until I can undo the last button. I let the pearl-plastic slip slowly through its slot, giving her time to protest. All I hear is the rasp of her breath, mingling with the background hum of the refrigerator, until I uncover her navel and rim it gently with my forefinger. She gasps. I grin, lean down, and tug on the sensitive skin with my teeth before allowing my tongue to spiral around and around the small indentation. When I stop, she whimpers—then moans as I deliberately fuck her bellybutton.

"Please," she whispers finally, her trembling fingers tugging at my short, curly hair. I look up and grin, finally absorbing the taste of her skin on my tongue. Salty, and also sweet. I want more.

"Please?" I'm teasing her, of course, but I also want her to be sure. No regrets in the morning.

"I need…" Her eyes are dark and hazy with desire, and I feel my body thrill as she stumbles over her words. Because of me. "I…can you…?"

I think it's cute that she can't quite get the words out. And I don't make her. Instead, I lever myself off her body, stand up, and extend my hand. Her palm is sweaty. I lead her, slowly, toward the bedroom.

"I've never," she whispers as we cross the threshold. "I mean, I did with –"

"Shh." I turn to her and kiss her again, and by the time we break apart to breathe I've undone two more buttons. My hands slide beneath the crisp material of her shirt to caress her stomach. Her muscles, strengthened by hours of training on the water, flutter beneath my fingers—velvet over steel. I tease her gently, sliding up over the crests and troughs of her rib cage until my hands find the edge of her bra. I dip one finger under the hem and run it lightly just below her breasts. She shivers.

"I want to take this off," I murmur, lips brushing her earlobe. It's so hard to keep my voice even, my hands gentle, when all I *really* want to do is back her up against the bed and *push*.

Her swallow is audible and when she speaks, her voice hitches. "I—I'm not stopping you."

My fingers fumble with the third button as I suck on her earlobe. It's only for a moment, but she groans. "Why not?"

She pulls away then—far enough to touch two trembling fingertips to my right cheek. But her voice, when she speaks again, is clear and strong. "I want this." I watch, searching her eyes as a lopsided smile chases away her intent frown. "But...I don't know what to do."

I grin back and reach up to caress the hand that's still pressed against my cheek. Lacing her fingers through mine, I guide her slowly down, down the side of my neck, along the prominence of my collarbone—down until the warmth of her palm soaks through the tank top over my left breast. "I'll teach you," I whisper, struggling to speak over my body's tumultuous response. Suddenly, I want to be taken—to feel her hands on me, in me. When she squeezes lightly, I can't stop the shudder—so I take a step forward, crush my body to hers, and kiss her hard enough to distract us both.

When the kiss ends, we're on the bed. I'm half draped over her, and her shirt is somehow completely open, even though I don't remember undoing those last two buttons. Her chest rises and falls in rapid succession, and it's a struggle for me to look away—to meet her eyes. Her pupils are dark and huge, almost entirely eclipsing the blue irises. As I watch, the tip of her tongue darts out to lick swollen lips—and I know I can't wait any longer.

"Off," I mutter hoarsely, tugging at her shirt. She sits up a little to shrug out of it, and I take advantage of the movement to hold her there, one hand splayed against her back. I push up her bra with the other. She gasps at the friction of the cotton, and then again as I begin to tease her with my tongue. Decreasing circles, spiraling closer and closer, until my tongue flicks against one nipple as I gently pinch the other. She arches above my hand, and I stroke her more firmly, thrilling to the sounds of her low, hoarse cries.

"Oh—oh God," she whispers as I let my teeth close around her. The long muscles of her back shudder against my hand, and I finally lower her down to the bed, shifting so that I'm kneeling between her thighs. Her eyes are closed, her body taut. Sweat glistens in the hollow of her throat, in the narrow valley between her breasts. She is need incarnate, vulnerable and open.

"Take off your bra," I order. My voice sounds thick and low, even to my own ears. As she stretches in obedience, I curl my fingers under the hem of her shorts and pull, taking her underwear along for the ride.

She lets out a startled little cry, the swatch of gray cotton hanging forgotten from the fingers of her left hand. She's exposed now, completely—tight brown-gold curls swirling around swollen, red lips. Glistening—for me.

She whispers my name, her voice saturated with desire and something that sounds like fear. Or hesitation. It's so very, very hard to move my eyes up her body, but when I do, the vulnerability of her expression slams into me—an unexpected wave.

"You're beautiful," I whisper. Fiercely. I hold her gaze for another long moment before finally allowing my eyes to feast again—to linger over the strong lines and gentle curves of her figure. I want her, *need* her to understand—to know just how desirable she is. To feel my appreciation, to absorb it into her skin. I undress quickly, feeling a rush of pleasure at her low intake of breath when I kick off my jeans and reveal my body.

"He's such a fool," I murmur as I stretch out on the bed beside her. But words and glances are never, will never be enough; there is no way to *speak* the message she needs. There is only my finger, trailing slowly down the center of her body, moving in teasing fits and starts. She relaxes and tenses simultaneously—thighs opening even as her stomach muscles clench. I return my mouth to her breast as I let my finger zigzag through the crisp maze of her hair, tracing both lips before finally settling against the slight ridge of her clitoris. Her body surges *up* as I touch her, and my finger slides down, into the waiting pool of moisture. I can't help but groan, before slipping gently inside. "You're so wet."

"Oh—" she breathes, then lets out a tiny whimper as my left hand tracks down her body to join its partner. As I part her swollen lips with my thumb and middle finger, she shifts restlessly, one hand clutching a fistful of blanket for purchase. "Is—is that…okay?"

"Okay?" I manage to choke out a laugh, somehow, as my index

finger presses down hard, then eases off in a barely perceptible circle. I watch her heels dig into the blanket, feel her hips and torso lift in a desperate attempt to get *closer*. Her urgency is infectious, and I stroke her gently but firmly, up and back, until her head is thrashing against the pillow and I can feel the anticipatory contractions of her internal muscles. "Oh, yeah. More than okay."

And then her eyes snap open, boring into me sightlessly as her body convulses, over and over and over. I hold still inside her, letting her clench around the length of my finger, drawing out her pleasure by continuing to massage the swollen knot of nerves with my other hand. She is so very beautiful. Unrestrained, responsive, passionate. Perfect.

When her body finally stills, I move my left hand up to rub the soft skin of her stomach. Gradually, I feel the muscles beneath start to relax. Her eyes, when she opens them, are bruises—equal parts black and blue. Still gloriously hazy from her orgasm.

I smile down at her, never stopping the soothing motion of my palm. She lets out a long breath, her eyes flicking back and forth between my own. "I've—" she begins hoarsely, then clears her throat. "It's never been like that. Before."

My smile grows, and I let one eyebrow quirk up, mischievously. "I'm not finished, yet." Her eyes go wide again, and I laugh—just before kissing her gently, teasingly, on the lips. My mouth gradually tracks its way down her body on almost the same path that my finger took earlier—except that it lingers for just a while longer on her breasts— biting and licking and sucking.

It's only when I feel her inner muscles begin to tighten once more that I move all the way down, so that the width of my shoulders forces her to open to me even farther. Her eyes—pitch black, now—meet mine just before my tongue darts out to taste her. She cries out and shudders, and I can't help but grin. When I taste her for the second time—the barest brush of my tongue against her dark red skin—she clenches hard around my finger. I withdraw it slowly, then push back in, all the while delicately flicking her clitoris with the tip of my tongue. She groans, loudly—then again as I slip another finger inside.

"More," she breathes, clutching blindly at my right shoulder, her fingers tangling in the curls along my hairline. "Oh God, I need—"

I lean forward and take her fully between my lips, hollowing my cheeks as I fuck her with my fingers. Her body stills for a long, perfect moment as she rears off the bed, back arched. And then she explodes again, hips trembling as the waves of ecstasy pull her under.

I don't realize that I've been holding my breath until it's all over and my cheeks are tingling from lack of oxygen. I release a deep, shuddering sigh as I move up the bed…and cry out when her right hand slips between my thighs.

"What?" I manage to choke, before my eyes close involuntarily at the feeling of her callused fingertips swirling against me. "Oh, yes—"

"Tell me how to touch you," she urges, her voice still thick with the memory of passion. Her fingers move back and forth, slip-sliding through my wetness, searching…

"There!" I gasp as she brushes one side of my swollen ridge. I can't stop my hips from bucking at the slight contact, and I know it won't be long when her single finger is joined by another in its gentle massage.

"Yeah," she mutters when I groan at her persistent touch. "Come on—let me feel you." She circles up and around, torturing me with glancing strokes against where I need her most. The harsh gasps of my labored breaths echo throughout the room.

"Please," I manage. "Oh, please—"

And then she is touching me firmly, pressing down hard on my clitoris with those exquisitely rough fingers, drawing out my pleasure until I am weak and heavy and drained. I can barely muster enough energy to slide closer—to pillow my head above her right breast and hold her close with one arm slung over her waist.

We lie entwined for a long time, in silence. As my heartbeat slows, I realize that I am breathing in tandem with her—that we have found a rhythm all our own. I smile at the thought and pull her a little closer. But finally she stirs, drawing away enough to prop herself up on one elbow and look down at me. Her expression is serious, nose wrinkled in a frown.

"What happens now?" The question is soft, hesitant. Her eyes squint as she asks it.

"We go to sleep," I reply, combing my fingers through the unruly strands of her disheveled hair. I do not frown—I smile. Somewhat mischievously. "And when we wake up, we do this all over again."

It's not the answer she was looking for, of course—but maybe, just maybe, it's sufficient. And sure enough, she grins back at me before settling herself more firmly in my embrace—her back flush against my torso and hips. I hold her close, treasuring that last image of her face in my mind's eye. Rosy-cheeked, eyes bright and expressive. Alive.

PEARLS OF WISDOM
ROUGE

I watch Carly order port for herself. Our waiter gives her a quick nod of approval, removes her wineglass, now tainted with lipstick, and darts off. Her features are soft in the candlelight and I see the woman I married twenty years ago as if no time has passed. She is still radiant; her high cheekbones have drawn her face a little thinner with the passing years and she wears her fawn-colored hair shorter to compensate. I catch her caramel eyes and they smile at me. If I had just finished a glass of cognac I couldn't have felt warmer inside.

"I know this trip to Paris is supposed to be our anniversary gift to one another, but I couldn't resist." She smiles as she lays a box on the table in front of me.

I recognize the shallow square box as one meant for presenting jewelry, though there is no logo embossed on the top. This is not like my wife—to buy me bobbles. As a rule I don't wear any jewelry except a nice watch, earrings, and my wedding band. I rest my wineglass on the white linen tablecloth and subtly shake my head in a scolding fashion. "You're awful," I whisper, my feelings for her just the opposite.

"I saw these in a store window this morning on my trip to get your breakfast pastry. I couldn't wait to see them on you, against your porcelain skin, resting underneath your dark hair..." She gives me a smirk that only I can interpret: the one that completes her thought— *when I'm fucking you.*

A server returns with her port, the white of his gloves in sharp contrast to the dark purple potion in the small glass.

I play with the corners of the box, at first because I'm overwhelmed and then because I want to tease her, make her wait. There is no one in the world more beautiful than my wife, no one more clever; certainly no one that can make me feel so good just by looking at me. She is my one vulnerability. I would be lost without her—me, the investment banker, the leader of the pack, top dog at one of the largest financial institutions in the world—unwilling to live another day without her.

The black leather box is hinged at the back, and I carefully lift the lid. Before me lie, in a perfect circle, a string of black pearls on a red velvet cushion. I knew such a prize existed, but had only seen pictures. "They're beautiful," I say, running the face of my fingers over them.

Carly stands behind me and fastens the strand around my neck. She takes liberties, kissing me below the ear. "I love you," she says, holding my shoulders.

We stroll hand in hand down the Champs-Elysees, the gas lamps casting weak shadows across the promenade. Cafés host small groups of young people—well, young to me—who sit around small tables set at the curb. You can't visit Paris and not think about love, romance.

Our lovemaking over the years had slowly changed: lust was replaced with trust, urgency with tenderness, adventure with knowledge; yet I still wouldn't trade being in my lover's arms for anything. Such intimacy is not gained in a few weeks, but earned over a lifetime. "How many times have we made love?" I ask and squeeze Carly's soft hand.

"I've never thought about it. Well over one thousand, I imagine."

My number crunching mind does an involuntary calculation. "Two thousand eighty." Carly turns to me. I can read her mind when I look into her twinkling eyes: she wants to make a smart comment about how lucky she is that I can add, and she wants to kiss me.

"Twice a week for twenty years," I explain.

"Future results cannot be based on past performance."

God, I love her wit. "I think we're about to have a windfall." I pull her to me and French kiss her, not caring about our lipstick. The kiss is so much more "French" in Paris.

Our hotel room is filled with blood-red roses, their sweet odor intoxicating. Candles have been placed throughout the room, waiting to be lit. "You did this?" I ask, frozen in the threshold, feeling the tears well in my eyes.

Carly kicks off her heels and lights the candles. "*Only* for you."

I feel so unprepared and thoughtless. I haven't done anything extra for my lovely mate. When I close the hotel room door behind us the familiar dance begins, only practiced at a slower pace, and the heat still races up my legs as she unzips my dress.

We take our time shedding our clothes, watching one another.

There is still something sexy about watching my wife reveal herself one part at a time. Even though I've admired the canvas many times, the vision is a masterpiece, always drawing a breath out of me.

She lays me on the bed and removes my nylons; I am left with nothing on but my pearls. I raise my knees, spreading them wide.

As she moves toward me, I gently hold her at bay, pressing the sole of my foot against her hipbone. "You have to watch," I tell her.

I move my hands over my breasts, down my trembling stomach, and rest my palms on the inside of my thighs, enjoying the smoothness of my own skin. I touch my unsheathed clit and feel moisture pump from my hole with a slight contraction of pleasure. Carly stares, lips parted. She keeps her eyes on my hands; as they stop to fondle my breasts she reaches between her legs.

"Elaine...you're so lovely," she pants.

My chest heaves with growing desire. I repeat this languid process, stopping this time to draw my breast to my mouth and trace my areola with my tongue. When our eyes meet, I am reminded how much I love her, how much I want to please her. I can feel her eyes take me in and I want to please her even more.

"Show me some more," Carly says, the catch of desire in her voice. Her thighs shining wet.

Reaching under each buttock, I hold myself open for her. She strokes herself faster, each upward motion exposing her clit. She wants to close her eyes—to give in—but can't take my dripping pussy from her sight.

"You should see how wet you are, baby," she coos in a heavy breath.

I dip a finger in my slippery hole and then suck on it up to the second knuckle, twisting it between my pursed lips. Carly rests a knee on the edge of the mattress. Her chest is as flushed as the roses. She exposes herself with one hand, allowing me to see her two fingers disappear into pink-purple flesh.

Wanting her, I pull my knees to my chest and fuck myself at a furious pace. I hear Carly's breath snag in her throat, then she groans. "Don't make me come without you," she says, her voice deep with desperation.

Her words reach my ears with the heat of a branding iron against my flesh. "Oh, I want to hear you come..." I whisper.

Her fingers increase their cadence as she rests the palm of her other hand over her mound, taking her clit between her fore- and index fingers, holding it hostage. Her hands move in unison now, her breath labored. I close my eyes and, keeping time with her panting, plunge my fingers into my tight pussy.

"Ah! Oh Jesus…watch me come," Carly commands.

Her nipples are the hardest I've ever seen them, her areolae the color of antique brick. She holds my eyes until her body convulses in small spasms; when the air escapes her open mouth in forceful gusts, her orgasm reaches my ears like a percussion grenade.

Carly's cry makes me so hot I can't wait any longer for her touch. "I need you to fuck me! Please!" I beg her. She wastes no time in complying, forcing her hips between my legs, her long fingers hard inside me. I wrap my arms tightly under hers. She knows what I want, taking my breast in her mouth and fucking me with such force our bodies inch toward the headboard, my heels dancing on her ass. Flashes of light race through my mind. *Oh God! Fuck me, Carly! I'm gonna come so hard*, are only thoughts—I can't manage to get the vowels I'm shouting to form words.

When our muscles go limp, I rock us gently, holding her between my thighs until she raises her head and looks at me. Her sparkling eyes tell me what words would destroy with their inadequacy: *I love you, I'm so lucky, I feel the sun deep in the middle of my chest.*

I roll over, putting myself on top of Carly, closer to the nightstand, and reach behind my head to take off my necklace.

She watches me in silence as I fold the string of pearls in half and dip the clasp into the wax that pools beneath the candle flame. The dark orbs are iridescent, like the inside of an abalone shell. I submerge the clasp several times until the small gold fittings are encased in a protective bulb of paraffin.

"Mmm…what are you doing?" Carly asks me in her "I've just been fucked senseless" voice.

"You'll see," I say, balling the pearls in my hand as I go down on her, first nipping and licking her breasts, then around her mound before moving into deeper folds. She smells of sweet, overripe fruit.

When she arches her pelvis against me, I work the strand inside her vagina, all the while keeping her hard bud exposed to the wandering tip of my tongue.

"Are we going to get those back?" Carly pants through a faint smile.

I leave two pearls dangling from her. "One at a time."

Kissing the inside of her knees and thighs, I let the tension build.

"Did you find your treasure, Sultan?" Carly spoke as her tight stomach heaved with anticipation, the delicate muscles rippling like snakeskin.

I smile in recognition of her wanting to play and grow serious with my response. "I have looked everywhere in my harem; I have not." My mouth took in as much of her breast as it could hold. She threw her hands above her head, pressing her palms against the headboard.

"When I find the thief I will take his hand, or worse." I run my desperate mouth down Carly's writhing side and up again, licking her underarm.

"Is there a reward for the return of your precious gems?" She sucks on my earlobe.

"I will share my bed with her forever." I kiss each rib. "Are you sure you do not know where my pearls might have gone?"

"I confess, Sultan, I've had them in safekeeping."

Reaching between her swollen labia, I take the first pearl between my index and middle fingers. "You shall be rewarded." I begin to tug on the string.

Carly gasps as the third small orb appears. Her pubic hair is cropped short, allowing me to see everything.

I suck on her engorged clit; it's hard and slick, reluctant to rest between my lips. Her hands position my head as she wants it. As other sisters on the strand slowly make their exit, Carly's sighs grow deeper and more labored. After years of translation, I understand her language and wait for the moment she will draw her deepest breath and hold it for a couple of seconds before the long cry of ecstasy begins. And when she does, I wait a beat before pulling the long strand out all at once, in a single motion.

Even with her hands pressed over my ears, I can hear her praise.

Carly pulls me on top of her and holds me tight; my rib cage can hardly expand enough to allow me to breathe. Aftershocks wrack her body as if she has a raging fever.

Carly caresses my face in front of hers. "You've never done *that* before," she says incredulously.

"I've never had pearls before."

NOTICE ME
GUN BROOKE

The first note came when I had just sat down and the waiter brought me my glass of Chardonnay. He placed a tiny silver tray before me, and on it was a tiny light blue envelope.

"A message for you, ma'am."

"From whom?"

The paper was thick and clearly expensive.

"I don't know. The maître d' gave it to me."

"Very well. Thank you." I waited until he left before I opened the envelope and unfolded the note.

> *If you knew me, you'd know how out of character this is for me and how long I debated with myself before writing this note, but I decided that I simply had to let you know.*
> *You're the most beautiful woman I have ever seen. The way you laugh, the way throw your head and your long blond hair streams down your back, sets me on fire.*
> *I don't have the courage to approach you directly, so I chose this way to say what's in my heart; you are amazing.*
>
> *Miriam*

The handwriting was neat and even, with no distinctive markings. I looked closer and it appeared as if it had been written with a fountain pen, not just a regular ballpoint. I drew a deep breath and furtively looked around, but none of the other guests seemed to be paying any attention to me. *Miriam.* I didn't know anybody by that name. The name was slightly exotic, and the note more than intriguing.

Caballeros was my favorite *tapas* restaurant, and I had been here more times than I could count the last two years. The maître d' knew me by name and so did the two bartenders. Sometimes men would try to chat me up, but I always declined. But for some reason…this note, it stirred a feeling of strange and bewildering anticipation.

On my way out I asked the maître if she knew who'd sent me the note.

"Yes, I do," she said. "Miriam Rosenberg. She's a regular."

A regular? *I* was a regular.

"Really? Could you point her out to me?" Quite unexpectedly, my heart raced and my palms grew moist.

"No, I'm sorry, Ms. Carr. She left shortly after you arrived."

"Where does she usually sit?" I was embarrassed at how eager I sounded, but the maître d' merely smiled politely.

"Ms. Rosenberg favors the bar or one of the corner booths."

On my way home in the cab I tried to remember the many faces I'd seen in the bar over the past few weeks. It was an impossible task since there had been an endless row of nameless faces and I was beyond the age when I had unabashedly checked out other women. After losing my partner, I focused on work, and I rarely allowed myself a night of pleasure with a stranger.

Except this note. I let my fingers close around it in my coat pocket. There was something endearing about her shy message.

The second note came a week later when I once again sat at the bar at Caballeros. The bartender reached under the counter and gave me an envelope; this time it was hot pink. "Ellie, I have a note for you."

Another one! I forced my hand to go slowly as I reached for it. "Thanks. Who from?"

"Miriam. She left just before you came."

I know now your name is Eleanor. The bartender calls you Ellie and it sounds wonderful. Soft.

I sit here with my favorite margarita, black currant, and the bartender tells me she thinks you'll be in later for a drink, since it's Wednesday.

I'm that predictable? Damn, it sure sounds boring. And true. I kept reading.

I can picture you perched on the tall stool next to me,

*your green eyes glittering down at me as you listen. You rest
your hand on my arm when you laugh...and of course this is
all a dream. You just take my breath away.*

Miriam

I reread the note. *She fantasizes about me looking down at her...
Down? She's short?* I had to smile at myself.

"Good news?" The bartender winked and placed another glass on
the shelf behind her.

"Humorous." I felt my cheeks warm and quickly tucked Miriam's
note into my purse. I had no intention of answering this strange woman,
no matter how curious I was. After all, she could be an axe murderer for
all I knew. *Oh right.*

I paid for my margarita, and only then did it strike me that Miriam
and I had the same taste in drinks.

I didn't get another note for the next two weeks, despite my
regular twice-weekly stops at Caballeros. I sat at home and stared at
my computer screen, my mind completely blank when I thought about
the article I was supposed to start working on. One minute my hands
rested motionless on the keyboard, and the next, they pulled my black
wool coat from the hanger and I was on my way out for an impromptu
visit to the restaurant.

"Ellie," the bartender, Sandy, said warmly. "You're a sight for sore
eyes. What a nice outfit."

I was dressed on the verge of casual in black gabardine slacks and
a black turtleneck. The only thing not black was the thick gold chain
belt around my hips. "Thanks, Sandy. I do try."

"Yeah, yeah, you're very trying. What can I get you? A
margarita?"

"No, not tonight." I didn't want to have what *she* usually drank.
It was probably stupid, but I didn't want to have the same taste as her
in my mouth. It felt too...intimate. "I'll have a glass of champagne,
please."

"There's a note for you again." Sandy handed it over; this time, a
light blue piece of paper folded in three. She had a funny little lopsided
grin playing on her mouth, which puzzled me. "You're popular."

"Oh. Thanks." My mouth was impossibly dry despite the
champagne, which I thirstily sipped again.

I opened the note, my heart seeming to slow to a standstill.

Ellie,

You are always in my thoughts, even if I haven't been able to go out for over a week. Isn't it silly how a case of the common flu can put a stop to most things in life? Here I was dreaming of you, and blowing my nose and taking cough drops at the same time. And you know what...it was still so romantic. Yes, I know you must be laughing, but it's true.

Now when I'm well again, and back at work, it's as if I see you everywhere. I shiver each time I spy a tall blonde dressed in black, hurrying down the street—sure it's you. What is that a sign of? That I'm losing it? Perhaps.

I wish I could just pick up the phone and call you, ask you how your day was. We could finally meet at Caballeros and have our margaritas together, perhaps exchange a few thoughts on life's hurdles and mysteries.

Perhaps.

Miriam

No matter how I tried, I couldn't see this note coming from a stalker. It sounded far too caring, and cautious, to come from someone about to haul out duct tape and a stiletto at any given moment. I reread Miriam's note. *Perhaps.*

I suddenly needed some privacy, if only for a moment. The note had left me with a prickly feeling on my skin, and I just wanted to splash some cold water on my hot cheeks and compose myself. As I passed along the bar on my way to the ladies room, I came to a quick halt when someone swung her legs, long, nicely shaped legs in black nylon stockings, into the aisle to leave. My eyes darted toward her face and looked into dark brown, surprised eyes.

"'Scuse me," I murmured, intending to circle her and keep walking.

"Oh, my."

"You okay?"

"I'm fine. No problem."

She sounded as breathless as I'd felt after reading Miriam's note...my head snapped up and I quickly glanced at the bartender, who nodded vigorously.

"Miriam?" The question left my lips before I had time to think.

"Ellie." She sounded taken aback.

Miriam was gorgeous—skin like melted dark chocolate and shining black hair, long and curly with subtle highlights, an exclusive hairdo that could only have been created by one of Chicago's premier hair stylists. Her emerald green skirt and jacket discreetly revealed enticing curves, and a gold locket rested just above the neckline of her white silk blouse.

"Nice to meet you." I grimaced, knowing how awkward I sounded.

"No need for pretense," Miriam said with a faint smile. "I'm sure the pleasure is all mine."

In fact it wasn't true. *This is nuts. Just get out of here and back to work.* My inner, sensible voice went unnoticed. "Ah…want to get a table?"

"Why not." She hesitated. "If you want to?"

"Sure," I heard myself say.

We sat down in the corner booth.

"So, this wasn't how I planned it." Miriam shrugged with an embarrassed smile. "I'm not a stalker—"

"I didn't get the impression you were, either," I quickly interrupted. "We wouldn't be sitting here if I thought so."

"Unless you're stalling until the cops show up." She winked.

The impish look on her face was irresistible and I broke into laughter. She smiled with apparent relief, and we went on to talk of ordinary things for more than an hour. I thought I could hear traces of immense loneliness and sorrow in her voice, but the more primitive part of my brain was on overload, checking out her stunning face and imagining her curvy body without clothes. It should've shocked me, but somehow I got the feeling she was doing the same. I had no idea what she saw in a woman like me, without a doubt looking colorless and dull next to her exotic beauty.

"You amaze me," Miriam suddenly said, her voice darker and full of fire.

"How is that?"

"You have this aloofness about you, and yet you seem to be the nicest person I've seen in a long time."

"Um, now you've lost me."

"As you might have understood from my notes, I'd been watching you from afar for quite a while." A faint blush crept up Miriam's cheeks, giving her complexion a reddish tint. "And you are always so nice to everyone here. They adore you. I think it was the kind way you treat people that first caught my attention."

"You must've hid rather well, because, believe it or not, I've never seen you in here." I knew I had to be honest, even if it was hardly a compliment.

"I'm good at being inconspicuous." Miriam raised her glass of water. "Here's to finally meeting. Cheers."

"Meeting. Cheers."

We sat in silence for a while, content with just looking at each other, or so it felt. Miriam's full lips parted and showed charmingly uneven teeth in a white smile. "You look so incredible," she whispered. "I can't take my eyes off you."

"You have got to be joking. You're the gorgeous one. I have no idea what you see in me, but…I'm glad you wrote those notes." I nearly choked on my iced tea when a stocking-clad foot stroked inside my pants leg. "Miriam…" One hot wave after another seemed to drown out all common sense. "Oh, God…" My stomach twisted into a knot and the sensation spread down between my legs. *And all this from the mere touch of her foot?*

"Want to go to my place? It's close, only half a block."

Did I? Dared I? My heart pounded and the wetness soaking my panties gave an undeniable answer. "Yes. I'd like that very much."

Miriam tossed bills on the table and we hurried out. The air outside was crisp and I wrapped my arm around Miriam's shoulders.

"That feels nice," she said and circled my waist with her arm. "It's cold."

We walked to her place in less than ten minutes. We spoke little. All I could think of was undressing this woman and searching out every single one of her secrets. The elevator ride was uneventful, since we stood two feet apart, looking at each other with hungry eyes.

Miriam's hallway was painted in red ochre and small spotlights gave it a cozy shimmer. I walked close to her and pressed her gently against the wall as I lifted the coat from her shoulders. Miriam's eyes were all fire, as if her body were about to ignite any second.

"Yes," she whispered. "Please, undress me."

Nothing would prevent that. I got rid of my coat and kicked off my ankle boots, then unbuttoned her jacket and let it follow the path of her coat. I gave a second long thought to hanging them neatly on a hanger, but the enticing outline of Miriam's breasts underneath the thin silk was enough to shove that thought to the back of my brain.

I cupped her left breast, rested it in my palm as I flicked my thumb across the nipple repeatedly. Miriam groaned and arched into the touch, her eyes locked on mine. "Ellie. Go on. Touch me. Please, touch me..."

"Don't worry. I have no intention of stopping unless you tell me to."

"Don't."

I released her and opened her blouse with trembling hands to reveal a white lace bra that contrasted stunningly against her satiny smooth brown skin.

In a sudden frenzy, I unzipped her pants and pushed them along with her hose down her legs. Her panties matched her bra, and her scent wafted to me. It was all dark chocolate, vanilla, and a trace of musk, and I inhaled greedily. I leaned forward and pressed my lips onto the base of her neck. Her silken hair caressed my face and I tasted her skin with pleasure. Legs unstable, I forced myself to remain standing.

Miriam's arms went around my neck as I nibbled her skin, tracing my way up to her mouth. Our kiss was feverish. "Miriam," I whispered against her lips. "Your bedroom?"

"This way." She took me by the hand and guided me through a small, but immaculate, apartment. Her bedroom was decorated in shades of white and grey, and the queen-size bed beckoned us with its velvet charcoal cover and a multitude of pillows.

I continued to lead, since Miriam seemed to sense that I was more comfortable that way. "Undress me," I said and placed her hands on the button of my slacks. "I need to feel you, skin on skin."

"I'd love to." Miriam's nimble fingers unzipped my slacks and pushed them down. Soon Miriam had me in the same state of undress as herself. "Oh my..." She swallowed hard. "Please..."

I wasn't sure what she was begging for, but I knew what I wanted. This was not going to be a fast, mindless coupling. I wanted this moment of passion to last, and unless I'd become completely inadequate in reading other people, so did Miriam. There was no need for power games, but it was in my nature to take charge. I did what felt right and moved onto the bed, stacking a few pillows in the center of it. "Trust me?" I asked and patted the pillows.

Miriam wet her lips and joined me on the bed. "How do you want me?" she asked with a husky voice.

"Naked, first of all." I smiled and cupped her cheek. "I'm going to make you feel so good." I brushed my thumb across her lower lip and her tongue immediately darted out to lick it.

I reached around her and unfastened her bra. It slid slowly down her arms and ended up on her lap where she knelt next to me. Her breasts were young, pert, and with plump, dark brown nipples. My mouth watered only to dry up instantly when I began to push her panties down. A neatly trimmed patch of hair did very little to hide her sex, and the engorged folds drew me in and I had to struggle not to spread her open and plunge my fingers inside right away.

Miriam managed to kick off her panties without changing position as she reached for the hem of my sports bra. She pulled it off and smoothed down my hair.

"Like spun gold," she murmured and raised a tress to her lips and kissed it. My heart ached with the tenderness of her gesture, and I trembled when she removed the last of my clothing.

I needed to feel her against me. I pulled her tightly to me and reveled in the sensation of her hot, slightly damp skin. Miriam groaned and I echoed her as we kissed again.

"God, Miriam, you're so wonderful, so sexy," I murmured in her ear. "I can't wait to have you, but I don't want to rush this. I want to pleasure you, so…tell me if I do something you don't like, okay?"

"I can't imagine you would," Miriam whispered back, her eyes dark with arousal. "Just touch me. Anything."

I pulled the small stack of pillows closer. "Then get on these pillows so I can give you your massage."

I half expected her to decline since getting on the pillows meant having her well-rounded bottom in the air and quite exposed. Such a position is vulnerable, perhaps too much so.

Miriam didn't seem to be of that opinion. She moved with grace and placed herself on the pillows as she pulled one more from the larger pile to hold on to. "Like this?" she asked huskily.

Oh, damn. Yes! I stared at the alluring sight before me. Miriam kept her legs slightly spread and her ass was elevated, which made it possible for me to see everything. The dark shadows between her legs were full of secrets, and the scent of her arousal was almost more than

I could bear. "Yes." I slid my fingers across her back and then repeated the caress with my whole hand, pressing gently. Miriam moaned and shifted a little. I kept up the almost-soothing motion as I wanted her to be comfortable with my touch, but also because it felt so good just to stroke her.

I massaged her shoulders and traveled up and down her spine several times before I moved to her legs. Her thighs trembled as I caressed them and I could see a dark patch on the top pillow underneath her.

I finally let my hand make contact with her bottom. I kept the caress light, teasing, to begin with. Miriam wiggled and turned her head toward mine with a whimper. "Ellie...kiss me..."

I was happy to oblige. I took a firmer grip of one butt cheek as I deepened the kiss. I examined every part of her mouth and lips as I kneaded her ass. Miriam moaned out loud with every breath. I got up, coaxed her legs farther apart, and sat between them. With my right hand I parted her folds and found her rigid, drenched clit. Once I had it firmly between my fingers, I moved over her and pressed my breasts onto her back. My hand was pinned between us, but I didn't need much space to milk her clit. With small insistent caresses I moved my fingers in a pattern that elicited even louder moans and whimpers from Miriam.

Her cries of pleasure made me wetter and I rubbed my center on the curve of her ass. "That's right," I whispered in her ear. "You're so wet. So hot. And all this for me?"

"For you," Miriam groaned. "Oh, yes, Ellie, for you."

Her hoarse voice nearly did me in. My own clit twitched hard several times and I feared I would explode before she came, and I didn't want that. I wanted to pleasure her, to give her what she dreamed of when she wrote those notes...for what she did when she broke my solitude.

"Ellie! Go inside...please!" Miriam was undulating hard against my hand and it was easy for me to push my thumb inside and still keep in contact with her clit. She gave a loud wail and tugged at the pillow she was hugging. "Oh, yes!"

I heard her voice turn huskier, and a fine shimmer of sweat beaded at the nape of her neck. I brushed my lips over the fragrant tresses and murmured my encouragement. "It's okay to come. Just let go, baby. Let it come."

Miriam was sobbing out her excitement, and I pushed my thumb farther inside, curling it slightly. Her orgasm started with small flutters, which grew into tight convulsions around my finger. Miriam's clit throbbed and grew impossibly large while more wetness coated my hand. I was a part of her body, and it seemed to welcome me in as Miriam's orgasm went on and on.

I was almost envious at the length and magnitude of her release, but also proud that I was able to bring her such pleasure. My body shivered against Miriam's as she rolled over and turned to me.

"Ellie," she murmured and held me close. "Oh, damn…" Miriam had tears in her eyes, and I thought she was overwhelmed by her own reaction.

"You're fine." I kissed her forehead and then her mouth. "I'm here."

"You are. You really are." Miriam sounded half in disbelief. "I've dreamed of this for so long."

"You have?"

"Yes." She sneaked one hand down between us. "I've dreamed of being with you and touching you…like this."

Small fingers slid along my drenched sex and I willingly spread my legs. I hooked one thigh across Miriam's hip as the burning sensation sent new tremors through me. She found my clit easily and circled it with quick fingertips. I gave a muffled cry as I pressed my lips into her neck and bit down on her damp skin. My center was burning and I knew it wouldn't take long until I came. Almost afraid of letting go, I tried to hold back the orgasm, but she brought her other hand down between us as well and began to push two fingers inside me.

I rolled over on my back and she followed me in a fluid motion. She only let go of me with one hand and it returned instantly, this time followed by Miriam's hot lips and her very agile tongue. I gasped aloud and arched my back when she flicked her tongue over my swollen clit and sucked at my folds repeatedly. It was right about then that I learned that I'm not above begging.

"Please, Miriam, please…take me," I whimpered in a strange and alien tone. "Don't tease. Just do it."

More fingers filled me, stretched me, and it was such an extraordinary feeling. She possessed me and I happily surrendered. I felt safe, even though we were virtually strangers. Or perhaps *because* she was a stranger. Waves of heat washed over me, closed around me, endless and overpowering. The orgasm erased everything else from my consciousness for precious seconds. My sex burned, and only these waves could put out the unbearable fire.

"My sweet Ellie." Miriam's voice whispered terms of endearment in my ear. "You're so beautiful. You come so *passionately*." She drew on the last words as if tasting something delicious.

"Mmm…"

"Come here." For being so small, Miriam was remarkably strong, and she held me safely in her arms for long moments in silence. I curled up, sated for now, and protected.

"Thanks."

"No need for thanks, but you're welcome anyway." Laughter permeated Miriam's voice. "God, you're the sexiest, most gorgeous woman I've seen or been lucky enough to hold in a long time."

Miriam looked up at me with her dark eyes and I saw how kiss-swollen her lips were, how her eyes shone with what looked like happiness. "I still have no idea what you see in me," I sighed, but couldn't help but smile. "But I'm glad you persevered."

"I'll make it obvious with time, what I see in you." Her face flushed. "That is, of course…if you want to see me again. I…I…"

It was painful to see her pretty face so uncertain and to hear her uncertainty. "Yes. I do want to see you again."

Miriam looked relieved and she quickly kissed my chin. "Good."

I let my eyes roam her body and a new surge of sexual energy stirred in the center of my stomach. Her nipples were still rigid, and they were irresistible. I lowered my head and sucked the closest one into my mouth. *God. She tastes so good.* Ripe and just the right size, her nipple filled my mouth, and my sucking motions made her whimper.

"Ellie! Yes, yes." Her voice trembled and her fingers combed through my long hair over and over. "That's it."

As I worked her nipples Miriam was squirming, spreading her legs wide and tugging at me.

"I need you. I'm burning up. Just feel how wet you've made me. Feel it."

I did. I plunged two fingers inside her without hesitation, and they met no resistance at all, merely silken wetness that enveloped me. I looked at her red sex and I knew it was now my turn. Her taste was a mix of something incredibly sweet and spicy, and I lapped greedily at her.

Miriam hooked her legs over my shoulders and kept them open as wide as I imagine it was possible. She gave me wonderful access to her vulnerable folds and I sucked at them gently as I kept up the steady movements with my hand. I'd already added more fingers and knew from the snug fit how full she must feel.

I moaned into her and nibbled gently at the outer lips. "So good."

"Yours!" Miriam cried out and at that, I locked my lips onto her clit and sucked it hard.

She came with a sharp cry that dwindled into sobs and whimpers. Miriam undulated over and over into my mouth and I made sure I didn't let go. Her orgasm lasted even longer this time and toward the end, I knew I didn't have long to go myself. When her tremors had subsided, I flipped her over on her stomach and I stretched out on her back.

"You drive me insane," I growled in her ear. "You're so fucking beautiful." My language was deteriorating, a sure sign that I was losing control. "Oh, God, Miriam…" I slid my legs down on the bed until I straddled her ass. Pressing my heated sex into her, I rubbed my aching clit against her sweat-slick skin. "I'm going to come."

"Come, then," she groaned and pushed back against me. "Take my ass like that and come for me."

Her language and the way she spoke, in a pressed, passionate tone of voice, nearly did me in. I moved against her, with her, and she was right there with me, urging me on. Her voice entered me as if she'd pushed her fingers inside again, and I needed…more. Just a little more, to push me over. I pressed my hands in between her and the mattress and found her hard nipples.

Her cry, and the way her body tensed, was all it took. My clit erupted and shot bullets of pleasure through my legs and my abdomen. My own nipples burned where I rubbed them against Miriam's back. In wave after wave, the orgasm took what strength I had left, and I slumped at Miriam's side on the bed, sweaty, tousled, and wetter than I'd been in a long time.

"I've got you." She wrapped one arm loosely around my waist, and it kept the connection going.

"Yes." It was all I could muster as I tried to find my bearings.

"You're amazing." Miriam was gasping for air and I realized that she had come again with me.

"You make me forget about everything else," she said. "And I love it."

I couldn't stop the satisfied, broad smile from appearing on my face. "I'm glad." I closed my eyes and listened to my heart slowly settle back to normal. "I'm really glad that I came home with you."

"I wasn't sure I was ready," Miriam said softly, "but I'm glad you noticed me."

COMING TO A HEAD

ANDREA MILLER

Aimee's soft, pink tongue wrapped around verb conjugations with a grace rare in French 101. And her first note (neatly folded and furtively pressed into my hand) said she planned to major in the language—for her the next best thing to aesthetics. Aimee hadn't wanted to attend university, but her parents had said they wouldn't pay for her to muck with lipstick. Looking at her big eyes and slender, snappable limbs, I would decide she'd enrolled because she was essentially a good girl. Then, looking at her chiselled cheekbones and straight back, I would decide that she'd enrolled because she was secretly sharp-shrewd. The compliant Aimee, after all, had a swanky apartment and a silver sports car. She didn't need a part-time job and she had ample pocket money for the creams and powders with which to practice technique.

Of course, by the end of September Aimee and I were as thick as thieves and she was practicing on me. On Friday nights she'd paint my lips a glossy red, perfect for dancing. And on Tuesdays she would slick hot wax on my calves, leaving me stone smooth. Weeks slipped by like this until it was mid-November. Outside, cold, the trees stripped bare. Inside, a warm, yellow light from Aimee's lamp.

"Hmm, how should we do this?" she murmured, fingering a strand of her blond hair. "I know—you lie on the bed."

Aimee had never before given anyone a bikini wax and I'd never had one done. But for the past week she'd been insisting that men like panties with a high-cut leg and that the style required a little grooming. As an incentive she'd even bought us lacy lingerie treats wrapped in tissue paper.

She laid an old sheet over the duvet and tested the temperature of the wax. "Perfect," she said. "Are you ready?"

We both looked down at my black pants, still neatly buttoned up, and a film of sweat suddenly glossed my skin. All my life I'd tried to avoid naked moments at sleepovers and in locker rooms. Moments just before nighties or gym shorts when other girls might catch a glimpse. And now here was Aimee asking me to be more naked than I'd ever imagined and somehow I couldn't avoid her. The rhythm of her voice was too compelling. The slope of her neck.

Fingers trembling, I undid the buttons one by one. Hesitated, then rolled the fabric down the length of my legs. But Aimee still stood waiting, looking at my thin covering of white satin. Finally I took a deep breath and pulled my panties off.

The bed had mounds of plump pillows and a wrought iron frame with shiny brass balls. I sat down and felt the sheet, cool against my bare skin. "Keep your bum close to the edge," Aimee said. "Lie down and let your legs dangle off the side."

As I got into position a blush burned from the tips of my ears to my chest. And I felt strangely like a mermaid or seal. Nothing separate about my legs. No possibility of a gaze falling between them.

Aimee sat down on a chair she'd dragged next to the bed and began to snip at the flat top of my triangle with tiny scissors. At first her touch jolted me like a bite. But quickly, I realized that being worked over with a cold silver mouth and warm fingers was not so terrible. In fact, it was giving me a strange, tingly feeling.

As Aimee made her way to the tip of my triangle, I let her part my thighs. My folds bloomed and I imagined how the glistening ruffles must look to her. I was now beginning to understand that my shame was burning into pleasure and the realization brought me, full-force, back into hot shame. I didn't want Aimee to know how delicious it all felt. I wanted her to stop; I wanted her to continue. I couldn't help but squirm.

Aimee's eyes—and mouth—were so close to me I could feel her soft, warm breath graze my now-clipped fur. She ran her fingers through her handiwork. "Beautiful," she said. "Now we're ready for the next step."

The wax, hot but not painfully so, was the color of honey and sticky like it, too. Aimee dipped a flat piece of wood into the vat and used it like a paintbrush to slick a small section of my hair. Then she pressed a thin, white cloth into her gooey art and in a single quick movement, she held down my skin with one hand and ripped the cloth off with the other, taking my hair with it and leaving a pink, tender spot.

Again and again Aimee slicked on wax and pulled it off. And I winced each time she yanked, but the pain felt necessary and right. Like it was my punishment for the pleasure I'd taken in her softer touch. Finally, when I had a neat triangle edged with what felt like fire, Aimee rubbed me with a soothing cream. The tips of her long hair brushed my inner thighs.

"Let's see how you look in your new panties," she said, gathering up the discarded strips of cloth and putting the lid back on the cream.

I wobbled to Aimee's dresser and found the panties in a bag between bottles of perfume. I stepped gingerly into each lavender leg, careful not to scrape the lace on my raw skin. And then I modelled for Aimee. Making a catwalk out of the bedroom. No longer shy.

"Next time," Aimee said, fixing me with her blue eyes, "let's give you a sphinx."

"What's that?" I wanted to know.

"That's when we take it all off—make you bare like a little girl." I shivered then, thinking how much it would hurt. How shamefully wide I would have to spread my legs and how good it would feel to have Aimee massage cream into every pink crevice. My breath caught in my chest and I felt a quick throb between my thighs. It would be so hard not to squirm, I thought. So hard not to squirm toward her warm breath and agile tongue.

I looked away and hurried to find my clothes. My new panties were damp with sticky traces of wax…and something else.

A few weeks later I was talking long distance to my mother. The reproach in her voice was heavy like winter layers and I was wavering, the phone cord drooping. Then I pictured Mum's fat fingers closing over chunks of fruitcake and Aimee driving away in a streak of silver. And I was suddenly firm; I was going, too. As soon as we finished exams Aimee and I were driving to Florida—to her grandmother's house. Her parents wanted to buy us plane tickets because they thought highways and motels could be dangerous for two lone young women. But Aimee sweet-talked their blessings out of them. We thought driving would be an adventure. And truly, it was.

We drove down the coast, peeling off layers with the crossing of each state line. We made up stories about the cars we passed and changed our own identities in every greasy spoon. But soon the sun was a hot yellow-white and we had the windows rolled down, our hair whipping in the wind. We had arrived.

After a sultry Christmas that smelled of salt and suntan oil, our skin was golden for New Year's Eve and we dressed in little more than heels and perfume. Aimee had gotten her hands on fake IDs and the plan was to have our midnight kisses at a dance club. "Since I'm driving, I'll just have one drink," Aimee said. "But you have as much as you like."

The bar was full of beautiful people bumping and grinding on the dance floor. And the air was thick with smoke and iridescent bubbles that were being pumped out of a machine. As it was my first time in a bar, I was nervous and piña coladas slipped down in remedy. After I'd twirled four paper umbrellas between my fingers, Aimee leaned over and said in my ear, "I bought myself a holiday treat and I've been meaning to share it with you…"

A bubble floated by and she popped it with her fingertip. Then she smiled, teeth flashing under the strobe lights, and I followed her out of the bar—not yet midnight. I wanted to know what the treat was, but she told me it was a surprise and that I'd have to wait. We drove to the outskirts of town—saying nothing, music blaring—until Aimee pulled into an industrial park and stopped the car on an empty dead-end. "It's in the trunk," she said. "Just a sec."

Aimee's heels crunched against gravel and she came back carrying a cloth bag with a pattern of tiny cherries. I had no idea what could be inside, but I felt tingles of anticipation and twinges of fear. Whatever it was, it had to be something important or else there wouldn't be this mystery.

Slowly, Aimee loosened the drawstring and pulled out a long, silver wand that flashed orange under the strange glow of the streetlight. I'd never seen anything like it before, yet I instinctively suspected what it was for. "What is it?" I faltered and Aimee cocked an eyebrow. "I'll show you," she said.

After adjusting her car seat so that she was slightly reclined, Aimee began to slide the wand's tip over the thin fabric of her dress, worrying her nipples into sharp, perverse points. A private act, crude even, and I looked away, caught my expression in the mirror—mouth and eyes circles of surprise. But there was something compelling about what Aimee was doing and I couldn't stop my gaze from roving back. Besides, she had her eyes closed; she couldn't see me watching.

Couldn't see me watch as she gently tugged on her low-cut dress and sent her breasts spilling out the top. Couldn't see me watch as she turned the base of the wand, and with it now humming, rubbed it over her naked nipples.

Aimee's dress was short and she already had her legs cocked open so that her panties were visible. But suddenly she spread her thighs a little more and ran the wand between them. Her chest started to heave then, her breathing change. She pushed her panties to one side of her folds, pressed the wand inside of her, and bore down on it, swallowing the silver while circling her clit with her fingers. Finally she made little throaty moans that made me throb and she buckled under her own touch.

For a moment Aimee sat panting, the wand still buried in her. Then she slipped it out and handed it to me. "Try it," she said. "It's fantastic."

Reckless with booze and the slick that had gathered between my legs, I accepted the wand—still wet and warm from Aimee—and slid it under my skirt. Through my panties, it hummed against my clit and it felt so delicious I almost forgot someone was watching. I threw my head back and rocked my hips until, soon, my panties were soaked and I was pulling them off, rushing to press the shaft to my bare skin.

Just before leaving for Florida, Aimee had given me a sphinx, making me as bald as a little girl. So that meant I could have been compared to a little girl in at least two ways, because on that New Year's eve at age eighteen I was also as tight as one, too. I had kissed several boys and let them grind their cocks into my clothed, indifferent thighs. But I was still a virgin. I'd not even had my own fingers inside. Nevertheless, I had liked the look of Aimee riding the wand, and I suddenly needed to know how it felt to be impaled like that.

I positioned the silver tip at the mouth of my snatch and for a moment I just let it rest there—the vibrations humming every crevice while my fingers worked my clit. Soon, however, my hips began to move with a life of their own. Made tiny thrusts that slowly swallowed the wand and ripped me open. My eyes watered, but the pain somehow made rolling my clit feel even more delicious. And my hips rocked faster, harder, until, with Aimee's eyes on me, I came against my hand, the rod jammed in my hole to the very hilt. Tears in my mouth and hair. Blood on the black leather seat, blood in my nails—even my French manicure blushing.

Quickly I shoved the wand back into its cherry bag and back into the trunk. Then Aimee and I drove to her grandmother's house, music blaring. Me looking out the window at inky landscape, shadowy houses, dark figures and her looking straight ahead.

And that is how it was for the rest of the trip—everything awkward, every space too small—the corridors in which I had to pass Aimee, the princess bed in the guest room we had to share. Looking back, I think it was probably me that made everything so uncomfortable. I was just so confused about what it all meant to me, to Aimee, to us. Still, I knew that I didn't want to lose our friendship, so back home I tried hard to make things return to normal between us. And for me that meant never mentioning the silver wand and it meant that instead of practicing with makeup and wax, we watched movies and drank coffee with two guys from school.

Though everyone said they were good-looking—Chris with his smoky eyes and Jason with his broad shoulders—I could never work up any excitement for either of them. Unlike when I watched Aimee wriggle on the dance floor, watching Chris or Jason never made it throb between my thighs. I simply admired their beauty the way I might admire that of curtains or show dogs.

Spring came and my true feeling became more and more painfully obvious to me. Perhaps it was watching pigeons strut with puffed-up chests and seeing flowers spread for bees. Or perhaps it was just that time had mellowed the shock of such a graphic night with the dildo and I was finally ready to move on. But either way, I was now explicitly aware of how I wanted to touch Aimee—how I wanted to trace her collarbone and taste her salt and perfume. The only problem that remained was my own virginal self-doubt. Sometimes I would look at her milky skin and decide that she'd never want to touch me. Then at other times I would look at the soft blue web just under the surface and I'd decide that she would—that secretly her blood rushed and throbbed just like mine. At any rate, it all came to a head one night at her place.

Chris and Jason were there, of course, and they'd brought beer—presumably to loosen us up for that inevitable moment when they would corner us and fumble with our bra straps. Chris doled out another cold round and cracked his open. "Have any of you guys ever played Truth or Dare?" he asked. Though I had not, I knew where his question was going and I wasn't surprised to find myself in the middle of a game.

What did surprise me, however, was that round after round we all chose truth.

I don't know about the others—maybe they were just warming up—but I avoided dares because I suspected they'd involve me doing something messy and unpleasant with Jason, that and because truth, unlike dares, could be dodged with lies. Unfortunately, lying was tricky. I had to come up with answers that weren't so green they would make me seem uptight, or so hot they would give Jason ideas. Walking that fine line left me without the energy to come up with questions and Aimee always had to think of something for me.

At first she asked stuff such as, "How often do you masturbate?" and "What is the most erotic dream you've ever had?" But eventually she hit on a question that got my attention: "Have you ever done it with another guy?"

Jason screwed up his face like the very idea tasted of sour milk and for a moment I thought he might even spit on Aimee's clean pink carpet. "No," he said. "That's disgusting."

Chris, sitting in an armchair by the window, nodded in agreement then suddenly flashed a sly grin. "Two girls, on the other hand," he said. "Now, that's all right. So what about you, Aimee? Have you ever gotten it on with another chick?"

"Hey, you can't just ask me a question. You have to wait until I choose truth or dare."

"Well, hurry and choose." But Aimee didn't hurry. Instead she took a long, slow swig of beer and looked in turn at the three faces watching her. Under her gaze, it seemed suddenly clear to me that Aimee knew. Knew explicitly how I wanted to trace and finger all her lines and crevices—the cleft of her heart-shaped ass, the curve of her hips. And I felt more exposed then than I ever had, even the first time she'd waxed between my legs. It was like I (not Aimee) had been asked the question and that it was about so much more than what I had actually done with a woman, but also about what I had wanted to do.

I tilted back my head and swallowed, polished off my beer, then discarded the empty can on the coffee table. Metal met wood and Aimee flicked a final glance at me. "Dare," she said.

The guys grinned at each other. "Okay," said Jason. "I dare you to kiss Heidi on the lips. Tongue and everything."

All at once the music coming from the stereo seemed loud and hard. And with its rhythm filling my throat, I couldn't breathe. Aimee was sitting on the floor a few feet away from me and I was sitting on the sofa. We locked eyes but didn't speak. I didn't know what she would do and it felt like a very long time before she did anything at all.

Finally, however, she crawled across the pink carpet until she was on her knees right in front of me and I could smell her perfume—sweet yet as heady as musk. She wrapped her fingers around my neck—under the hair, right on the skin—and she pulled me to her. Kissed me softly at first, then insistently. Her tongue curling around mine. Her teeth on my lips. But too soon it was over and she was back in her spot on the floor, my mouth watering for her.

"What do you want, Heidi?" Jason asked. "Truth or dare?" The guys were apparently getting off on this and hoping it would go further. I didn't, however, care what they wanted. The only important thing was that their presence seemed to free Aimee and me to do what *we* wanted to do. To choose dare.

Jason tapped his feet, cracked his knuckles. "I dare you to feel Aimee up," he said. Without a second thought I got up from the sofa and walked over to her. Got down on the floor so that we were sitting face-to-face, kissing hard. Her dress so thin and slippery my hands instantly fell into place.

I leaned into Aimee until she was lying on the floor and I was on top of her, one of my legs wedged between hers and one of hers between mine. In that way, we slid against each other, panting, as she worked my skirt up to my hips and squeezed my ass. Finally she rolled me off her and pulled down my soaked panties. She kissed the thin, sensitive skin of my inner thighs and ran her tongue along the thrust of my hipbones. Then when she had me squirming, she brought her mouth to the vee of my crotch and licked a steady rhythm. I whimpered and rocked faster and faster. Almost like I wanted her to swallow me whole.

I thought, this may be a dare but it sure feels like the truth. And then I thought nothing. Just ground into her tongue until I came.

DEBUT
CHERI CRYSTAL

From the very first page of her first novel, I was enamored. She wrote the way I wanted to be held. She took me prisoner while I frantically turned pages, sitting at the edge of my seat, my tight jeans digging into my swollen clit. Sometimes I actually came in my pants in the middle of reading a sex scene. She wrote some of the hottest I'd ever read. I had to e-mail this author. I had to convey how deeply her writing touched me, how her words resonated in the core of my soul and at the same time caressed my body like tongue and fingers.

I was over the moon when she answered my first shy note, and within a few weeks we were exchanging e-mails regularly like old friends. We wrote and chatted online for almost a year but never met. Through e-mail we shared photos, secrets, desires, and laughter. We discussed everything from writing styles to how she wrote her first tantalizing sex scene. Her descriptions of fisting had me intrigued. I wonder if she knew I had never tried it but was dying to.

Her name was Angel and at first sight I truly believed she was sent to me from heaven. I was already in love with her mind but I knew it was her body I was going to worship. She was a few inches taller than me and stunning with her spiked red hair, small straight nose, and emerald eyes. Her shoulders were broad, her waist was slender, and her snug, man-tailored shirt showed off ample breasts. The top two buttons were undone, revealing a throat I wanted instantly to lick. Her long legs and the way they led to her firm butt had me drooling. With a jacket slung over her shoulder and boots with two-inch heels, she looked like an Amazon.

I wondered if she'd seen me. The cocktail hour was all abuzz and I busied myself mingling with the other guests, waiting for our paths to cross. The champagne was going to my head and elsewhere. It wasn't even *my* big night. Well, not for a literary award but for something I longed for from the first moment I started having these fantasies. Perhaps my latest romance novel would be in the running next year, but I couldn't think about that now. I was about to meet her face to face. I was presenting the award for Best Lesbian Erotica—how appropriate; I could almost smell the lust oozing from my pores. She was up for the Debut Fiction award, and I wished I were presenting that one. If it were up to me, she would win in every category, especially Romance and Erotica.

When she finally glanced in my direction and our eyes met, my pulse quickened, my heart pounded hard in my chest, and I could feel my clit spring to attention. I had dreamed about this moment for what seemed an eternity and as she looked me over, the anticipation of breathing the same air as her was unbearable. My skintight black strapless dress with the plunging neckline seemed to do the trick. She smiled as she checked out my cleavage. *Thank you Victoria's Secret for helping Mother Nature.* I knew I was blushing furiously, but I watched her take me in, loving her slow sensual appraisal. I ached to run my fingers through her short spiked red hair. I wondered if she was a natural redhead and yearned to find out. Her eyes lingered at my breasts once more before they lifted to mine, gorgeous green eyes that sparkled just for me. Her mouth parted in a mischievous smile.

"Finally," she said.

"Finally," I replied.

It was hard to believe that two critically acclaimed authors couldn't come up with anything more poetic than that. After months of being the biggest flirt this side of the Internet, I was finally meeting the recipient of my corny jokes, endless prattle, and long-winded beating around the bush about what I really wanted. A mixture of amusement, pleasure, and outright lust flitted over her face as if she was recalling every e-mail we'd exchanged over the last year. For a moment, all of the secrets, laughter, unquestioning friendship, and tentative exploration of new sexual territory showed in the way her eyes gleamed.

We grabbed beers from a passing waiter, clinked bottles, and said, "Cheers," in unison. We laughed. She had beautiful even white teeth.

"You look great," I said. *Good enough to eat.* Her Internet photos didn't do her justice.

"So do you," she answered, her eyes locked on mine.

I touched her arm and wanted to touch so much more. "Good luck tonight. You're sure to win."

"Thanks, but have you read the others in the category? I think I have some stiff competition."

"'Stiff' as in dead. There's no contest. You may as well claim the prize so the two of us can go back to your hotel and fuck our brains out." I couldn't believe I just said that. From the surprise on her face, neither could she, but then she grinned.

"You wanna?" She said it jokingly, but her gaze belied her nonchalance.

"Sure, let's blow this joint."

We both laughed, knowing there was no way we were going to leave before they handed out the awards. It was fun to tease, though, except the teasing was making my clit twitch. Now that I'd met her I was more and more sure that the things we'd hinted we'd like to do in a night of passion were going to happen. Part of me started to panic, but I looked at her again and I felt safe. It was going to be hard to concentrate on the ceremonies.

"Shall we go in?" she said when the lights flashed.

I nodded, and she downed the rest of her beer. I had hardly touched mine. We gave the bottles to the waiter collecting empties, and she led the way into the auditorium with her arm loosely around the small of my back. Her touch was light but it sent electricity shooting through my body directly to the heightened nerve endings of my clit. I shivered slightly.

"Are you cold?" She put her arm around my bare shoulder. "Would you like my jacket?"

How sweet. I shook my head. "You're so hot…I mean, your body is exuding enough warmth to keep me toasty."

"You're pretty hot yourself. You smell so good too." She rubbed her cheek against my hair and I nearly fainted. Fortunately, we found our seats just before my knees gave out.

Sitting close with only the armrest as a barrier, I leaned into her. "You nervous?"

"Nah."

"Liar. I can feel you shaking in your boots."

"That shaking has nothing to do with the awards." Her eyes were hungry, as if she wanted to devour me in a single gulp. If she leaned toward me one more inch, our faces would touch. I longed to kiss those lips when she moistened them with her tongue. I wanted to *be* that tongue.

The lights went down and she nonchalantly put her hand on my thigh just under my dress. I moved ever closer as her hand inched its way up the inside of my thigh and spread my legs farther apart. It took all my strength not to scream out, *Don't stop. Claim your prize.*

I prayed that she would keep going, knowing the thin silk of my panties would not get in her way. She pushed the material aside. My clit was about to explode. Her nimble fingers caressed my soft curls and I sighed. It was delicious. *Keep going. You're almost there, almost...* and just when I thought I was about to get my wish the emcee took center stage and began his shtick. Angel cleared her throat and readjusted herself in the chair. If her clit was pulsating as frantically as mine, she was likely to miss her category being called, so I reluctantly let her go.

I delivered my well-rehearsed speech, laced with as many jokes as I could muster, and announced the winner for Best Lesbian Erotica. I didn't wait onstage for her to thank everyone, but made my way back to my seat. Once seated, I could tell that Angel was sweating with anticipation for her award. Best Debut Fiction was up next.

I took her hand and squeezed it. "Good luck," I whispered in her ear, purposely tickling her with my breath. The lights from the stage were just enough for me to make out her hardened nipples beneath her shirt.

I heard her name and jumped out of my seat. The cover of her novel was larger than life on the two-story screen. She sat there stunned for a second but got her legs to work and regained her composure. She stood up and I hugged her in congratulations. The heat between us ignited my fire even more. I was bursting with excitement. Seeing her stride to the podium, so confident and poised, made her that much more desirable, if that were possible. I wanted her so badly. My favorite book had won, but more importantly, my favorite author had won, and I planned to be the one to help her celebrate.

Angel looked radiant as she came back to her seat and, impulsively, I kissed her on the lips. She flashed me one of her dazzling smiles, took my hand in hers, and I lifted it to her lips. I put my hand on her knee and slowly made my way up toward her inviting crotch. There were people all around us, which only made me more excited. I was so turned on that I would have fucked her even if we were in Grand Central Station during rush hour. Applause erupted just as I reached the goal. I lost track of which category they were up to as I focused on Angel's need. I imagined I could feel her stiff clit under my fingertips, so swollen and hard that even her pants couldn't conceal its prominence. She twitched when I fingered her. My nipples hardened and the muscles tightened deep within my pelvis.

"I need the restroom," she whispered urgently in my ear and got up suddenly.

She made it almost out of the auditorium before I got up to follow her.

I couldn't believe what I was doing. My heart thumped hard, and it wasn't just from the steep incline of the auditorium and my three-inch heels. I was so swollen that my clit was squeezed with each step. Making my way out of the auditorium and opening the door, I quickly headed to the ladies room. I made it there in record time.

Angel turned around as if expecting me and put her award down on the counter. I practically flung myself at her, frantic for the taste of her lips, kissing her as I made my way down to her breasts—undoing buttons two at a time.

She stopped me. "Hey, who's the butch here, anyhow?"

"You are, but I want you so badly I can't help it. Besides—you like to think you're so tough, but I know what a mush you really are."

She laughed. "So take me, then."

As I fumbled with her shirt, she led us into a stall. Since I was all over her, she barely got the door locked. Possessively, she wrapped her arms around me. *Now look who was* taking *whom!* Relinquishing control for the moment, I felt safe in her embrace. Never having felt this way about anyone, I trusted her implicitly. The restroom was empty and the thought that someone could walk in at any moment titillated me. I soaked through my panties. If we kept up this fevered pitch, I knew I was going to come and it was going to be quick; I was on the brink and she hadn't even touched me yet.

I pushed up her bra and pulled one well-rounded, delicious nipple into my mouth. I was teasing her hardened nipple with my teeth and tongue when she groaned and stopped me.

"Oh, God, not like this."

"Was it too hard?"

"No, perfect. Just perfect. But let's get out of here. Our first time needs to be better than this."

"What could be better than being with you?"

"Let's get out of here."

"But what about your publisher's reception..."

"We'll come back, maybe. I'm so hard—I need you now. My hotel is around the corner." She interlaced her fingers in mine and grabbed the award with the other hand. "Come on."

We practically ran to the hotel. The night air cooled my flushed, hot skin, but it did nothing to alleviate the fire inside. We reached the lobby of the hotel in record time and made out in the elevator on the way up to her room.

Shivering from anticipation, I knew in my heart that I was about to embark on new territory and realize my dream. Suddenly, I knew what I wanted and I was surer than ever. The mere thought of her kissing me, caressing me—*fucking* me, made me wet. The reality of it overwhelmed me. I felt as if I had finally arrived at the place I was supposed to be.

Angel didn't waste any time getting her key out and opening the door. In one fluid motion, she lifted me into her arms and carried me across the threshold. My limbs were putty. Again, I relinquished all control to her. She set me down beside the bed.

My strapless Lycra dress slipped off easily as Angel grasped the hem and pulled it down. She sucked on my neck as she removed my Victoria's Secret bra that wasn't a secret anymore and playfully teased at my breasts. She returned her attention to my waiting mouth and penetrated me with her tongue. I heard myself moan as her thigh made its way up against my clit. I had my hands on her head pulling her closer.

Angel pulled away just long enough to kick off her boots, remove her shirt, sports bra, pants, and underwear. She was a true redhead. I smiled. Her curves were beautifully accentuated with smooth muscles that rippled slightly as she moved. Her skin was a creamy white that I often dreamed about. She was flawless. We backed onto the bed, her touch never leaving my tingling skin.

I couldn't take it a moment longer. "Please...I need you... inside."

"Soon. Let me look at you first."

She removed my lace panties, slowly torturing me as she spread my legs as far as they would comfortably go. She licked her finger and opened my lips before touching my tender, swollen clit. I thought I would die.

"You are so beautiful. Just as I imagined you'd be," she said and continued to stroke the length of my clit on either side with her thumbs, slowly easing her finger inside me.

"So good." I'm sure I dug my nails into her arms, but she didn't even flinch.

"Deeper," I begged. I wanted her inside me. She took her time. "I'm going to come…"

"No, wait. Hold on. I want to taste you." Before I knew it, she had my swollen clit in her mouth and was sucking it in a way that I had never felt before. I was so wet, so close…instinctively she looked up for a second. "Soon," she said.

And I obeyed.

The hints and the innuendos in a year's worth of e-mail and chat had prepared me for this moment. I wanted her in ways I never trusted any woman before. She inserted one, then two, then four fingers inside me as she sucked and licked. The combined effort was sensational. Enthralled, I held my breath to avoid even the slightest distraction each time I got closer to orgasm. I didn't care if I died just then from asphyxiation.

"I want all of you in me," I begged.

"Have you ever?"

"No, but I want to with you."

"Are you sure?" she asked.

"Yes…please."

"I don't want to hurt you."

"You won't. I trust you. Please, Angel. Take me. Fuck me, please!"

"Can you relax for just a minute, baby? I won't do that without lube."

"Okay," I said shakily. I didn't want her to, but her concern that I not be hurt touched me.

She was only gone a moment or two, and after a hot, reassuring kiss, her slick hand was between my legs again. Carefully, watching my expression, she guided her fist inside me tentatively, at first compressing her fingers to fit in the tight space. I leaned on my elbows to watch as she skillfully guided her fist up and in me as high as it would go. It cut like a knife at first but then, ooh, it felt soooo good in a wicked way. The more turned on I became, the more delicious it felt.

A mixture of concern and awe on her face made me feel special—loved, even. She looked like she was in a wonderful place and I was right there with her. I concentrated on relaxing as she worked her hand inside me, but my muscles had a mind of their own, tensing and flexing with each thrust. I swallowed her up as she went deeper still. Watching her excited me further until I could not bear it any longer. I lay back and enjoyed the sensation as she eagerly entered me at an increased pace. I brought my legs up over her shoulders. She fit inside of me perfectly. I was so wet, and I cried out in ecstasy again and again with each thrust, "Harder, harder." I was so close—the rougher the better.

"You sure?"

"I'm sure! Do it! I'm almost there."

The last thrust accompanied by one last lick sent me convulsing as I came all over Angel's fist. I shuddered again, letting the orgasm take me over and over again until the last ripple ceased and all I could feel was the calm of a warm glow. It was everything I'd imagined my first time being fisted would be, but more importantly, it was Angel who took me to that special place. Slowly she removed her fist, taking her sweet time, and when she licked her fingers, I quivered. "Ooh, baby…"

"You like?" She kissed my thigh, her voice sounding smug.

"Oh, I like. Come here. I want to give you *my* award for outstanding performance. Turn over." I wanted to please her so badly.

"Two awards in one night. I don't know if I can stand it."

"You can stand it." Luckily, I had pored over Angel's every word and knew what she liked, but I was happy I had a few tricks of my own. Her reactions reassured me that I was a bona fide sex goddess.

After we were sated, dressed, and freshened up, we walked back to the auditorium hand in hand with the gentle breeze in our hair and lightness in our step. Her arm was draped protectively around my shoulder, and I had my arm around her waist with my hand in her back pocket. She kissed my neck and I pulled her closer. Finding my soul mate on the Internet was unbelievable enough, but our first encounter and my first experience with fisting exceeded my wildest fantasy. We made it back to our seats just in time for the lights to come up, signaling the ceremony was over. If we had been missed, nobody mentioned it. Angel accepted congratulations from all who offered them, then finally reached for my hand. She smiled at me and I melted at the heated promise in her eyes.

We both had won debut awards.

PERSPEX WINDOW
CHEYENNE BLUE

Kate pushes her way ass first onto the promenade deck. The wind curls around the door, threatening to slam it back on her, and the sea swells enough that she lurches along the deck with a rolling gait. Carefully, she cradles her glass of Chardonnay. A second quarter bottle sticks out of her pocket.

She staggers along the deserted deck until she finds a sheltered corner. Metal and Perspex windbreaks divide the open area, and she presses up against a bulkhead, carefully setting down her glass on a ledge and turning away from the wind to light a cigarette. She huddles into the merge shelter and turns her collar up for the illusion of warmth. Here, the wind isn't strong enough to be unpleasant, which is a good thing for an addicted smoker on a nonsmoking Irish ferry. Kate inhales, holds, and feels the nicotine steal through her blood.

She's the only one on deck as far as she can tell. One o'clock in the morning, and the ferry is rocking its way from Rosslare to Cherbourg, packed with holidaymakers and Irish couples on swift shopping jaunts, off to buy cheap booze and cigarettes in France. Down on the car deck, her Suzuki waits, its back seats removed to fit more cases of wine. Shopping bags are piled on the passenger seat.

Kate pulls on the cigarette and the small lines crease above her upper lip. The wind whips a strand of graying hair across her mouth, and she pushes her free hand deeper into her jacket pocket. She can smell the sea, taste its briny sharpness. Seven hours into the crossing, and her body leans with the boat.

Inside the ferry's heated interior the corridors are nearly deserted. There's a faint smell of puke creeping out under the door of the toilets— probably from the group of underage lads determined to put the pints away. The restaurants have closed, and most people have shambled off to their tiny cabin bunks to close their eyes until morning.

Kate likes the sea air and she needs her nicotine, so she's here, on the promenade deck, watching the moon carve a path across the slatey sea. Out here, she is alone. Only the white bench seats stand solemn sentry duty in the night.

A door crashes open behind her. Laughter, slurred and female, reaches her across the nonslip blue matting.

"For feck's sake, Annie, can't you walk in a straight line?" The voice is young and Dublin and has an indulgent lilt to its censorial question.

"I can so. It's this bleedin' boat that can't sail straight."

Kate watches the women making their stumbling way to the railing. One bird-thin and fragile, the other stout with drafthorse buttocks; one with cropped hair, the other with a mess of tangled curls. They hold each other's arms as they weave their way across the deck.

"Not here," the thin one with cropped hair, Annie, mutters. "Anyone can see us."

"There's no one around."

Annie is led back to a dubious shelter, to a nook behind one of the entrance doors, sheltered from the wind by a sheet of rust and Perspex.

Kate waits, watching idly, as she finishes her cigarette and takes a sip of Chardonnay. She can see them clearly, but obviously they haven't noticed her.

"Here," Curly-head says decisively.

She turns Crop-head and wraps her arms around her. Her mouth comes down, and Kate stifles a gasp. The kiss is long. Kate huddles deeper into her jacket and sips. Women. Kissing.

She's not naïve; she knows it happens, and happens here in Ireland, in spite of the church's stranglehold. And she has sometimes wondered, in a sort of vague afterthought way when the TV showed a lesbian kiss, what it would be like. But never has she seen it unfold in front of her. The cigarette burns down to the butt as the women kiss, and Kate watches. It's a long kiss, a deep, drugging kiss, and the two figures merge in the moon-wrapped night, blend into the deep blue of the deck matting, fade into the shadows of the lifeboats. And still they kiss. Kate can hear the short pants of breath merging with the lap of the water against the sides and the creak of the boat as it rolls. She waits, not wanting to interrupt them now, although will they even notice?

They break apart. "I love it when you kiss me like that," the one called Annie says.

"You'll like what I'm about to do better."

"Orla, no, not here—"

"Here, yes here." Orla is insistent. "There's no one around. All the families have gone to bed. The football has finished. And if you'd booked a cabin we'd be in it now, loving our brains out in peace and privacy instead of out here on deck."

"It's cold," Annie whines, but Kate can see her hands burrowing around Orla's waist, pushing up the bulky sweater to reveal a line of white flesh. Is it really that ethereal white, or is it the moonlight?

"You were hot inside," points out Orla.

She's the one choreographing this. Kate can see her pressing Annie into the Perspex, her hands moving purposefully over the waiflike body.

Kate knows she should move. Her cigarette is finished, and she should return to the privacy of her own cabin, go to bed, and sleep. But instead, she takes a sip of wine and continues to watch. Orla and Annie. Annie and Orla. A nice coupling to their names.

With a swift movement, Orla moves back, pushes up Annie's shirt, flicking the buttons so that the garment falls open. Kate sees pearlescent flesh and small high breasts, tipped with moonlight. No bra. Annie's nipples are raised to the moon. A brief moment of clear sight, then they are covered by her girlfriend's hands, thumbs flicking her nipples. Annie's head falls back, hits the Perspex.

Kate tilts her head the better to see, peering slightly around her shaded alcove. She tries to breathe quietly, although it's doubtful the women will hear her above the thrum of the diesel engine and the creak of the boat as she cleaves through the inscrutable sea. In front of her, the women are kissing again, and although she can't see, she senses that Orla's fingers are working the fastening of her girlfriend's hipster jeans.

"Ker—iste! Don't bloody bite!" Orla's fingers muffle Annie's shriek. Orla holds her hand over Annie's mouth, even as her face is buried in her neck.

The objection fades to a sigh, and Annie kisses those same fingers as they stroke across her lips. Orla stoops, and one of those high, tight breasts is engulfed in her mouth. Annie's hands wind in those disordered wild curls.

Kate fancies she can feel a mouth on her own breasts. There's a tingle between her thighs, a sensation long absent. The scene in front of her has a surreality to it; the moonlight, the dark night outside its path, and the two girls, edged in gilt and silver.

Orla kneels—how hard the deck must be on her knees—and Annie's jeans descend. There are bowed white thighs and black panties banded across her narrow hips. Then the panties are gone, slipped down below her knees.

Annie spreads her legs as wide as the bunched jeans and underwear allows, there's the dark shadow, the hidden cleft. Fingers part the bitter sea, and then Orla's mouth ducks down, her nose wedged firmly in the forest. She's there a long time. Annie's fingers wind in her hair, holding her there. When she lifts fractionally, Kate sees her chin is wetly shining. Her hand shakes as she takes a sip of wine, and her mind spirals back to the last time someone's face was between her legs. How long ago? She's forgotten the exquisite sensation, forgotten the feeling of being completely loved, forgotten the feeling.

Kate is so caught up in her own memories, her own cunt throbbing hotly, that when Annie comes with a glass-shattering shriek, she's caught by surprise. Kate's wine glass slips from shaky fingers and crashes to the deck.

"What the fuck?"

Orla rises, wiping her mouth with her hand while Annie struggles to pull her jeans up. They are impeded by her panties, which have twisted around her thighs. Both women are peering into the long shadows that spill from the bulkheads.

Kate waits until Annie is decent again, then moves forward. "Sorry," she says. "I dropped my glass." She moves as if to retreat back to the ferry's interior, but Orla's harsh words stop her.

"Have a good look, did you? Like what you saw? Going off to complain to the steward?" And under her breath, "Fecking middle-aged puritan."

Kate pauses, turns slowly. "Guilty on the middle-aged part. But I'm not going to complain. You were..." She hesitates, knowing she should simply offer a frosty smile and leave, but is compelled to tell them how they made her feel. But the words are too clumsy for the poignant feelings of love and loss entwined within her. She settles for, "You were beautiful."

Silence greets her answer, and the girls exchange surprised looks. Suddenly, they're no longer the confident young lovers; they're shy and used to censure from strangers.

Annie moves to stand with her lover, wraps an arm around her waist and leans her head on her shoulder. "How so?"

"I like to see young people in love. It gives me hope that sometimes there's a happy ending."

"What do you mean?" Orla stands protectively of Annie.

Kate shrugs, aware she's said too much. She considers several replies, but simply says, "It's not always a fairy tale."

"And don't we know it." Shared smiles, and a tentative bond strings between them all.

Kate moves again, makes to sidle past them and away, out of their lives, but an impulse makes her say, "I have a cabin to myself. Why don't you take it instead of me? Then you can continue uninterrupted."

The women exchange wary glances. "Why would you do that?" says Orla. "Where will you sleep?"

"Where were you going to sleep?" Kate watches them. She's already slightly regretting her impulse. Her bones are too old to sleep on the floor.

"In the children's play area," replies Annie. "There's foam on the floor, and there's only a couple of people there."

"Then that's where I'll go," says Kate, decisively. She fishes the key out of her pocket. "Come with me now, let me get my stuff and I'll be out of your way."

They hesitate, so she adds, "I promise I won't disturb you, and you can have some privacy." She addresses her comment to Orla. "Besides, I think you'd like to let Annie return the favor."

A snort of laughter. "Indeed." She makes up her mind. "That's very kind of you. Come on, Annie."

Kate leads them through the ship to her tiny cabin. "Let me get my bag." Swiftly she gathers her toilet bag and her nightie, stuffing them back in her case with her clean underwear.

When she turns, Orla is right behind her.

"Two bunks." Orla states the obvious. "Why don't you have one and we'll have the other?"

Annie giggles; a breathy sound, hastily choked off.

Kate arches an eyebrow. "Privacy. Remember? You don't want me listening in."

Orla advances so that she's practically nose to nose. Kate fights the urge to step back. "But you wouldn't mind listening in, now would you? After all, you stayed and watched on deck."

Kate draws herself up to her full five feet three. "I didn't have a choice then."

"You have one now."

A beat of hesitation, then Kate shrugs, feigning a nonchalance she doesn't feel. Her heart is leaping like a spooked rabbit. "If you insist. I'll have the bottom bunk." She takes her nightie back out of the bag and disappears into the tiny bathroom. When she emerges, hair hanging loose and nightgown brushing her calves, the others are in bed. There are muffled giggles from the top bunk, and two heads crammed in together. She arranges herself in the lower bunk, turns to the wall, and closes her eyes.

For a minute or two, all is silent. Slowly, Kate releases her pent-up breath, aware of a faint sense of disappointment. She didn't really want to hear them making love. No, she didn't.

The lights are out, and it's velvet black in the inner cabin with no porthole. The only glimmer of light is the slight luminescence of the safety notice on the wall. Kate tries to steady her breathing, self-consciously aware of its fast, uneven pitch, fast above the steady throb of the boat's engines. Finally her body relaxes, limbs twitching on the edge of sleep.

That's when there's a noise from the upper bunk. A thump, and the sound of a body turning awkwardly. Something hits the wall, and there's the slide of skin over sheets. A sigh; Orla's, thinks Kate. She turns on her back and opens her eyes. Too dark to see anything. More rustling, then the sound of soft kissing. Kate imagines lips sliding over heated skin, imagines the taste of another woman.

"Yes. Like that." Orla's voice, gruff and tight.

Then there's only the sound of Orla's breathing, faster, loud in the quiet cabin.

When she starts to moan, breathy little murmurs of encouragement, mumbled affirmations of pleasure, the knowledge of what is happening pierces through Kate in a vivid dart of imagination.

"Oh yes," Orla says. "Oh yes, yes, yesyesyes." And Kate's arousal swells out into the cabin to mingle with Orla's. Her own cunt is throbbing, in sweet, pulsating waves, and she feels molten. The sound of pleasure—even a pleasure not her own—is compelling.

Quietly, slowly, she inches her own thighs apart, and even though no one can see, or care if they could, she casually rests a hand on her own curved stomach and concentrates on keeping her breathing slow and even. Her hand inches down to her panty line and farther, down to the patch of hair, stealing ever onward until she can slide a finger along her slit, finding her pleasure point.

Orla's litany of joy is continuous, and Kate's mind runs through a flickering kaleidoscope of possible scenarios. Is Annie kneeling between her parted thighs, her face plastered to Orla's slick and swollen gash? Or are they lying entwined, with Annie's fingers pressing and rubbing between Orla's legs? Maybe Annie has three, even four, fingers in her lover's pussy, curling them around, pressing on pleasure points, filling her, stretching her so that she knows that engorged feminine fullness. What endless possibilities they have. Kate's mind spins, and her fingers rub tiny concentric circles over her clit.

"Faster," commands Orla, and there's another bang, as if her head has contacted with the wall.

Kate pulsates in time to the breathing she hears. Stealth and silence are abandoned, and she spreads her legs, rubs faster, uncaring of her hitching breath.

Orla comes in a crash of noise, a howl of pleasure, and the bunk above Kate shakes. Her fingers push her over the edge into her own orgasm, a more muted pleasure than Orla's although she's sure her rapid breathing has given her away.

The flutters still twitch around her fingers. She withdraws them and raises her fingers to her own lips. Tentatively, she tastes. Above, mumbles of pleasure, a small whisper of love. Then a strange, hung tension permeates the room. Do they all simply roll over and go to sleep now? Talk? Get to know each other? Kate wishes for a cigarette. But, in the darkness, here in the company of strangers, she's content.

As the ferry noses its way into Cherbourg, Kate stands on deck with a cigarette. She sniffs her fingers. She can smell the sea.

HER
KI THOMPSON

I am not a greedy woman. In fact, I pride myself on my sense of self-restraint and a "moderation in all things" approach to life. I was shocked, therefore, to discover that these tenets could so easily be abandoned, all because of her.

The day I met her began auspiciously enough when I decided to alter my usual routine by walking home instead of taking the train. Looking back now, I don't recall why I decided to make this five-mile jaunt on foot and in heels, except that it was such a lovely October afternoon. The leaves in the park displayed colors of autumn fruit and the air held that crisp expectation of mulled wine and evenings spent fireside. As I exited the park and crossed the street, I was enveloped by the heady aroma of baking bread emanating from a patisserie adjacent to the corner. My stomach growled in anticipation of café au lait and a warm, buttery croissant, so I diverted from my intended path and entered the quaint shop.

It wasn't her looks that initially attracted me to her, though even now, the thought of her full lips and topaz eyes arrests my soul. Rather, it was the way she moved, like quicksilver unrestrained by its container, free-flowing and sensual. She was placing a fresh rack of baguettes on the shelf when the tiny brass bell hanging over the doorway called out its welcome. Stopping in her tracks, she glanced up at me and the temperature in the already warm room spiked.

"Good afternoon," she greeted, looking intently at me.

"Hello," I returned.

I watched as a graceful hand rose up to place an errant strand of silken jet hair behind a delicate ear. When it lowered, a streak of white flour smudged her cheek, contrasting sharply with the porcelain skin. I smiled inwardly and approached the glass counter with confidence.

A sample plate sat near the register and I selected a piece of pain au chocolat, popped it into my mouth and let it dissolve between my tongue and palate. She watched as my eyelids closed with pleasure.

"Good?" she asked.

"Oh my, yes. Very good." I opened my eyes and found myself lost in hers.

"I've tried to make bread at home," I said, "but it just doesn't compare with this."

"You can't be afraid to handle it firmly." At this, a slow smile made its way leisurely across her face. "But don't overwork it either." She hesitated, her thoughts reflected in her eyes. "I'm about to make more bread right now. I can show you how, if you like."

"I like," I said, returning the deliberate smile.

She stepped out from behind the counter and my eyes pursued as she sauntered to the front door. Grasping a hanging sign that said Closed, she flipped it so it faced outward onto the street. Then with a loud click, she shoved the deadbolt to the locked position. Turning, she crooked her finger at me in a conspiratorial manner.

"Follow me," she whispered with a look that harbored no refusal.

How could I resist? She led me behind the counters and through a door that meandered back to the kitchen. The apron she wore in front exposed a small ass from behind and I ogled salaciously as it swayed irresistibly in front of me. I was at least six inches taller than she was and knew my large hands could cup those cheeks easily. The thought made me weak in the knees. She stopped suddenly in front of me and I nearly teetered forward into the very backside I was admiring.

We were standing in front of a stainless steel table that shimmered from the fluorescent light overhead. It gave a clinical feel to the room and made me shiver, whether from anticipation or the cool feel of it under my fingertips I couldn't be certain. A miscellany of baking items occupied the center of the table including a bag of flour, its top cut open with a small amount spilling onto the surface, and a half-full pastry bag. She lifted my hand, drawing my attention away from the table, and deftly inserted my index finger into her mouth. The warmth and wetness of her tongue as it wrapped itself sensually around my fingertip instantly dispelled any sense of chill I had and I groaned, pressing the length of my body against hers.

"Mmm, that feels good," I breathed as she sucked rhythmically.

Removing the digit slowly from her mouth, she pulled me by the back of my neck with her other hand until our lips met. Tentatively at first, then with greater force, she entered my mouth and explored its depths. She took my tongue into her mouth, sucking slowly and gently as she had with my finger, while at the same time pushing me down onto the surface of the table. When my feet went out from under me and my back hit steel, my head almost collided with the sack of flour left haphazardly near the edge. Climbing on top of the table, she swept the bag off to one side in a single motion, knocking it over in her haste. To keep from sliding off the slippery surface, I reached out to grab the edge of the table, only to smear flour onto the sleeve of my suit jacket. I didn't care.

"You are so hot," she rasped.

She knelt over me, straddling my hips, and then slowly sat until her buttocks rested lightly over my crotch. I pushed upward, trying to connect with that soft ass, and felt her press down and undulate above me. I could feel myself getting wet, and the throbbing that always accompanied that feeling began to pulse its urgent demand. Needing more contact, she reached down and pulled my jacket off my shoulders and down my arms, pushing it to one side of the table. Her mouth descended and took a hardened nipple between her teeth, sucking it through my silk blouse.

"Oh, Jesus, yeah," I exhaled sharply.

I craved to feel skin on skin and, sensing the need, she began to unbutton my blouse. Frantically, I fumbled behind her back at the apron strings, yanking it off her waist, and then returned to the zipper on her pants. Almost simultaneously I had her unzipped while she had me unbuttoned. Shoving her pants down her hips, she rose up to help me lower them while I leaned up so she could push my blouse down my shoulders. We helped each other remove the pants and blouse and then removed the rest of our clothing on our own.

"God, you are so beautiful." I looked at her in awe.

Her breasts were small and firm, the nipples bright rose against her pale skin. Like the hair on her head, the triangle between her legs was dark and thick, and I could see moisture glistening in its depths. I couldn't resist; my hand snaked out to gently caress between her thighs, my thumb gently stroking the soft nodule I found cocooned there.

"Oh God," she moaned.

I looked up to see her eyes closed tightly in concentration and her mouth slightly open, breathing erratically. As my thumb continued its exploration of her clit, I allowed my index finger to search out her opening. When I found it, I teased the sensitive area by lightly flicking in and out around the edges, like a butterfly flitting from flower to flower. She began to move faster over my thumb and finger.

"Please," she gasped, "go deeper. Fuck me as hard as you can. I am so ready."

My efforts doubled as I plunged two fingers fully into her and felt her come down hard in response. No longer capable of sitting upright, she collapsed forward, her hands planted firmly on either side of my head with her breasts dangling tantalizingly in front of my mouth. My free hand reached out once again to seek the edge of the table for support, but something soft and pliable found its way into my hand instead; the pastry bag. I grasped it firmly and brought it between us. When I squeezed it upward, a ribbon of chocolate spurted unexpectedly across her left breast. Liking what I saw, I repeated the process on her right breast. Tossing the bag aside, I took possession of her right and left breasts with my mouth, alternately sucking and tugging and lapping up the chocolate.

"Fuck yeah, that feels so good! Bite my nipples too. Yes, yes, like that. Oh God, yes, harder. Yes!"

She was pumping up and down like a piston on overdrive. The juices pouring out from her center and running down my hand and arm definitely told me I was on the right track. When her thrusting changed to a steady rhythm, I felt her thigh muscles clench spasmodically and I knew she was almost there. My free hand slid around to her backside where I slipped the middle finger in unceremoniously and after a few thrusts, she blasted off like a rocket.

With her sprawling on top of me, I could feel the pounding of her heart against my chest, and rather than soothing me, I found it highly erotic. The beat mimicked the throbbing between my legs and I found myself pulling her hips downward to relieve the pressure. She slowly rose up to place more of her weight where I needed it. She looked down at me, an easy grin forming on her lips, and her eyes glittered to see the reaction she was causing in my body. Rocking gently, she dropped one hand to find its way between my legs.

"Mmm, so wet," she purred.

Bringing her fingers to her mouth, she closed her eyes and sucked in apparent ecstasy. Then she moved down my body until her face came level to my crotch where she spread me fully open, her lips finding my aching clit, hard and extended, in need of attention. She drew it into her hot mouth, gently at first, and then as I began to push upward, more fervently, swallowing her approval of what she found.

"Oh baby, that's it, that's perfect, don't stop!" I wasn't sure, but I think I was shouting. "Keep sucking just like that. Now go inside...ohh, yes, yes, yes."

I didn't need to tell her how to do it. She anticipated my every need, sucking and fucking with just the right amount of intensity and speed. I arched up, grabbing both of her shoulders, and held on. When the storm hit, I didn't even try to seek shelter. I just let the elements take me to the inevitable conclusion.

Lying on top of me once again, she turned her head sideways so that it nestled just under my chin. We rested like that for a while and I stroked her back soothingly, coaxing our breathing pattern to a more normal pace. When we finally got up to dress, I noticed I was partly covered in flour, and she laughed good-naturedly at the sight.

"Well, I may not have shown you how to make bread, but I hope I've shown you how to do something else." She traced a finger down my arm and brushed flour from my cuff.

I took her hand in mine and brought it to my lips, placing a brief kiss inside her wrist.

"I hope you'll continue to teach me," I murmured. "I have so much yet to learn."

We kissed. It wasn't a sexual kiss, but one of future promises.

I returned to the little bakery on the corner many times after that, but I never did learn how to make bread.

WORD PLAY
RADCLYFFE

When you edit someone's work, it gets to be pretty personal. You touch on a lot of private places, catch glimpses of so many secrets. I mean, we all know that anything worth writing, or reading for that matter, has to have a little of the author in it, right? Sometimes maybe even a lot. I don't mean an autobiographical "how I first got laid" blow-by-blow, but the underlying experiences and emotions that inspire the prose—the fantasies and fears, and sometimes—between the lines—the needs and desires.

It's always a challenge, offering criticism without damaging an oft-fragile ego, but after a while, there's an ebb and flow, a give and take, that feels more like a tango than a tussle. At least, with luck, it does.

So, when I sat down to work, my mind wasn't on the pacing of the final action sequence in my latest thriller. The deadline was closing in fast, and I prided myself on never missing a deadline. But I wasn't in the mood for writing; I'd been thinking about her all day. About her last *book*, I mean, the one I was editing. About the love scenes that I couldn't read without seeing her as the star. And, okay, seeing myself there, too—the co-star to her dark hero. I resisted, just barely, pulling up one of her e-mail messages to reread, not that I didn't have them all memorized. We'd gotten close, maybe a little bit inside each other's skin. It happens, when you share a passion.

The last message from her had been different—filled with taunting phrases and teasing innuendo. I had resisted rereading it for days, afraid that the longing, already so close to pain, would paralyze me for good. Mostly, I was haunted by the fear that everything I *thought* I'd read beneath and in between her words was merely a projection of my own furtive desire. As with fiction, I would discover that I had created the reflection of my own desire.

I couldn't deny the attraction, but I was far from certain of the source. Despite what the theoreticians and critics say, I firmly believe it's impossible to separate art from the artist. So how could I know if it was the heat of her words or the cool, amused distance she projected in the flesh that was so compelling? At first, I decided it didn't matter—that twinge of discomfort that masked unwanted arousal—because it could not, *would* not, lead anywhere at all. We had to work together, and while a little lust might stir the creative juices, too much just clouded the mind. Like the last drink that would have been better left on the bar. And if that weren't enough, there were rumors she was heavily involved. I don't share, not even my casual fucks.

But then somehow, when I wasn't paying attention, or maybe just when I was pretending not to look, we'd exchanged a few e-mails that morphed into something far more than one writer pushing another to the edge. We'd crossed a line; extended the invitation. *Try me. I'm ready.*

Finally, after rewriting the opening paragraph four times and ultimately hitting *delete,* I relented and opened the folder of e-mail messages to the last message. To the last sweet suggestion that could have meant nothing, or everything.

I read it and heard her murmur the words in my ear, her breath warm and teasing. I reread it, and felt her fingers skim my jaw.

I stared at the screen and felt the tremble of desire. And then I wrote.

> When I wake in the night, I reach for you, the smell and feel of your body so near drenching my senses.

First sentences define the world, paragraphs the universe. For a writer, the tone and flavor and rhythm of the lines create texture, sensation, heat playing over skin, fire simmering in the belly.

I stared at the words, knowing I could not take back the truth. I had awakened in the dark, wanting coiled deep inside. I had reached out a hand, so desperate for the feel of her, craving the touch of her fingers to relieve the aching need that had ascended while I slept. When her image shattered like promises tossed into the wind, I stroked myself, imagining it was her.

```
      I am always wet, always so ready for
you then, when I have shed control and
surrendered my defenses.
```

I read what I had written, my body tight, throbbing to the rhythm of my fingers on the keys. All because of a few words on the screen. Just a few words that crossed time and space, slipping through, over, around every barrier I had ever constructed—like the slick slide of fingers through the channels of my engorged flesh. I read, and remembered— the silvery sheen of passion streaking my thighs.

```
      I whispered your name, a desperate
plea in the night. I parted my thighs,
baring my soul.
      "What is it you need?"
      "You know. You know. Please. Please
just touch me."
```

I saw her so clearly as the words filled my vision, the curve of her mouth, the length of her fingers, the intensity of her gaze. I remembered laughter and a quick toss of thick, unruly hair. I recalled a moment's hesitation, and that instant when she wondered if she had revealed too much. I saw her hands, lifting as she spoke, certain and sure. I saw them now, traveling up the inside of my legs, a slow taunting journey of pleasures waiting to be called. My fingers hovered above the keys, my clitoris hard, a reminder I was flesh. Her fingertips only a breath away. I ached. I ached.

I forced my hands to move.

```
      "What is it that you need?"
      "You. Only you."
      "Tell me."
      "Touch me. Feel what you've done to me
in my dreams."
      You trace a single line down the center
of my abdomen, your fingertip burning
my skin. I wait, breathless, until you
reach my weeping clitoris, exposed and
```

```
vulnerable, wet with the tears of my
desire. You hesitate, cruelly probing-
the flick of your nail steals my breath
on a whimper.
```

As I typed my sex twitched, and without thinking, I stopped and slid my hand under the restraining layers of clothes. I squeezed, pressure screaming along jittery nerve endings, annihilation a breath away. I worked my clit, faster, harder, my vision blurring for an instant, and I lost the words. I stilled my hand, bearing down with brutal fury, trapping my wild need in impotent rage. If I could not find the words, I would lose her.

I let go, leaving my desire to beat helplessly alone.

```
"Please…"
"Not until I say."
"I need…"
"No."
"Oh…you're making me…"
"No."
Fingers clamped around the pulsing
shaft, the pleasure-pain driving my hips
into the air.
"I need to." My voice an unrecognizable
scream.
"No."
I am dying to come. For you.
```

My body quickened as the word images took shape. Her body weighing me down, her hand inside me. A relentless scream fluttered around the edges of my consciousness and drove me into the scene, through it. The desire burned in me to touch, to be touched. To be her, them, you, *us.* My orgasm thrashed like a raving beast, clawing its way to freedom, threatening to let loose despite my fight to chain it down. A wild thing, devouring me with pleasure. I was so close, my clitoris alive with a heartbeat of its own, poised to rage with a well-placed caress.

```
"Do you want to come?" Your voice a
```

soft whisper, your fingers instruments of
sweet torture.
  "oh yes yes…want to…need to…"
  "Ask my permission."
  "please please…please may I come…"
  I hear you laughing through my
screams.

I wondered if she would hear my moans, feel the slick come on her hands as the eruption escaped from the hard core of my sex. I wondered if she would fuck me back, with her words.

Beyond the Blue Horizon
Fiona Cooper

You are lying limp on the chaotic surface of our planet, your beautiful strong arms spread wide. Your fists have punched the shattered pillows like meteors hurtling through space, your bruised neck is bright with sweat and a vein jumps there, your heart is racing so loud I can hear it. I am on all fours above you, my face and chin are dripping with you, I stick my fingers between your laughing lips so you can taste you too…

"Wonderful," I tell your perfect nipples a thousand times. "You are wonderful, you taste wonderful, you smell like heaven, and I adore you."

Your teeth graze my fingers and you run your tongue round your lips…

"Well, I don't do anything for *me*," you say. "When I land I need to eat *you…*"

Your arm moves in a slow circle like the beating of a snow angel's wing and you rub your hand on your perfect thigh where I have spurted all over you. Another slow wing beat and you suck your fingers and smile and nod with infinite wisdom.

"*You*," you say, drawing out the word like it was a mile long, "mmm—the best taste in this world or any other."

I arch my back and breathe on your glistening fur and your whole body shivers like a hologram. My tongue hovers on your steaming secret skin, sleek and rosy and pulsing like a sea anemone, spread taut by my fingers, and your head thrashes from side to side as ecstasy seizes you over and over. Then your hand is in my hair, your fingers digging into my scalp, dragging my face to yours as you growl into my mouth, your eyes electric.

"You are in serious trouble."

I grin like some crazed slime-fanged alien and my hands are green-scaled claws as I pin your fabulous wrists to the starstruck sheets and my eyes shoot lasers that glorify your naked beauty.

"What kinda trouble, lady?"

Now I am a grease monkey, chewing gum, an idle pelvic thrust letting you know who's in charge.

"Big trouble," you say, wrapping your thighs round me, digging your heels into my ass, pushing me into you.

"How big is big?" I say, deep and impassive like the guy who tore the doors down in *One Flew Over the Cuckoo's Nest.*

"Big enormous mega mighty universal deep deep deep poo," you say, cool as the best poker bluffer on the 24/7 stud gambling channel.

"I am sooo scared," I say, and my fangs clash the air by your ears. You grip me tighter, thrusting up at me so our bones singe through the flesh.

"I am teeerrrified." I burn your throat with my breath. "You're the only trouble I want to be in."

Now you struggle, and we wrestle—when we fight like this, you really fight, and that takes my breath away, but if I hang on to your wrists I'm okay, I'm the boss, my baby, because if you tickle me, well, I'm finished.

I tug both your wrists into one hand and kiss you so our teeth clash and our tongues rip at each other and our eyes lock and we are one.

My free hand slides through the swamp of our bellies and I thrust my fingers inside you. Hard.

"Is that okay?"

"Mmm."

Your thighs clamp on my arm hard as the petrified jaws of a giant clam and you throw me over, climb on me, knees on my shoulder. Jesus, woman, you bowled me over the first time we met and I knew in my guts that without you I am only half alive. When we let our eyes meet all those years ago—a hundred people in the room and not one of them existed—there was a deep space explosion like the proud and ancient star we came from. A cigarette paper between us is too much distance. Call it destiny, call it karma, call it fate, call it hey diddle diddle, shoo-be-doo, call it si si, oui oui, da da, doo wop, words cannot hold it—even the word *love* holds only a microcell of our truth.

Your eyes are multidimensional as you look down into my soul. Your hair is spiked and dripping and you smile wide as all the Osmonds rolled into one. Then you drop your drooling mouth onto mine and our faces slide together. You smell like a rainy field as the sun rises, you with rainbows in the eternal skies of your eyes.

You arch your back and wriggle your thighs between mine, resting one wrist on my neck, flipping the lid of our magic gel open, squeezing the tube until your fingers are thick with a clear web and you flex your hand into a fist. I am burning for your touch, I need to leap that first bruising edge of almost pain and you know it, your wild smile shows it.

I spread my arms like a crucifix as you glide down my shaking body. I push up to meet your mouth and you seize me between your lips, suck me, your tongue huge and soft as you lick me over and over. Then your tongue is stiff and delicate thrusting into me, circling me until I could scream for needing you deep deep inside me.

One of your fingers joins your tongue, then your knuckles nudge against me and I open wider and wider and drag you into me. You swim up to my face, your fingers take it slow, nudging into me, your eyes very still and glowing.

"You are mine," you say.

"I am yours," I breathe, dizzy with the feeling of your fist sliding into me. My body jackknifes over the edge of pain, blood roaring in my ears, and I break every sound barrier, you shoot me higher than anything that ever squandered rocket fuel and TV footage from a NASA launch pad.

"Mine," you say and I feel your fingers peel from your fist one by one and probe me as I shudder from head to toe, gripping your wrist and needing you—my God is it possible—more and more.

Now you rock your hand inside me as galaxies fly by bright as pixie dust. This is the bit that drives us crazy—crazier?—because we are one and I need to swallow all of you, our mouths are a vacuum of desire, and we cannot be close enough. All at once you are fierce and strong, my soft-skinned gentle love, my lover, you possess me completely, I flow like a flood dam. Every deep thrust and twirl of your beautiful hand and I am in deep space, your blue eyes are liquid gold, and I have no body, no skin, I am nothing but a creature born to love you, be loved by you, I am a zillion formless cells merging into you.

"I'm...

nothing without you

coming

close to tears
to
we two are one
you…"

My perfect love, I am sobbing, biting your face, thumping your shoulders with my fists, spouting like a geyser, laughing like a madwoman.

You hold me close as I rematerialize from eight miles high, from our waist down we are in the Everglades and clinging to each other, you rescue me as wordless and tender as the Swamp Thing, take me to your world which is our world, oh God my darling I was utterly lost until I found you.

You pat me and totter to the loo and pee loud and laughing. Somehow I crawl to be where you are and fall to my knees, bury my head in your breasts and tongue your navel. As you stand I push my face between your thighs and eat you, we fall to the cold tiles, then you pat me again as I drag myself up to pee too. You are curled in front of me, and I slide my smallest finger into your ass and let my hand splay and play with you. I bend so I can cup your breasts and pull you to me, squat behind you and bite into your neck as you whimper and shiver and fill my palm with liquid ambrosia.

Millennia ago, we would have lived in a cave high on a hill where a trickle of water and sunlight created a haze of ferns on the dark rock. Our skin was shaggy and our feet were wide with long strong toes. Our eyes were wild, our hands greedy and needy for the feel of each other…well, these days I guess we're less hairy and the water comes from taps and plants grow in pots. We love through all time.

Half drowning and delirous, we crawl back to our wrecked bed and you splash icy fizz into our glasses. An empty glass is a crime and we should have been arrested a thousand times. Someone a thousand miles and years away grew luscious rosy grapes and a dozen people stripped the vines in the sunshine, someone trod those grapes to pulp, someone let them ferment and let their essence fill bottles and fly over the oceans—and all for us. *Because we're worth it, we are worth everything and anything.*

We drink holding hands and look around—your stilettoes hurled against the wall, black velvet pants inside out on the table, silk shirt like a crash-landed parachute, electric blue thong a butterfly on the floor, electric blue lace bra crushed under the chair. My boots lie gawping on the sofa, twin socks their laughing tongues, jeans concertina-ed over the waste bin, somehow my shirt has flown to the overhead lamp shade, and my leather jacket lies in a deflated heap.

"I love wrecking rooms with you," you say, refuelling our glasses.

"We need a big house," I say. "Lots of rooms and a cleaner whose middle name is discretion."

"And no visitors," you say.

"I don't think they could cope," I say. "We could do a dinner party—just about—then you'd turn into the She-Hulk and they'd be very polite and wonder what they'd been drinking and why I'd dissolved into a pool of desire."

"Me—the She-Hulk?" you say, all convent girl prim.

"Or the Blue-Eyed Thing," I tell you, "smashing down any barriers I might be fool enough to imagine could keep you away."

"Even more trouble," you say. "You have no idea how much."

"Show me."

"Only if you close your eyes and lie back," you say.

So I do.

I feel you slide the black blindfold round my face. This is familiar. As is the feel of knotted silk on my wrists and the way you tether my wrists to the legs of the bed. I like the trouble I'm anticipating. Then there is silk at my feet and you are very quiet as you tie my unresisting ankles wide apart. *Okay.* Less familiar is when you slide a gag round my chin, the way you slide a pillow under my bum. And though I can hear the soles of your feet on the floor, recognize the sound of you changing the CD, then there is only the sound of music. God, I want you, where are you? Every pore of my skin is electric.

I feel the mattress dip a little and I open for you, wanting, needing, expecting your tongue. Your hot skin brushes my inner thighs and my fingers and toes curl into hyperspace—your mouth? Your hand—God my love, touch me…

And then there is the warm weight of you on top of me and your breath on my neck. Your hands on my breasts and you are glorious and suddenly you are inside me, hard and wet, and I need to be free to wrap myself around you, but I can't move, just feel you pushing into me, pulling a little back then thrusting your hips against me, my darling, this is amazing.

"I want to fill you," you growl, tearing off my blindfold with your teeth, one hand on my throat now. Your eyes blaze like a solar eclipse and your head clamps between my neck and shoulder, I can see your ass clenching and plunging and a wide band of leather gleaming above the cleft and I am choking on this gag until you tear my mouth free and fill it with your tongue.

"I want..."

"Just wait. This is what *I* want," you groan, thrusting slow and hard with every word.

"I want..."

"No," you say like steel, "You want this. I know you do."

"I want this, I want you," I gasp.

"We're going to come together," you say, grinning, still slow and deep.

"Yes," I say, "I'm coming already, I can never stop coming to you."

Now your neck is pulsing and you are staring wild-eyed somewhere above my head.

"What *do* you want?" you say intensely.

"Untie my ankles," I say. "Please. I need you to."

You curl over me, reach down and pull me free and I am suddenly empty—your leather belt twitches the deep purple strap-on against my thigh. I keep my legs flat until you are on me and in me again. Then my legs clamp around your waist and you go deeper into me, your eyes wide.

"Is that what you want?" you ask me like a high priestess.

"Yes," I say.

And then you thrash into me over and over faster and faster and on and on and I am yours. Forever. And you are loving me like we've never loved before and you scream as we come and still you invade me, still I surrender over and over and it's never over until I shoot you right out of me and you free my wrists and your hands dig deep into my ribs and to the heart of me. Our total ecstasy slides like an electric eel over my heart and curls right into our guts and pours from us like the turbulence where a river meets the sea.

Now, my love, you have nothing, I have absolutely nothing left, just us flying like the diamond rings of Saturn round our galaxy as our bodies collapse together and melt like the wax of twin candles lit in some ancient church and holding the prayers and hopes of the world.

We sparkle like a star being born, we meld, we melt, we blend, so that even more I am part of you, you are part of me, we are one, I am you, you are me, I am yours, you are mine.

I groan into your cheek.

"Forever…"

Your twin whisper fills my head…

"*Forever…*"

Then we lie together dizzy and silent.

In a while I know I'll unstrap you and tie you face down, the soaking pillow under your belly. And I'll put on our new toy and push it between your lips and into the depths of you, both arms free to hold you.

But for now we crumple against each other, for now I can feel you twitching very gently as sleep comes over you.

You open your eyes all of a sudden and look at me, proud queen of my soul.

"I declare world peace," you murmur and your eyes close.

I lie and hold you sleeping.

My love, you are the ruler of my universe.

DISTRAUGHT TRUTHS
ASHLEY BARTLETT

I was a little drunk and I stumbled as she pushed me against the wall. Her mouth was on me, hot against my frozen skin. One hand pushed beneath my T-shirt while the other worked open the button on my jeans. Her fingers squeezed my nipple and I groaned, rocking my hips into her. Silently I begged for her to touch me. When she forced her hand down my jeans, my head jerked back and hit the wall. I dimly felt the pain in my head, yet I was too far gone to care. Her fingers slid through the wet heat between my legs. My hands found the flesh beneath her sweater and I pulled her against my body, needing the touch, not caring who she was. Slowly she pushed me closer to the edge. She began to bite my skin, sucking on my neck. I knew it would leave a mark.

"No. No. Stop that. No marks," I gasped.

"Shut up, baby, I know you want it," she growled.

I forced my eyes open at the sound of her voice. She was not Finch. The breath escaped my lungs and my stomach tightened. I knew it was coming the moment Finch entered my mind. I felt my body go rigid as I rode the waves of pleasure. My head snapped back again. My fingers curled in the air, seeking someone to hold. I bit my lip and tasted blood. Faintly, I felt her pull away, leaving me gasping against the wall.

I pulled a cigarette from my back pocket and lit it, inhaling deeply. The wall dug into my shoulders as I sagged against it. I buttoned my fly while I glanced around, wondering if anyone was watching. I couldn't have cared less if they had been. I didn't care that I never asked her name or that she was cheapened by the fact that I wished it was not her who touched me. She was not the woman I wanted.

I pushed through the crowd back to the table. Caitlyn and Sylvia were still huddled by it, watching women pass by openly staring at them. The club was mostly women with a few men scattered about. The occupants were all in tight jeans and skimpy shirts. The long bar spread the entire length of the back wall, the crowds of people lined up to get drinks keeping the three bartenders in constant motion. A DJ and dance floor took up nearly all of the remaining space. Women moved to the beat of the music, all one being. The music was their heart. I could hear it moving them. As I came closer to our table, the crowd pushed me around and I felt a woman press against me.

"Nice display," a deep voice said into my ear. I could feel her breath on my neck. Her voice aroused me more than the sex minutes before. I looked back at her. Finch's distinctive smell flooded my senses; smoke and surprisingly feminine perfume. Her dark green eyes bored into mine, deep and hazy. I saw some emotion pass through them. I told myself it was jealousy.

She gestured with her chin at her hands. Four cold beers were carefully dangling from her fingers. She shouted, "I've got beer. Come on, don't hold up traffic." To emphasize her point she thrust her hips into my ass.

I felt like I was going to melt; her body was fire against mine. I couldn't tell if she knew how turned on I was. Maybe she thought it was left over from my performance against the wall. Her eyes clouded again.

I found my voice. "Yeah, yeah." My attempt at nonchalance came out as a choked whisper. I turned back into the stream of people.

We managed to regain our seats at the table. Finch passed out the Corona. Taking a deep swig, I resigned myself to getting drunk and hoped the night would end. Hoped that I would stop wanting her. I felt the light fuzziness spread to my limbs. My emotions were almost less harsh, less poignant. I looked at Finch again. She was so beautiful it hurt. Dark shaggy hair fell into her eyes. Her shadowed face seemed like a mask of pain; a recent acquisition. I wanted to know what was making her hurt, I wanted to make it stop.

Caitlyn broke into my thoughts, "I liked the show." She made her voice deep. "It was very sexy."

Sylvia laughed, adopting the voice. "Yes," she breathed heavily, "it made me so hot." She emphasized the last word while leaning down to show off her cleavage.

"Fuck off," I shot back. I took a swig of beer.

Sylvia looked hurt. "Jeez, don't get so pissy."

"Yeah, you're a bitch when you're drunk." Caitlyn scowled. She turned to Sylvia. "Wanna dance?"

"Yeah, I'd love to." Playfully she ruffled my hair. "We'll be back when you're more human," she laughed. "You know, not post-orgasmic."

I tried to smile but it came out as a grimace. The weekly outings to floating clubs were beginning to drain me. I had been evading my best friend for the last month, but she was starting to get suspicious. Soon Finch would ask point blank why I was avoiding her. I pulled out my cigarettes. Finch leaned close and lit it for me. I handed her one and she accepted it, her long fingers lightly touching mine.

"You wanna tell me what's bothering you?" Her voice in my ear made my stomach tighten.

"Nothing," I grumbled, "absolutely nothing."

"Don't give me that shit, Tiff."

"Oh, would you like to tell me what's bothering you?" I punctuated my words by poking myself, then her in the chest as I spoke.

"Don't do that." She shook her head at me. "There's something going on in that head of yours."

This time when I looked at her, my eyes begged along with my voice. "Not now, okay?"

She put an arm around me. It was meant as a comfort, but I was finding it harder and harder to resist her touch. I shuddered. I could feel her stop her motion so I leaned closer, wanting the feel of her. She tightened her grip, slowly rubbing my back. I felt her lips press a kiss into my hair.

"I want another beer." I began to get up. As much as I had needed her a moment before, I now needed her to stop. If she didn't, I would embarrass myself.

"Don't worry, I got it." She abruptly pushed off her seat. I watched her tall, lanky, boyish figure disappear in the direction of the bar.

When Finch returned she was carrying two bottled waters. "I thought this might be a better idea than beer." She smiled. "Otherwise we'll hate ourselves tomorrow."

I managed a grin. "I guess you're right."

"You wanna go outside?" She nodded at the door.

"Sure."

She grabbed my hand and led me toward the exit. We walked away from the doors. I realized we were still holding hands only when she let go to sit on the curb. The only company we had was a burned-out streetlight. I looked at our feet in the empty gutter. Our Chuck Taylors were equally scuffed; however, hers were about four sizes bigger. She had a good five inches on me, so she seemed to tower when we walked together. I liked it.

"You want?" I held out a freshly lit cigarette.

"Thanks." She took it from me. This time our fingers did not touch. Finch wrapped her gangly arms around her bare knees, which stuck out of the holes in her threadbare jeans, and rested her head on her arms. Periodically she lifted her lips to take a drag. I raised my hand to touch her, then lost my nerve and lowered it slowly.

"Tiff?" Her voice came out as a whisper.

"Yeah?"

She took a deep breath and exhaled it slowly. "Never mind."

I put my hand on her bare forearm. The sleeves of the oxford shirt she had on were rolled twice, revealing an expanse of tanned skin. A large band of leather was tied around one wrist and a wide watch covered the other.

"What?" I probed gently.

"Really, it's nothin'." She pulled at the thin tie around her neck with both hands. The black silk folded and slipped through her fingers. She scratched her neck. The unconscious motion made the shorter, dark hair on the back of her head stand up. I loved when she did that. Her hair would stick out at odd angles when she was nervous. I wondered what was getting at her now; she had been acting weird for a while. I realized I was staring when she looked directly at me. The shadows in her eyes spread, making them deep as fathoms. It gave her that brooding look that made her so fucking sexy. Her mouth was slightly big for her face, and her wide, soft, pink lips were slightly parted.

"Finch, I..." *love you.* Yeah, right. I looked away from her, afraid I might embarrass myself. I tried to look really intrigued by the streetlight above us. To stress my point I got up and walked toward the post. It was metal with bits of paper, tape, and filth clinging to it.

"Why do you do that, Tiff?"

Confused, I turned around. "Do what?"

She stood and stared at her shoes. "You know. Hook up with chicks like that." She seemed nervous. "You deserve better, you know?" She shuffled her feet.

My mouth was hanging open, so I closed it. "I…I don't know." What was I supposed to tell her? I do it because I want to touch you so bad I feel like crawling out of my skin to escape? I shoved my hands in my pockets to hide their trembling. "Why do you care?"

"'Cuz it seems like all you do is get trashed and screw around and…and it freaks me out."

Her words cut into me. Without thinking, I lashed out. "Well, babe, I learned from the best." I nodded my chin at her. I knew I was being a bitch but I held my ground. She looked like I had slapped her. Her mouth thinned out and turned down at the corners. A muscle twitched in her cheek and her jaw trembled. I thought she might cry.

My words fell out. "Ah, damn. I'm sorry." I brushed her hair out of her eyes, so dark they were almost black. "I didn't mean that. I'm a bitch."

"Yeah. You are." Her voice was cold. She turned and began walking away.

"No, Finch, wait! Let me explain."

She stopped walking. Without turning around she said, "You don't need to explain to me."

"Yeah, I do." I took a deep breath and stepped closer to her. We were only a foot apart, yet she still faced away from me. My voice was a whisper. "I do it to get you outta my head. I can't stop wanting you. It hurts so bad. I just wanna stop imagining your hands on me, waking up thinking about you." I stopped talking when her shoulders started shaking. She finally turned around.

When she raised her tormented eyes to mine my stomach plummeted. Silent tears left small tracks down her cheeks. I had never seen her look so timid and unsure.

"Tiff, I want to believe that so much. I've spent months pining over you." A small grin crossed her face, lighting her rakishly handsome features. My breath caught in my chest. "You don't want me"—she gestured at the club, her smile fading—"you make that pretty obvious." She started walking away again. My heart stopped.

"Finch." I grabbed her hand and made her turn around. I brought my lips to hers. In an instant she pressed her body against mine. My head was tilted up, hers bent down protectively over me. I could still feel the fresh tears on her cheeks. An eternity passed before her tongue met mine, so soft. I moaned deep in my throat. She wrenched her lips away. Our bodies still touched.

"No. Stop." Her plea came out tinged with pain.

"Why?" I knew I sounded like a petulant child, but I didn't care. I reached for her again. "I want you so bad. Please."

She took a step back so our bodies were no longer in contact where a moment before, her body was liquid heat against mine and I could feel how much she wanted me. Now her posture was stiff, her gaze chilly.

"You don't want me."

"You're kidding me! I can't get you outta my goddamn head, Finch." My voice cracked when I said her name. I tried to grab her hands but she moved them. "Why not?"

Her voice was lethal. "Because I just watched some chick fuck you in a bar." Her eyes never left mine. "Because I watch you leave with a different woman every night and I can't take watching them screw you." She stepped closer, still not touching me. A note of tenderness penetrated her anger. "Look at this." She placed two fingers under my chin and lifted it to show the hickey my earlier companion had left. "Oh honey. Why?"

Angrily my words burst forth. "'Cuz I can't touch you. I keep trying to forget you, but your face is burned into my skull." I felt hot tears well up and pushed them away. "Every time they touch me all I see is you. All I feel is you." I reached for her again. Deliberately, she stepped away from me.

With a low, calm voice she spoke. "Fuck you, Tiffany. You expect me to believe that shit? You fuck other women to replace me?" Her voice broke and a small laugh escaped. "Fuck you." She stalked away.

"Finch!" I called to her retreating back. "Finch, I'm an idiot! Come back." She couldn't hear me anymore. "Finch, I love you," I whispered to myself, but I knew she was already gone.

Cautiously I knocked on Finch's apartment door. The lights were out. "Finch," I called, "Finch, if you're in there answer the door!"

The other door on her landing opened and a grungy kid stuck his head out. "Dude, stop yelling, she hasn't been home all night." He rubbed his bloodshot eyes and closed the door.

I stole a glance at my watch; just past midnight. I settled on the cement stairs, prepared to wait until dawn if I had to. My cigarette pack was digging into my ass again, so I pulled it out. Almost half full. I placed one in my mouth, unconsciously touching my tongue to the filter to make sure it was not backward. The bars of the handrail felt like ice, but I leaned against them anyway. If I didn't, I was afraid I might fall apart. I hated myself. The alcohol had left my system and was replaced by a killer headache. I smelled like a bar: cigarettes, booze, and sweat. None of these things mattered, though, because all I could think of was Finch. I could feel her touching me—her lanky, muscled body warm against mine, those soft hands pulling me into her. I let my head fall between my knees wishing I could just do the damn night over again.

"What the hell are you doing here, Tiff?"

My head jerked up at the sound of her voice. "I had to talk to you." I stood up, placing myself between her and the door. "I'm not leaving until I do."

Finch walked toward me with smoldering eyes. I thought she might hit me for a second, and I flinched when she stepped closer. I could feel her breath on my face, her perfume flooded my nostrils again, and my nipples hardened when her breasts brushed mine. My stomach tightened at the onslaught of feeling. I knew I was wet; but I tried to ignore my arousal. Any second she would tell me to leave, probably forever. I braced myself.

"Don't talk," she whispered through damp eyes. She kissed me hard and backed me against the door. I felt her fumbling with her keys, trying to open the door. When her tongue finally met mine I lost control. I grabbed her hips and pulled her against me, sliding my thigh into her crotch, moving my hands down to her ass. Then I bit her lip, sucking it into my mouth. I heard the keys drop. My hands found the skin beneath her shirt and I drew my nails up her sides hard enough to draw blood. She gasped when I found her breasts, my thumbs brushing across her sensitive nipples. Unconsciously I moved my leg higher between hers. I tried to bring her closer to me, but the only barrier separating us was clothing. I tore my lips from hers only to bite along her neck down to her collarbone. With one hand still on her breast I pulled the knot from her tie and began unbuttoning her shirt.

"Wait, Tiff, wait," Finch pleaded.

"No." I resumed kissing down her chest to her now-bared nipples.

She threaded her fingers through my hair, pulling back so I would look at her. "We need to do this inside."

I nodded and silently waited as she groped for her keys and unlocked the door. Once inside, Finch walked in the direction of her bedroom. I made it as far as the hallway. I moved directly behind her, then I slid my hands up her stomach to her breasts, lingering for a moment before I slid her shirt off her shoulders and dropped it behind us. Carefully I inspected the red tribal tattoo that ran from Finch's golden shoulder blade up her shoulder and wrapped around her toned arm. With my lips I followed the tattoo, kissing, biting, and licking. My hands roamed down her taut stomach to the curve of her hips. I trailed the natural line of smooth skin, dipping just below the waistline until I felt her shudder and moan. She turned to capture my mouth in another kiss. Groaning at the touch of her lips, I pushed until she was against the wall. An almost painful cry escaped her.

"What did I do? Are you okay?" I brushed a shaking hand across her cheek.

"The wall's just cold." She grinned.

"Deal with it." A laugh escaped me as I ran my tongue along her ear. When I drew my thumb under the elastic of her briefs, she arched against me.

"Please, you gotta touch me." She raised her hips to mine. I gasped at the pressure. Desperately I tried to ignore the heat between my thighs. The button and zipper on her jeans seemed to open themselves at the touch of my fingers. I brushed my fingers down the soft shaved skin; the thick moisture flooding the tight space between Finch and her underwear made me groan. I tried to draw a full breath but the air had left my lungs. My lips found hers again as I began the slow circles I knew would drive her insane.

Finch twisted away from the wall. "Please." The air escaped her lips in short gasps. "Now. Please, Tiff."

The sensation of Finch was killing me. She smelled the way she always had; only now, I could smell the sex on her skin. The way she smelled and sounded and felt would have been enough to make me go off. I heard myself moan when I entered her. A cry tore from her lips as she stiffened. I came the moment she did. The orgasm shooting through my body almost crippled me. I concentrated on standing and threaded an arm around her waist, whispering assurances in her ear as she quieted. Her knees did not seem to work properly and she fell against me. I slipped out of her feeling like my brain and body were no longer connected. When I wrapped my arms around her she molded against me. I waited in silence still unsure if she was angry.

"Bed," she whispered before calmly taking my hand and leading the rest of the way. Once in the room, Finch stripped off her jeans and made a move to climb under the sheets. "Aren't you coming?" The look on her face was uncertain.

Awkwardly I stood by the door, not sure if I should leave or stay. "I... I don't know if you want me here."

Finch motioned me closer. When I stood in front of her she lifted off my T-shirt and unbuttoned the fly of my jeans and pushed them down until I could step out of the tight material. Gently she tugged my hand until we were lying facing each other.

My hand wandered up and down, tracing the planes of her bare body. Finch was clearly exhausted judging by the look in her eyes. I pushed the dark locks off her forehead and kissed her. "Finch, I'm... I'm sorry," I said, "about earlier."

She nodded and curled closer, her eyes now closing. "Don't worry about it."

"But..."

"It's okay, really. Just go to sleep."

"All right." I watched as Finch surrendered to sleep, hoping that tomorrow she would feel the same.

THE ART OF RECYCLING
REMITTANCE GIRL

*E*lena, do you like girls?
      Well, how else could she put it? Beatrix didn't think it was appropriate to proposition someone working in a restaurant; it was a little like exposing them to secondhand smoke. After all, that person was stuck there, working, a prisoner to the whims of the patrons. She had always smiled very sincerely at Elena, regardless of whether the interchange was an offer of more coffee or a request for the bill.

Beatrix stubbed out her cigarette and clicked her pen in consternation, staring down at the scrawl she'd made on the paper napkin. Second thoughts clawed at her belly and she whipped the tissue off the table, balling it in her hand. Why couldn't she just go meet someone in a bar like everyone else? Why was it that the only women she really noticed were the ones she was never sure about? Perhaps it was a subtle sort of masochism.

The couple at the next table broke out into peals of laughter. Beatrix drained her cup of mocha, leaving enough at the bottom to soak the wadded-up napkin and make the note unreadable, irretrievable, when she dropped the thing into her cup.

"Ehr...ju want another mocha?"

Oh, the short, sun-streaked Eton crop and the serious wire-rimmed specs. They made Beatrix quiver. But nothing was as lovely as that Hispanic accent. Elena stood by the table waiting, pen poised at her order pad, weight shifted to one hip. She had tiny hips. Beatrix imagined that underneath the black waitress pants, delicate bones stretched white skin, taut, sinewy, a protrusion to nibble on.

"Eh, chica! Up here! Look at my face. More mocha?"

Beatrix's eyes flitted up Elena's body. "Yes. Yes, please."

"Por fin!" grunted Elena and whisked the empty cup bearing the soggy missive away.

After a year of late Sunday breakfasts, their interchanges had become less formal. Elena had slowly begun to take on the character of a harried, abrupt, but warmhearted mother. Beatrix was disconcerted by this; her feelings for Elena didn't run along familial lines. Moreover, there couldn't have been more than a couple of years' difference between them. Still Elena managed to make her feel like a wayward, daydreaming child.

The new, steaming cup of mocha arrived. Elena slid it onto the table in that inimitable way waitresses have of putting something down in front of you with considerable force but still managing to keep all the liquid neatly in the cup.

"Thank you." Beatrix beamed upward, trying to look as grateful as she could without actually appearing insane.

"De nada."

It's nothing.

Oh, it's not nothing to me, thought Beatrix.

The slim, work-worn hand slapped the bill down on the table with determination. The gesture said, "Drink up and leave, there are other people waiting for a table."

Patisserie Valerie was always a very busy place on a Sunday. The gold lettering on the door stated proudly that it was established in 1926. It had been a meeting place for radical students in the sixties. Now it was full of late-blooming yuppies coaxing toasted hot-cross buns down the throats of their screaming offspring.

Beatrix left the restaurant with the second paper napkin sitting unused and unblemished on the table along with the tip.

The January drizzle turned the quiet London street to watercolor as she walked back to her pokey studio flat. Sunday mornings were set aside for brunch and Elena (although Elena didn't know it), and the afternoons were dedicated to playing domestic catch-up.

Beatrix let herself into her flat; it smelled of must and cigarettes and was furnished in postmodern skip. The overstuffed sofa where she often fell asleep was slowly spilling its guts onto a worn Afghan rug. The walls were lined in raw plank and cinderblock bookshelves, overflowing with ratty paperbacks and even rattier hardcovers. A mournful aspidistra corpse sat in a dried-up pot by the window awaiting proper burial. It was her Sunday custom to prod it and consider throwing it out, only to spot some minute but encouraging sign of life. She watered its leafless skeleton with a mugful of tap water and opened the window wide, letting in the damp breeze.

Her sleeping area was screened off from the rest of the room by an enormous and very bad oil painting rescued from the back of the London School of Art. It had cost her eight pounds to get it home, strapped to the roof of a minicab. The monstrous abstract had no artistic value that Beatrix could see, but it made a decent wall.

Beatrix opened the window beside her bed as well and looked down at the nest of rumpled bedclothes on her futon. It always looked so empty. Sometimes when she lay in it, she saw herself from a perch somewhere near the ceiling. It still looked empty, even with her in it.

A goose-necked reading lamp sat atop a pile of encyclopedias, doing duty as a bedside table. Along one wall, obscuring the baseboard, books stood in line, waiting to be read.

Pulling the bedclothes off, Beatrix wondered what it might feel like to have a bundle of linen, warmed with someone else's body heat, in her arms. She'd had women in her bed before, occasionally, but they had never stayed long. Invariably, they couldn't stand her silence. She, for her part, could never understand why people needed to talk so much. They always seemed to need to fill up the silent spaces, flooding time and volume with chatter, as if it would collapse if it weren't stuffed full of noise.

Right at the moment, of course, her inability to talk was clearly a problem. She wasn't ever going to be able to ask Elena out if she didn't get around to popping the question. But it wasn't done to just come out with a question like that; one had to build up to it with inane chitchat. Beatrix thought about this dilemma as she gathered up the hospital sheets from her bed and made a bundle. In the tiny bathroom, she pulled the Excelsior Hotel towels off the rail and sorted her clothes by smell, finding the ones that needed washing.

Finally, having stuffed everything into a large bin liner, she selected a book and set off for the launderette.

❖

There was almost no one at the launderette and Beatrix finished her washing in record time. She folded the clean clothes and linen and put them back in the black plastic bag.

On her way home, she approached the bus stop. It was Elena, standing propped up against the post, waiting. Beatrix's pulse raced as she walked toward her, trying to order the sequence of banal sentences she knew she was expected to deliver. At the very end of it all, she had mentally tagged the question: "Would you like to have a drink, or dinner or something?" Did that sound too desperate? Too needy? Well, it would have to do.

But as she came close, all that careful planning had to be dispensed with. Elena's face was tear streaked and miserable. Her eyes were red. Her mouth shut in a determined line, her throat moving, swallowing, as if she was trying hard to keep herself from crying out loud.

Beatrix hesitated for a heartbeat and then touched the other woman's shoulder. "Elena? Are you all right?"

Elena looked at her mutely and handed her an open letter.

Notice of Termination of Employment

> *We regret to inform you that we currently find ourselves overstaffed, now that two of our long-term employees have returned from their maternity leave. Unfortunately this means we can no longer offer you a position in our establishment.*
>
> *We will be happy to provide you with an excellent letter of reference which we are certain will enable you to find alternate employment.*
>
> *Yours sincerely,*
> *The Management*
> *Patisserie Valerie*

"Oh dear," murmured Beatrix.

"Eh, it's nothing. Stupid to cry about it." Elena took off her glasses and smeared the flat of her palm over her cheek. A new flood of tears spilled down over the wet skin.

It had started to rain again and the light was fading. Some of the streetlamps were beginning to flicker on, making little difference to the twilight. Colder now, a gust of wind picked up the droplets of rain and hurled them sideways.

"Would you..." began Beatrix. She swallowed and tried again. "Would you like to come and have a cup of tea? My flat's just around the corner." Suddenly she could hear the blood pushing against her eardrums, her pulse throbbing in her dry throat.

Elena put her glasses back on and looked at her seriously. Beatrix was almost sure she was going to be told to fuck off and mind her own business. Then, quite suddenly, Elena's face broke into a small smile.

"Oh... so in de morning I esserve ju and now ju esserve me? So ironical! Why not?"

The response shocked Beatrix and, while she was waiting to find out that she'd hallucinated the answer, Elena slipped a strong hand into Beatrix's. She stood there, feeling it grow warm.

"Well? Ju change jor mind?"

"No! Not at all," Beatrix said hurriedly and began to stride up the street, pulling Elena and her bag of laundry behind her with indecent haste.

They didn't speak as they walked, or as they climbed the stairs to the flat. It was only when Beatrix opened the door and led Elena in that she mumbled, "It's a mess, I'm sorry."

She dropped her bag of clean laundry and rushed to slam the windows shut against the cold gusts of rain-heavy wind. The room was freezing and dark. Suddenly Beatrix was heartily ashamed of where she lived. This woman deserved better—somewhere welcoming and warm, cozy. Elena's expression did nothing to assuage her embarrassment. She took in the surroundings looking stunned. Her eyes fixed on the canvas that separated the living area from the bedroom.

"Oh... it's my wall," said Beatrix sheepishly. "Look, sit down and I'll put the kettle on." She led Elena to the sofa and practically pushed her down on it.

In a frenzy she filled the kettle, lit the gas ring, and pulled out the mugs. She ran into her bedroom and grabbed the electric heater, yanking its cord out of the wall plug. Finally she pulled the quilt off her bed and dragged it back, along with the heater, into the living room.

Beatrix plugged in the old three-barred heater into a socket near the sofa, pointing it in Elena's direction. The quilt she wasn't so sure about. She thought a moment and then shrugged, jumping a little as she heard the kettle start to scream.

"Here, look, you'll be warm in no time!" she insisted, draping the quilt over Elena and tucking it in around her.

It suddenly struck her that Elena must think she was a bag lady or something. But the woman said nothing. She had started crying again, silently, sitting like a stone statue as Beatrix wrapped the quilt around her legs.

She warmed the chipped teapot with boiling water, made the tea, and bore it all into the living room on a tray that she set down on the floor, near the heater. Lacking a sugar bowl, she plunged a teaspoon into an old coffee jar full of sugar and looked up at Elena.

"How many sugars?"

"Two."

"Milk?"

"Jes."

"Do you like girls?" It had just tumbled out with the other questions. Beatrix held her breath and waited. Suddenly she realized what a stupid question it was, considering the circumstances.

"Jes."

"That way?"

"Jes, dat way."

Beatrix brought her the mug of tea, on bended knee, by coincidence. She smiled and watched Elena wriggle a hand out from underneath the quilt to take it.

She went back to fix her own. The electric fire's artificial heat washed over her face, roasting it red, or perhaps she was blushing. But she kept her face toward it as she asked, keeping her voice casual.

"Do you like me?"

Elena gave an abrupt little grunt that made Beatrix turn her head. "Maybe... let's see how ju make tea." The voice was stern, abrupt.

Beatrix watched Elena take a sip out of the unchipped mug with a FedEx logo. She held her own cup in both hands, trying to equalize the temperature difference between her cheeks and her fingers.

"Mmm. Come sit here," said Elena. She pulled an edge of the quilt up and looked at the empty expanse of ratty sofa beside her.

Gingerly—very gingerly—Beatrix rose and walked to the couch. She settled herself at a discreet distance, not touching her but close. Elena smoothed the quilt over them both and clucked her tongue loudly.

"Bery good tea. But der is a ... a... gap. Jes, a gap. All de cold air is coming in," she said huffily.

Beatrix shifted herself closer, till she could feel the line of Elena's seated body right next to hers. It made her feel all squirmy—warm, too.

They sat in silence for a while, sipping tea and staring at the fake wall. The colors on the canvas were dark and brooding, but the red glow from the heater lit them in a new way, converting the whole painting into a womblike cavern.

Beatrix set her empty mug on the arm of the sofa and turned to Elena. Warmed now and feeling the heat radiating from the other woman's body, she put an arm around Elena's shoulders and kissed her on the cheek.

"Are you still sad?"

"No."

It wasn't that Beatrix didn't like glasses, but they got in the way of a good kiss. She reached up to pull Elena's off. Beatrix grinned and pressed her lips against Elena's.

She had wanted it to be a gentle sort of kiss. She'd thought about kissing Elena many times and she'd always envisioned that it would be very gentle and languid. But now that it was happening, she couldn't help herself. The knot in her stomach and the throbbing between her legs drove the kiss desperately, and soon she was straddling her beneath the quilt as she wrapped her arms around Elena's neck and pressed against her fiercely as she fed at her lips. Her tongue flicked and plunged into Elena's mouth, stroking and coaxing until she heard a low growl freed from the other woman's throat.

Between them, Elena worried the buttons on her sweater, even as Beatrix consoled herself with sliding her hands over her clothed form. Nice plump little breasts pressed against Beatrix's hands as she cupped them through the wool. And even through all those layers, she could feel two hard, prominent nipples. She squeaked with need and fumbled beneath Elena's pullover, shirt, bra, finally closing her spread fingers and trapping the big, burning hot nipples between them. They were as big as raspberries and had the same effect on Beatrix as she buried her mouth in the crook of Elena's neck. She pictured them dark pink and plump; her mouth flooded at the image, her cunt flooded in response. As she squeezed her fingers closed, Elena's hips arched up beneath her. The fabric of their jeans slid and caught as they ground against each other, so hard it almost hurt.

"Jesus, mujer. Donde está tu cama?"

"Sorry?" Beatrix looked up from where she'd been feeding on Elena's neck.

"Where de hell is jor bed?"

"Behind the wall," Beatrix whispered.

Elena glared at her. "Dat is not a wall. Dat is a piece of art."

"Yes... behind there."

"So, are ju going to invite me?"

"Absolutely, yes!" Beatrix was at it again, grabbing Elena by one hand and the quilt by the other, pulling her around the painting, collapsing onto her futon and dragging Elena down with her.

What followed was a madness of layer shedding. Boots were discarded, pullovers and shirts and jeans and bras and panties all followed. Wriggling against Elena beneath the quilt, Beatrix suddenly felt like a terrible host again. The heater was in the other room, there were no sheets on the bed. Still, it didn't seem to matter to Elena, who was plunging her fingers between Beatrix's cunt lips. The chilled fingers made Beatrix twitch and chirp.

"Ah, Christ!"

"What?"

"Your fingers are freezing."

Elena sniggered as she slid her fingers back and forth through Beatrix's wet slit.

"No problem. I warm dem up a little, jes?" And with that she pushed two fingers deep into Beatrix's passage.

Just for a moment, it felt like she was being fucked with an ice-lolly. Then everything melted and turned to syrup.

She pressed her own hand against her stomach to feel how cold it was. Her fingers were freezing too and she copied Elena, plunging them into the nest of hair and through Elena's furrow.

She felt Elena shudder and clamp her legs closed around her hand, trapping it there.

"Friction—friction creates heat," panted Beatrix. "Open your legs."

Elena relinquished her death-hold on Beatrix's hand and allowed her to slide a thigh between her legs. Beatrix rolled on top and began to move her body, rubbing the top of her thigh against Elena's mound, pressing hard against her outer lips until they splayed and Beatrix felt the hotter inner flesh slide against her skin, wet and warm and lovely.

She tried to be goal focused and sensible; nothing cheered a person up like a good, hard orgasm. But it was difficult not to get waylaid by the sheer pleasure of being in contact with skin, the gorgeous taste of another's mouth, the curious electric shocks she got from grazing her nipples against Elena's.

Beatrix mourned the normal sequence of events. Elena would come, she would come, and then it would all be over. The prospect of an empty bed, so recently warmed by the body of another... *no, not this time.*

Beneath her, Elena's hips rolled and arched. Warm, strong hands clutched at Beatrix's ass, pulling her hips down. Her thigh was slick with juice, every undulated thrust designed to drag Elena's clit over her skin. To hell with body contact, she needed to taste her.

She coaxed Elena to loose her grip on her ass. Perhaps Elena was close to coming—and that only fed Beatrix's urge to burrow her face in Elena's cunt. Wriggling down the bed, squirming between Elena's legs, kissing a long line of salty-sweet skin along the way, Beatrix finally got to her destination and pulled the swollen, matted lips apart.

Pointing her tongue, she traced the harder, solid line of each inner lip from Elena's hole up to where they joined to above the hood. She damned the weather and the darkness under the quilt. She would have loved to see the color, the blush of blood beneath the surface of those delicate membranes.

Elena panted and arched her hips, protesting at the tease with animal sounds and fingers that threaded through Beatrix's hair. Then, with the flat of her tongue, Beatrix dragged a heavy path from Elena's passage all the way up to her clit, pushing the hood up as she lapped. She worked slowly, taking her time to find all the other little spots that made Elena twitch, not just the protruding little nub. Finally, she settled her lips around the neat, small bud and sucked at it as if it were a nipple, lashing it with the point of her tongue all the while.

"*Ay, Dios mío!*" The fingers buried in Beatrix's hair grew frantic, pulling her head down even as Elena's hips thrust upward.

It was then that Beatrix eased her finger into Elena's tight, dark passage. The walls fluttered and clamped around it, pulling it in deeper, resisting each time Beatrix withdrew. As she added another finger, and then another, Elena's legs began to quiver and Beatrix felt those warm, lithe thighs close around her head. She sucked harder, flicked her tongue cruelly at the clit that was now clearly throbbing. Thrusting her fingers deep into Elena's cunt, Beatrix could feel the very start of the orgasm.

Fluids flushed between her fingers, soaking her hand and the mattress beneath. Elena arched her hips and froze, a belly-deep guttural cry breaking from her throat, but Beatrix kept on fucking her, dragging her tongue over Elena's clit again and again with even heavy strokes, prolonging the climax until she felt the spasms that squeezed at her fingers subside.

Then she withdrew them, slowly, and moved her mouth to surround Elena's entrance. She slid her tongue inside, shallowly at first, and then deeper, drawing out the flood of juices and feeding off them. It was delicious, hypnotic to feel the aftershocks clutch at her tongue. Her own cunt fluttered and throbbed in sympathy. She encouraged the tiny tremors by pressing her thumb against Elena's clit and rolling it.

Above her, Elena was keening softly. The hands that had, just moments before, grabbed desperately at Beatrix's hair were now stroking and gliding over her head.

Beatrix knew she should wriggle up beside Elena for the traditional post-orgasm kiss, but she just couldn't bear to leave the wonderful wet cave between her legs. It was too nice, too warm, and the tiny convulsions that gripped at her tongue each time she pushed it into Elena...they weren't stopping.

She pressed inward, as deep as her tongue would reach, and let her thumb slip and slide over the proud little clit that still pulsed so clearly beneath it. And slowly she felt Elena's hips begin to move again, not violently, but in time with the tongue that fucked her.

Another torrent of liquid spilled over Beatrix's chin and all of a sudden, without any warning, Elena was coming again, quietly, shuddering and making different sounds this time. Like a puppy crying.

It was Elena who sat up and dragged Beatrix on top of her. She licked and sucked at Beatrix's face until she found her lips. The kiss was long and deep and soft, and when it was over, Elena said, "I think jor turn now."

"No," whispered Beatrix. "Tomorrow...not now. Just sleep with me."

And even though Elena tried to insist, sliding her hand between Beatrix's legs to try and persuade her, Beatrix refused. She didn't care about coming; she just wanted to lie beside this lovely body. From her imagination's perch, somewhere up near the ceiling, she wanted to look down and see two bodies in the bed.

On the edge of sleep, Beatrix heard Elena speak.

"De painting. Where did you find it?"

"Um...the wall? Behind the London School of Art, I think."

Elena curled around her body, spooning it. Beatrix nestled back and covered Elena's arms with her own. "Why do you ask?"

"Dat painting—it's mine. It's bery bad. In de morning, I will make ju a new one."

Here Endeth the First Lesson
Renée Strider

You're out of your mind!" Stunned, Jo gaped at me. "You can't be. Not her. It's…It's…"

"It's what? A sin?" I had to laugh. I had just told my longtime friend and colleague that I was in love. Well, in serious lust. I had to tell somebody, and she was really the only one I dared confide in. Because the woman I thought about day and night, especially night, was a nun.

"Well no, but… How could you let that happen? Robin, it's not right. For God's sake—so to speak." She snickered at that.

We were sitting in my office in the hall attached to the church. Not the Catholic Church, nothing to do with nuns. Jo and I did outreach work with street kids for our church. We had just finished writing up a report about sponsoring a halfway house.

I sighed, closing my laptop. "I didn't *let* it happen. It just did. I can't get her out of my mind."

"After all the women I've been trying to fix you up with." She looked at me accusingly.

"Well, nobody was as gorgeous as she is."

"Yeah, she's pretty hot all right. If you don't think of her as a nun."

"I don't." That wasn't quite true. I couldn't forget what Antonia—*Sister Antonia*—was, and that was why I hadn't made any real moves. Yet. That had to change soon or I was going to lose it. Or go blind. I had to do something, and I intended to at a retreat that weekend. The theme was Women's Spirituality in World Religions, with workshops, panels, and meditation sessions. Antonia was the organizer.

After Jo left, more preoccupied than I'd ever seen her, I was free to think about strategy.

In case you're imagining the object of my fixation concealed in a black habit and veil, hands and generic face the only proof of a body underneath, you can stop. Antonia was a modern nun in regular clothes—trousers, even—if a little subdued and conservatively styled. And she didn't live in a convent but in a very large brick Victorian house with other nuns downtown near the cathedral. Technically, they weren't called nuns—as in cloistered—but sisters.

She and her housemates worked in the community. That's how we had come to know her. She was a social worker, and we often attended the same meetings and events related to youth welfare.

The first time I saw her she was sitting halfway down the table from me at a meeting. As I sat down she looked over at me with the clearest, lightest gray eyes I'd ever seen. I didn't separate out the other details till later: full red lips, straight nose, and dark lashes and brows beneath an unruly lock of straight black hair falling over her forehead. I was undone. By the time I found out she was a nun it was too late.

I think that she knew from the beginning how she affected me. She must have seen it when our eyes first met because immediately her color had risen, the kind of delicate blush you see only on very pale, translucent skin. I wanted her and she knew it. My eyes said so. It was a tacit acknowledgement that lay there between us in all of our subsequent meetings in the year that followed. She also seemed to sense that I wouldn't do or say anything about my desire because of what she was.

We didn't exactly become friends but we had many encounters and conversations. We talked about my denomination, the most liberal of the traditional churches in the country. We talked about the Roman Catholic Church and its restrictions, and about her congregation of sisters. I told her about my beliefs and philosophy. She told me how hers had evolved and changed over the years since she had taken her vows as a young novitiate.

She asked me to call her Antonia, without the "Sister."

I could never tell whether she wanted me, too. If she did, she hid it much better than I. At times just the sound of her voice made me wet. She couldn't see that, of course, but when her gaze fixed on me, my heart beat faster and the hot blood rushed through my veins, heating my face. That was surely obvious to her, even through my tan and freckles.

Antonia was probably a virgin. I imagined her opening up to me. I wanted to be the first to penetrate her with my fingers, enter her with my tongue. Some nights that vision would shudder through me to release. I was obsessed.

One day, not long before the retreat, she touched my hair. "I love the color of your hair," she said as she held a dark red curl between thumb and forefinger and raised those eyes, clear as water, to mine. Sometimes I thought I saw desire in them, but I wasn't sure.

Ste-Thérèse Spirituality Centre is a stone villa on a wooded estate on the lakeshore, an hour's drive from the city. It used to be a convent but now serves as a retreat for both religious and secular groups. It's still owned and run by nuns, though, and some of the retreats are directed by them, the congregation of sisters Antonia belongs to.

In the enormous, light-filled lobby of the Centre stands a replica of *The Ecstasy of S. Teresa di Avila* by the seventeenth-century Italian sculptor Bernini. Ostensibly, the statue represents the mystical ecstasy the saint experienced during a vision. In this vision God's love entered her in the form of a flaming arrow thrust into her by an angel.

The saint's ecstasy certainly doesn't look spiritual to me. The sculpture is incredibly erotic. From the position of her bare foot you know that the saint's legs are splayed wide under the agitated drapery. She's lying back. Her neck is arched, her face enraptured, with eyes closed, flared nostrils, and full lips open. The smiling, bare-breasted angel beside her, holding the arrow pointed at her, could be female, or at least androgynous. The figures are life-size.

I had been here before, conducting workshops or attending meetings in which Antonia was also involved. This tableau is what greeted me every time I visited the Centre. It was the last thing I needed when I was already in a state of anticipation about seeing her. The provocative sculpture just intensified my desire. I wanted to see the same rapture on Antonia's face. I wanted to be the angel, not standing beside her but bending over her.

That Friday was no different, and the sexy saint was even harder to ignore because this was the weekend that I was determined to get Antonia off somewhere and seduce her. However, I also had professional obligations here, so I went to my assigned room to unpack and go over some notes. I was to lead a couple of workshops on topics such as "Spirituality without God?" and to take part in a panel discussion.

I had arrived early and the place was still quiet. Not even Antonia had arrived yet. I walked through shadowed halls with gleaming floors that smelled of new wax. As always, I could almost hear the sounds of the women who lived here long ago—the murmur of voices, the swish of habits, the soft click of beads.

My room on the second story was somewhat larger than the nun's cell described in books, but not much. It was all white and the furniture was plain and dark—a straight-backed chair, a small desk with drawers serving also as a bedside table, and a wardrobe. On the wall above the bed was a simple cross, without the tortured figure hanging on it.

In another century this bleakness would have been relieved only by the tall window stretching almost to the high ceiling and opening out to a spectacular view of lake and sky. Now there was also a bright throw on the narrow double bed and a colorful mat on the hardwood floor.

I sat at the desk and worked steadily for a while. When I heard cars in the drive, I stretched and went to the shared washroom down the hall to freshen up before joining the others.

By late Saturday afternoon it was still the status quo. My time hadn't been my own since the day before. Antonia had also been busy with her duties, and I hadn't really seen her except when she introduced speakers and facilitators—and this morning at breakfast.

We sat at the same table, across from each other. I noticed that a few ends of her short hair stuck out from her head, and her eyes were still heavy-lidded from sleep. The intimacy of that sent an unexpected shock of lust to my groin so strong that I started. I managed to cover it up by reaching for something on the table and making small talk with my neighbor. When I dared look at her again, she was looking at my hands. Slowly her gaze moved up to mine. *Oh God.* This time there was no mistaking the longing I saw in her eyes. I walked around in an erotic haze for most of the morning.

Now it was late afternoon. The rest of the time was mine as I had no more official responsibilities and could simply enjoy the beautiful surroundings and the company of the other participants. And think about how to get Antonia alone and in my arms.

I strolled across the front lawn and down to a small wooded area by the shore. A tree with low branches provided shade in the hot sun, and I stood with my back against it, looking out at the sparkling water. The sun was still high. Nothing moved in the still air. I could hear only faint voices behind me in the distance and the murmur of the lake swells moving slowly to and fro over the pebble beach.

I decided that I would ask Antonia to go for a walk before the string quartet performance to be held out on the lawn that evening. My stomach tightened as I imagined pulling her against me within the protection of the trees. I closed my eyes and suppressed a moan. When I opened them I almost collapsed. She was standing in front of me, the bright sun behind her casting her in shadow. She had followed me. I moved so that I could see her face, and we stared at each other, lips parted but speechless.

"Antonia? What is it?" I finally managed.

For the second time that day I saw hunger in those clear eyes, and I was mesmerized. I would have stood there forever if she hadn't said something.

"I want to come to your room tonight," she said in a husky voice. "After the concert. May I?"

I tried to hide my shock. In all the seduction scenarios I had created in my mind, I had never pictured her as being the one to initiate our first erotic encounter.

"Yes. Yes, I'd like that." I almost gasped the words. My heart thudded so hard I hardly knew what I was saying.

She nodded and smiled as if she had come to a decision and had expected my yes. By unspoken agreement we both turned to walk back up to the house. My legs were weak. When she brushed against me on the narrow path I could feel her whole body trembling, and I knew that she wasn't nearly as cool and collected as she'd seemed down by the water.

I pulled myself together and reentered the villa. As I walked through the spacious lobby, I winked at the saint.

❖

During the recital I sat cross-legged on a blanket at the edge of the audience. Antonia sat on the other side on a low camp chair. It was hard to keep from looking at her, and when I did, her gaze would be fastened on me. Her eyes appeared hooded at that distance and I couldn't read them. But I could imagine. By the time I was back in my room I was wet from arousal.

I stood looking out at the gathering dusk. The concert was over but still the poignant echoes of violin and cello playing Barber's *Adagio for Strings* seemed to drift up from the lawn to my open window. To the east a full moon shone on silvered water. To the west the sky was still tinted rose.

I was getting impatient. I wanted her right now and wondered how much longer I would have to wait. As organizer, she would have to stay downstairs to say good-bye to the musicians, who had driven from the city only for the evening.

It was dark now and just as I switched on the lamp near the bed, there was a soft knock. My insides turned to liquid. I opened the door, and she was standing there in a thin, white cotton bathrobe with a delicate blue pattern, like a Japanese kimono with wide sleeves and belt tied high on her waist. Her hair was damp and she smelled faintly of soap.

I moved aside and she came in and stood against the closed door. We just looked at each other, neither of us saying a word.

"I just got out of the shower," she said finally, smiling tentatively.

"I can see that," I said softly. I placed my fingertips on the triangle of skin at her collarbone and drew the robe apart very slowly, exposing her cleavage and the swell of her breasts. I could see her throat move as she swallowed. I opened the gown a little further, baring her shoulders and the areolae of her nipples. They were dark pink. I knew her nipples would be redder. Their hard points were pressed against the flimsy cloth. I could hardly breathe. Antonia's breathing was erratic.

I caressed her bare shoulders and kissed her throat, then moved up. Our mouths came together and I opened her lips with my tongue, sliding it along and around hers. She moaned into my mouth. I moved my lips down to her throat again, leaving a moist trail, and kissed the rapid pulse. I wanted to bite her there and suck her.

She groaned, and with her hands on my buttocks, pulled me against her. I was beginning to lose control and started to shove my thigh between hers, then suddenly stopped. What was I doing? This was probably her first time, and I had been about to take her up against a wall—me fully dressed, her almost naked.

I held her close. "I'm sorry," I said hoarsely. "I'm going too fast."

"I'm not going to say 'Please be gentle,' if that's what you think," she said into my shoulder, breathing hard. She pulled away and looked at me, her eyes dark with passion. "I want you to teach me, show me—things."

I searched her face. Those words and that look in her eyes caused a fresh rush to my groin. I was so wet for her. I pulled the zipper of my chinos down and guided her hand inside.

"Touch me, Antonia," I whispered. "Please."

Without any hesitation she stroked down my belly into my briefs, and farther down between my legs. Long fingers slid through my swollen folds.

"Oh, yes, I've wanted this for so long," she breathed.

I stopped her hand and pulled it away because I was so close to coming, and it was too soon. "See how wet I am for you? Are you as wet as that?"

"Yes," she said, her voice shaking. "Touch me and see."

I undid the cloth belt and it fell to the floor. She spread the robe open herself, displaying small, white cotton panties. She looked so vulnerable and so sexy at the same time. I moved my hand slowly down her stomach, caressing the warm smooth skin, then cupped her outside the panties. They were damp. We both moaned as my fingers moved to the heat between her thighs and found their way into her briefs at the crotch. She was drenched and so very slippery. She cried out and arched against me as my fingers slid along the base of her clitoris to her entry. I pushed gently but it was closed.

"Has anyone ever touched you before?"

"No, just me." Her laugh was almost a sob. I knew she was close to the edge, too, so I withdrew my hand. I wanted her in bed. I wanted her to climax there, to see it in her face.

"Don't leave," she begged. "Don't stop."

"I won't." I drew her to the bed. "I want you here, under me."

"For now, anyway." She gave me a knowing smile and sat down. "Are you ever going to take off your clothes?"

I stripped as Antonia watched me. I had expected her to be shy, uncertain, but she wasn't. When I was naked, she stood up and reached for me, and explored my body— breasts, buttocks, the small of my back. Her searching hand slid between my thighs, and I closed my eyes, pushing back the orgasm.

"I've dreamed of this," she said, and her voice caught as she stroked my abdomen with wet fingers.

Slowly I removed her robe. As I held her breasts in my palms, my thumbs skimmed her nipples, rigid and golden red and so beautiful in the lamplight. I got down on my knees and tugged her briefs down to the floor, kissing the soft black triangle. She was trembling wildly, and I held her tightly around her thighs to keep her from falling as I pushed my face into her and licked her. I craved the taste and scent of her arousal and thought I could die for them. She pulled my head harder against her and thrust her hips forward.

I pushed Antonia onto the bed and as she lay back, I knelt between her legs, spreading them with my knees. We looked into each other's eyes as my hand parted her dripping folds, then my own. As I ground my pelvis into her, our swollen flesh slid together. The sensation was excruciating. She gasped, hands clutching my shoulders.

"Oh, God, Robin, I never imagined…"

I wanted to bring her to the edge without going over so that she would be so aroused when I penetrated her that the pain would be indistinguishable from the pleasure. When I knew we were both on the verge I moved up her body, clenching my jaw to keep from climaxing.

"No, come back," she protested, writhing against me.

"Wait. I need to be inside you." I slid my fingers through her slickness, pressing against the tight opening. I drove my leg between hers, riding her thigh. We were both frantic. Then one stroke with my thumb against her engorged clitoris, and the orgasm tore through her at the same time as my fingers thrust into her through the barrier. Her body went rigid as she convulsed with a strangled shout. When I saw the rapture in her face I came instantly, jerking against her. We were shattered, and the aftershocks went on and on.

We had fallen asleep on our sides with my head pressed forward into the nape of her neck and my arm wrapped around her hip with my hand tucked between her legs. When I woke up we were still in exactly the same position. I had managed to turn out the lamp just before passing out and awakened to a study in black and white. The moon shone directly through the tall, open window. It was almost as bright as day in the room but without the colors.

Slowly and gently I pulled my hand out from its warm hiding place. It was still sticky. I examined it closely in the moonlight. I couldn't see any blood. I smelled it and licked it, and my stomach swirled with remembered desire. Very carefully, so as not to wake her, I raised myself up and leaned across her, barely touching her, and examined the white sheet we were lying on.

"See any blood?" Antonia murmured sleepily as she stirred and rolled onto her back. Startled, I laughed.

"No," I said, pulling back. I lay on my side, leaning on my elbow. "Your lips are black in the moonlight, just like your hair."

"So are your freckles—and your nipples. Amazing."

She smiled and tugged me toward her and kissed me, her warm smooth tongue sliding slowly between my lips. Our breathing picked up. I felt the familiar rush low in my guts.

I groaned. "I'll be wrecked tomorrow. I still have to go over my sermon for the eleven o'clock service, and then officiate at a wedding in the afternoon. I'll have to leave here right after breakfast."

"Have you got your collar with you? I like seeing you in it." She raised her eyebrows suggestively.

"I hardly ever wear my clerical collar." I sucked the soft hollow between her neck and shoulder. "But I have one with me. I'll put it on before I leave, just for you." I paused and looked at her. "What are you going to do?"

She looked away. "What do you mean? Tomorrow?"

"No. You know what I mean," I said, caressing her cheek.

"Yes. I don't know yet." Her eyes met mine again, as clear as ever. "But tonight I just want you to show me more." Her hand slid down my side and over my buttocks. "It's not that late," she whispered into my ear. "The moon is still high, and I'm so wet again. What about 69?"

"Oh God." I took a shaky breath and whimpered a little, then rolled over on my back. "First, how about this. Kneel above me, here." I patted my stomach. She straddled me in the moonlight, pushing down on me lightly with her sex. I clasped her hips. "Now move up to my face…"

THE CASE OF THE STOLEN SHORTS
THERESE SZYMANSKI

Author's Note: This story depicts the absolute truth, except when it does not. The reader is advised to continue at the risk of her own suspension of disbelief and imagination.

"Well, this doesn't seem to be getting any hotter..." I said to Karin as we sat in the hotel sauna.

"We've worked the temp control and the door guards—maybe there's a basic on/off switch we're missing?"

Brains, beauty, sense of humor... She was married, though. I *so* needed to get away from her. She was off limits to the nth degree. "Hey, do you want something to drink?" I held up my now-empty beer bottle. "I'm just gonna run on down and get a refill."

"Oh, okay," she said, looking as if she couldn't believe I was fleeing.

"I'll be back in just two shakes," I explained.

"Yes, please, another rum and Coke would be great."

I thought about hopping back out to the pool area to collect my shorts. I was only wearing my dark blue Fruit of the Loom boxers and a Vail T-shirt with a sports bra underneath and it was too nice a hotel to wander into the bar quite so undressed. However, the hot tub out by the pool was full of many lovelies and, knowing me, I'd sober up before I finished flirting. Instead, I grabbed a nearby towel to wrap around the boxers and headed down on the elevator.

I wasn't sure if the hotel bar was still open, but the mini-bar in my room might suffice if it wasn't.

I wrapped the towel around my waist and brushed my fingers through my hair, standing it slightly on end into what a friend had dubbed "baby bird" hair. It was now my trademark. Just as I finished properly mussing the 'do, the elevator dinged and stopped at a floor, which elevators are wont to do. An attractive brunette strode in. She wore red come-fuck-me heels, a red halter, under which she obviously wore no bra, and a black miniskirt shorter than the black dress worn by one hot author who was at the awards ceremony earlier in the night.

Damn, I was like a dog—or cat—in heat. This woman had obvious itches and I wanted to scratch them all for her.

The little lovely smirked at me, obviously noticing my attention. "See something you like?" she drawled in a faint Southern accent. Leaning back against the wall, she crossed her long legs in front of her, showing them to their best advantage as she assessed me.

I was emboldened by the many beers I'd had, so I suavely replied, "Uh...Yeah." She laughed at me. I reckoned that wasn't a bad thing, since laughter showed she was comfortable.

"Interesting outfit you've got going on there," she said, raising an eyebrow. "Should I even ask what you've got on—if anything—under that towel?"

"My boxer shorts. I was just up at the sauna and was heading for the bar."

"Barefoot in your boxers."

"Ayup."

"Listen, is it just my imagination, or are there a lot of...you...here this weekend?"

"I think I'm the only me here this weekend. Least, last time I checked nobody had cloned me. And actually everyone who knows me thinks one of me is way more than enough."

She glared at me in a truly adorable way. "You know what I mean."

There was something about her clear blue gaze that was familiar, and I needed to keep her talking to figure out why. I had to keep her interested and occupied.

The elevator dinged as it hit the ground floor. I held my towel on with one hand and with the other gallantly indicated that she depart first.

"I'll tell you about it if you'll tell me where you're from," I said.

"I live in Chicago."

"Originally. That's not a Chicago accent."

"But it is the answer to your question."

"Fine. It's a convention."

"You have conventions?" she said, putting her hand on my forearm to stop me from walking away. Her eyes were huge with disbelief.

Her perfume swirling around my head was intoxicating. Maybe more so since I really was intoxicated. "Where are you from—*originally*?" There was no particular reason I wanted to know, I just wanted to be able to identify that absolutely yummy accent. And I still had to figure out where I knew her from.

"Virginia."

"I come from *Dee-troit* originally myself, but I live in D.C. these days." I shrugged and leaned close to her. "I'm here for a lesbian *literary* convention."

"It's a lesbian *literary* convention?" She looked me up and down, a teasing smile dancing on her lips and a playful glint in her eyes. "What? Are you some sort of a writer?"

"Uh, yeah." I recognized that glint—that teasing smile—that single arched brow. She'd had her eye on me earlier tonight.

"Really? What do you write?"

She was interested. I just had to reel her in. "Sleazy lesbian mysteries."

"Really? Get out!"

"So you want me to leave?" I turned to go, knowing she wouldn't let me.

She didn't. She again put her hand on my arm. "No, I mean... Stay."

"Well, you know, you'd better watch out. I'm actually rather well known for being a bad girl."

"And just how bad are we talking about here?" she asked, running a fingertip lightly up and down my arm.

I grabbed her hand and pulled her into my arms. "I remember you, you know. You were in the bar earlier," I whispered into her ear, burying my face in her silky hair. I'd been well aware of the gathering of straight girls eyeing the dykes and blushing.

She gasped and made a token protest, trying to push away from me. "I'm sure I don't know what you mean."

"Yes, you do. You knew earlier, in the bar. And you knew when you saw me in the 'vator just now. It's why you started talking to me, in fact." I wrapped an arm around her waist, pushed her up against a wall, and shoved my thigh hard between her legs, against her heat.

"Uh, ah, you maybe might wanna let me go now," she panted into my ear, grinding against me.

"So no follow-through, eh?" I growled, running my lips softly up her neck. "You've been flirting with me all day. Are you trying to say now that you're not interested?" I dropped my hand to her bare leg, tracing up the soft skin to cup her ass, running my finger along and just under the edge of her silky panties.

She gasped, closed her eyes, and leaned into my shoulder. "I'm straight."

"Sure you are, sweetie." I slipped my fingers inside the crotch of her underwear, dipping into her wet to lube both her and my fingers. "Tell me—you're not really all talk and no action, are you?" I pushed her underwear aside with the fingers of my left hand, then dipped my fingers into her.

"Uh, God, yes, please," she moaned, then pushed her face from my shoulder, even as she humped my hand. "Your name, please, what's your name?"

I thought about answering a la *Pretty Woman*, all with the "what do you want it to be," but I didn't think we needed so many words. "Reese."

"Reese, yes." She buried her face in my shoulder again. "I'm not sure if I like you better all in black or half dressed. Or maybe that should be half undressed?" I'd been in black jeans and a black long-sleeve shirt earlier. With black boots, of course.

She was able to talk too much, which meant my hand didn't have her full attention. I went knuckles deep inside her and flicked her clit with my thumb, playing it back and forth.

"Oh, oh God," she moaned into my shoulder.

"Not so straight anymore, are you?"

"Take me back to your room," she said, pulling away ever so slightly.

"No. You're gonna come for me the first time right here."

"The…" She jerked against me, trying to pull away. "The…the clerk…"

"No," I said, still fingering her. "You're gonna come for me the first time right here, straight girl." I toyed with her plump nipple through the thin material of her top with my other hand.

"God, I can't, not here. He's watching!" She was grabbing at my arms, squeezing my right forearm, half trying to push it away and half encouraging me further.

"Then let's give the clerk a little show, shall we? Come for me, baby."

"Fuck me. Now. Hard. Yes."

I wrapped her left leg around me, opening her further so I could fuck her hard, in and out, while I flicked her clit back and forth. I glanced back and saw that the lobby was empty. The only person in sight was the clerk, standing behind the counter. We had his rapt attention.

I lowered her halter, revealing a tit in its lush entirety. I licked all the way around the nipple, then pulled it into my mouth as she humped my hand, her ragged breathing filling my head. I fucked her, in and out, teasing her clit harder and faster.

I ran my teeth over her hard nipple, then bit it.

"God, yes!" she choked out, convulsing against and around me before she fell into my arms.

"Why don't we get a little more comfortable?" I whispered, reaching down to pick her up.

"Yes, please," she said, wrapping her arms around my neck and hiding her face against my shoulder.

I turned, hit the elevator call button, winked at the clerk, and carried her into it. I touched the button for my floor, put her on her feet, and pushed her against the wall.

She practically sagged onto my thigh, which she began rubbing lasciviously against. "So, how bad are you?"

"Very bad," I growled, pulling her hard against me while shoving my thigh harder between her legs.

She wrapped her arms around my neck and jumped up slightly to wrap her legs around my hips. "Take me to your room."

I claimed her mouth with my own, enjoying her soft lips against mine for just a moment before I slipped my tongue into her. Our tongues tangoed, dueled, and the 'vator dinged again.

I carried her off, enjoying her mouth, her lips, the feel of her body wrapped around mine. She was soft and warm in all the right places, and she could represent whomever I wanted her to. Her soft curves belonged to me, she was mine right now. She was giving herself to me, for whatever I wanted.

"Strip. Now," I said once she was on my bed.

She sat up, kicked off her shoes, and looked me right in the eyes as she pulled off her halter, then stood, unzipped her skirt, and let it drop to the floor.

"You're still not naked."

She stepped out of her panties. "You've had me already."

"But I haven't made you scream yet."

"Then fuck me inside out." She lay back on the bed, draping herself artistically across it.

I walked casually over to the TV and turned it to play some light music. "What do you want, straight girl?"

"I...I..." Her bashfulness was at odds with how she stared at me almost defiantly.

"Say it."

"I've heard that...well..." She got off the bed and came to me. "I want you to fuck me, hard. Take me. And use whatever you want to." She pressed her naked body against mine, wrapping her arms around me. "Fuck me, Reese. Hard and fast."

I picked her up. Threw her on the bed. I opened a drawer and pulled out lube and a dildo, complete with harness. She was, literally, fantastic and having all the right accessories ready was equally so. I dropped my towel and boxers and let her watch me strap it on. I went to her with the lube in my hand.

"Get me nice and slick."

"How about this way first?" She sat on the edge of the bed and took me into her nice wet mouth. She worked up and down my long, hard cock, taking me deep into her mouth and down her throat before working her mouth back up. She gave me a blowjob. She let me fuck her face. She blew me, relishing every moment of it, and the sight of it was doing things for me I hadn't thought any straight girl could do. And then I put the lube into her hands so she could give me a hand job.

This very naughty straight girl deserved a really good time. I pushed her onto the bed, putting her on her back, and climbed on top of her as she gripped my shoulders.

I entered her slowly, pushing in all the way, easily and surely. She arched up against me, urging me to go deep. She wrapped her legs around me, forcing me to stay inside. She pushed my shirt up so her hands were on my back. So she could run her nails up my back. Dig them in. Scratch me and mark me.

And I fucked her. Slowly. Then faster. In and out. Riding her.

Fucking her. She used her legs to keep me inside her even as her nails cut jagged lines down my back, hurting so much I groaned. I moaned. And I slid in and out of her. I licked her collarbone, kissed her neck, sucked her earlobe into my mouth, gently pulling on it.

I put some of my weight on one of my hands and used the other to caress her body, to make sure she realized she was completely naked. I felt her beautiful tit, cupping its lushness, and tugged on her hardened nipple.

She arched against me, helping me fuck her. Her pelvis went up and down even as I pistoned in and out of her.

"God, yes, please—harder! Faster!"

I twisted her nipple as hard as possible, pulling it so her tit stretched from her body.

"*Yes!*"

I was brutal and forward, and once she came, I stayed inside her for a few minutes, our sweaty bodies all but glued together. I lifted myself and looked down into her incredibly blue eyes.

And then I kissed her and fucked her again. Fantastic.

And then I put her on the table so I could fuck her while I stood, giving me better leverage and also allowing me to finger her clit while I fucked her. And still be able to enjoy the beauty of her entire body laid out bare for me.

And then I pulled all the way out of her, sat her up, coated my hand with lube, and shoved my fist into her. No warning. No gentle fingers first. Just my whole hand, my fist, ravishing her.

"*Fuck!*" she screamed, pushing against me, urging me on.

Her nails were biting into my bicep and her fingers were hard against the other forearm. I knew I would be bruised later. But still, I barely gave her a chance to acclimate to my hand buried deep inside her hungry, luscious cunt before I started fucking her with it.

"Look down," I demanded. "Now. I want you to see my hand inside you."

I felt her tighten around me as she looked. She choked with little moans as she fell back on her elbows to reveal her entire body to me. She met my every push and the table got very, very wet.

"That was awesome," she breathed finally, lying back on the table.

I none-too-gently extracted my hand, trying not to hurt her, but not minding that it did a little—in such a good way.

She looked up at me dreamily. "Let's go to bed and do all of that again."

"Hmm," I said, going to the bathroom to get some water. I helped her sit up and drink some, soothing her parched throat from her heavy breathing, screaming, and sounds of excitement and coming. "I think I may have had all the fantasy I can handle for one night."

Her lips full and inviting, she offered, "Maybe tomorrow? Nooners?"

"Maybe." My evil mind had no trouble imagining it.

"So, what happened to you before?" she finally said, once she had her breathing under control.

"What do you mean?"

"You were dressed so…well…dapperly before. What happened?"

Oh shit. Karin. My shorts. "Y'know, I need to run up to the pool. A friend was waiting for me in the sauna. Give me your room number, and I'll get back to you."

I grabbed some drinks from my fridge, dropped off the woman-without-a-name, as I've now come to refer to her, since I never did get her moniker, and went back up to the sauna.

Karin was staring at the controls and looking as if she wanted to kick them. "I don't think we're going to get it to work."

"Oh. Here's a drink for you. The bar was closed."

"You didn't have to break into your mini-bar."

"That's what took so long." I was thinking very fantastic thoughts. "Why don't we get our stuff, then, and call it a night?"

"Sure. It's late and we're signing books at eight."

"Oh, that's right." We walked back to the pool. Or at least, the hotel doors that led out onto the roof, which contained the pool. There was a wicked thunderstorm going on, and the doors were chained and padlocked shut. I tried opening them as much as possible so I could push out between them, to no avail.

"Reese, I don't think that's a good idea. You might get stuck. Or dislocate your shoulder. Or worse. So you should stop that. Now."

There was no arguing with Karin when she used that Moogie voice. She grabbed the phone next to the door and called the front desk, quickly explaining the situation. A security guard came up and opened the doors for us. He waited as we ran out into the pelting rain to where we'd left our belongings.

Karin put on her shoes, and I looked all around. "Hey, where are my shorts?" I asked.

Karin laughed and said, "No one will believe they walked off by themselves. Who got into your shorts, Reese?"

That's when I knew I had all the makings of a good short story.

GETTING IN AND OUT OF HER SHORTS
KARIN KALLMAKER

Author's Note: This story depicts the absolute truth, except when it does not.

Okay, I'm the woman who ended up with that writer's shorts—you know, the pair that went missing from poolside. I was naked, they were apparently abandoned, so I put them on. Given that we'd been trading glances all day it was quite a turn-on to be in her shorts.

There was also a pair of shoes, cute ones, too, and I was about to slip them on—thinking I'd turn both shorts and shoes into lost and found in the morning—when I saw the writer was coming back. There was good news and bad news about that. Good news was she had a security guard with her. Finding myself without my swimsuit and locked on the roof during a thunderstorm hadn't been fun.

I grabbed a soaking-wet towel to wrap around my upper body. The bad news was that the writer wasn't alone and the security guard was lingering. Damn, the owner of those cute clogs was back, too. I just couldn't be seen like this, in a borrowed pair of shorts and a towel that was only making it more apparent I had nothing else on.

Back behind the big potted plants I went.

I heard the writer, in that silken butch voice of hers, ask, "Where are my shorts?"

The other woman, some femme, laughed. "Who's in your shorts now, Reese?"

Oh, she liked to be called Reese? I'd only heard Therese all weekend.

"I love those shorts. They had great pockets and I didn't bring another pair."

I fingered the hem guiltily. They were nice shorts. I hoped she didn't look behind the plants and discover me. It looked bad, but really, the only mistake I had made was thinking my ex was capable of some fun for "old times' sake." A lot hadn't worked between us, but the sex always had. So when she proposed a quick, hot tryst behind the plants, only a few feet away from the hot tub party, I'd agreed.

And then, once she'd coaxed me out of my swimsuit, she'd walked off with it. Now you see why she's my ex. Truthfully, the only reason I was so willing was this writer, Reese. The baby bird hair, dark eyes, and little looks she'd given me that said she appreciated the style of a high femme put me in very warm mood. Her gaze seemed to appreciate the light pink polish on my fingernails and the glitter of my earrings, and a girl likes that. It had been a while since anyone noticed the little things.

I realized with a start that Reese and the other woman were leaving. I couldn't remember the other woman's name—another writer but I don't think I'd read anything by her. Reese's books I'd studied, certain parts more than others. She writes great sex and, well, a girl's got to wonder if it's all fiction, doesn't she?

The other woman, ringing for the elevator, was laughing and it seemed to me that everyone around Reese laughed a lot. I love a sense of humor. I mean, I love the kind of sense of humor that creates laughter, not the kind that thinks swiping someone's swimsuit and leaving her abandoned in a thunderstorm was funny. My ex was so dead when I found her.

The elevator came and went, taking the other woman away, and I watched Reese head for the fitness room, probably still in search of her shorts. To my profound relief the security guard had not relocked the doors. The hotel air-conditioning had me shivering instantly—wet clothes and fifty degrees will do that.

No doubt I should have called my roomie on the house phone to wake her up so I could get into the room. But I felt bad that I had Reese's shorts and she was obviously going to search high and low for them. The least I could do was tell her she'd get them back. So I followed her into the fitness room, which was even colder, and realized she'd really been aiming for the bathroom, which made a lot of sense.

She had a really annoyed look on her face as she was closing a stall door, and it only took her two seconds to look me over. Her expression was funny, then, because the wet towel made her do a double-take as she checked me out, but she was still a little annoyed.

"You have my shorts on."

"Yeah, see, I, uh…" I couldn't help but glance at myself in the big mirror to see what she saw. The pool towel was translucent and her shorts were tight on me. "Someone swiped my swimsuit."

"Oh?" She stayed where she was and a little smile was dancing in her eyes. "Skinny dipping?"

"No, I was, uh, doing something I shouldn't have been." She was definitely checking me out and I was shivering not so much from the cold as from the way her eyebrow arched. "An ex played a practical joke."

"An ex? Say no more." She was openly grinning at me now. "So, how am I going to get my shorts back?"

"You could take them off me." God, where had that come from? I wasn't usually quite so…blatant.

She crossed the room slowly toward me, her gaze never leaving mine. I backed up against the sink, not breathing. The shivers became more pronounced as she planted both of her hands on the counter to either side of me. "Hasn't anyone ever told you there are certain dares you never try on a butch?"

I shook my head. My mind took off at warp speed, imagining her reclaiming her shorts and discovering that—and it was all her fault with that look in her eyes—now they really needed to be washed. I closed my eyes and gave myself to her voice.

"You're shivering," she said. "It's very cold in here."

"Wet." I indicated the towel.

"Is that all that's wet?" She leaned into me, then jerked back as the dripping, chilled towel touched her sport bra and skin. "I could warm you up but the towel has got to go."

She arched an eyebrow again, didn't move an inch and just waited. It was up to me.

After a hard swallow I slowly unwrapped the towel.

Just as slowly she wrapped her very warm, very strong arms around me and pulled me close.

She felt like a fantasy, like her heartbeat was in her hands, pulsing on my naked back. I closed my eyes and gave myself completely to it. "I've been watching you all day."

"And thinking what?" Her fingertips lightly traced the nape of my neck, then drifted down my spine.

"Thinking things that made me say yes to my ex tonight."

She sighed like she understood. "If you weren't playing with her heart I don't think there's anything wrong with a…stand-in."

"Well, she was playing with me, that's for sure. I got locked on the roof, stark naked."

"Oh, poor baby. And no one to rescue you. Okay, I forgive you for taking my shorts."

With a shudder I whispered in her ear, "Do you want them back now?"

She growled. "We're getting to the point of no return here. If you mean it, tell me so because you're making me crazy."

I managed to lift my head from her shoulder. "Was I wrong thinking you were watching me today?"

"No. I like red hair and I like a femme who is comfortable with her sexiness, and you obviously are. It's a pleasure to watch you move."

"Oh." I took a deep breath. "Do you make love the way you sweet-talk?"

Her fingers went to the zipper on the shorts. "Wanna find out?"

"Yes."

She hesitated, then ducked her head to look in my eyes. "I'm going home tomorrow."

"So am I," I answered, understanding what she meant. Tonight only, and that was fine with me. This kind of fantasy only worked for a night and it had been a really long time since I'd been this bad.

She kissed my bare shoulders as she loosened the button and carefully unzipped me. With a mutual wiggle the shorts slipped down a little as she swept her hands firmly around my waist, then down to cup my ass. "Oh, very nice," she murmured.

I wasn't shivering anymore. It was something else flooding over my body, ripples of tension and awareness. Her bare midriff was warm and her lips soft against my collarbone. I arched back as she leaned down to flick her tongue over one nipple. I saw her smile at my little gasp, then her teeth closed over it and she bit down just enough to make me shudder.

Part of me couldn't believe this was really happening. "How do you know I like that?"

"I don't—I'm just listening to my dance partner." She gave me a long, intent look, wrapped me very tight in her arms, and the next thing I knew my bare ass was on the counter.

She stripped off the shorts and moved between my knees. I had to brace myself with my hands behind me to keep from swooning onto my back.

"Perfect," she said, then she bit my nipple again, a little harder. "Stay just like that, baby."

I should have worried someone would walk in on us, but the idea of it excited me too much to care. It was unlikely at two o'clock in the morning, but if someone did we'd cover up and find someplace else. Or let them watch. God, I was in a mood tonight. Her teeth felt fantastic and she seemed to understand what my body was saying. Her hands were feeling my thighs and hips and ass like she could read my desire through her fingertips.

I lifted myself on my hands enough to press my crotch to her swim trunks. Something hit my clit just right and I pressed against it with a stunned gasp. I was already so close.

"Uh-uh," she whispered. "Don't you dare."

"Touch me, then. Please."

"I thought you'd never ask." She ran her lips and teeth over my shoulder, making my skin burn.

I groaned, loud and long, as her hand cupped me between my legs. She was taking possession of me, and I could feel it in the tingling soles of my dangling feet and my burning, sweating scalp. Had I been cold? I was on fire now.

She made that growling noise again. "You're ready, aren't you?"

"Yes." I put my weight on my hands and pushed myself against her.

She turned her hand over, rubbing my swollen lips with her knuckles, bumping along my clit as she opened me. "Oh. God, you're wet."

"What did you expect?"

She bit my lower lip in response. "That it would be really fun to fuck you off those stiletto sandals you were wearing this morning. I like you naked."

She slid into me then, not slow, not fast, but firmly. My choked cry drew a moan from her as she spread her fingers inside me. She massaged me on the inside, immediately finding the right nerves and muscles. It was so quick, so hot. Gasping, I couldn't hold back a hard, wrenching climax.

It was over so fast I wanted to cry. Once was always enough to put me to sleep.

"Uh-uh." She squeezed my nipple between her finger and thumb. "You're not done. We're just getting started."

"Oh, fuck," I breathed out.

Her fingers danced on my clit, then dipped inside me, withdrew and played again. "This is really fun. Your body can really move."

My thighs trembled as I held them as far apart as I possibly could. I drove myself down on her hand, dying to put out the burning fire she was stoking higher and higher.

She pulled me to the very edge of the counter, one muscled arm holding me firmly down while she leaned hard into me. I realized she had four fingers inside me and it was her thumb rubbing my throbbing clit. She pushed in with the force of her whole arm, knocking the breath out of me, and I responded with a hoarse cry, feeling as if I was clinging to my sanity by a rapidly thinning thread.

She could have anything she wanted. She could take everything I offered. I tried to grind myself on her hand but she was holding me down too firmly. She did all the moving and I surrendered to sensation like I never had before in my life. She fucked me the way I'd always wanted someone to fuck me, so good and so deep it was a fantasy come to life.

My eyes tightly closed, shivers ran up and down my body as another climax rolled over me.

"Wet," she said, "is going to give you a cold in this air-conditioning."

My eyes snapped open. Her hands were still planted to either side of me. She was starting to look at me as if I was odd, and that wasn't at all what I wanted. I had to say something, but I could still hear the fantasy echo of my eager, hoarse cries. "About that dare…"

Her smile was slow and sexy. "You should be careful who you say things like that to. Another butch might have stripped you."

My inner femme wailed, "Aren't you going to?" but I wisely kept my lips clamped desperately together. Thank goodness she couldn't read my mind.

She finally leaned away from me and my entire body wanted to go limp. "You can leave my shorts at the front desk or something. I understand why you need them."

Gazing at her, at a loss for words, I knew exactly how her arms would feel if she embraced me, and exactly how her hand would feel learning all my secrets. She was a fantasy and yet she was reality, too. I was sure there were surprises about her that would be delightful to discover. "Maybe I could mail them to you after I wash them. They're a little…wet." Like me, I wanted to add.

She shrugged and then tried to cover a yawn. "I'm so sorry. It's late and that's not usually what I do in the presence of a half-naked beautiful femme."

God, she was sweet and sexy. I bet she was cuddly when she woke up in the morning. It didn't look like I was going to find out. Not now, not here, at least.

A true gentleman, she walked me to my room to make sure I arrived safely in my half-clad state.

I said shyly, "If anyone saw us now they'd never believe we behaved."

Her grin was genuine. "It's because I'm so tired. It's one of those times when what didn't happen is far more interesting than what did."

She gave me a peck on the cheek that I'm still dreaming about.

Here's the big confession. I never did send her shorts to her. I figured I'd give them back at the next convention. Maybe invite her to take them off me again, if I really could get up the nerve.

Meantime, they're great shorts with all those pockets. And I even got a free Chapstick out of the deal.

Every Life for a Thousand Years
JC Chen

I was swimming in a lake in the first memory I have of my
Beloved. She pretended to enjoy the water as she waded out
knee deep to greet me. I've learned since then that she loves everything
about water except swimming in it. It is one of my favorite memories
of her: one hand holding the hem of her dress high above the waterline,
exposing the leanness of her thighs, the other hand shading her eyes
from the sun while watching me intently and possessively. I asked her
what her name was but she only laughed. Her laughter was clear and
joyful; the sound of it drew me to her.

We spent that first day talking on the bank of the lake. She was
wise and witty and her stories were exotic and grand. I felt naïve and
awestruck around her but she never seemed to tire of my company. At
dusk, we agreed to meet again the next day at the shore of the lake. We
met every day for a month. She would bring journals with her. Some of
them contained pictures and stories of places she had been. I would lie
with my head in her lap as she read to me from her memories. She also
brought journals of places she wanted to go. I would sit side by side
with her, equally engrossed by the silkiness of her skin and brilliance of
her smile as the maps and paintings of these faraway lands. I had never
much imagined the world beyond my lake before she brought it to me
in her books.

I was the one to suggest that we go. On the last day of the first
month we were together, I turned to her while she was reading aloud
about a land with a thousand waterfalls. Although I wasn't looking at
the pictures, I could see the landscape in my mind: cascades of silver,
rolling green hills, the serenity of a perfect azure sky. I wanted to see it
with my eyes and I told her so. She looked at me then with eyes full of
hope. I felt a new kind of warmth burn through me like fire in my veins.

I would go with her to this land of a thousand waterfalls. I knew I would go with her to the ends of the earth.

It is still dark outside and the sun is not due to rise for a while. The wind is brisk and cool against my naked skin and I can hear the surf crashing wildly against the rocks far below. I hear my Beloved approaching and I turn to greet her. Despite the darkness, moonlight ignites the highlights in her hair like smoldering embers in a blanket of coal. She sets a large velvet satchel down on the ground and steps into my embrace. Her long silken robe is warm where I press against her and cool where it flaps loosely around my back and thighs. She smells like autumn, and standing this close I catch just a hint of our morning lovemaking.

She presses a soft kiss against my neck before pulling away from me to unfasten the silk tie around her waist. The robe slips from her slender shoulders toward the ground where the wind grabs hold and whisks it away. She stands radiant before me. Her pale and flawless skin gleams in the moonlight and the darker tips of her nipples are just beginning to harden against the cold. My breath catches in my throat and my heart beats fast and heavy.

Our home consists of three buildings: two small bungalows—each with a large workspace and a smaller sleeping alcove—and the main house. The three buildings are situated on the corners of a perfectly square courtyard. The fourth corner—diagonally across from the main house—is open, offering an unobstructed view of the valley below. These days we spend most of our time in the main house, although my Beloved still keeps her painting studio in one of the bungalows.

I can be found most often in the library. Our collection spans centuries, but our most valuable tomes are not literature at all. Along the eastern wall, behind a thick protective brocade curtain, are the shelves that hold our personal journals. There are hundreds of volumes, each leather-bound and inscribed with our names and the years covered within. Most mornings my Beloved and I read together from them. It is a curious and wonderful experience akin to remembering and learning at the same time. I do most of the writing, but she is responsible for the numerous maps and pictures that adorn the pages. The journals serve as the collaborative visual memory of our time together.

Along the back windowed wall of the library is my Beloved's pride and joy: a large screen composed of eight panels with ebony frames encircling gold that has been beaten paper thin and stretched across the frames like a canvas. On this golden canvas is painted a story like no other. It took my Beloved over half a lifetime to complete the painting, and even now she cannot resist fussing over its finer details with her brushes and her colors. Reading from left to right like a book, the panels depict the legend of the Dragon and the Phoenix and their never-ending quest for the Pearl of Knowledge. The first few panels are dark and violent, with the Dragon and Phoenix battling mightily for the Pearl, but successively the images become lighter and more peaceful, ending with the final panel: a triumphant joining of souls with the Pearl as a unifying rather than dividing force. It is a familiar story, painted on gold in vivid colors but also rendered in black and white throughout our journals.

The sky is slowly illuming. The glow of the predawn is dim above the horizon but strengthening with each passing moment. My Beloved picks up the satchel from the ground and unties the drawstring holding it shut. Her fingers pluck away at the old, heavy knot with confidence. When the bag is finally open, she reaches in with reverent care and pulls forth a large and luminous pearl. The diameter of the pearl is such that her fingertips cannot quite touch when she grips it. Tentatively, my Beloved offers it to me, cradled in the palm of her hand. The surface of the pearl is smooth and iridescent. As I step forward to take it from her I can see the writing etched just beneath the surface, catching and bending the light like facets in a gemstone. It reads:

> *Every century a Race to run*
> *For the Pearl. From rising sun,*
> *Around the world, 'til day is done.*
> *Memories kept for She that won.*
> *For She that lost, a life redone.*

The cliff upon which we stand is atop the mountain where our home is built. We only come up here for the Race since the climb is difficult and the view is almost as grand from the safety of our courtyard. Yet every time I come here I am struck by the majesty of it all. It is the top of the world and on a cloudless day like today, I can see the horizon extend in a perfect circumference around us.

I take my Beloved by the hand and walk her to the very end of the plateau. Her footing is firm and confident despite our tremendous altitude. I slip behind her, wrap my arms securely around her waist, and urge her closer to the edge for a better view. My body melts into her curves as I pull her against me.

"Beautiful," she whispers.

"Yes, beautiful," I reply.

She turns in my arms to face me. Her eyes are wide and brimming with tears. "Is it always like this?" she asks.

"Yes, my love. Always." I kiss away the tears that roll down her face.

The night after I told her that I wanted to see the waterfalls, my Beloved brought me home. She set me up in one of the bungalows, which had a workspace that looked like a small library with a table in the center. There was a stack of blank scrapbooks on the table that she said I could use as I pleased. I spent a little time exploring my new space but it wasn't long before I wanted to see her again.

I found her in the courtyard with an ancient journal she had never shown me before. She was wearing a dress made from multicolored layers of translucent silk and when she moved, I could see tantalizing hints of her body beneath. She motioned for me to sit across from her on the grass.

"There's a story I want to tell you," she began, "about two immortal souls, the Pearl that binds them, and a fantastic Race."

I watched as she set the journal down before her and caressed the weathered spine with reverence and tenderness. A gibbous moon floated in the night sky, bathing the courtyard with an ethereal glow.

"The souls are immortal, but their memories are not. Every one hundred years, the two souls must race each other around the world to see who wins the Pearl. The winner retains her memories for another one hundred years. The loser is reborn with no recollection of her past life. The Race must occur or both souls will lose their memories forever.

"In the beginning, these two souls were fractious and vicious. Each viewed the Pearl as power over the other and they spent their lives battling for advantage over the Race.

"Over time, the fighting wore them down and they realized that this power they sought so mercilessly brought them only loneliness. This legendary hatred ultimately dissipated and in its place, these two souls discovered something far greater in love."

Her voice, like her laughter, was clear and melodious. She spoke the words of the legend with a lyrical cadence. It was a hypnotic and romantic fable that made my heart pound with yearning and inspiration. I reached over and clasped her hand gently in mine. When she didn't resist, I brought it slowly to my lips, rotating slightly to place a single, soft kiss on the inside of her wrist. The sensation was electric, a pulse of desire and intensity that raced from my lips through my entire body. I saw, too, the effect of my kiss on her: the slight tremble in her body and her sharp intake of breath. Emboldened, I reached out and traced my fingertips over the smoothness of her face, imprinting the tactile memory of her beauty. Her skin, normally fair and luminescent, was suffused with a warm flush that extended down and over the curve of her bosom. I leaned in and pressed another kiss gently to the side of her neck, savoring the staccato rhythm of her pulse beating beneath my lips and tongue.

She was able to undo her dress with her free hand while guiding my mouth to the soft swell of her breast. I continued my kisses around her nipple, feeling it harden with my touch. I took one, and then the other, into my mouth, reverently loving her with only instinct and her gentle moans to guide me. As absorbed as my senses were with the nearness of her, I forced myself to memorize the way the light played across her body as she arched beneath my caress.

I wanted to wait, to indulge myself in the feel and taste of her, but she urged me onward, her hand on my wrist pushing me lower.

"I've waited so long…"

She gasped when I stroked her but her hips moved against my hand in hunger, not pain. I traced a path of kisses from her breast over her stomach and down to where my fingers were warm and slick with her desire. I inhaled the intoxicating scent of her arousal—for the first time and the thousandth—and she writhed beneath my tongue as I tenderly stroked her open. Her hips responded to my touch, bucking against my hand and mouth in urgent need. I felt the reciprocal heat that rose within me, flaring ever higher in rhythm to my stroking until we became united in fire, burning beyond thought or feeling. I wanted to wait a little longer, to luxuriate in the wonder of the moment, but her need was insistent and I couldn't stop. I found myself swept up in her passion, cresting immediately with the first spasms that clenched deep inside her.

When the frantic beating of both our hearts finally subsided, I brought her wrist once more to my lips, returning to the spot that began my journey. From her wrist I traced a light path following her pulse with the tip of my tongue. I kept moving over her shoulder and up the slender column of her throat until our lips touched and fused.

The sun is moments away from breaking the plane of the horizon, signaling the start of our Race. I turn to my Beloved and see the stiffness in her stance and the clench in her jaw. I reach out and touch her face ever so gently. This is her first race and she is anxious. I lean toward her and kiss the furrow in her brow. The muscle in her jaw relaxes infinitesimally. I won't push her further. This is the tenth race I remember, and worry still sits in my gut like a stone.

What if I lose and she doesn't love me in my next life? What if I win and I can't find her? Every lifetime is a first time for one of us.

When the sun rises, she will take to the skies as a Phoenix and I to the sea as a Dragon. It will take us the day to circle the earth with the winner arriving back to this spot before sunset. Then the two of us will return to our home for one last night together. In the morning, the one who won the Pearl will remain and the other will be reborn somewhere in the valley below our home.

As the arc of the sun edges above the horizon, I turn to her one last time and capture her eyes with mine. "I will find you," I promise.

I see the last of her tension melt away in the daybreak as her easy confidence returns. She smiles at me with a love I have treasured over every life for a thousand years and replies, "No, my love, I shall find you."

FUCKING: A VIGNETTE OF THE MIDWEST
LYNNE JAMNECK

Was it because she was leaning up against the red brick wall—was that why I noticed her? Navy cargo pants, Doc Martens that were probably fraying at the seams. Her hugger T, black and slight from age, showed that, despite her butch appearance, her breasts were nothing but womanly. Not small. A generous handful. And fucking perfect.

That would only be the first time that particular word would come to mind where she was concerned.

I find it terribly amusing that my male friends are hard pressed to believe that I work in a lesbian strip club. That, in fact, such an establishment exists at all. Their favorite argument is that lesbians just *aren't that way*. What way? They don't enjoy having another woman's tits shoved in their faces? Getting a lap dance from a chick with an ass you can bounce coins off? The only difference is a dyke can maybe hide her hard-on better. If she wants to. Well. In her pants. It always shows on her face.

It's Saturday night. My favorite day of the week. Saturday nights the club is always full. At eleven p.m. they lock the doors and no one else gets in. It's a sort of unofficial private party. The right people are in the know, you know? Things get real rowdy behind those locked doors.

It's early evening when I see her leaning back against the wall like that. She's real lean and sleek. Short blond hair gelled back just like that.

Half past eleven and the crowd's going insane. Fuelled with enough alcohol and free-floating pheromones, everyone's intentions are set to overdrive.

Dylan's turning on libidos as she does her cowboy thang onstage to Sheryl Crow. "Maybe Angels." Hell yeah!

My set starts at twelve. I like that; on the cusp of the old and the new.

I watch from behind the bar as Dylan struts. Her legs are strong and confident as she kicks them out in front of her in that brash swagger. She's wearing Levi's so worn they'll probably dissolve beneath the first insistent caress. Scuffed cowboy boots and a Stetson round the picture off well. But it's the brown leather chaps and that "come-on-over-here-darlin'" smirk of hers and the substantial bulge in her crotch that drive the girlies crazy. She works those beautiful boy-hips of hers, working the crowd into a frenzy until a sexy redhead bounds onto the stage amidst a howl of coercion and applause.

The bouncers here don't drag people off stage. It's not necessary. And there seems to be an understanding amidst the spectators of who they can do it with. No one has ever invaded my space while I strip. They watch me. Somehow they never try and touch.

Dylan's John Deere T is on the stage. Her nipples are stiff beneath the overhead glow, her skin tanned. Dylan really works on a farm, see. Stud farm couple of miles out of town. The Midwest sure has its perks. Dyke cowboys are beautiful creatures.

Dylan pulls the redhead against her, hand splayed on the small of the woman's back. Their hips move together slowly.

"Get a room!" a voice yells from a corner, laughing.

Angels, yes. Not maybe. Definitely.

Heather's up after Dylan, right before me. She's playful and teases the butches into clamping their beer bottles until their knuckles go white.

Heather does her thing to Tori Amos's "Sweet Dreams." Every time Tori croons "Who's your daddy?" several women volunteer with gusto. It helps that Heather mouths the words down to the crowd with her glossed, red cherry lips.

I'm still behind the bar with Sinead, the bartender. My little ritual. I have one or two vodka straights before I go on. Fluids the limbs.

I'm making a sexist joke with Sin when I look up from my drink and see her there. The lean and sleek girl. She looks a little mean, huddled within the shadows. All the lights are focused on the stage. "Who's your daddy?" Tori croons again. Heather blows a kiss at one of her prospects and the leather madam sticks a collection of bills in the barely there elastic of her panties.

Sin's gone, relating to the needs of customers at the other end of the bar.

"You're one of the strippers." Mean girl doesn't ask. She states.

"I'm up after Heather." I lean in closer because I don't want to have to shout. She smells of sandalwood. I notice her arms are really muscled. I feel a faint flutter between my legs at imagining the rest of her body. "I have to get ready. She's almost finished. Let me buy you a drink. For while you're watching."

She notices I'm flirting with her right away but she remains cool. I smile. She says a cold beer would be great. I practically order Sinead to give her the coldest motherfucking beer she can find in the fridge before dashing off backstage.

While waiting in the wings for Heather to finish her set, I hear the unmistakable sounds of fucking from somewhere in the shadows. Then I see Donna, our stage manager, looking at me slyly from a nook in the wall, her hips pumping into the dark.

Don't forget my cue, I mouth as the applause outside starts to drift and Heather, naked, slips past me. A muted moan in the shadows is all I get for a reply.

Heather smirks. Her body glows with sweat. "Donna's fucking the hired help again, isn't she?"

Just then my cue sounds. I'm amazed at how Donna can make an announcement with such a steady voice while I know she's doing what's she's doing back there.

The song begins.

❖

I've always loved the Boss. I wanted my girlfriends to be like him.

As the strains of "I'm On Fire" start, the club abruptly goes still. The rumble of mixed voices falls in a hush. No one even clinks a glass. Sin stops serving drinks and I notice how she winks at me just as the house lights go down.

The club is dark now. A subdued spotlight bleeds on me as I move to the song, tempting the need of the music into my legs, my back, shoulders, hips, arms.

I'm barefoot. I can't walk for shit on high heels.

Part of my appeal, I know, is my androgyny. The butches and the studs come to see the vulnerability that hides behind my dark eyes and to appreciate the tone of my curves. The femmes come for the danger in me, my ability to play the switch. And the bois... They come because they see parts of themselves reflected in my angles.

She's sitting down, almost right at the back, watching me. Her legs apart and feet planted firmly on the ground, beer bottle in one hand and smoldering cigarette in the other. *Jesus, she looks hot.*

There is a hushed, burning appreciation as my clothes come off. What I wear isn't fancy. It's not lacy and it's not silk. It's gender functionality. Maybe if you walked past me in the street you wouldn't look twice.

That's why the crowd gives me such reverence. I make the everyday untouchable.

❖

"Where you from?" I ask her.

"New Jersey."

"Yeah? You got that grit. It fits."

She smiles. "That there—that's a great compliment."

We're standing outside on the curb. It's two o'clock in the morning. The chill in the air makes me shiver as she lights a cigarette for me.

I inhale and blow smoke. "Listen, what the hell is your name?"

She laughs. A comforting sound, low and easy. "Jake."

"Jake," I repeat, rolling the name around my tongue. "What are you doing in Michigan?"

She hitches her shoulders. "Guess I started driving one day and ended up here."

I watch the muscles in her arms flex.

She's renting a room, but I take her to my flat. I'm not exactly sure why, but I don't want to have sex with her in a motel.

We both know that's the deal. And that's good, because it's what we both want.

I already saw it back at the club in the way she looked at me while I stripped. Those Docs of hers firmly on the ground. She was solid. Her intentions were clear in every move she made, whether blowing smoke out the car window or stroking her big square hand intently up and down the inside of my thigh. We don't talk much in the car on our way to my flat.

"Actually, I don't usually go to strip clubs." She says this and looks at me intently from the passenger seat. I can't remember if I'd actually asked her about it.

We're going to fuck the way I strip. I can feel it.

I've just closed the heavily padlocked door behind me when I feel the touch of her hands. Her fingers trail down the sensitive skin of my hips…

When I touch her it's her back I feel, all muscled and coiled and hard. Our bodies aren't touching yet. We're just breathing. I take hold of her wrist and guide it up inside the front of my shirt. I neglected to put my bra back on after my set. Her fingers brush skin, making my nipples strain. My hands travel down and massage her ass through the coarse material of her navy cargos.

"I'm not going to fuck you up against the wall or something trite like that."

"Umm…okay?"

The corner of her mouth tilts as she looks at me. I want to kiss her real bad. She shakes her head. "Where's your bed?"

I lead her to it. It's unmade, of course. It's not like I was expecting company.

Jake pushes me down. She stands at the edge of the bed, legs slightly apart, feet firmly on the ground.

"Get over here." I can't believe I'm telling her what to do. Jake takes her shirt off, but the undressing goes no further. Her stomach is ripped. Fucking washboard flat. Chiseled. She crawls on top of me and we finally kiss.

Her tongue is hot. I taste cigarettes and beer and smell sandalwood and the faint musk of aroused sweat. I pull her down on me and sigh into her throat at the weight bearing me down into the wasted mattress. I can't move. She holds me down with no effort at all.

Jake doesn't stop my fingers from pulling at her button fly but I'm having a hard time because she's heavy and her hips keep bearing down on me. Frustrated, I try to push against her stomach, push her away, just for a moment.

Our kiss breaks wet and breathless. The morning air feels tight.

"Want me to fuck you?" Jake asks.

"Jesus, yes." I've never had a butch show such respect, such restraint. The girls I sometimes pick up at the club usually can't wait to get my clothes off. Sure it's a kick; and a compliment.

When they buy into the stripper fantasy.

I feel Jake's hand touch mine down between her legs. Our fingers tangle and I hear metal buttons pop. I force my hand inside her pants and feel the substantial cock she's packing. Jake exhales loudly when I start fondling it leisurely.

"Not so fast," I say as she tries to push me away. Where is her restraint now? With my other hand I reach out without looking and fumble on the bedside table until I find half a tube of KY. I take my hand away from her only long enough to squirt a generous blob of the warming liquid into my palm and then return it back through the fly of her boxers and smear it slowly up and down the length of her cock.

My hand moves slowly up and down. I'm all too aware of the effect it has on Jake as the base of her cock applies subtle pressure on her clit every time my hand disappears way down.

"Fuck…" Jake growls. Her eyes are half closed, generous lips slightly parted. She looks as if she's momentarily forgotten about me.

My hand keeps up its pace, never faltering; steady and slow while Jake's breathing becomes shallower and faster.

I sit up until my mouth reaches her ear and say, "Let me jack you off."

Jake grunts as my hand inside her cargos suddenly becomes more insistent. "You're going to make me come," she hisses between clenched teeth.

I don't say anything, but my hand starts to stroke her cock faster. I'm surprised when Jake suddenly seems to gain her awareness again. With one strong arm she pushes against my chest, pushes me flat on my back. She suddenly remembers—she's the one in control.

She rips my hand away from her crotch and holds it down against the mattress so hard it hurts. With her mobility restricted, lying on top of me and holding me down, she nevertheless manages to free her cock. For a moment she struggles with it and I fight against her to even up the ante, but fuck me, she's just too strong.

Jake pushes herself into me with a sneer—the first sign of dominance I've seen in her all night.

The breath catches in the back of my throat but I make no sound. Instead I hear the bed knock hard against the wall. There's the sudden release, a *whoosh* of blood as Jake releases her grip on my wrist. Quickly—before she can restrain me again—I lace my hands behind her neck just as she starts fucking me.

Her strokes are long, slow and deep. Her eyes don't leave mine for a second. She starts to breathe hard and move harder too. I start to say things; even, I think, beg her to please, pleaseplease not ever stop.

I feel like I am going to detonate. My head is spinning and I'm mumbling half-formed words. Jake pulls herself up to lean over me and starts fucking me really hard and fast, barreling me toward a swiftly approaching orgasm that on the one hand I want and on the other want to postpone, to chase away.

Neither of us can stop ourselves.

I shudder and buck beneath Jake and she keeps pushing, keeps riding me until she comes herself. I think she shouts some obscenity at the wall behind us. Either the wall or at me, I'm not sure. Both prospects are equally erotic.

❖

I wake up early in the morning, thirsty as hell. Jake is sleeping, her broad, strong back toward me. I sneak out of bed and go to the kitchen.

I'm swallowing mouthfuls of Fresca when I feel her behind me. Neither of us says anything. She pulls down my clean pair of panties and fucks me from behind against the cold kitchen sideboard. And rough. This time she lets her fingers do the talking, all the while whispering harshly just below my ear how goddamn beautiful I am.

Wouldn't *you* want that? Such devotion and aggression in one perfect package. I'm drunk on her. I'm lucky that she's fallen in love with the Midwest. Every night when I strip she's at the back with her beer. Watching me. She sets me on fire.

Mirror
Eva Vandetuin

S he's not afraid of me yet, but she wants to be.
I've left her alone in the bedroom, told her to strip and put on the black leather cuffs I've left out for her. Now I'm watching her through the keyhole. This rickety Victorian house allows old-school peeping, and I appreciate that. The room is just a little drafty, and I've left it cool, knowing body heat will warm it once we get started. In the meantime, she's kneeling on the bed with an expression that's both nervous and a bit sulky. There are goose bumps on her skin, and her nipples are taut with the chill. I've left her waiting long enough so that she's gone through at least one cycle of tension and calm and back to tension again. She is, perhaps, just a little annoyed. My mouth twists in a half smile. The waiting is delicious. So is watching her while she doesn't know she's being watched. Her hands move restlessly on her thighs, the rings on the cuffs glinting in the light; she chafes her torso, arms, and breasts for warmth, and maybe for comfort.

I choose that moment to open the door and she looks at me, faintly embarrassed to be caught touching herself, even in such an innocent way—and the embarrassment annoys her too, and puts a bit of defiance in her eyes. She stares at me coolly, like an ordeal is about to begin, as if we're not both here because we want to be. My breathing quickens a little, pleasantly restricted by the corset I'm wearing; I feel armored next to her nakedness.

Standing in front of her, I catch her hands in mine and hold her arms out away from her body to take a long, hard look. Her chin tips up a little, but she gazes at me steadily as I admire her: teardrop-shaped breasts with prominent blue veins, nipples clenched and flushed red, generous hips, a sparse triangle of dark hair below the graceful curve of her belly. I trace a finger down her breastbone and abdomen, teasing her cleft. "Show me," I tell her, and still holding me with hard eyes, she spreads her legs to display a lovely smooth-petaled flower of a cunt, flushed deep pink with blood. I take my time, then look her in the face, smiling, letting the hunger show. She looks back at me unwavering, gray-green irises set under long, straight black lashes. She wants to be touched and she won't say it. I'll make her wait.

I sit on the bed behind her and pull her against me so she can feel the leather and hard boning of my corset against her back, how exposed she is next to the thickness of my shell. My lips trail down her ear and neck as I pull her hands behind her, joining the cuffs with a metal clasp from my bodice. There's a set to her shoulders that tells me she won't resist physically, but she's wary, not at all ready to surrender, not yet. I have something to prove. For now, though, I just keep kissing her, biting at her neck gently, rolling her nipples between my fingers. Her breathing changes; she's leaning against me now, her head against my shoulder, her eyes drifting shut. I can feel her hips longing to thrust forward, but there's nothing there to touch. Still too early for that, yes.

And I am behind her, so she can't see when I reach to free the knife that's sheathed at my back and bring it to her exposed throat. But she twitches when she feels the edge, and her eyes open, her breathing a little faster. "That's my athame, sweet," I purr in her ear. "Traditionally, they're blunt, but mine is sharp. Feel?" She nods almost imperceptibly in acknowledgement, and I turn the knife, let her feel the cold flat against the artery in her neck, then drag the point slowly down her body. My left hand comes up to grasp her jaw, holding her arched against me as I reverse the knife and touch her exposed clit with its metal pommel. She shivers; her hips shift forward again, and when I bite her earlobe, she moans. In her ear, I whisper, "I would so love to make you bleed. It would be so beautiful, all that red on these white sheets," and I rub the ridged hilt of the knife against her clit for emphasis. She makes a strangled sound, her bound hands move restlessly against me. "But there are so many other pleasures we can subject this soft white body of yours to. Why should we rush?" I ask her, and with a slow pressure I allow the hilt of the knife to slide into her cunt. Her pelvis moves to accept it, but I don't let her have much; I keep my grip on the hilt near the blade and stroke her clit with my thumb as I carefully fuck her with the knife. Her eyes roll, but she says nothing. It's too quiet, but I don't really want to hear myself talk. I'd rather hear her scream.

I pull the knife from her with a final caress and she moans a little, a disappointed sound. The knife goes back in its sheath, anointed with her juices, and I lick my fingers, then give them to her to suck, turning her to the side a bit, cradling her. She lets me do it, but her eyes are guarded again as she looks at me, daring me to try harder. I love her resistance; looking at her, I have to fight the urge to rub up against her hip to satisfy my tingling cunt. How unseemly it would be, when really we're just getting started. Instead, I lunge forward suddenly and close my mouth on her exposed throat, pricking her with my teeth. She stiffens for a moment, then relaxes again, feeling the vulnerability of the pose, and I reward her with an open-handed caress on her mound. Her body is deliciously responsive, her cunt already dripping; my excitement is growing with every shiver of her skin.

I release her, then turn her and push her down on her stomach, freeing her arms only long enough to attach them instead to the bedposts, along with her ankles. Having her thus comfortably spread-eagled, I caress her body, then leave her alone again to gather my tools and to let her nervousness rise. On another day I might take her up gently with feathers and horsehair brushes to peak with a painless flogging, but today I think that would disappoint her. She doesn't like pain, but she wants a little fear. Returning, I rub her back, buttocks, and thighs vigorously, bringing the blood to the surface, then slap her lightly, three times. She doesn't flinch. I feel my smile stretching my face, my teeth beginning to show. I know it's not a pleasant expression, but she can't see. I am so hungry. I can barely wait.

Still, I start with light blows, dragging the soft tails of the flogger across her skin between lashes. As first I'm not causing her any pain, but after a few minutes I begin to increase the speed and intensity, and I see her wincing now as I hit the same spot on her thigh over and over, the skin turning a rosy pink. I move back to her buttocks, strike her harder, and she gives a short, painful bark. Again. She's pulling at the restraints now, thrashing a little as I beat her. Harder. "Fuck!" she says, involuntarily. Again. "Ow, goddammit, *fuck*!" I hit her again, pushing her, and with each blow a little more profanity escapes her with a little more force, until she's screaming the words at me, cursing me, pulling hard against the cuffs. "Goddamn you, you fucking—*ah*! Bitch! You fucking whore! You—shit! Ow, ah God. *Fuck*!" "You're full of flattery, my dear," I purr in between breaths, moving my hips with the rhythm of my blows. She's out of words now, just screaming, growling, biting at the sheets beneath her, incoherent with rage. "You want me to stop?" I ask her sweetly, but the only answer I get is a strangled roar as she again struggles with the bonds. "Then beg," I tell her, and she screams again, curses me. "Beg," I say again, "Beg, beg, beg," timing the word with the blows, and after a few more enraged screams she chokes, "Please stop hitting me, please please *ow fuck* please lady I'll do whatever you want *please* oh fuck oh God *please*—" and suddenly I do stop and there is silence except for our breathing, hers ragged, mine deep with exertion but steady. For a moment I struggle with the urge to turn the flogger in my hand and ram the handle into her, but I hold back; this is more for her than for me, and I don't want to hurt her in ways she doesn't want to be hurt. Instead, I kneel beside her, stroking back her short brown hair, and she heaves a sob, tearlessly. When I touch her face, she turns her head to kiss my fingers, and I know this was what she wanted. I lean down, murmur nonsense endearments in her ear.

There's a bottle of aloe vera by the bed, and I take it down and stroke the gel into her skin, cooling the angry heat of the beating. I rub tension from her shoulders and knots from her thighs, telling her how lovely she is, how gorgeous, how desirable. I reach between her legs and gently touch her outer labia, feeling the heat that lingers there. A little more aloe and I'm rubbing her clit, she's moaning softly, unresisting. And as much as I loved the fierceness of beating her, I want to do this much more. Slowly, I unhook the corset, baring my torso, and toss it to the side; I pull off my panties to let the short, thick cock I'm wearing swing free. Wiping the aloe from my hands, I replace it with a generous dab of lube, slicking her up and then my equipment, already warm with my body heat. I put my weight on her, my nipples tightening at the chill of the aloe evaporating from her back, and slip inside.

She groans and moves against me as I grind her pelvis into the bed, pushing her clit against the mattress, and my own cunt throbs with the pressure as my cock pulses into her, just enough length to push firmly against her cervix at the end of each thrust. Her moans are half sobs, and it's the sound of her more than the pressure that gets me close. I slide a hand under her to stimulate her clit more directly and she's screaming again, in pleasure instead of pain this time, but she sounds just the same, only with a bit less profanity—and then she's thrashing, coming, and I let her finish before jamming my fingers under the harness and into my own throbbing wetness. It only takes a few desperate thrusts before my orgasm explodes through me and I catch myself, remember not to collapse on her, so much more exhausted than I am.

I take my time unbuckling the harness, detaching her from the bedposts one limb at a time, and then I gather her up into my arms, both of us naked now. For the first time this evening I give her a real kiss, my mouth tender on hers. As I pull back, she looks up at me, her eyes finally vague, no longer hard. But there's still a flicker of mischief in them, and after a moment she whispers, "Bitch."

I smile, playing the game with her. "Slut."

"Whore."

"Floozy."

"Tramp."

"Jezebel."

"Harlot."

...until we run out of insults, and one of us starts to giggle, and then we're both laughing, voices raised in identical cackles, equally shameless, equally spent.

The Decision Coin
NYRDGYRL

A ll roads lead to therapy." After making this pronouncement, the patient settled back and folded his hands in his lap to await his therapist's return volley.

Oh God, I need some relief. Losing the battle of keeping her posture erect and her demeanor interested, Dr. Odessa Martin slumped back into the shadow that crossed her desk. Pressing her fingertips together, she pretended to evaluate the declaration, then said, "I believe that's all roads lead to Rome, not therapy."

"Rome...therapy, what's the difference? I'm here, aren't I?"

The pencil Odessa habitually twirled suddenly snapped, scattering wood slivers across her desk and eliciting a self-satisfied smirk from her patient. She quirked an eyebrow at her least favorite client, then selected another pencil from her stockpile. He'd bested her again. Odessa's profession required patience and neutrality, two qualities that she grappled with constantly. Over time, she'd realized that most people were reluctant, at best, to deal with reality. Without volition, her hand rose and rubbed a crescent-shaped scar that creased her hairline. It was a parting gift from a former patient who'd found another use for her summer heels.

When she was a child, her grandmother had filled her head with stories about Sojourner Truth and Martin Luther King. God knew she'd never heard his call, but making her people proud had been woven into the very fiber of her being. Every day of her youth, she'd endured lectures about the importance of service until she bristled with purpose and grabbed the shield, eager to take her turn on the field of battle. Before her conversion, the pictures of Martin Luther King that graced every wall in her gram's house seemed benign. Afterward, she always felt like the man himself was beaming down on her with approval. Most people contented themselves with one formal portrait, but her gram collected his picture like other people did thimbles.

Service had been her calling; unfortunately, lately she'd grown tired. Nothing she said or did seemed to provide anyone any relief. Especially herself. Her normally cocoa brown skin was drawn and her soft "good hair" had dried out and become as brittle as the tumbleweeds that skittered across the highways of this godforsaken part of the country. Misguided love had lured her away from Georgia and landed her deep in the Sonoran Desert.

Killing time, she doodled in her notebook, knowing that the session was very near its end. Within seconds, her patience was rewarded when the clock struck five.

"Well, Mr. Clement, looks like our time's up. Same time next week?" As much as she hated dealing with this man, Odessa had bills to pay and he was one of her few self-paying, private clients. All he really needed was someone to harass, and she'd filled that role nicely. No one else would have put up with his nonsense.

Heaving a huge sigh of relief, she ushered him out the door. He was her last patient of the day. Now all she had left to do was finish her notes and close up the office before heading home for another solo dinner. Afterward she'd drive to the clinic to facilitate her codependency group.

The next morning she overslept, then broke her favorite coffee mug while hurrying to keep her appointment with her friend and department head, Dr. Leslie Craven. She'd called in desperation, needing to talk to someone, so Leslie had cleared an hour out of her busy day just for her. Despite her best intentions, Odessa was late and her hastily applied makeup failed to camouflage her state of mind. Leslie met her at the door to the suite, then ushered her directly into her office.

"What's wrong, Odessa? What's upsetting you?" Leslie settled her onto the cushioned sofa, then drew a chair up close enough to touch Odessa's twitching leg. "Is it Carmen?"

Odessa dropped her head into her hands and scrubbed her face, trying to dam the tears that trickled down her cheeks. She wept silently for a few moments, then gathered her composure and faced her friend. "No," Odessa said. "Not Carmen. We're through. I've told you that."

"Then what *is* it?"

"It's *everything*, Leslie. I can't take it anymore." She looked around for a pencil, then ran her fingers through her carefully styled hair, a sure sign that things were not right in her world. She said, "I can't face another patient or student. They're sucking me dry." Raising her tear-stained face, she whispered, "I'm going crazy. I'm distracted and disorganized and I want to…"

Leslie pursed her lips, then motioned for Odessa to continue.

"It's everywhere. I see the tops of people's skulls popping open like washing machine lids and I'm pouring detergent into the open hole. It's crazy. You've got to help me, Leslie. I can't stand it."

Leslie's eyes widened. "I have an opening for Tuesday and Thursday mornings at say…7:30? I also think you should clear your schedule and—"

"*No*. Not more therapy! I tell you, I can't stand it." Odessa's bottom lip quivered as tears once again coursed down her cheeks. "I want…I mean I *need*…time. That's all. I just need some time."

Wrapping her arms around Odessa's body to buffer her ultimatum, Leslie said, "Time! Girl, all you've had is time. You've been skipping your session regularly and look what's happened. Absolutely not, Odessa. Those sessions are mandatory. I won't settle for anything less. Not if you want to keep working, that is."

"That's…that's just it, Leslie. I'm not sure I want to…that I *can* keep working."

"You can't mean that, Odessa. You're too good and do too much for people in this community to turn your back now."

"But what about *me*? What about what *I* need? What *I* want? When does that matter to anyone?" Odessa threw her soggy tissue into the wastebasket and snatched three more from the box by her side.

"You need to recharge your batteries. Why don't you use my condo in Sedona? Take some time to reflect on where you're going. After you come back, we'll talk about this some more."

Odessa nodded eagerly. Getting away might be just what she needed. Her enthusiasm waned when she asked, "But…my students and the clinic? What about them?" As an afterthought she added, "My clients, who'll see them if I go away?"

"I'll handle all of that, Odessa. You just go ahead and take care of yourself."

❖

Odessa steered her Lexus convertible onto exit 298 on I-17, trying to let the muted pastels that painted the desert landscape ease her worries about her car. It had been acting up for weeks, intermittently cutting out for no discernable reason. She'd been to her mechanic three times, and each time he'd returned it hinting that Odessa was mistaken because he'd never been able to duplicate her complaint. On the way up from Phoenix, the car had shuddered twice, but after a quick prayer, the engine smoothed out. It would have been just her luck to stall out on the way to a much-needed vacation.

She'd forgotten her sunglasses, so when she turned west on Highway 179, the brilliant sunset dazzled her eyes and forced her to the side of the road. When her vision cleared, she put the car in gear only to have it stutter, then stall. Her dead car brought fresh tears and she cried until her sinuses ached, grinding the ignition again and again in frustration, unconsciously mimicking her clients' senseless repetitive behavior.

She was still crying when a loud metallic tapping made her clasp her chest in fear. She whipped her head around squinting through her tears to make out the features of the figure standing beside her car. Whoever it was backed away and was standing with her arms extended sideways, assuming a harmless stance that went a long way toward relieving Odessa's fright. After wiping her face, she cracked the window and asked, "Can I help you?"

Stepping closer while still keeping her hands out to her sides, the stranger said, "That's what I was going to ask you. You're the one sitting by the side of the road."

Bristling at the stranger's tone, Odessa ground the engine. She pounded the wheel in frustration. "My car won't start."

"I see that. Pop the hood, ma'am." The stranger sauntered to the front of the car, rapping the fender with a knuckle when Odessa was slow to comply.

Rubbing her freshly bruised hand, Odessa climbed out from behind the wheel and walked toward the front of the car. Dangling legs and a muscular green-clad butt greeted her. The stranger had practically climbed into the engine compartment and was whistling tunelessly while she tinkered with the visible wiring. Absorbed in admiring the mechanic's physique, Odessa had to jump back to avoid a collision when the stranger pushed herself from under the hood.

"I'm going to have to give you a tow, lady. I can't fix this here."

"A tow?"

"Yeah, I even brought my truck along. See?" The stranger peeled blue nitrile gloves from her hands and waved them behind her at an idling tow truck. She sketched a bow. "Wendy Harper at your service."

Odessa blinked, oddly discomforted by her timely rescue. Her luck usually wasn't that good. She eyed the driver's pixie face and spiked hair and said the first thing that popped into her mind. "*Really*," she drawled. "Are you sure it's not Darling?"

"Darling? Why'd you call me that? We've just met." Wendy stuck her hand out, then pulled it back to stuff the gloves in a pocket. "My name's Wendy. Wendy Harper. What's yours?"

Blushing at her runaway mouth, Odessa extended her hand. "Oh, Odessa. Odessa Martin, but I didn't call for a tow."

"I know. I was just taking a ride and saw you sitting there."

"In a tow truck?"

"How else would I tow your car?" Wendy tucked her hands into voluminous pockets and rocked back and forth on her heels.

"Of course." Odessa eyed her rescuer warily, watching for any sudden moves. This woman had a manic gleam in her eye that many would mistake for enthusiasm. Odessa's experience led her to believe that the tow truck driver was clinging to the edge of the sanity abyss with her steel-covered toes.

As Wendy pulled the tow chain and was hooking it to the Lexus' undercarriage, Odessa asked, "What's wrong with it?"

Straightening from her crouched position, Wendy shrugged her shoulders. "Dunno, Om, but whatever it is, I can't fix it here."

Odessa growled, "It's Odessa, not Om."

"That's what I said, Om. You know, your initials, O-M. Like those meditation things."

"Mantras?"

"Yeah, mantras. Om is a pretty common one, according to the TV."

"Do you meditate?"

"Nope, no need. I've got my coin." She pulled a hand from her pocket and flicked her thumb, sending a flash of brightness spiraling into the air. Once it landed, she opened her palm with a flourish and displayed its well-worn surface. "Frowny, next answer's no."

LESSONS IN LOVE

Odessa stared at the coin nestled within the mechanic's small palm. "Excuse me?"

Speaking slowly, as if she were explaining the miracle of birth to a small child, Wendy said, "Smiley face is yes, frowny face is no. Came up frowny so the next answer's no."

"You can't mean that you make all of your decisions by flipping a coin?" Odessa fumbled in her pocket for a pencil, her expression incredulous. Every time she thought she'd plumbed the depths of bizarre behaviors, someone deepened the well.

"No, I don't, not all of them. Only the ones I'm not sure about." Wendy smiled. "See, it worked. You asked a question and my answer was no. Works every time." Finished with hooking the car up, Wendy waved Odessa into her truck.

Resigned to meeting lunatics at every turn in the road, Odessa prodded, "And *where* did you get this idea?"

"I saw it on TV."

"On *television*?"

"Oh yeah. I've got a great one too. It took me years to save up, but I've got a flat screen TV that's *this* big." Wendy spread her arms out to their full span, which outlined pert breasts under her jumpsuit. "I watch it whenever I can. *Bubblegum Crisis* is my favorite."

Odessa was now certain that Wendy was still mentally with Peter and the boys but, still, something about her made her skin flush and her belly heavy with longing. She shook herself mentally, surprised at her suddenly surging libido, and forced her attention back to the peculiar conversation. "Tell me more about the coin."

Scowling, Wendy said, "I'm trying, but you keep interrupting."

"Sorry, go ahead." Odessa schooled her features to present a picture of complete attention and twined her traitorous fingers together in her lap to keep them from tracing Wendy's sharp cheekbones.

Shifting into gear, Wendy said, "All right, then. The Science Channel said that everything on a computer happens with either a one or a zero. That's like my coin, except I made it with smileys and frownys."

"Smileys and frownys..."

"Uh-huh. I tried thumbs, but I never could remember which one was up."

Odessa turned her face toward the passenger window to hide her smile. "So smileys and frownys work better for you?"

"Yeah, I made it myself. See, it's cool." Wendy rummaged through her pocket until she found the coin again and then offered it to Odessa.

Odessa took the coin, snatching her hand back when a spark leapt between their fingers. The coin was well made and obviously had seen lots of use; both sides were worn from repeated rubbing. Wendy kept glancing out of the corner of her eye as Odessa turned the coin repeatedly. Something was niggling at her subconscious that Odessa couldn't bring to the forefront of her mind. "Go on, Wendy. You were telling me about how you came up with this."

Wendy grinned. "Anyway, the show said that lots of things happen because of one and zero. If computers can do everything with them, I can too."

Intrigued, Odessa asked, "Why didn't you just use yes or no?"

"'Cause not everything's a yes or no answer. Sometimes I have two things I can't decide between and the coin helps me choose. It works great! You should try it."

Something about Wendy's simplistic logic made Odessa reconsider her initial opinion of the tow truck driver. Maybe there was more to this woman than first appeared, her physical response to her notwithstanding. She sat in silence until just after they had passed the sign that announced Sedona proper.

"Wendy, would you mind dropping me off? I'm staying at a condo on Arroyo Roble Road." She waved a hand at her rumpled clothing. "I'd like to change and get something to eat before I have to tackle my car again."

"Sure, Om. Not a problem. Just tell me the address and I'll take you there."

They pulled up in front of the address and exchanged information, Wendy licking her pencil stub before copying Odessa's insurance information and having Odessa sign the paperwork consigning her car to Wendy's care. Each time they touched or made eye contact, Odessa's skin tingled, making her blush and duck her head to hide from Wendy's knowing grin.

Wendy carted Odessa's substantial luggage out of the car and into the condo, grunting with effort. Odessa tried to help but Wendy waved her off saying, "I've got it, Om. You just watch."

Odessa willingly complied, manual labor being something she avoided at all costs. Besides, she was only too happy to watch Wendy work, admiring the wiry muscles that the woman revealed when she unzipped her jumpsuit and tied the dangling arms around her waist. Her muscle T-shirt was sweat stained, but Odessa ignored that to think about how nicely Wendy's small breasts would fit in the palms of her hands. It had been a while since she'd been with a woman. Carmen was her last; sex with her had been infrequent and one-sided, with Carmen always on the receiving end. Odessa licked her lips, imagining Wendy's fingers tangled in her hair, holding her in place while she ravaged her breasts with her teeth and tongue. She shivered awake when Wendy brushed her fingertips against her arm.

"You all right, Om? You had a funny look on your face just then. Anything else I can help you with?"

Blushing furiously, Odessa shuffled her feet, embarrassed to be caught fantasizing about sex with a stranger. She cleared her throat, hoping her voice would sound normal. "I'm fine. I was just… thinking."

Waggling her eyebrows playfully, Wendy teased, "Must have been good, you were really moaning. I thought maybe you were in pain or something."

Odessa cringed, then climbed the stoop, shuffling backward when Wendy followed her. She was at least nine inches taller, placing Wendy's mouth even with her breasts. Though it was still warm out, her nipples rose and stiffened, reaching out for contact. Seeking distance, Odessa pressed her shoulder blades against the door, unintentionally thrusting her breasts forward even more. Instead of moving away, Wendy stepped closer until there was less than an inch separating her lips and Odessa's straining nipples.

"Something tells me you want me to stay."

Wendy's breath brushing against her nipples almost made Odessa come on the spot. She opened her mouth, nearly panting her denial. "Yes…I mean…no. I want…you…to…go."

Wendy cocked her head and stepped away, giving Odessa some much-needed space.

Maybe I tapped into a ley line. Sedona was riddled with energy vortexes but as far as Odessa knew, none of them were sexual.

"Are you *sure*? I'd love to stay and…" Wendy stepped closer and ran a fingertip across Odessa's nipple. In a singsong voice she chanted, "Stay or go, yes or no. Stay or go, yes or no. Stay or go, yes or no."

Odessa writhed under Wendy's fingertip, her blood pounded in her belly, making it difficult to think, and still Wendy chanted, "Stay or go, yes or no."

Finally following her body's lead, Odessa said, "Yes. Stay."

Wendy's gray eyes twinkled. "And you didn't even need my coin."

Odessa fumbled behind her for the doorknob, stumbling into the room when the door opened behind her. Wendy followed, catching Odessa by the wrist and raising it to her lips to nibble the pulse point.

Legs close to buckling, Odessa groaned, then leaned in for a kiss—she *had* to slow this down or she would come in her pants before Wendy even really touched her.

Wendy deepened the kiss, maneuvering Odessa down the hall toward the open bedroom door. When the back of Odessa's knees bumped into the bed, she fell backward, finally breaking the suction that bound them together. She raised her hands to Wendy, beckoning her to join her on the bed, frowning slightly when Wendy raised a hand and said, "Stay there. Don't move. I need a shower."

Breathless and confused, Odessa flopped back onto the bed and traced a crack in the ceiling with her gaze. She'd never had such a physical response to a stranger before but knew that she wanted whatever magic Wendy possessed. Needing to take the edge off her desire, Odessa slid a hand under her waistband, inching her fingers toward her aching center. Just before she touched herself, Wendy poked her head back into the room and said, "Ah ah ah. No touching. The wait will make it better." She grinned at Odessa's groan and flashed her naked ass as she returned to the bathroom.

Odessa lay still, listening to Wendy singing in the shower. She couldn't make out the words or even the tune but found herself somehow mesmerized by Wendy's voice. She couldn't wait until that mouth, those lips were snugged in her most intimate places, sucking her neatly shorn lips. Lost in her daydream, Odessa didn't hear the shower stop, didn't hear Wendy moving around, didn't hear anything until Wendy was standing naked between her legs, holding out her hands to help Odessa stand up.

Wendy turned her around to face the bed, rubbing her naked breasts against Odessa's silk-clad back. When Odessa pressed backward into her, Wendy slapped her ass and said, "Stay still, this is my rodeo."

Breathing raggedly, Odessa tried to comply while Wendy unbuttoned her blouse. Cool fingers pinched and pulled her nipples through her bra, and Odessa sagged. Her nipples had never been as plump and sensitive, and Wendy played them like a jazz pianist, interspersing herky-jerky tugs with smooth finger riffs. On the verge of coming just from nipple play, Odessa tried to turn around again.

"No, no." Wendy pushed her onto the bed, trapping her arms in her shirt sleeves by rolling her over onto her back.

Nipples pointing to the heavens, Odessa swallowed thickly when Wendy licked her lips.

"We need to get that bra off, but...not...just...yet." Wendy bent over and tugged Odessa's slacks and panties from her hips, leaving them crumpled around her ankles. "Now I think I'll—"

Eyes glazed with desire, Odessa panted, "Touch me, Wendy. I need you to touch me."

"Oh, I will. I will. Don't you worry." Wendy dropped to her knees and peeled Odessa's shoes off, massaging her feet, then taking the time to run her fingertips up the inside of her thighs, stopping just before she reached Odessa's aching slit. Odessa's hips rose, seeking contact, but Wendy denied her by kneeling on her pants, pinning Odessa's feet to the floor. "Now I've got you, my pretty. If only I had some lube."

"In my bag. The blue one. Please, Wendy. I need you."

"Just a sec." Wendy left the room, then returned with the blue bag, upturning its contents onto the bedroom floor. "Pantyhose, underwear, socks, bras..." She paused to finger a lacy edge, making Odessa wish those fingers were fondling her nipples instead of her underwear, "Ah, lube. Now where's my jumpsuit?" Odessa's eyes tracked her as she moved around the room, then widened when she snapped on a pair of blue gloves.

"What...what are those gloves for?"

Wendy resumed her position between Odessa's legs, pouring a generous amount of lube onto her gloved hands before dripping some on Odessa's fiery slit. Odessa jumped when the cool lube hit her clit and Wendy once again stomped on her pants, forcing her hips back onto the bed. Rubbing her hands together, Wendy said, "Now where was I? Oh, right here." She touched her lubed fingers to Odessa's opening and probed gently to gauge its elasticity.

Odessa moaned deep in her throat and her eyes rolled back in her head when Wendy inadvertently brushed the tip of her clit with one of her fingers. "Oops. Sorry about that." She pushed a little deeper, curving her fingers upward to press on Odessa's g-spot, then asked, "Have you ever been fisted?" Odessa's head thrashed and the only sound she produced was a series of grunts and moans that increased in volume and intensity every time Wendy moved her fingers. "I'll take that as a no, then." She poured more lube onto the palm of her right hand, pushing three fingers, then four, into Odessa's wide-open snatch. Finally, she tucked her thumb into her palm and Odessa swallowed her hand whole, grunting when Wendy's fist pressed against the walls of her womb.

Wendy stepped off Odessa's pants and straddled one of her long legs, twisting her right hand and gently massaging Odessa's lower belly with her left.

Odessa moaned, "Oh...my...God! What are you doing to me? I've...never...felt like this before." Rising up on her elbows, she pried open her eyes, falling back when she realized Wendy's hand was completely inside her body. Coherence deserted her when Wendy pressed her wrist against her g-spot, reducing her to grunting, moaning and sobbing in pleasure.

Wendy rode Odessa's straining leg, waiting until she was on the edge of coming before she moved her left hand down to Odessa's cleft. Using her thumb, she massaged Odessa's lips, avoiding her clit completely until Odessa called out, "Touch me! Touch me!" So Wendy did.

When Odessa's mind cleared, Wendy was kneeling between her legs, her right hand still being squeezed intermittently by Odessa's womb. She was wet all over, sweat dotted her forehead, and moisture seeped around Wendy's wrist, running down the crack of Odessa's ass and drenching her asshole. She sighed gustily, twitching whenever Wendy moved, too weak to protest when Wendy withdrew steadily until the thickest part of her hand popped free. Wendy snapped off her gloves, wiping her hands on a towel she'd placed beside Odessa's hips, then climbed onto the bed, kissing her way up Odessa's quivering body.

Wendy said, "That was some ride, huh?"

The edges of Odessa's lips turned up and she whispered, "I'll say, cowgirl," then closed her eyes when sleep dragged her under.

A slash of sunlight woke her and Odessa stretched, pleasantly sore from the previous night's activities. Wendy was snoring, back turned and curled around herself. Odessa resisted the urge to run her fingertips down the knobs of Wendy's spine. She chuckled softly; one leg was still entangled with her pants, but Wendy had taken the time to free her from her blouse and bra at some point during the night.

She shook her leg free and Wendy stirred, then rolled over, throwing a leg over Odessa's hips. "Ready for round two?"

❖

They spent the next two weeks together, mostly in bed, only occasionally venturing to Wendy's garage to check on Odessa's car. Wendy used her coin frequently for decisions both large and small, and each time, Odessa felt an idea niggling at her subconscious. They were lying in bed, sharing their last afternoon together, when Odessa was stuck by a thunderclap that she eagerly shared with her new girlfriend

Wendy said, "I don't know, Om. It doesn't seem right to sell it. I thought it up for free. Maybe I should just share."

In a million years Odessa never imagined herself saying the words that were about to come out of her mouth, but she was desperate enough to take the chance. "Flip your coin, Wendy. See what it says."

❖

Odessa changed her name to Charon. Life was good on the talk show circuit; she'd even introduced her grandmother to Oprah, which almost made up for the disappointment she'd seen in her grandmother's eyes when Odessa had resigned from the university. Wendy was especially pleased because she was the star of their infomercials. As the spokesperson, she could watch herself on TV anytime she wanted. The only thing she liked better was dragging Om off to bed for a midafternoon romp.

Odessa/Charon was ecstatic because in an odd way, she was still helping people. It didn't hurt that they'd made a mint within three months of marketing the coin. She didn't even feel guilty about her new livelihood. The coin was Wendy's idea, but she'd come up with their instruction manual and sales pitch all by herself. The Decision Coin: two extremes that lead to infinite possibilities.

TOP OF THE CLASS
RADCLYFFE

Allie punched in the first three digits of Cindy's phone number and then hesitated. With a sigh, she pushed the off button and surveyed the mountain of clothes that had sprouted in the middle of the bed as she'd tried on and discarded outfit after outfit. Somehow, the excuse that she couldn't go out because she had nothing to wear felt thin, even to her.

"I can't believe I let them talk me into something as stupid as this." She fingered the leather chaps she had purchased one summer for a horseback camping trip. Smiling, she recalled that the concept had been a little bit more glamorous than the actual event, but it had still been fun. Of course, most of the clothes she'd purchased for the eight-day excursion never saw any further use. "And they're not going to tonight, either."

Eyeing the black leather pants and mesh top with a shake of her head, she scooped up the whole pile and dumped it on a chair, then marched to the closet and pulled out what she usually wore for a night out with friends—jeans and a scoop-necked, ribbed white T-shirt. All right, so it was true that the simple attire always got her plenty of attention. The jeans hugged her high, tight ass, and with no bra under the form-fitting T-shirt, her breasts just screamed for a warm palm to cup them. The thought of fingers playing across her tight nipples caused her belly to twitch. "Okay. Okay. So maybe they're right and I *do* need a little recreational sex, but vanilla will do me just fine."

A glance at the clock told her she had less than ten minutes before Cindy and Jeri arrived to pick her up. She still wasn't certain how she'd let them talk her into going with them to Chances, the local leather bar. Just because she'd played that stupid Truth or Dare game at Jeri's birthday party and had even more stupidly told the truth about one of her favorite fantasies was no reason to repay her honesty by dragging her out to a club where she would only feel out of place.

"So come on, Al, tell," Cindy *prodded. "What's your favorite jerk-off fantasy?"*

"What makes you think I—"

Cindy and Jeri *hooted her down, and Allie grinned.*

"Okay okay. Truth." She sighed. *"I want to top this incredibly hot butch and have my way with her."*

"So why haven't you?" Cindy *asked.*

"I haven't a clue how to go about it. Afraid of being turned down, I guess."

"Yeah, but," Jeri *chimed in, "if you didn't have to worry about any of that…what would you do?"*

"I'd tie her up and torment her and then fuck her silly."

And after that, they'd badgered and cajoled until she'd agreed to at least go with them, *just to see.*

"So, I'll stay for a drink or two to keep them happy, and then I'll beg off," Allie muttered as she leaned close to the mirror to apply her eye makeup. "At least then they won't call me a chicken any longer."

At the sound of her doorbell ringing, she shouted down the hall from her bedroom, "I'll be right out!"

Hastily, she grabbed her keys and pulled open the door. "Oh!"

The woman standing on her front porch looked like she'd stepped directly out of Allie's favorite wet dream. Short thick dark hair, cobalt blue eyes, a lopsided grin, and even, white teeth. The package was spectacular, and the wrapping even better. Long lean legs sheathed in skintight black leather, a matching vest over nothing but flesh, and a suggestive swelling below the wide studded belt that signaled a surprise tucked behind her fly. Her bare arms and stomach were tight with muscle. A silver bar pierced the top of her navel, and a tribal band tattoo circled her left biceps.

Allie resisted the impulse to touch her just to see if she was real.

"Allie?" Gorgeous Creature inquired.

"Yes?" Allie replied in a high, thin voice she barely recognized. She cleared her throat, feeling foolish. "Can I help you?"

Again the megawatt grin, this time accompanied by a subtle shrug of broad, strong shoulders that set off ripples of pleasure in the pit of Allie's stomach.

"I'm Ryan." Fantasy Lover extended her hand. "And I'm yours for the evening."

Allie stared. Heartbreak Material was obviously a nutcase. "There's been a mistake."

Ryan smiled as if she'd heard that one before.

Allie hurried on, "I was just on my way out." She started to close the door. "If you'll excuse me."

"Cindy and Jeri won't be coming, so there's no need to hurry."

The little voice of reason in Allie's head screamed, *Close the door!* but the part of her brain ruled by Id won out. She leaned against the half-open door. "How do you know them?"

Ryan slid two long tapering fingers into the slit pocket on the front of her vest and teased out a folded piece of paper. She held it out between her fingers. Clever fingers. "The work order."

"I'm sure there's..." Allie took the note, skimmed the few lines, and laughed in disbelief. "They paid for you to be my...slave?"

"If you desire." Ryan nodded toward the paper. "Apparently they thought you would prefer that. However, if you would like to reverse the scene, that can be arranged."

"I'm going to kill them," Allie muttered under her breath. Still, she was beyond intrigued, and there really didn't seem to be anything overtly crazy about the woman standing in front of her. Well, if you didn't count the fact that she...hired out...as a sex slave. She looked Ryan up and down. "And if *I* want to be the slave, do you just...switch?"

"I can," Ryan said seriously, "but you might prefer a replace—"

"No!" Allie spoke so quickly that she surprised them both. Blushing, she added hastily, "I mean, this...arrangement...seems fine."

"I'm glad."

Allie studied Ryan's face, certain that she had heard gentle sincerity in her voice. But then, nothing about the situation was real. So what did it matter how she sounded? "You're serious?"

"Yes, quite."

"Are you...is this...safe?"

Ryan nodded. "If you mean me, yes. If you mean anything that might happen, the answer is also yes. I'm experienced, and you can trust that I won't allow anything to happen that either of us would regret."

Allie released the door, and it swung open as she leaned her back against the doorjamb, her arms crossed just below her breasts. The very idea of having sex with Ryan, a perfect stranger, was perversely exciting. She *was* hot. But every time Allie thought of actually dominating her, of being free to do anything she wanted with her, she felt a thrill that was entirely new. It went beyond physical excitement. It was as if every cell in her body buzzed with sexual anticipation. "And you'll enjoy it?"

Ryan bowed her head, dropping her gaze from Allie's for the first time. "It would be my pleasure to serve you."

"I don't know wh—"

"Perhaps you wish to bring me inside where it is more private. So you may examine me and determine if I please you. Mistress."

Allie's breath caught as heat raced over her skin. She knew if she thought about what she was doing, she'd close the door and leave Ryan standing alone in the dark. And she'd never know if her fantasies were any more than that—unrequited dreams. She'd imagined just what she'd do so many times—she'd only been waiting for permission. She stepped inside. "Follow me."

Then Allie turned and walked to her bedroom. She did not look back when she flicked on the small lamp just inside the door, but she knew Ryan was behind her. She could smell her. The thick, hot odor of desire. She sensed as soon as Ryan had lowered her gaze that she was saying Allie was in charge, and Allie didn't intend to pass up this chance to do what she'd been dreaming of.

"Kneel by the bed," Allie said, pleased by the quickly muffled gasp. She slowly circled Ryan's kneeling form, all of her senses inexplicably heightened. She saw the tiny hairs at the back of Ryan's neck flutter as she passed and heard the breath rush in and out of Ryan's chest. Seeing all that power and beauty harnessed and waiting, hers to command, drove the last whispers of resistance from her consciousness. Everything in the room receded from her awareness except Ryan and the steady rush of blood into her pulsing clit.

She stopped and traced her fingernail along the edge of Ryan's jaw, over her chin, and down her throat. "Take off your vest."

Wordlessly, Ryan unbuttoned her vest and dropped it on the floor. Her breasts rose proudly, tight cones tipped with hard dark nipples. Allie grasped one and twisted slowly. With a groan, Ryan tipped her head back, her eyes half closed.

"Oh did I hur—"

"I am here for your pleasure." Ryan caught Allie's free hand and drew it to her other breast. "Pain arouses me. You can trust me to say *enough.*"

Allie heard the unspoken message. *She won't tell me what to do. She'll only tell me to stop.*

Allie caught Ryan's other nipple and set up a back-and-forth rhythm, tugging and squeezing, first one then the other. After a few minutes, Ryan's thighs flexed and her hips jutted up with each jerk on her breasts. She panted, her hands lying palm up by her sides, the supplicant before the altar of desire.

"You like this," Allie grunted through the heavy curtain of lust that clouded her vision. Her jeans cut into her swollen sex, riding over her clit, rough and raw and almost hard enough to make her come.

"Yes," Ryan said through gritted teeth. "Christ yes."

"Get up."

Allie barely gave Ryan time to get her balance before she grasped Ryan's breast and sucked the nipple into her mouth. Ryan's flesh was hot, so hot. And sweet. She bit down, unthinking, aching inside. So hungry for her. She pressed her crotch against Ryan's iron-hard thigh. She wanted to get off, needed to. She bit again, mindlessly.

So softly Allie could barely hear, Ryan whispered, "Harder."

Allie shivered and fanned her fingers over Ryan's throat. Blood raced wildly beneath her hand. "Would you like that? For me to suck on your breasts, leave my marks on you?"

Ryan swallowed convulsively, her hands trembling on her thighs. She had not been given permission to touch. "Yes."

"Then why should I?" Allie mused, struggling to appear calm when all she wanted was to rub her hard, wet clit over Ryan's skin and drench her in come. But that would be too easy. For both of them. "I'm not here to pleasure you, am I?"

"No, Mi—"

"You may call me Allie," Allie said, molding her palm to the soft, warm leather between Ryan's legs. She squeezed and massaged the firm cock inside. "Say my name. When you beg me to let you come."

Ryan's legs jerked and she moaned. She panted out, "I...stop, please...I want...oh..."

She's good. I wonder just how much she's playing. Allie jerked her off methodically, relentlessly, until she knew it wasn't an act and that Ryan would come with a few more twists of her wrist. She wanted her to, wanted to see this strong, sexy woman writhe on the floor, coming for her. But she hadn't reached the end of her fantasy just yet.

"Should I stop now?"

"If it pleases you to stop," Ryan gasped. "I want...I..."

"What, Ryan. What do you want?" Allie demanded harshly.

"Let me make you come...Allie."

Allie yanked her hand away and in one motion stripped off her tee. She cupped her own breast and fisted the other hand in Ryan's hair. She jerked Ryan's head down. "Not until I say."

Ryan's mouth was warm, her tongue just rough enough to burn her nipple with rapid swipes in between the tease of teeth. Eyes closed, Allie swayed beneath the onslaught, releasing Ryan's head to fumble with her own jeans. She got them open and the zipper down.

"Stroke my clit," Allie gasped. When she felt Ryan's hand skim down her belly, she grabbed her wrist and forced it down the tight vee of her jeans. "Oh yes...hard, I like it hard."

The force of Ryan's arm pumping and Allie's hips thrusting in response propelled them toward the bed. Allie's knees hit the edge and she fell, Ryan following her down. The fingers on Allie's clit drove into her cunt, impaling her with pleasure. She arched off the bed, screaming as she came.

Before the last electric jolt pulsed from her clit to her core, Allie shoved Ryan off and onto her back. Just as fast, she pushed her jeans off, straddled Ryan's hips, and pinned her to the bed with her hands clamped on her shoulders. "I did not tell you to make me come," she panted, sweat dripping from her face onto Ryan's.

"I...I'm sorry, Allie," Ryan murmured, licking the drops from her lips. Her chest was damp, washed gold in the slanting lamplight, her stomach tight, muscles rippling.

"I don't care if you're sorry." Allie ran her nails down the center of Ryan's stomach, twisting the silver bar in her navel as she passed. Ryan groaned. "You do not make me come without permission."

"Yes, Allie."

Allie tugged loose Ryan's belt, then cinched it around both of Ryan's wrists and looped it over the bed frame, tethering her arms above her head. "You do not come until I say."

"Ye-yes, Allie." Ryan's thighs twitched.

"You ask to come." Allie flicked open the button on Ryan's pants and pushed her hand inside, watching the pulse jump in Ryan's throat. She pulled out Ryan's cock, raised her hips, and took it in to the hilt. She nearly came with the sudden pressure on her clit. Her head snapped back and her breasts heaved. She closed her eyes and rode. "Oh, so good."

"Please," Ryan whispered. "Touch my breasts."

Allie tugged on Ryan's nipples to the tempo of her pistoning hips. Ryan's thighs went rigid and she arched from the bed. "Fuck my cock, Allie. Fuck it."

"Yes, yes," Allie chanted, sliding almost all the way off the thick length before plunging back down, one long stroke after another. "Yes yes yes."

Ryan thrust to meet her. Faster, harder, deeper—"I'm going to come!"

Allie's eyes snapped open. "You are not!"

"Please, please," Ryan gasped, head thrashing as she struggled to free her wrists. "Allie, please…oh please…I need to co—"

"Ryan," Allie shouted, pulling Ryan's head back by her hair. "You will not come before I do."

Ryan's eyes were glazed, her mouth soft and vulnerable. "Yes, Allie."

Allie's cunt spasmed and clamped down on the cock. Her clit turned to stone. "Ohh, here I come." She brushed her breasts over Ryan's face and shuddered, bearing down, forcing the cock into the base of Ryan's clit. "Come with me."

"Thank you, Allie," Ryan gasped, her mouth against Allie's breast.

Allie came twice as Ryan plunged into her, coming long and hard with broken shouts of pent-up pleasure. When Allie's muscles were too weak to hold her up any longer, she fell onto her side. Ryan's cock slipped out. "Unh, miss you already." She released Ryan's wrists, then dragged her hand down Ryan's hip and grasped the shaft, tugging it until Ryan twitched and groaned. "Nice."

"Thank you."

Allie opened one eye. "How did you know I'd want it?"

Ryan grinned. "Didn't. Just wanted to be prepared."

"Good idea." Allie sighed contentedly and skimmed her fingers over Ryan's mouth. "Mine for the night, you said?"

"As long as you desire. Mistress."

"I can see you still need instruction." Allie kissed her. "This time, try to do as you're told."

Ryan laughed. "Yes, Allie."

MAKING IT EASY
SASKIA WALKER

Sometimes it's hard to say hello. Saying "I want you" can be harder still.

I want you. The words were drumming in my head and in my heart, louder, louder, daring me to blurt them out. But how would she react? My body was on fire with need to see her, to touch her, to taste her—but my stomach was balled with anxiety. Chill, I told myself. *Chill.*

Chrissie was so self-assured, so knowing, and I was a bundle of nerves. The last thing I wanted to do was stutter and stumble my way through a conversation, when what I really wanted to do was to tell her how I felt, to ask her if she was interested in more. *Damn it.*

I sighed, rested back in my seat, and eyed the road ahead. The creak of the shelves behind me had become familiar now and I didn't need to look back through the hatch to reassure myself the books were safe. They were captured in angled metal shelves, the mobile library taking on the road like a loaded barge, sturdy and resolute.

The rolling landscape of the Yorkshire moors filled my vision. The road was a gray ribbon unfurling across the expanse of fields, the English countryside made up of patches of green, marked out by old stone walls. A line of cottages rose up to break the horizon, signaling the village of Etherington. We'd be there inside five minutes. Tension beaded up my spine. I'd waited impatiently to see her again, to be here and to absorb the smile that fueled my imagination so vividly. At night, I twisted in my sheets, thinking about her, wet with longing to lose myself in her arms.

She'd known as soon as she caught sight of me standing there in her shop, gawky and mesmerized by her smile. She'd known and she'd responded. Gently, soft and all woman. I wanted her from the first instant, and what had been a gem of desire that I had nurtured and treasured had now become a nagging need to confide and take action.

I'd first met Chrissie when I went into the small village shop to pick up a chocolate bar and a newspaper at the end of my first week in the new job. It was also the first time we had pulled into Etherington. Brian, my senior, announced we took lunch there and that meant he visited an old pal for an hour. When I glanced round and asked what there was for me to do, he nodded over at the post office sign.

"Village shop, post office too. Get yourself some lunch. I'll meet you back here in an hour." He hauled the brake on, drawing the mobile library to a halt in the bus lay-by.

"Isn't it illegal to park here?"

"It's a peaceful place. The buses only come by every other hour, we'll be fine."

"Do we have any customers here?" I nodded back at our store of books, the stock that kept the isolated villagers supplied with reading material.

"Three. Ida has a large-print romance. I've got three new ones for her to choose from. Bill likes something on bird watching, and he won't remember if he's read the book before. Jonathan will read anything on politics or health, but be prepared for a lecture on the state of the world when we hand it over." He glanced at the clock on the dash. "No need to think about that until one thirty, though. Union rules." He winked and opened his door. "There's a pretty bench overlooking the churchyard. P'raps get yourself some food to fatten you up and head over there." With those words of sage advice he climbed out of the cab and disappeared.

"Fine. Whatever," I murmured to myself. Brian was okay, a likeable person, even if he had assumed a rather fatherly role in my life. We'd established a reasonable working relationship in the week since I'd started on the mobile library run, and he'd even promised I could drive the wagon on occasion. "In time," he'd added, "when you've discovered your confidence."

Fine. I rolled my eyes but couldn't argue. His teasing about my scrawny figure was beginning to wear thin, though. He was a stickler for rules too, so we couldn't work through lunch even if there was nothing else to do. I'd climbed down and locked up, pacing over to the post office and village shop with grim determination.

As soon as I walked in the door and the chimes overhead announced my presence, Chrissie had turned toward me. The whole world and all its irritations fell away.

She had a wide smile and shaggy wheat-colored hair. Her green eyes seemed to tease me, sending naughty messages as they twinkled my way. A black cobwebby garment over a jade T-shirt drew my attention to her outline. Full. Lovely. Her jeans were as worn as mine. She looked as if she wrote poetry, but I would later find it was sketching that gave that creative edge to her character.

"Hello there, you're a new face."

I would learn soon enough how direct she could be.

"Are you out walking on the moors?"

"No, I"—I gave up pretending to choose chocolate and gestured outside onto the road, awkwardly—"I'm the new assistant on the mobile library."

"Oh, right." She put out her hand. "In that case, welcome."

I took her hand. "Thanks."

She squeezed me, slowly. "Some of the villagers couldn't manage without the service."

"So I gather, and that's good news for us." I felt loss when she took her hand away. "Do you take any books yourself?" I was hoping I could deliver some for her.

She shook her head, smiling. "No, I go up to town once a week or so and stop by the main library then, but you never know, you could convert me."

I grinned. "Just let me know what you like, I'll make sure we stock some."

We talked, for an age. I didn't notice the time flash past. A couple of people stopped by for goods or for the post office service, and she managed to serve them unobtrusively, never breaking away from our chat.

"Have you always lived out here?" I asked, when the last person left.

She looked at me with searching eyes. "No, it's about three years now. I split with my partner, and when she'd gone my life in the city felt wrong. I used to come out here to walk on the moors and take photos for sketching. When I saw this place going onto the market, I made it my fresh start."

A fresh start. She felt like my fresh start. If I could make it happen. Four weeks on from our first meeting. Just that one hour spent together, once a week, and I'd fallen for the postmistress at Etherington. I had to let her know.

Brian clicked his fingers in front of my face, snapping me out of my thoughts.

"Sorry. Miles away."

"So I see." He hauled the van into the bus lay-by. "I said Fred's away from home, so I suggest we deliver the books, then get off to Skipton and have a hot lunch there."

"Oh. Sure." *Damn.* I'd been living for this moment. I had to see her. But Brian was the boss. "I've brought a letter to post, I'll just pop over." I gestured at the shop. Brian nodded as he got out of the cab.

She was on her stepladder, stocking the high shelves, her long trailing skirt swishing around her shins.

"I can't stay," I blurted when the door shut behind me. The door chimes seemed to echo sadly around me. I stood with my back to the door.

"Fred's away, isn't he?" Chrissie smiled, stepping down and turning toward me.

I melted inside, then nodded, peeling myself away from the door. "I just came by to…" What? What could I say?

She watched me move, her gaze touching me. *Everywhere.* "I'll miss our chat, Joanne." She did it again, she made it easy.

"Me too." Relief hit me. She knew.

"In that case, why don't you come over this evening? After hours."

I stared at her, taking in the teasing look in her eyes. Had I imagined it? "Really?"

"Why not?" She rested one hand on her hip, green eyes twinkling.

My thighs clenched, desire pumping hard in my veins. Try as I might, I couldn't wipe the grin off my face. "I'd love to."

"Come over about eight, I'll open some wine."

"I will, thanks." When I walked back to join Brian, I might as well have been walking on air.

❖

Her mouth on mine, opening me up. Shock hit me, then it melted away, leaving me boneless, speechless. She turned away and lifted our wineglasses, nudging mine into my hand. I drank deeply, focusing on the glowing embers of the fire in the grate.

She reached over and brushed my hair flat. "We both knew it was going to happen, Joanne."

My hair bounced up under her hand, as awkward and prickly as I was. "Yes. Sorry, I'm not very experienced. I want this so much but I just look at you and I lose it."

"What's your body telling you?" Her glance was teasing, but only in a good way. She knew already.

I smiled. "It's telling me all the right things, you know that."

"Yes, I do. And mine is the same." She took my fingers to her nipples, nut-hard through her sweater.

I bit my lip, my hand shaking as it rested over her full breast with its knotted peak.

"All you have to do is stop thinking about it," she breathed. "Trust your body, let it run free. It will guide you."

I lifted my gaze from her shirt, where her breast burned an imprint on my palm, making me want to stain it with my mouth—if I was brave enough. "Easy to say—"

"Yes," she interrupted. She lifted my hand from her breast and kissed it in the palm, sending my nerve endings crazy. "But I can show you a way to make it easy to *do*, as well."

A disbelieving laugh escaped me, but my fingers were clutching at hers, hopefully.

Her gaze locked mine. "Will you trust me to show you how?"

I about managed to nod.

She stood up and took me by the hand, leading me out of the sitting room and up the stairs to her bedroom. My heart thudded loud as I looked at the bed, so inviting with its colorful patchwork quilt and plump pillows. Here we were, at the heart of the matter.

Chrissie flicked on the bedside lamp and then walked back to where I stood in the doorway. She switched the overhead light off. "Don't worry, love." She ran her fingers against my cheek. I turned my face into her palm, kissing it gratefully. She smelt of musk, of woman, of desire.

She took my hands and stepped backward, step by step easing me into the space, closing the door behind us. She kissed me, holding my face in her hands as her mouth opened me up.

I moaned, gasped against her mouth, trembling with need.

She drew back, giving a throaty chuckle. "You're like a nervous little bird about to take its first flight, aren't you?"

I nodded.

"Close your eyes."

I did so, immediately putting myself in her hands. *Entirely.*

She moved away and I felt loss. I heard her opening a drawer, then returning. "Don't peek."

Fabric touched my face. It shimmied into place over my eyes. *A blindfold.* My fingers automatically went to it, curious. It felt light, silky, like a scarf. She tied it in place and then began to unbutton my shirt.

"We need to teach you to trust your body more, to respond to your desires and be confident in pursuing them." Her voice was like an aural caress, soothing and arousing all at once. She pushed the shirt back over my shoulders, exposing my breasts. "By depriving you of your sight, it will force you to focus on your other senses." As the shirt fell away, her fingers traced the outline of my breasts, tantalizingly, making me reach after they'd moved on.

"I see," I replied, and then laughed at my own comment. I was indeed absorbed by what she was doing to me, wondering what was coming next.

"Good, that means I can enjoy you without you flying away, little bird." Her fingers popped the buttons on my jeans and she shimmied them down my hips. Her breath passed over my skin as she ducked low to steady me while she stripped me. I was so focused, I was like her doll. Her trick was working.

And then she was standing, her arms lifted, and she moved closer. I started when I felt bare flesh against mine. Her breasts and mine, touching. Hers large and soft, nipples peaked and squashed against my smaller tits. She kissed my mouth and my hands reached out for her, touching her bare arms, her shoulders, her neck. I wrapped my arms around her, sinking into the experience.

I threw my head back when she moved to kiss my neck. "Oh, Chrissie, I've been aching for you."

"And me for you." She continued to undress and then guided me toward the bed, sitting beside me. Her fingers traced along the insides of my thighs, her hands easing them open.

I had to bite my lip to stop from crying out when I felt her head dip down between my legs. She kissed me, opening me with her tongue, sending shivers of pleasure through my entire groin. I clutched at the bedcovers.

"As soon as I saw you, I wanted you," I blurted. The words were tumbling out now, my fears, my needs and my knotted nerves all unleashed under her tutelage. "At night, I wanted you so much, I dreamed of you."

She rested her tongue over my clit, pressed firmly, rousing me to fever pitch, and then lifted away. "I know, I've been thinking about it too." Her warm breath swept over my aroused flesh as she spoke. "But we're here now." Her mouth engulfed my clit again.

She was so right. *We are here now.* And it was more special than I could ever have dreamed. My entire body was wired into her mouth. Sensation swamped me. Her body rolled closer and she stroked one strong finger at the mouth of my cunt, dipping inside, where I clenched her, making her chuckle. She lapped and probed, rocking back and forth in time, and her actions hammered the breath out of my lungs. Her thumb replaced her tongue and I felt her mouth move up against my belly and then rest on my breast with a hungry kiss.

Urgency hit me. My hands moved into her hair, my hips rising from the bed.

When she moved again, lying alongside me, and kissed me, I needed to respond so badly that I went to lift the blindfold off. She must have been watching. Her fingers caught mine.

"No, feel your way, trust your instincts." She returned her attentions to my cunt, where she stroked one finger inside, hooked it against the plump pad of flesh on the inner front wall.

Desperation made me bite my lip, but I wanted it all and I reached for her. I stroked her shoulders, my fingers raveling themselves in her tousled hair, then shifted to cradle her full breasts, my thumbs tracing over the diamond-hard tips of her nipples. Each and every time I touched her, she swayed closer, moaning aloud. That did strange, powerful things to me, sending me deeper, further than I might have gone, making me brave. "I want to taste you," I whispered. "Please. I want to make you come."

She turned around on the bed, never ceasing her attention to my clit. Pleasure spangled through me when I felt her climb over me and I breathed her in, my face between her thighs, her breasts resting over my belly. I reached up, my mouth groping for her, and then we were totally joined, each engulfed in the other. Her mouth on my clit, mine on hers. Our hips rolled, fingers stroked. We moved in time, drinking each other in, stroke after stoke leading us on in the dance. I was adrift on a hot tide of pleasure and my hands groped for the solidity of her thighs to ground me as I hit home and my hips lifted, my clit throbbing, my core in spasm.

She groaned, nursing my tender clit in her mouth as she rode out my moves, her thighs trembling with pleasure on either side of my head. Her sticky juices ran down into my mouth and onto my cheeks as she shuddered to completion.

I squinted into the light when I took off the blindfold and then smiled when I saw her glowing face smiling down at me. She looked even more gorgeous, her cheeks flushed with pleasure. My chest ached with pride.

She lifted the scarf in her fingers. "Did it work, little bird?"

"Like a dream." I nodded, laughing, and pulled her into my arms, brave at last and no turning back.

The road to Etherington didn't look like an unfurling ribbon anymore. Nowadays it looked like Chrissie's blindfold, wavering across the landscape, tempting me in for more lessons in how to lose myself to her love. My heartbeat lifted when I saw the road rise and the outline of the cottages appeared at its end, marking the spot.

"You look happy," Brian commented over the drone of the engine and the creaking shelves.

"I am."

"You're settling into Etherington well enough, since you moved out here?"

"Oh yes. Indeed I am. Feels like I found home, you know?"

He nodded. "It's a beautiful spot to be, no doubt about it."

"That it is," I replied. *That it is.*

When we reached the village, I hauled the mobile into the lay-by, pulled on the brake, and looked at him for his feedback.

He gave me a wink and a nod, signaling approval of my first trip at the wheel. Apparently he'd decided that I had discovered my confidence.

I smiled and shook his hand. *And isn't that just the icing on the cake.*

THE FRENCH LESSON
KIM BALDWIN

Waterloo Station, London

The Eurostar looked fast and futuristic with its streamlined shape and smooth conical nose, all bright red and brilliant blinding chrome. And I was going to travel in the very poshest car, on this, the poshest train around. When you're out to fulfill a fantasy, it's best to do it up big, I say. I'd dreamed all my life of going to Paris, and getting there was part of the whole experience. The Chunnel Train would deliver me to my destination in less than three hours, providing unmatched accommodations and the scenic splendor of the English countryside on the way, while freeing me from the hassle of airport security checkpoints and endless waits.

Of course, you can't have everything. Though I hadn't minded exploring London by myself, my fantasies of romantic Paris—with its candlelit cafes and moonlit bridges—had always involved seeing it with a lover. But I hadn't been very lucky in the romance department, and I just got tired of waiting. So instead of having wild sex on the train to Paris (as I'd always fantasized), I appeased myself with an upgrade to premium first class.

The car was nearly empty when I got on board. An attendant in a crisply starched uniform was serving drinks to the only others on board—a young couple, seated halfway down the long car. I paused in the aisle to admire what was undoubtedly the most luxurious train I'd ever been on.

The gray and burgundy seats were wide and plush, with deeply cushioned headrests and ample legroom. Each seat reclined and had its own folding table made of cherry. The floor was gray carpet. The décor had touches of Art Deco, with etched glass accents on the windows and stylized sconces providing soft, subdued light.

I chose a seat in the back, on the aisle, facing forward. It's a good place if the car is empty, like this one, because I get the maximum view out of both sides of the train.

A moment after I settled into my seat, the steward approached with a smile.

"Welcome aboard the Eurostar. May I get you a beverage?" he asked with a Scottish brogue.

Now, I've always been a sucker for accents, and hearing a variety of British dialects during the past week had been a real treat. But it was Paris I was really looking forward to. French really does it for me, if you know what I mean. Ooh la la. Gets me all hot and bothered, though I haven't a clue beyond *oui* and *par-lay-voo* what any of it means.

"I'd like some Earl Grey, please," I told the steward, and he gave a little bow of his head and retreated toward the back. I returned my attention to the young couple. They were oblivious to everything but each other, holding hands, their heads bent together, talking in low tones. They looked very much in love.

Suddenly, she was standing there—near the front, her presence filling the aisle. I hadn't seen her come in. I sucked in a breath at the sight of her as all the air rushed out of the car.

She was tall and sleek and beautiful, dressed head to foot in form-fitting black leather—pants and jacket and laced-up boots that came to mid-calf. Powerfully sexy. Subtly dangerous. Perfect androgyny. Her hair was dark and fairly short, with shaggy bangs that half hid her dark eyes and long, lush eyelashes. She looked about the car, taking in its accoutrements with a pleased nod. Her glance fell on the young couple and lingered on them a moment, then continued on toward the back, toward me. I felt a chill of anticipation run up my spine.

When her eyes met mine, she froze—and when I did not look away, a smile curled at the edge of those dark red lips, making her even more beautiful. She raised her eyebrows and cocked her head in question.

Still I could not look away, or breathe, or swallow, or think a rational thought beyond *oh, please.*

"Miss?" The spell was broken by the steward, who'd materialized beside me. I glanced up dumbly as he served my tea, blocking my view of the apparition.

He had a small silver tray in his hand containing cream and sugar, cup and saucer, napkin and spoon, and a small teapot of tea. There was also a plate of assorted cookies and freshly made scones, normally a real favorite, but I couldn't wait for him to set it down and leave.

"Thank you," I mumbled, finding my voice.

"Just ring if I might be of further service," he said, indicating a call button by my hand. "I'll be serving brunch in an hour." He retreated toward the back again as the train began to move.

I saw her then. She had taken a seat on the aisle, several rows away, facing me. Watching me. Of all the available seats, she had taken one where both of us could see each other easily and also get a view of the couple sitting in between us.

The steward reappeared and took the woman's order. Her eyes never left me, just as mine never left her. She licked her lips in a most inviting way and appraised me with a candor that I found both unsettling and unbelievably exciting. As her gaze skimmed over my body, her hand absently caressed the armrest of her chair. I felt something twitch in my belly, a stirring of heat. I missed every bit of the scenery flashing by, and my tea grew cold.

She glanced toward the couple sitting between us, and I did, too. They were kissing now with abandon, their arms around one another, unmindful of their surroundings. That twitch in my belly got worse. My eyes went back to the woman. Her smirk reassured me that she was getting as aroused as I was.

Without warning, we were in the tunnel, and the car darkened dramatically. A mild case of claustrophobia kicked in. I took a deep breath and tried not to think about being under the English Channel for the next half hour or so. I was suddenly aware that it was particularly dark right where I was sitting. I glanced up and noticed for the first time that the wall sconce nearest me was burned out.

During that momentary distraction, she appeared beside me.

"Je peux me joindre à vous?" she asked with an amused expression. I stared up at her, transfixed, letting her rich, fluid voice wash over me, understanding not a word and never more frustrated to be lingually deprived.

When I didn't answer, she frowned and said, *"J'ai fait une erreur?"*

"I'm sorry, I'm afraid I don't speak French," I said. It must have been clear from my desperate tone of voice that I didn't want her to leave.

Her frown disappeared and that rakish smile returned. *"Oh, ça va être amusant,"* she said, almost to herself. And then, gesturing toward the seat beside me, added, *"J'ai demandé si je pouvais me joindre à toi."*

It was at least clear now that she was asking if she could sit with me, so I nodded like an idiot and got up to let her in, fumbling with the tea tray.

She paused briefly in front of me and brought her hand up to lightly stroke my cheek. *"Et polie avec ça! C'est mignon,"* she purred seductively.

Speaking French to me was like pouring gasoline on a fire. Every time she opened her mouth, I got hotter. On the other hand, it would be nice to know what the hell she was saying. "Do you speak English?" I sputtered as she withdrew her hand and we took our seats. "Par-lay voo ang-lay?" It was the one phrase I had learned.

"Non," she answered, shaking her head. *"Désolée."* Those luscious full lips of hers stuck out in a disappointed pout.

"Damn," I muttered under my breath, and she understood that well enough to laugh—a throaty, rich peal of delight that broke the language barrier and made both our intentions clear.

Her dark eyes bored into mine as she moistened her lips provocatively with the tip of her tongue. I could feel my heartbeat pick up. *"Fini?"* she inquired, tilting her head toward my tea.

I nodded.

She picked up the tray and rose to set it on the seat in front of us; then she folded my table back out of the way and very deliberately raised the cushioned armrest that separated us. When she sat back down, she turned to face me, tucking one leg up beneath the other, and I did the same.

"Tu es belle," she said, her eyes falling to my breasts and lingering there. *"Très belle. Et très sexy."* That last word was clear enough. I wondered for a moment whether I really was dreaming, but she reassured me I was very much awake when she leaned forward and

placed her hand lightly on my thigh. I swear I could feel the warmth of her hand through the thick denim of my jeans.

Restraint slipped away. I didn't care where we were or who might be watching. I wanted her, as I'd not wanted anything in a very long while. My heart was hammering in my chest, and I was finding it a little difficult to breathe. I couldn't contain a soft moan of pleasure.

She smiled again, obviously pleased at the encouragement. *"Je t'excite?"* she murmured as her hand began to move, fingertips tracing an excruciatingly slow path up my thigh.

Excite. Okay, I got that one. She's asking whether I'm getting excited, I think. No problem there. I nodded mutely as my mind willed her hand to continue its teasing path of exploration.

She didn't disappoint. Her fingertips skimmed the fly of my jeans, danced across the soft plane of my stomach, and then grazed my painfully erect nipple. "Mmm," she purred. *"Délicieux."*

Delicious. Got that one, too. Suddenly I was feeling pretty bilingual after all. My body leaned toward her of its own accord. I was on fire. "Please," I groaned.

Her lips curled upward in a satisfied smirk. *"Non."* She shook her head, correcting me. *"S'il te plaît,"* she instructed, grazing my nipple again with a fingertip. A promise.

"S'il te plaît," I dutifully repeated, my voice unrecognizable.

"Très bien, chérie," she said, rewarding me with a firm pinch of my nipple. It sent a jolt of desire through me and ratcheted up my arousal to a fevered pitch.

"S'il te plaît," I begged again. "Oh God, you're making me crazy…"

She silenced me then with a scorching kiss, thrusting her tongue into my mouth, claiming me with searing intensity. Her hand slid around my waist and she pulled me tight against her body.

If all the blood in my brain hadn't fled to the lower regions of my anatomy, I might have been grateful I'd splurged for the roomy seats of first class and that the premium car was so blissfully empty. But I was beyond rational thought by then, immersed in the overwhelming sensations of her hands on me, her warm breath on my face, her body pressing mine against the seat back.

"Touche moi," she whispered as she unzipped her jacket and led my hand to her breast. She was wearing a thin, silky top and no bra, and

her nipples were already rigid and sensitive, too. I pinched one lightly between my fingertips, then the other, and she groaned, reclaiming my mouth in another kiss as she shifted her weight to straddle me in the oversized seat.

She tasted like chocolate and espresso, and she kissed me hard and long, as though she, too, had fantasized about an encounter such as this.

I was lost in her, oblivious to all but the sensations roaring through me. I cupped her breasts in my hands, fondling the weight of them, caressing the nipples roughly with my thumbs. She moaned into my mouth and pressed her body more firmly against me, grinding against my stomach. My hips rose to meet her, and we rocked together, both seeking greater contact.

She broke the kiss. She was breathing hard, and so was I. *"C'est fou ce que tu m'excites,"* she whispered next to my ear as her hand slipped between our bodies, seeking the fly on my jeans. I didn't need to know what she said. We were speaking the same language now.

She was only fractionally faster getting into my pants than I was getting into hers—our hands found each other at almost the same moment. I'm not sure which one of us was wetter—it was probably too close to call.

We stroked each other in unison, working in an unspoken, teasing tandem to prolong the experience. When I felt her nearing her peak, I would back away—lighten my touch just enough—just as she kept me on the edge of my precipice, until both our bodies screamed for relief.

"Please," she begged in a ragged voice, her face pressed against my neck, and we came together then, in a shattering burst of frenzied strokes. We collapsed against each other, gasping for air. I had not yet regained my wits or my strength when a burst of light filled the car. We were out of the tunnel.

My companion gave a disappointed sigh and gently extricated herself from my embrace, smiling at me mischievously as she straightened her clothes and sank into the seat beside me.

I managed to zip up my fly just before the steward reappeared. He tried to hide it, but the trace of a smile on his face as he addressed us suggested he was probably well aware of what we'd been up to and had timed his entrance accordingly. "Are you ladies ready for brunch?" he asked.

Since I was blushing profusely and hadn't yet regained my ability to form a coherent sentence, I was rather glad my companion spoke up.

"Quelques fruits et croissants, s'il vous plaît," she told him. *"J'ai des projets pour elle à Paris, mieux vaut s'assurer qu'elle garde toute sa vigueur."*

Whatever she said made the man smile. The fruit and croissants part I understood. But I didn't get the rest.

"Comme vous le désirez," the steward replied and turned to go.

I hadn't considered that the train staff would be bilingual, though it made perfect sense. "Wait!" I called after him.

He turned back around with a puzzled expression.

"I got the fruit and croissants part. What else did she say?" I asked him.

He chuckled. "She said she has plans for you when you get to Paris, and she wants to make sure you keep your strength up."

I had a feeling that by the end of the week, my French would be perfect.

LONG ROAD HOME
LC JORDAN

Whaddayagive, whaddayagive, gimme forty, forty dollar, now fifty..."

The auctioneer's voice droned on, competing with the chorus of cicadas perched somewhere high in the maple trees on this September afternoon. There was a decent crowd milling about, numbered paddles in hand, rising and falling in some random dance set to the cadence of the bidding.

My parents were having a belated midlife crisis. At least that was my theory. In truth, they were tired of the Midwest winters and had decided to become nomads, buying a motor home and following the sun with the seasons. Most of the contents of my childhood home were being auctioned, but my parents were leasing the house and not selling. I suspected that was an insurance policy of sorts in case their new lifestyle didn't agree with them and the wanderlust only lasted a year or so. As for the liquidation of the furniture, I would bet a year's salary that my mother agreed because it would be the only way to get my father to part with the living-room couch and chair and provide the possibility of getting new ones.

I had flown in for the weekend to be on hand for the auction and stick around until Monday when the new tenants would arrive. Friday night I saw my parents off, waving as they maneuvered their RV out of the drive and feeling very much left behind even though I had moved out years ago. It is a sobering thing to realize that you are old enough for your parents to be retired, much less to have them run away from home. The fact that they had me later in life didn't help any with my complex about aging.

My one contribution to the whole affair was a '65 Ford Galaxy in good condition. It was my first car, a gift from my parents my junior year of high school. Most kids that age want something new and fast and foreign, but not me. I fell in love with the burgundy body, white top, and fender skirts. The same fuzzy white dice were still hanging from the rearview mirror.

So many bittersweet memories were tied up in that car. I lost my innocence right there on the front seat, but not exactly in the usual way that comes to mind. When I left for college, my father agreed to store it for me, and I'd kept it all these years as some sort of connection to a part of my life that I had carefully locked away otherwise.

Now, with everything else moving forward, I reasoned it was as good a time as any for me to stop looking back. I had told my father to consign it to the auction with a minimum price of seven thousand dollars. It was the last thing to be sold, and the crowd had gathered around it in the driveway, waiting for the bidding to start.

I leaned back against one of the rack wagons parked in the yard, a glass of iced tea in my hand. The chilly condensation dripped onto my jean-clad leg, soaking through the denim and leaving a dark spot. Reaching down to try and brush it off, I heard a soft voice speak from directly in front of me.

"Cat?"

I froze. No one had called me that in years. The blood pounded in my ears from bending over and I slowly straightened. Everything in the background faded as I faced the woman standing two feet away. With the exception of a very few more pounds and a small scattering of early gray in her chestnut hair, she looked exactly the same as she did the last time I saw her. We were eighteen then and she had just bolted from both my arms and my car.

"Cat?" she repeated. I still hadn't spoken. I never expected to see her here, today, or ever, for that matter.

Not waiting any longer for me to confirm my identity, she hesitantly continued. "I thought it was you." With a wave of her hand, she indicated the yard filled with people. "I saw a flyer and couldn't believe it."

Finally finding my voice, I spoke more harshly than I intended. "Couldn't believe what, Ashley?"

Pausing a moment before answering, she replied, "I couldn't believe your parents were leaving. They've just always been here, you know? After I saw the advertisement last week I called your mom and she told me about their plans. And I couldn't believe you were selling the car." The last sentence trailed off as she looked away. "I knew you'd kept it. I've seen your dad driving it from time to time."

Everything was instantly just too close to the surface; the old pain, the disappointment in both Ash and myself, the effort spent trying to forget and remember. "I held on to it too long as it is," I answered flatly.

Taking a deep breath and meeting my eyes, Ashley spoke with determination. "We need to talk, Cat."

"Stop calling me that, and no, we don't," I shot back immediately.

"Stop calling you what?" Ashley asked, confused.

"Cat. Nobody calls me that now. My name is Catherine." In truth, everything about me became longer as the years passed; my name, my hair, my regrets.

A little glimpse of Ashley's rarely seen temper was beginning to show. "Fine. *Catherine*, we need to talk," she clipped out.

"We have nothing to talk about," I stubbornly replied.

Just then, the auctioneer announced that bidding on the Galaxy was about to start. Abruptly, Ashley turned her back on me and walked toward the driveway. My traitorous eyes watched her retreating form, and it was then that I spotted the paddle in her hand. Something in my stomach did a little flip, and I quickly sat my glass down on the wagon and made my way toward the crowd.

The auctioneer began his chant, starting the bidding at seven thousand. Several numbered paddles went up, but I was only interested in one in particular. When the bid increased to eight thousand, the paddles decreased by a third. At nine, only half were left and as I scanned the group I saw Ashley holding hers up, staring straight at me.

It was already a warm day, but I swear my body temperature rose ten degrees with the look she gave me. Waving my arm wildly, I shouted, "Ten thousand!"

The auctioneer stopped his chant and patiently explained, "You don't have a number; you aren't registered. You can't bid."

It took a second for that to sink in, then I shouted, "It's my car! Like hell I can't!"

His round face becoming red, the auctioneer peered down at me from below the rim of his straw cowboy hat. "The car is consigned

and bidding already started. The minimum selling price has been met."
Pointing with his gavel to the small trailer hitched to his pickup truck,
he yelled back, "If you want to bid, get a number."

At this point the crowd was far more interested in the crazy woman
who was shouting than in bidding. All of them except Ashley, that is.
In the brief silence that followed, she held up her paddle and sweetly
said, "Ten thousand."

That damned chant resumed and I made a mad dash for the trailer.
In the space of time it took me to produce my driver's license for
identification and wait for the infuriating man's wife to register me, I
heard him shout, "Sold to the lady for twelve thousand!"

As I exited the trailer, the crowd was slowly dispersing. I could
see Ashley standing by my Galaxy, waiting. I stopped a few feet away
and asked, "Why?"

"You tell me," she retorted. "Why keep this car all these years if
it meant nothing?"

Ignoring her question, I countered, "I can refuse to let you have
it."

"I can call my lawyer," she said, not backing down an inch.

Suddenly too tired to fight, I brushed past Ashley and leaned in the
driver's side open window. Reaching in, I grabbed the black-and-white
fuzzy dice from the rearview mirror.

"Take it," I said as I walked toward the house and closed the front
door.

I sat on one of the stools at the bar in the kitchen until the evening
sun slanted low in the west windows above the sink, bathing the room
in a pale coral glow. The auction company had left after distributing
all the sold items and collecting the fees. The two rack wagons, the
crowd, and my Galaxy were gone. The only evidence left of the entire
afternoon's events was the trampled grass in the yard and the license
plates that Ashley had evidently removed from the car and laid on the
front porch step. They were on the counter now, and I traced my finger
along the raised letters and numbers. One last time I let the memory
replay of the final drive Ashley and I had taken over ten years ago.

It was our senior year of high school and our volleyball team had
finally won the state championship. Everything had been golden that

year; perfect grades, perfect win record, perfect friendship. Graduation night we flipped our tassels and posed with our diplomas for what seemed like a hundred photographs for our families. Deciding to skip the usual parties, Ashley and I took the Galaxy out on Highway 45 and just drove, singing loudly and off key with every song that came on the radio. We were still a little wound up from the euphoria of passing that first major milestone in life, but we were also starving, so we decided to head back to Ashley's house and raid the kitchen.

I pulled into her folks' driveway and cut the engine. We sat there a few minutes, talking about what we were going to do that summer and what college would be like. Somewhere between listening to Ashley's laughter and watching the happiness radiate from her face, I thought to myself how beautiful she was. She was the embodiment of strength and innocence and she made me feel so alive. There was no way I could help falling in love with her, right then, right there.

Dimly I realized she had stopped talking and was just quietly sitting there, looking at me. My hand reached out of its own volition and brushed back a strand of dark hair that had escaped her tie. It seemed the most natural thing in the world for me to lean over and kiss her.

To say I was unprepared for the jolt of electricity that touching her lips with mine caused would be a vast understatement. I pulled back suddenly, afraid of what I would see in Ashley's eyes. They were closed, and when she slowly opened them, a myriad of emotions swirled around in their dark blue depths. Desire, love, and panic were there, and not necessarily in that order.

Without a word or a glance back, she opened the car door and hurried inside her house, leaving me at once both lost and found and forever changed.

I didn't see Ashley again all summer. It felt like I'd lost my best friend, and I guess I had. Anyway, it hurt like hell. In the fall I left for a West Coast college on a volleyball scholarship. As far as I knew, Ashley had gone to her school of choice as well.

That winter when I came home over break, there was a card waiting for me. Inside was a note with Ashley's new dorm address and phone number, written in her distinctive script. Over the next four years my mother became a messenger service, dutifully forwarding two cards a year from Ashley; one for Christmas and one for my birthday. In each card was a request to meet but I never replied, not being able to bear hearing some placating speech about how she liked me a lot, just "not that way." To her credit, Ashley never asked for my address, and after eight cards, she stopped trying.

After college, I joined the AVP and began playing open beach volleyball tournaments. Once or twice, after I began to make a name for myself, I could have sworn I saw Ashley at some of the matches. During year two a rotator cuff injury simultaneously ended my playing career and began my coaching career. Over the next four years our university managed to make it to a Division I championship twice. The stats for my personal life were far less impressive; I never seemed able to sustain a relationship for more than a few months.

Ashley had fared well, or so my mother kept me informed. Surprisingly, she had returned to our hometown high school and began teaching chemistry, no less. I knew she had never married, and I wondered why someone so wonderful stayed single.

The persistent honk of a car horn drew me from my musings. The image of what my father would have had to say to whoever the unlucky driver of that car was provided me with a much-needed moment of comic relief. Another long blast sounded and I slid from the bar stool and walked to the front door to investigate. The neighborhood had always been a quiet one, and I didn't blame my folks for leaving if every weekend had become this noisy.

Stepping out onto the porch, I waited a few seconds for my eyes to adjust to the waning light. There in the driveway sat Ashley, parked in the Galaxy. Just to be sure, I blinked a couple of times. Before I could even form a thought, she hit the horn again.

"Get in!" she shouted loudly enough for the entire block to hear.

"Are you insane?" I answered back, glancing left and right, hoping none of my parents' neighbors were witnessing this exchange. After the free entertainment of the auction that afternoon, I was certain that at least Mrs. Perkins would be on the lookout for any further drama at 503 Mulberry Lane.

Another drawn-out honk shattered the otherwise still evening, and somewhere nearby a dog began to bark. Taking the porch steps two at a time, I quickly covered the distance to the driveway and stopped inches from the driver side door. When I opened my mouth to speak, Ashley cut me off. "Get in."

"There is no way I'm getting in that car with you," I said calmly. "I don't even know why you'd think I would."

"Oh, I think you will," she answered just as calmly. "Either that, or I'm going to sit out here all night honking. You can either get in or call the police and have me arrested for disturbing the peace or trespassing or whatever," Ashley said with a hint of anger in her voice.

I just stood there staring at her, cursing whatever fate made her still so beautiful after all these years. Part of me wanted to climb in that car and roll back the odometer ten years and another part of me wanted to just finally move on, whatever that meant. If there was any shortcut I could take somewhere between the two destinations, I wished I knew which way to turn and find it.

Sensing my indecision, Ashley got out of the car and leaned back on the door, folding her arms across her chest against the cool air of the evening.

"Listen, Cat," she began, then corrected herself, "Catherine, please. Just come for a drive with me and I promise if afterward you still don't want to see me, I won't contact you again. Ever," she said quietly.

The finality of her tone made me realize that this was it. There would never be another chance to resolve this part of my life, for good or bad. Ashley was watching me, those blue eyes melting a path through my heart.

"I should have my head examined," I said with conviction as I walked back to the house to lock up. Returning to the car, I opened the passenger door and paused. "I don't suppose I could drive?" I ventured, trying to gain some control over this situation in which I felt very much out of control.

Breaking the tension, Ashley nearly snorted with laughter. "Hell no," she finally got out. "You never would let me drive this car. After all it's taken for me to get behind the wheel, do you honestly think I'm going to just hand over the keys?"

"Hope you're a better driver now than you were then," I commented dryly as I sat down on the wide bench seat.

"Funny, Cat...therine." Ashley grinned as she started the engine and backed out. "Nice to know your sense of humor hasn't changed."

I couldn't keep the small smile from my face. I had missed this, the teasing and verbal sparring. The ache in my chest made me admit just how much. We rode on in silence for several miles as Ashley took us out beyond the reach of the lights of town. I rolled the window down an inch or two, letting the crisp night air pass over me, trying to clear my thoughts. The hum of the tires on the pavement was calming and I turned a little in my seat, studying Ashley's profile.

Suddenly, I had to know. Right here, right now.

"Did you hate me?" I gave voice to the fear I'd kept inside for so long.

Ashley's head jerked in my direction and the Galaxy swerved a little. "No!" she shouted, the word filling the space between us. "No," she repeated, softer this time. "I could never hate you, Cat. I…" Frustrated, she took a deep breath. "Let me find a place to pull over, okay?"

Parker's Pond was just up the road and Ashley turned in, cutting the engine but leaving the dash lights on. For a moment, neither one of us seemed able to speak and only the crickets broke the silence. I was about to make some desperate comment on the weather when Ashley found her courage and continued.

"You turned my world upside down with that kiss, Cat."

I sank down in the seat, not sure where this was going.

"I was afraid," she went on. "Afraid of you, afraid of me, afraid of what I felt. I was angry with you for changing everything, and I was angry with myself for being such a coward. By the time I had sorted it out in my head, you were gone and wouldn't talk to me. I didn't know how to fix it at that point. I could never hate you Cat. I love you. Always have, always will. So I guess the real question is, do you hate me? I wouldn't blame you if you did," she said, sounding resigned to hear the worst from me.

Replaying her words in my mind, I felt a little light-headed. This was not what I had expected. Trying to process it was nearly impossible at the moment and I just sat there, not saying a word.

Mistaking my silence for an answer, Ashley reached for the ignition. "I understand, Cat. You don't have to say it."

"Wait," I said, covering her hand with mine. "Just give me a minute, okay? You always were so damn impatient."

Turning her palm over and lacing her fingers with mine, Ashley slid from behind the steering wheel and faced me. With a look that sent every available ounce of blood in my body straight south, she lowered her voice and asked, "Why don't you shut up and kiss me?"

"What?" I almost shouted. My senses were on overload from her thumb stroking my wrist and the thought of tasting her lips again, even for a moment. I could smell her scent, sweeter than I remembered, and it was becoming difficult to breathe, let alone form sentences.

Gaining confidence, she moved a little closer until our bodies touched from thigh to shoulder. Leaning forward until I could feel the warmth of her breath against my cheek, she spoke in a tone of voice I had never heard until that night. "I said, why don't you shut up and kiss me? I can pretty much guarantee you'll get an entirely different response this time."

"It's not that simple!" I protested, not really able to come up with one good reason not to at the moment.

Looking me straight in the eyes, Ashley spoke with emotion. "Yes, it is that simple if you want it to be."

I wondered if it actually could be. It took me all of ten seconds to decide that it could, and was. Laying my palm against her cheek, I captured her lips in a kiss so full of desire that it took us both by surprise. Ashley recovered quickly, however, and returned the kiss with an equal amount of passion. As she tilted her head a bit more, I felt her open to me and I took the invitation. My tongue traced her full lower lip, sucking it gently before gliding over the sensitive skin inside.

I felt Ashley shudder and surge against me, her breasts pressed against my arm. The immediate flood of wetness between my legs tore a groan from my throat as I gradually ended the kiss with one last stroke of my tongue and several nips along her jawline. Keeping my eyes closed, I rested my forehead against hers, trying to ignore the almost painful throbbing of my clit.

Ashley was having a hard time getting her breathing under control, and when she finally did, she laughed nervously. "Wow."

"Wow?" I echoed, teasing. "That's all you can say?"

"How about I'm sorry," she offered.

Frowning, I opened my eyes. "You're sorry? For what?" I started to pull back, but Ashley brought both hands around my neck, keeping me right there.

"I'm not sorry for this, Cat. I'm sorry for the past, for hurting you. And I'm sorry I missed out on ten years of kissing you." She ended with a small smile, searching my face for some sign of hope.

I closed my eyes again, overcome. When I opened them, Ashley was still gazing at me intently, waiting. Not able to find adequate words,

I tried instead to show her what was in my heart. Grasping her hips, I tugged her forward, guiding her over me as I leaned back across the seat. My hands found their way under the hem of her Henley, slipping beneath the waistband of her khakis and coming to rest at the small of her back. This time when my mouth found hers, it was gentler but filled with meaning. It was a kiss of absolution and love, and I did my best to let it speak for me.

Ashley understood and threaded the fingers of one hand in my hair, pulling me even closer. The other hand trailed down the front of my shirt and came to rest low on my stomach. I felt the heat of her palm through the material, shivering when she began to tug it loose from my jeans. A firm thigh pressed between my legs, rocking hard against my crotch. Groaning deep in my chest, I tore my lips away from hers as my hips lifted up off the seat. Insistent fingers freed the buttons on my shirt, tracing random patterns on my skin until finally circling my left breast through the fabric of my bra. Ashley bent lower and I felt her moist breath on my nipple, causing it to harden even more. When she grazed the tip with her teeth, I almost threw us both off the seat.

"Wait," I managed to protest. "We can't do this here; there isn't enough room. Besides, I don't want the first time we make love to be in a car." My face flushed at the confession.

Ashley seemed to consider this for a moment but made no move to sit up. Instead, she just shifted to the side, allowing me to lift my torso and lean back against the door. A thin sheen of perspiration covered my body and I reached up to brush the hair away from my neck.

A smile slowly spread across Ashley's face as she drew an imaginary line down my chest to my naval. "Cat?" she spoke in my ear, her tongue coming out to taste the lobe as she flicked open the top button on my jeans.

"Yes?" I replied, my voice higher than normal.

"Cat?" Ashley repeated.

I sucked in a breath as I felt the remaining buttons surrender.

"Have you ever made love to anyone in this car?" Playfully, Ashley grasped the elastic of my bikinis and snapped it back against my skin. I nearly came right there.

"What? No, why?" I managed to answer.

"Because," Ashley explained, "this is where we began, Cat. I want another chance. I want to put life in reverse and then shift into high gear." Her hand dipped inside my bikinis. Finding the wet heat there she parted the swollen folds, stroking, once, twice. "Unless," she whispered against my neck, "you want to drive."

My eyes slammed shut as her fingers closed around my clitoris. "That's okay," I ground out. "I have a feeling it's going to be a short trip." Blindly, I cupped her face and claimed her mouth as she entered me, taking me home.

The trunk lid closed on the Galaxy, Ashley's luggage packed inside. I took a final look around the old neighborhood, waiting for her to make one last check of her house before we left for California. She came out the front door, closing it for the last time. Walking to the car, she stopped in front of me and placed a quick kiss on my lips.

"Who's driving?" she grinned, daring me.

Reaching into the back seat, I pulled out the fuzzy dice and hung them from the rearview mirror again, making them twirl.

Turning around, I held out my hand to Ashley. "Give me the keys," I answered. "You're dangerous when you drive." Laughing, she complied.

"So can this thing make it all the way?" Ashley asked as we headed west on I57.

"Are you serious?" I answered. "Look how far it's taken us already!"

THE TEMPLE
AMIE M. EVANS

The Temple is quiet except for the steady, soothing sound of the water being returned through the filter back into the turtle pond. I sit with my back perfectly straight on the wooden bench facing the mirror. The sheer material of my dressing gown reveals the form of my breasts and the darker color of my areolae. The silver hoops that pierce my nipples flash as the light hits them.

Sixteen years ago, Kate held my wrists over my head as the strange woman put surgical clamps on my nipples and rammed the sharp silver needle through my flesh. It happened over there on our bed. I touch myself now, and I am wet from the memory.

I woke, confused, a ball gag in my mouth, my shackled ankles attached to the rings in the floor, my head in Kate's lap, as she stretched my arms up toward her. I could see her face, the intense look in her eyes, but I couldn't lift my head to see my own body or anything else. I could feel the weight of the mysterious stranger as she straddled me. I twisted in revolt, thinking Kate would allow someone else to fuck me. I cried out, but it was muffled and deformed by the gag. I pleaded to her with my eyes. For the first time, I was afraid.

"Shh, Isabella," she said, soothing me with a warm look from her ice blue eyes. "It's all right. Don't move."

I'd heard those words before, seen that look in her eyes, and I believed her—trusted her. She wouldn't let anyone else take me. I belonged to her. I relaxed and stopped fighting against my bondage. I felt the stranger's fingers touch my nipples. I felt the clamps—like no other clamp I'd ever felt before—being put into place. My cunt got wet from the pressure on my nipples; then Kate kissed my forehead and her hands slipped from my wrists into my palms. The prick of the flesh didn't exist, just intense pain and a burning as a rush of endorphins hit my brain. An unfamiliar voice said, "Breathe for me." And again pain, burn, pleasure—as the stranger pierced the other nipple. I moaned and grunted a mock protest.

"Almost done," Kate's familiar voice said as she looked away from my breasts and into my eyes. "There." She released my hands and stroked my forehead. She lightly touched the healed cuts on my breasts that had just thickened into scars, then attached the leather shackles around my wrists, hooking them to the O-rings on the wall at each of the bedposts. She cupped my face in her hands, softly kissed my nose, stood up and gave the woman, whose face to this day I have not seen, her money. Turning back to me, she slid a finger between the folds of my labia as she lay half on top of me, half next to me. I was wet and euphoric from the fear, the piercing, and the realization of what my love had just done.

She unzipped her pants and the hard silicone cock popped out. "You're so wet," she said as she fingered me. I twisted and squirmed at her touches. Played outraged. Played resistant. She pushed her cock into me, fucking me hard while lightly pinching my nipples, sending increasingly stronger jolts of pleasure through me. Kate clamped her hands onto my bound wrists and fucked me like I was an inanimate object and when I came, she kept fucking me until I came again.

I was brought up Catholic, attended a parochial school and church until I entered college. In high school, I researched alternative religions with fevered passion. I spent hours reading books on Taoism, Buddhism, Satanism, and Islam. I searched mythologies and cults for proof or even a sign that a god, goddess, or multiple divine beings existed. I wanted desperately to believe. I wanted to find something that sparked the spiritual fires inside of me, lit up my soul. I never found any proof. I never even found any hints. I stopped believing in gods.

In college, I looked for a spirituality that wouldn't leave me empty and needing. I waded through texts looking for something that would touch my soul and stir the powers I felt inside myself. I practiced yoga, transcendental meditation, and tai chi. I played with Wicca and paganism. I build altars and shrines and participated in ceremonies to honor the seasons. I dabbled in voodoo and tarot cards. None of it filled me up. None of it stopped the aching desire or the longing need for completeness. None of it enabled me to save my soul, tap my spiritual energy, or move into a higher plane. I was always left empty—a spiritual void.

Then I met her.

❖

I let the robe fall from my shoulders, then slide the silk slip with the antique white lace over my head. It fits the curves of my body perfectly, holding my breasts taut and high, cutting in at the waist and flaring out at the hips. I pull stockings, new from the package, onto my legs. The sheer black nylon clings to my freshly shaved skin and stops at mid-thigh. I attach them to my pink and black garter belt, then apply a small spray of perfume to each wrist and the back of my neck. Returning to my original position at the dressing table in front of the mirror, I select a black eyeliner pencil and apply it close to the lashes—thin, even lines emphasizing my lids to complement the makeup on my lips and cheekbones.

The prick of the needles was new to me twelve years ago. That Kate wanted me so completely yet still wanted me as an individual, separate from her being, was not something I had experienced, nor had I imagined that those contradictory impulses could exist in the same person.

She instructed me to sit straddling the weight bench. A small table with her equipment on it stood next to the bench. Kate ran the blade of a straight razor over the flesh of my upper back, removing the tiny layer of soft baby fuzz, then treated the area with a disinfectant. She laid the transfer on my back, placing it carefully, then removing it. Using a hand mirror, Kate showed me the ink design—two cherries with a stem.

Her hands felt foreign; she touched my back as if it were a canvas. Gone were the soft, firm strokes of reassurance, replaced with the artist's hands seeking, searching, ready to create, transform. "Don't move," Kate cautioned me, and I heard the buzz of the tattoo gun. I clutched the sides of the bench as the new sensation moved through my flesh and Kate adorned my body with her art.

She owns me, not because of a mutual contract, an agreement, or an exchange of money. She is not my Mistress; I am not her slave. She is not my Daddy; I am not her little girl. Sex is my religion; she is my God. I worship her—not in the way that little children worship

Santa Claus and their mothers, or the way priests worship their idols. I worship her in the intimate way prophets worship their gods. I have seen the burning bush, and my God has spoken directly to me. She has laid her hands on me, marked me physically and mentally. I worship her not with blind faith, but because she has been tested and proven. She has demonstrated her divine powers. I am her high priestess. Like Moses, I will lead my people out of servitude and into the Promised Land through her word alone. She reveals the divine prophecy and the mystical secrets. She places the holy manna in my mouth. I am nothing before her, and yet she has chosen me.

❖

I open the jewelry box on my dressing table. An assortment of necklaces lies on the velvet lining—sparkles, thin chains, elaborate stone settings, and her favorite, classic white pearls. I select the medium-length strand and clasp it around my neck. The necklace belonged to my grandmother, a stern woman of English descent who was a social snob. I attach a bracelet to my wrist. It belonged to Kate's grandmother, a flamboyant woman who seized life with gusto. I think they would approve of my use of their pearls, if not of my erotic choices.

I like the pearls because they hold our families' history. Intact in the mucus and dirt that are of such value to society, our families' struggles, lives, and loves are held fast. Kate chose a pearl, small and silky, as the bead for my labia piercing. It was our sixth anniversary. The room smelled of sage and musk. The piercer, a young, tattooed girl, had agreed to allow Kate to watch. The lace of my dress pushed up around my waist, my feet in stirrups, and my genitals shaved bare, I felt oddly exposed.

Kate sat slightly to the side and behind the woman as she prepared my clit for piercing and talked in a singsong voice indicative of how many times she'd repeated this procedure and its instructions. No sex, she said, for six weeks. She clamped my hood then pierced it, all in Kate's view. The ring with the pearl holder was in before I was even able to process that she was done.

In the car in the parking garage, Kate placed a dental dam over my genitals and softly stroked my clit until I came.

I have always, from the first time I met Kate, felt as if I've known her forever. Forever. The word was incomprehensible, meaningless, mystical until her. Our bond is from a long time ago, as if we'd shared the same womb. Comfortable and safe. Someone I know, love, honor. And yet, she has felt new each day. New and unknown. Someone to explore, learn, consume. Her marks on my body are a road map of our time together. Gentle strokes of affection, passion-filled yearnings to strengthen our bond.

Offerings of my flesh, my spirit, I give to Kate.

❖

Offerings of my flesh, my spirit, I give to Isabella.

I cannot think of anything more important to me than touching her. I'm addicted to the feel of her flesh under my hands. Addicted to the scent of her skin, the taste of Isabella's cunt. I'm addicted to the sound of the moan she makes when I slip a finger into her and the little noise that seems to fight its way out of her when she comes. I'd do anything to make her happy—to satisfy her needs. Sometimes I'm afraid I can't. Afraid she'll want too much—more than I can give her.

I search my soul for a sign that I am worthy. I pray for strength. A vision that I deserve to receive the great honor Isabella has bestowed upon me. I am her vessel, her tool, and through me she will be able to reach the Promised Land. My fear is great, but my desire is stronger.

I swing the blade separating the shrublike weeds from their bases, then pull the roots out of the dirt. The weeds will grow back—they always do—since I am unable to remove all of the roots despite how hard I try. In a few weeks, I'll have to return to the yard with my blade and hack them away again. Some cuts don't last. I could remove them permanently with a chemical herbicide, but I like the ritual of cutting them. The process of cutting and pulling, cutting and pulling. The battle that these weeds and I are engaged in endlessly. I like the solitude of the act, the weeds and their resistance, the shine of the blade, and the gleam of the sharp edge when it is held just so. The secure, heavy feeling of the handle in my hand, the pump and rush of my muscles as I use them to hack, chop, cut, and pull the plants from the soil in which they grow—defiantly.

The first time I ever marked her body was eighteen years ago, with a blade—my blade. A smooth metal dagger with red stones set into the black handle in the form of a cross. I bound her arms to the overhead beam with fur-lined leather cuffs attached to silver chains. Then I put a spreader bar on her legs. The sound of metal on metal excited me, but not like the sight of her. Her body in a barely there leopard-print teddy. Her thighs exposed almost to her waist by the high-cut sides and the low-cut back. Her limbs spread open. The G-string bottom with just enough material to cover a quarter of an inch stripe across her lower back. "Two snaps at the crotch," she'd told me when she bought it, "so you can get inside me without taking it off." She knows exactly what I like.

But it was the breasts I wanted now. The nipples almost showing, raised up and out by the shelf design of the top and pushed toward me by the X-form of her bondage, her cleavage the focal point. I turned my back to her and withdrew the dagger from its black leather scabbard. I could hear the chains clank as she stirred and strained to see what I had, what I would do to her first. Turning toward her, I wasn't sure if I could do it. Maybe I'd tease her, taunt her with the dagger. Trace a pattern on her skin without breaking it open. I knew I was ready; I wasn't sure she was.

I stepped close to her, lightly kissed her forehead, and grabbed a handful of her black hair. I jerked her head back, exposing her neck, and ran the very tip of the dagger down the side of her throat to the valley of her cleavage. Isabella sucked in air, then stopped and held her breath, her body completely still. I allowed the point of the knife to push against her left breast, just hard enough to be felt yet not break the skin.

She moaned and slowly released her breath. I let go of her hair and lifted the dagger from her flesh. I traced a path with the point down her back and up her side. She moaned again. "I want your blood," I said in a low voice without the emotion I felt. "I want your flesh and your blood." She moaned again, slightly rocking her hips.

I repositioned the dagger in the small gap between her breasts, pressed lightly, and reached down and undid the two small snaps to expose her. "I want your blood and your soul," I said as I slid two fingers into her wet cunt.

She moaned and carefully rocked her hips toward my hand.

"You're wet," I said as I pumped my fingers deep inside her. Isabella was warm and soft and felt so ready. I wanted more of me deeper inside her. I pulled my fingers out and grabbed her chin, leveling her eyes with mine.

"This is forever," I said, holding her gaze.

"Forever," she repeated.

"Don't move, sweet. Don't move at all." I placed my hand on her breast and held it so it would remain still. She whimpered, a small helpless sound, and I looked into her eyes. Deep, dark black pools full of trust, fear, and excitement met mine.

The dagger pushed into Isabella's flesh just deep enough to release her blood and leave a light scar when it healed. I drew a two-inch line across her right breast. Her skin resisted for a moment before the blade bit through it and released her blood. It ran slow at first for a moment and then dripped down in a steady, almost even stream. As I withdrew the dagger, Isabella groaned and moved her hips toward me. Her eyes were closed and her head hung back, exposing her neck to me. I watched the stream of crimson, red against her pale white flesh, trickle down between her breasts and pool in her cleavage.

I made the same mark on her left breast, then reached down and touched her clit. Her wetness had spilled out, allowing me to easily slide my fingers across it. Isabella's body rocked as she made sounds of needing more. I bent my mouth down to her breasts and licked from the collected blood. I turned my attention to the wounds I had inflicted on her body and lapped at both of them. Her blood tasted like iron as it coated the inside of my mouth. I locked my lips over the incision on her left breast and sucked, pulling more blood to the surface as I stroked her clit.

I consumed her, pulling her every essence into me, then used the dagger to cut a gash across the palm of my own hand, allowing my blood to come forth. I placed my bloody hand over her mouth, and Isabella sucked my fluid from it.

Joined forever through the power of blood magic, I am chained to her—bound to her needs. Her hunger is all consuming and within that hunger lays my power. Without her belief, her want, I am nothing but another fake prophet. Her endless desire gives me strength and power. Her lust for more gives me purpose and drive. Her trust makes me confident. Her belief makes me real. Her love gives it all meaning. All I want to do is satisfy her and I never want her to be satisfied. Her body is the spring of life, the Garden of Eden, the seed of existence from which all things come. It is my responsibility to reach deep inside of her and pull forth from that dark space what lies hidden there—to release her soul. I am honored that she has chosen to allow me to have unlimited access to her body and mind, that she believes I am strong enough to lead both of us through the darkness—her darkness—into the light of salvation.

I take my vows seriously, for eating from the wrong tree will tumble us into eternal ignorance, expose our nakedness to each other, and prevent us from seeing the beauty. But sampling the fruits is part of my charge, and she has left it to me to be the ferryman and guide her across the river of bones inside her own being.

❖

I pile the hacked stems, leaves, and assorted plant materials into a heap. Later I'll feed them into the chipper to reduce the pieces to manageable sizes. The chips will be added to the top of the composter along with a bit of soil and water. Then I'll turn it once each day so that the contents will ferment, mix, and decompose into what will ultimately become a highly compact, intensely fertile growing material for the flower beds. Because of this process, from the remains of the resistant, defiant weeds will come the delicate buds of the bleeding hearts, irises, and tulips. But only if I handle them correctly with care to every detail, remembering each day to attend it, mix it, and watch over its transformation. Adding just enough of what it needs, protecting it from too much and not enough; from carelessness, overindulgence, and neglect.

The sound of flesh sizzling like steaks on a hot skillet, the scent of human meat cooking crisp fills the room. I am overcome by the pink-red of her meat, the piercing cry of her voice, her unrelenting compliance to allow me to mark her body with symbols of my own unworthy devotion.

I place the burn pack on top of my newest offering and sob, overcome by the moment. Her ass had been in the air; as the iron imprinted its tribal pattern deep into her flesh, it sank into the mattress. I feel as if our flesh has become one. I cradle her in my arms and gently stroke between the folds of her labia. She is, as always, during these intimate moments, wet. Her desire confounds me as it honors me. For I am a heathen in the Vatican, ignorant of the correct rituals, what words to say, when to stand or kneel; but not of the power and glory around me. Her body, like the consecrated wafer, has been lifted up on high before me. The sanctified host has been offered and I have responded, "I am not worthy, but only say the word and I shall be healed."

And she has said the word.

Amen.

I have been called like Abraham to sacrifice my best, my favorite, and my offering has been received. I wandered in the desert, tempted by false prophets and the devil himself before I saw the divine spirit made flesh in Isabella's form and all of my pain and suffering were washed away by her blood. She's mine. Her body is my responsibility. She's the temple and I have to make sure everything is in order. I'm the priestess sworn to protect the goddess and to perform the rituals in praise and honor of her.

❖

Isabella walks down the steps to the second floor, wondering if Kate is done with the yard work. She holds herself perfectly still four steps from the bottom when she hears the front door open. Kate's eyes sparkle as she takes her in head to toe. A vision of loveliness. Isabella's dark hair is pulled up into a bun held in place by rhinestone pins. A red satin dress in a style out of fashion before either of them was born, but cut perfectly to accent Isabella's hourglass figure and display the cleavage Kate has loved for so many years, clings perfectly to her body. Matching ankle-strap high heels with rhinestone clips and opera-length gloves finish the dinner outfit. She is stunning in Kate's eyes despite or perhaps because of the fine lines around her eyes, the extra fullness of her belly, and the gray in her temples. She is every bit the femme fatale Kate first met twenty years ago—and yet so much more.

"You're too much," Kate says, putting her arms out to her. "You hot thing." Isabella moves down the remaining steps. "I'm all dirty," Kate says, stepping back from her.

She's wearing a one-piece work suit, faded from years of use. The sleeves are cut off, her muscular tattooed arms are pumped from the labor she has been doing. She is covered with dirt and grass from an afternoon in the yard. Kate smiles at Isabella, sweat dripping from her, the veins in her neck popping. Her blond hair hides the silver and her Nordic ancestors' blood has served her well, allowing her to age gracefully. From where Isabella stands, the lines on Kate's face can barely be seen and softness in her middle abdomen is hidden by the jumpsuit.

"I don't care." Isabella steps into her and Kate wraps her arms around her. Kate smells of earth and sweat, of comfort and love. Isabella smells of musk and exotic oils, of sex and desire.

It's been twenty years since Kate first took her metal blade to Isabella's breasts and made her hers. Twenty years since she embraced her in the folds of her arms and promised it would be forever. Twenty years since Isabella lay open and exposed the deep darkness, and Kate agreed to explore, control, and indulge it. Twenty years since they first shared in the flesh and the spirit. It has been a lifetime, but today as they stand together, arms around each other, they kiss with all the newness and excitement of two lovers sharing their very first kiss.

REUNION
LISA FIGUEROA

The last thing I wanted to do was go to another family reunion. Is there anything more boring than a bunch of relatives gathered together to drink beer, grill fajitas, and chase after small children? My mother had other ideas and piled on the guilt about how both sets of grandparents weren't getting any younger and that I had cousins whom I'd never even met. The woman is a connoisseur of passive aggression, so there was no point in trying to argue. Rosa and Blanca, my younger, identical twin sisters, would simply smile back at her when met with resistance, themselves students of the school of manipulation in which our mother gave daily classes. If it hadn't been for my grandmother, Abuela Frida, insisting, I wouldn't have gone at all. She was a woman who, at age eighty-two, had survived three husbands, a bout with breast cancer, and as she liked to often brag, still drove her own fucking car.

My family has known I was a lesbian from the time I was twelve, starting with my first devastating crush on Serena, my best friend since kindergarten. Their way of dealing with it was not to mention it or ask too many questions they didn't want answered. My mother finally stopped trying to fix me up with boys in high school when I discussed the futility of such attempts with my Abuela Frida. She was the only one who accepted me for the person I was and even respected me more for being true to myself.

"Mama doesn't understand, Abuelita. I never have, nor will I ever be interested in boys."

"My daughter is a hardheaded fool. I told her to back off, but she never wants to listen."

"I don't know what to do. I'm thinking I shouldn't bother going to college. What's the point? I'll never be able to live my own life."

"Emilia, don't worry. I'm going to have a long talk with your mother. I'll remind her about her great-aunt Cuca. Even back then we knew about women who loved women. To each her own, I've always believed. I respected your mother's decision to marry your father and live her life, so why shouldn't she let you live your own life? You're not a child anymore."

"Thank you, Abuelita. You always understand."

So, my Grandmother Frida became the emissary of peace in my family when she at long last convinced my parents, my mother in particular, to give up on useless dreams.

Now that I was home on spring break from UCLA, I was ready to relax and have some fun, and as always, was open to the possibility of finding love. A family reunion wasn't exactly what I had in mind, although I was looking forward to some good home cooking. After too much Taco Bell, I had almost forgotten the pleasure of handmade flour tortillas.

Breakfast had been over for hours, but I had to help myself to one last warm tortilla and generously slathered it with butter. I took a huge bite, savoring the heady taste and textures combining in my mouth. Too much of this sort of thing might start expanding my backside to an uncomfortable point, but for now, I had a feminine plumpness that still turned the heads of both sexes. What mattered to me most was the attention I received from soft butches. They were the sexiest women on earth as far as I was concerned, and never failed to attract me.

My last girlfriend, Davila, had been femme like me. She was pretty in a classic Latina way, full chest and mouth and not much of a backside. Her best feature were her dark chocolate–colored eyes framed by striking thin eyebrows like Greta Garbo's. We met at the beginning of my first semester, breaking up amicably by the end of it when we decided we were better as friends than lovers. In our last conversation, we had talked about what we both wanted from a relationship and how we would never find it together.

"Emilia, I knew we wouldn't last from the minute we first kissed," Davila had said.

"Why is that?" I asked.

"Remember how we looked at each other waiting for someone to make a move? You finally kissed me, and although it was enjoyable, I felt like you were taking on a role you really didn't like."

"Well, that's true. I don't like to be the one who makes the first move. I like a woman who knows what she wants and then grabs it, especially when it's me."

"Exactly. That's why you will never be completely happy with a femme. You need a more butch woman. A woman who is more comfortable taking charge. I'm not that kind of a woman and neither are you."

"You make us sound completely helpless. I'm a strong, single-minded Chicana, like my mother and grandmother before her. It's just that when it comes to intimacy, I like my lover to take control. There are enough other areas in life for me to exhibit power in the relationship. Besides, control isn't just physical, is it?"

"Emilia, I was never your match, but I do hope you find her someday."

"So do I. I hope we both find what we're looking for."

Thinking back on our conversation made me feel vulnerable and melancholy. I wondered if I would ever find that missing link, that other half to make me complete. My mother bustled into the kitchen carrying several bags of groceries with my grandmother Frida following close behind.

"Are you going to sit there all day, *mi hija*? I have your sisters scrubbing the bathrooms, your father cleaning up the backyard, and your abuela is going to help me cut up meat and vegetables for the fajitas. Maybe you can bring in the rest of the shopping bags," my mother said before she had set down a single bag of food.

My abuela smiled and winked at me conspiratorially. "Your mother has been barking orders all morning. I even saluted once," she said.

Her daughter sighed dramatically, hands on hips, until I nodded and went to bring in the last of the bags, wondering if we were planning on feeding the entire neighborhood. My mother continued to direct the family as if she were in command of an intricate military operation. There was no choice but to go AWOL. I went upstairs and got ready for the reunion.

❖

By the time I reemerged downstairs, the first of my relatives were arriving. I hugged favorite aunts, uncles, nieces, and nephews, needing to be introduced to many I hadn't seen before or in a long time. My parents always made sure to mention proudly that I was home from college. The attention embarrassed me a little, but it was nice to be bragged about. I wandered into the backyard, dug a soda out of the ice cooler, and sat down on a wicker chair. The warm weather had been perfect for shorts but now I regretted the decision when the wicker fibers kept pinching the backs of my legs. I adjusted my shorts self-consciously. There was nothing to do but try to get through the long, boring night with as little pain as possible. I studied the stars, looked at the faraway tiny suns, and imagined my true love out there somewhere among the cosmos. A shooting star caught my attention and I thought about making a wish. Some cynical part of me resisted, though I gave in to my hopes and dreams and made it anyway.

I was in the midst of a large gulp of soda when the most attractive woman I had ever seen came into the backyard. My throat closed up and I coughed and sputtered loudly, causing her to turn and look at me. I felt my face blossoming into a sunburned shade of red as I wiped my eyes and tried to smile. She was devastatingly gorgeous.

The stranger wore tight blue jeans and a blouse with its long sleeves rolled up. She wasn't wearing a bra; her small bust didn't need it, though what gave her away were adorable, pert nipples that insisted on pushing through the blouse's flimsy material. Her dark hair was very straight and short, reaching only the nape of her neck, but it seemed shorter because she had both sides tucked behind her ears. She had soft, honey-colored skin tone that matched my own and large, almond-shaped eyes. The firmness in her jawline intrigued me the most, as it gave strength to her face along with a boyish handsomeness. My legs trembled and for once I was glad to be sitting in that uncomfortable wicker chair. The backs of my knees were sweating at the same rate that the heat and moistness grew insistently between them.

She looked at me and our eyes locked as the intensity with which I had stared at her was equally returned. I wondered for a morose second if maybe she was a cousin or niece and thought about the possibility I might be contemplating incest with a close relative. Such an awkward complication must be considered when anyone falls into lust with an appealing visitor at a family reunion. As she approached, I drank my soda as if dying of thirst.

"Do you mind if I sit down here?" she asked, motioning to the chair next to me.

I was trying not to imagine the places where I wanted her to sit, preferably naked, so I simply shook my head in the negative.

After all that staring, we now both couldn't make eye contact, even though I was sure she was looking at me whenever I glanced away. She opened her can of soda as I gazed at her hands. They were large and smooth. There wasn't any jewelry on her fingers, though she wore a slender leather bracelet on one wrist. She also had a necklace with a single charm of the letter *L. L* for lesbian, perhaps?

I finished the last of my soda and before I set the can down, she stood up.

"Would you like another one? I'll go get you one," she said before I answered. I watched her walk away, staring at her tantalizing backside, so perfectly framed in those tight pants. There was a confidence in her step, a certain glide I had often noted in butch women that made my insides tingle and my ears itch. On her way back I noticed her eyes on my bare legs, so I crossed them as sexily as I could. She tripped, stumbled, and dropped right into my lap. Exactly what I wanted, although not in front of all my family members. The wicker chair rocked dangerously, then tilted backward as we both fell in a heap on the soft grass. I laughed, huge bursts of giggles that broke the tension.

"I'm sorry, I'm sorry," she kept saying until she realized we weren't hurt, then joined in my laughter.

"Let's get out of here," I said as I noticed some of my relatives watching. I grabbed her wrist and led her out a side gate into the front yard where it was quiet. We went over to the sidewalk and sat down on the curb.

"My name's Emilia," I said.

"I'm Louisa. But you can call me Lou."

I leaned in very close, obviously startling her, although she didn't pull back. I noticed her lips parting as if expecting me to kiss her. I didn't.

"What are you doing?" she finally asked.

"I'm trying to see if there's a resemblance or anything to my side of the family."

She laughed lightly. "You won't find one. Although you're very beautiful and I wouldn't mind looking like you, I'm not related to you."

I was so abuzz over her compliment that it took a moment to register what else she had said. "We're not relatives?"

"Well, technically maybe, though not by blood. I'm the half sister of your cousin Ricky's ex-wife."

"So, you mean there's no chance of our children being born with two heads?"

"Not a chance." Lou grinned and tilted toward me as if searching for something. My lips parted slightly but she didn't back off as I had done. Instead she looked around quickly, then cupped my chin with one hand and kissed me once, firmly. Our tongues barely touched, but the thrill of contact made my pussy contract.

"I don't usually kiss strangers," I said playfully.

"Hey, I thought we were *familia*."

I laughed, breathing in her scent, a rich woodsy freshness that intoxicated me. I felt lost in her aura and wondered if perhaps I was falling in love. It was as if I had found my true mirror image, the femme counterpart of myself reflected within her butch masculinity. She had the potential to be everything my ex, Davila, could never be or hope to be. I wanted Louisa like I had never wanted any woman. But what did she want of me? Maybe just a quick exchange of fluids and then *adios*?

"I still don't know anything about you," I said breathlessly.

"Ok, let's see. I'm twenty-eight. Single. Chicana, of course. I'm a nursing student at USC in my final year. And most important, I think I'm falling in love with you."

I kept finding it difficult to focus. Her eyes were alight with intelligence, and something more, love? A part of me was afraid of moving too quickly, afraid of being disappointed.

"Well, you don't know anything about me," I countered.

"You're wrong. Your grandmother, Frida, filled me in when I first arrived. She cornered me in the living room and told me all about you. I have to say I agree with her. I happen to think we would be perfect together, too."

I stared at her with my mouth open, which she took as a signal to move in for another kiss. This time when our lips met, our tongues had time to explore and taste each other. When we parted, both of us breathing fast, I said, "Come with me."

I took her inside, past several staring relatives in the living room, including my smiling Abuelita Frida, up the stairs, and into my bedroom. The moment I turned the lock in place, Louisa had me in her arms in a tight embrace. I secured my fingers behind the back of her neck, entangled in the thick silky hair as our lips met and parted in a lingering, wet kiss. We devoured each other's mouths while our bodies pressed together, my generous curves yielding to her leaner, firmer build. Her large hands, which I had so admired earlier, were now smoothing themselves over the contours of my heavy breasts, down the soft swell of my belly and backside. Every place she touched rocked me with desire, and I perceived a similar need building within her as well. She abruptly pulled her mouth away, gasping in an effort to catch her breath.

"I want to make love to you, Emilia. If you don't want to, we should stop now. You're driving me wild. I know this is crazy but I feel like I'll die if I don't have you right now."

I opened my eyes, my mouth still pursed in motion of a kiss. Every nerve was on fire, as if I might go up in flames ignited by nothing more than the warmth of her breath on me. Only her touch could quench the overwhelming yearning inside of me. I answered her by unbuttoning her shirt. With each button I released, I kissed the soft, warm flesh I exposed. I had been right earlier. She wasn't wearing a bra. My efforts eventually uncovered two small, pert breasts with large erect nipples. I licked each one teasingly as she panted and reached for my top, pulling it up over my head. Before she could get hold of my bra strap, I undid it myself more easily and my full breasts came tumbling into view. She buried her face in them, drawing me closer, her soft moans echoing my own. I noticed her intention of catching one of my hard nipples within her mouth, but I stopped her by backing away toward the bed. There was a look of lusty determination in her smile as she took off the rest of her clothing while I did the same.

She wrapped her arms around me and carried me to the bed, then settled in next to me. I watched the joy on her face as she scanned me from head to toe, all the while running her hand down the length of my body. My juices were overflowing by the time she reached my warm mound. Her gentle fingers spread its lips, exploring the liquid desire she found. As her fingertips brushed against my hard clit, she withdrew them and put them in her mouth, smiling at the taste. She kissed me again, hard, her lips bruising mine, as I too shared in the essence of my inner folds. Our bodies crushed against one another, burning flesh rubbing, squeezing until she ended up on top of me. My thighs opened and at last, our aching pussies converged, the heat and wetness we generated mingling together. She released my mouth to give her full attention to my breasts, pausing just briefly within the valley between them and then flicking over my right nipple with tongue and teeth until she finally drew it completely into her mouth. She sucked greedily and steadily, first one and then the other as I writhed in delight.

I reached down between her thighs and spread her warm pussy with my hand, her slippery wetness allowing my fingers to move with ease up and down her engorged clit. She was forced to release my nipples as she tried to muffle her groans by burying her face between my breasts. No longer able to stand the pleasure my hand produced, she grasped both of my wrists and held them above my head as she stared at me, her face aglow with love and longing. She kissed me once more, then traveled her way down my body, ending her journey between my pussy lips, kissing them open with her face. Her soft groans matched my own as she teased my clit with her tongue in steady, demanding flicks. I was already so wet it didn't take long before a huge orgasm erupted over me, and I grabbed a pillow to muffle my scream of release while I rode the waves of bliss.

Afterward, Louisa lay next to me, again rubbing my belly as I slowly came back to my senses. Desire and hunger still gleamed in her eyes, needs that hadn't been quenched yet. I moved on top of her, my breasts and long hair spilling onto her chest as she wrapped her arm around my waist.

"Wait, what are you doing?"

"It's your turn," I said, sliding down her body. She stopped me with shaky hands.

"You don't have to do that. I'm happy just making you happy."

I shook my head. "It's not going to work like that. Don't you see? I want you the same way you want me. To me it's not making love unless we both are satisfied."

She gave me a strange look as if she'd never thought about it that way or never had the opportunity to and slowly, reluctantly parted her legs, her pussy opening like an exotic flower. I dived in like a bee drawn to nectar as I explored her inner warmth, licking and sucking until, trembling, she strove to open them even farther apart for me. I was relentless in my pursuit of both of our pleasures, capturing her clit between my gentle teeth and strong tongue until she began to buck wildly against my mouth with her hips. Her hands clawed the sheets as she shook with the force of her orgasm's onslaught that made her call out, "Emilia, *mi amor!*"

I lapped up the last traces of her sweetness, kissed her now-reposing flower, then reclined beside her. Her eyes were closed as I searched her face, feeling a sense of contentment that I had pleased her so fully. When she opened them to meet my eyes, the depth of love I saw reflected there was almost overpowering. Louisa gathered me into her arms and we held each other tightly, both of us giving silent prayers of thanks that our years of longing had finally been assuaged.

Since that first night, we have been inseparable. It wasn't long after spring break that we moved in together in an off-campus apartment, both of us intent on finishing school. Last year we celebrated our fifth anniversary in my parents' backyard where we had first met. We decided to have a small commitment ceremony and invited the family for another reunion. Even though some members didn't show up, my parents and sisters were there. My mother insisted on calling it simply a family reunion, but Abuela Frida made sure everyone remembered what it truly was by throwing rice and singing her version of "I Love You Truly" in Spanish. It wasn't just a family gathering, but a ceremony celebrating the union of Louisa and me. For me, it was a true reunion with the lost part of myself, *mi otra mitad*, Louisa, my other half, who had been missing for so long and was found at last.

BONUS NIGHT
RADCLYFFE

W e're causing a stir," Allie murmured as she and Ryan waited for the elevator in the lobby of the Four Seasons Hotel. A woman in a floor-length gown and dripping with diamonds stared at them with an expression of distaste. Allie supposed it wasn't every day that the guests of the five-star hotel saw two women dressed in leather from head to foot. Allie ran her gaze over Ryan's long, rangy body. As always, she was dressed totally in black: tight T-shirt, studded belt, motorcycle pants and boots, and—Allie knew from personal experience—a thick black cock strapped around her lean hips. Allie smiled and jutted her hips so that her already short black leather skirt rode dangerously close to her crotch. "You are just too hot to go unnoticed."

"I think it's more likely to be you, babe." Grinning, Ryan traced an index finger down the center of Allie's chest, dipping inside the deeply scooped Lycra top to skim over her breasts. A gasp of outrage was audible behind them, and Ryan laughed.

"I love you when you misbehave, but I'm not so sure about the rest of this," Allie said as the elevator opened and they stepped into the empty car. Not surprisingly, the woman waiting with them did not get on. "What if the client isn't happy about me coming along?"

Ryan leaned her shoulder against the wall. "Trust me, I know her."

"She might just see another top as competition."

"She's hinted at things. She'll like it."

"Well, we know she likes *you*," Allie said, "since she calls you every time she's in town."

"Jealous?" Ryan teased.

"If I got jealous every time you went out on a call, I wouldn't have time for anything else." Allie leaned close and cupped Ryan's crotch. "Considering how popular you are."

Ryan murmured in approval but the tiniest bit of unease flickered in her eyes. "It's just work. You know that, right?"

"I've known since the first night we met that women pay to top you, baby," Allie said, "since that's *how* we met." She laughed. "I still can't believe Cindy and Jeri hired you to be my slave for the night. I'll never be able to repay them for *that* little present."

"Neither will I." Ryan nuzzled Allie's neck, sucking hard enough on the soft skin at the base of her throat to elicit a groan.

"I don't remember hearing you ask if you could do that," Allie said in a dangerously soft tone of voice, pressing her palm flat against Ryan's chest and pushing her back against the wall. "Have you already forgotten that tonight you'll *still* be a slave?" She edged her thigh between Ryan's and quickly drove her knee into Ryan's cock. "Hers *and* mine."

Ryan stiffened from the unexpected pain and the pleasure that followed immediately from the pressure on her clit. "I'm sorry."

"Not as sorry as you'll be if you forget your manners, especially in front of another mistress."

"She's not my mistress," Ryan whispered.

"For however long she pays you to be, she is," Allie said sternly. Then she kissed Ryan softly and stroked the thick lock of dark hair that fell over her forehead back from her face. "You have my permission to please her in any way she requires."

"Yes, Allie."

The elevator opened into a quiet hallway, dimly lit with sconces at intervals along the corridor. They made their way to the corner suite, where Ryan knocked. A moment later, the door opened and a woman with collar-length, honey blond hair regarded them silently. Allie judged her to be somewhere in her late forties or early fifties. She was Ryan's height and several inches taller than Allie, statuesque in a classic way. Her full breasts were evident beneath a black silk shirt, the top three buttons of which were open to reveal creamy cleavage. Her waist, circled by a thin black belt, was not narrow, but appeared solid beneath tailored charcoal trousers. Her hands, one of which rested loosely on the doorknob, were large and elegant.

"Ryan," she said by way of greeting before her gaze shifted to Allie and traveled slowly over her body. "I didn't realize we were having company."

"If it pleases you," Ryan said softly, "Allie will see that you are well served."

"Really," the blonde said with interest. She turned her cool blue eyes to Allie. "Is she yours, then?"

"Yes."

"May I ask why you're willing to share?"

"I've never seen her work. I'd enjoy that."

The blonde nodded thoughtfully, then held the door open wide. "I'm Deirdre. Please come in."

Deirdre led the way through the suite, to where an iced bottle of champagne stood in a gold-plated cooler beside a king-sized bed. A platter of cheese, fruit, and crackers had been placed on a nearby table, next to which was an oversized silk-upholstered chair. She indicated the food with a sweep of her arm. "Please, help yourself."

Ryan stood next to the chair while Allie poured a glass of champagne and handed it to Deirdre. Then she poured one of her own and lifted a plump ripe strawberry to her lips. She bit into the strawberry, then sipped the champagne, noting the hungry look in Deirdre's eyes as she stared at Ryan.

"Ryan, you haven't properly greeted Deirdre, have you," Allie said softly.

Wordlessly, Ryan knelt before Deirdre. "Good evening, Mistress."

Deirdre stroked Ryan's head absently, sifting dark strands of hair through her fingers as if Ryan were a favorite pet, her eyes on Allie. "Will you allow me to command her?"

Allie savored the last of the fruit, licking the juice from her lips. "Of course."

"Please make yourself comfortable," Deirdre said to Allie, nodding nearly imperceptibly toward the chair. "More champagne?"

"Thank you," Allie said as she stepped around Ryan's still form and settled into the large chair. She extended one arm along the broad armrest and held out her champagne glass for Deirdre to fill. As she sipped, she watched Ryan while Deirdre idly caressed her face and neck, judging by the rapid rise and fall of Ryan's shoulders that she was already excited. Allie knew from experience that just the thought of being dominated was enough to arouse her lover.

"She's a lovely animal, isn't she," Deirdre murmured, tilting Ryan's face up and rubbing her thumb over Ryan's mouth. "And so talented."

"Yes," Allie agreed, imagining Ryan's lips and the magic they were capable of. She saw Deirdre take a step closer, thread her fingers through Ryan's hair, and rub her crotch over Ryan's face. She knew Deirdre would feel the heat of Ryan's breath on her clit even through her trousers, and her own clit twitched as she watched. She hadn't known what to expect when Ryan had suggested that she come along, explaining that Deirdre had intimated more than once that she enjoyed watching a good scene. Allie was discovering the same was true for herself. "She has a marvelous tongue."

"Let's put it to work." Deirdre smiled lazily at Allie, then leaned down and kissed Ryan. "Help your mistress with her clothes, Ryan." When Ryan reached for Deirdre's belt, Deirdre stepped back. "Allie's."

Ryan couldn't quite hide her look of surprise as she turned toward Allie, but Allie carefully kept her expression neutral, even though her pulse jumped. She sipped her champagne as Ryan moved to kneel between her legs and slid both hands along her thighs beneath her skirt, guiding the leather up her hips. Allie had worn nothing under it and she was wet. She knew Ryan could smell her excitement and wondered if Deirdre could see the glistening evidence of her passion. Ryan caressed Allie's hips but made no further move until Allie cradled the back of Ryan's head and drew her gently forward.

"Slowly, Ryan," Deirdre said as she stepped to the side of the chair. "Let me see you lick her."

Allie caught her breath at the first touch of Ryan's warm tongue separating her swollen lips. She released Ryan's head as Deirdre's hand gently brushed hers aside. When Ryan delicately ringed the hard prominence of her clitoris, she shuddered. When the tip of Ryan's tongue teased at the hood covering her most sensitive spot, she drained her champagne glass and set it down with a trembling hand. Ryan knew her body so well that she could keep Allie on the edge of orgasm for hours, but her stomach was already fluttering and she was afraid she would come too quickly.

"Don't suck her yet," Deirdre whispered, as if hearing Allie's fears. She looked at Allie, her own lids heavy, her voice husky. "She makes you want to come right away, doesn't she?"

"Yes," Allie admitted thickly. Lids nearly closed, she rested her head back against the chair, a trembling smile on her face. Ryan's head moved in time to the steady thrusting of Allie's hips. "Especially when she flicks her...oh!" Her eyes opened wide. "She's making me come!"

"Ryan!" Deirdre said sharply, tugging Ryan's face away from Allie's sex. Allie cried out, her hand flying to her clit. Even though a stroke would push her over, she did nothing but press her thumb to the base of the rigid core, forestalling her orgasm. Her chest heaved, nipples straining against the tight Lycra shirt.

"Did I tell you to make her come?" Deirdre demanded.

"No, Mistress," Ryan gasped, her eyes dark with desire.

"Take out your cock," Deirdre ordered, walking around behind Ryan. "Quickly."

Ryan yanked open her heavy belt buckle and tugged at her fly. Then she dug inside and pulled out the long, thick length of her cock. When she started to rise, obviously expecting to enter Allie, Deirdre pushed her back down with a firm hand on her shoulder. Then Deidre knelt beside her, angling her body so she could see Allie's face. She wrapped her fingers around Ryan's cock, making an appreciative sound deep in her throat. Ryan groaned when Deirdre worked her hand quickly up and down the shaft.

Looking at Allie, Deirdre said, "Are you ready to come now?"

"God yes."

"Suck your mistress, Ryan," Deirdre ordered softly, her arm vibrating rapidly between Ryan's rigid thighs. "She wants to come in your mouth."

Ryan leaned forward, her eyes on Allie's, and closed her lips around Allie's pulsing sex.

Deirdre smiled at Allie. "I'm going to jerk her off when you come. Tell me when you're coming."

"Soon," Allie gasped.

"Is she making your clit hard?"

Allie nodded, her head twisting from side to side. "Her mouth is so damn hot."

Ryan was panting, her clenched fists pressed to Allie's thighs. Her hips jerked unevenly as Deirdre pounded the cock into her tortured clit.

"Lick me, baby," Allie sobbed. "I'm so close."

Deirdre ran her tongue over the rim of Ryan's ear. "Your mistress needs to come, Ryan. Suck her now, harder."

"Oh I'm coming!" Allie cried, grasping Ryan's head.

Deirdre pumped the cock furiously and Ryan stiffened, moaning into Allie's cunt while Allie rode her mouth. Tears leaking from her eyes, her gaze riveted to Allie's face, Ryan came against the base of the cock while Allie's clit exploded between her lips.

Allie wasn't aware of Deirdre moving until Deirdre yanked Ryan's head from between Allie's legs.

"Get your cock into her," Deirdre ordered.

Ryan, still shaking from her own climax, struggled to guide the fat head of her cock between Allie's drenched lips. The added pressure against her overly sensitive clit as she pushed inside made her stomach tighten reflexively. "I'll come again," she gasped. "Please...may I come?"

"Wait, baby," Allie said gently, bending her knees around Ryan's leather-clad thighs and setting the rhythm by pushing herself up and down Ryan's cock. "Fuck me nice and slow. You can come when I come."

"Allie..." Ryan's face was contorted, her face and hair dripping sweat. She braced both arms on the chair. "I don't think I—"

"Listen to your mistress," Deirdre commanded, her voice strained. She hurriedly kicked off her shoes and pushed down her pants and underwear. She stepped close to Ryan, one hand opening herself, exposing her fully aroused clit. "Bring me off while you fuck her."

Allie stared at Ryan's face pressed between Deirdre's trembling thighs. "Suck her clit, baby."

Deirdre cupped the back of Ryan's head and, groaning quietly, smiled shakily at Allie. "I'm going to come on her face. Soon. Are you...oh *fuck*...she's so good." Deirdre's eyes closed for a second but she forced them open. Her breath came in short pants. "Is she making you come?"

"Uh-huh." Allie arched, slid her fingers to her clit, and masturbated, the cock buried to the hilt inside her. "Coming now…so hard." She screamed, her shoulders jerking up from the chair.

Ryan thrust blindly, driven to climax by her lover's cry.

Deirdre laughed harshly, shooting off in Ryan's mouth.

When Allie opened her eyes, Ryan was slumped between her legs, her head resting on Allie's stomach. Allie caressed her damp cheek. "Okay, baby?"

"Mmm," Ryan murmured, eyes closed. "Wasted."

Allie sighed and turned her head, searching for Deirdre. She was leaning against the bed, dressed once more, lighting a cigarette. "I think we might need to pay you."

"Oh, I don't think so." Deirdre drew in the smoke and exhaled with a satisfied smile. "Ryan alone is priceless. Tonight? This was bonus night."

MARKS
RONICA BLACK

The cigarette tip glows orange against the night, hypnotizing as it grows. The sound of it burning, like crinkled paper, is a strange comfort. The wispy trail of its tail makes me cough, reminding me that I hate smoke. Yet I keep inhaling, relishing the pain and coughing it brings on. The brown liquid in my glass hits my lips, cold and aggressive. I don't usually drink either, but the raw emotions that are eating me alive have led me to open the tiny bottles from the hotel mini-bar. I blink back against the sting of tears and wonder at the cause. The smoke? The alcohol? The pain? I stare out at the night settling in around me and accept that it's all three. The sky is dark and clear, not a cloud in its wake. I look to the moon, small but proud, and wish for rain. The evening air is comfortably warm but I wish it were cold. I down more of the burning liquid and wish that everything around me would reflect how I feel. But that's not the way it works, I guess. The world doesn't care about your pain. It only cares about continuing. Am I going to be able to continue? Christ. I don't know. I know I have to, but my heart is beaten.

It started weeks ago, gradually. Just like everything does. We stopped making love. She stopped kissing me back. I would wake up in the middle of the night all alone and rise to find her on the couch. She started drinking again. They may sound like huge red blinking signs of trouble now, but when you live it, you don't see it that way. You stumble upon each sign, like a pebble in your path in the dark of night. It's small, but it still trips you up. And yet you recover quickly, regain your balance, acknowledge it almost unconsciously, and move on. You continue on your path and don't give it a second thought. Not until the next pebble comes.

Eventually there are so many pebbles, you find it difficult to walk. Then and only then do you actually take a moment and step off the path to examine what it is that's happening. That's where I am. Right now. I'm off the path, rubbing the back of my neck and examining each pebble. They're not all her, though. A good number of them are from someone else.

I caught her staring at me about a month ago, and later on caught myself staring at her. I found myself watching the way her mouth moved when she spoke and the steady, alluring pulse of the vein in her neck. I began to realize that I held my breath when she was near and then breathed deep as she walked away, wanting to capture her scent. Sounds pretty and pink and romantic, doesn't it? It probably would be if it weren't for three other tiny little things. Actually they're monumental.

One: I'm taken.

Two: She's taken.

Three: She's my boss.

But those three enormous factors can be cast aside, swatted away like mere gnats when you want what you want and need what you need.

But they always come back. They never die. They simply wait. Wait for you to open the door to your hotel room after leaving her. They slip inside with you just before you ease it closed. You're in a daze, lost in her aura as you lean back against the door. And that's when you feel it. The sudden, hard slap against your cheek. The three things hit you hard, one right after the other, inflicting a pain and guilt you never could've imagined.

You need to hear more to fully understand. Let's go back to yesterday. Back to when I was still innocently stumbling along my pebbled path.

"Good, good. That's it. Pull the tank top down a little farther in front."

The model complied and my camera raced, clicking a mile a minute. My body moved equally fast, circling her, ensuring I captured every possible angle.

"Excellent. Now lean down, rest your elbows on your knees."

My brain was flooded with the excitement of creativity. I had her now, suspended in that realm where everything was perfect. The sunlight, the sand, her eyes, her skin. She gave a cocky grin from her pose on the old wooden chair. My camera continued, every click sounding like it had its own heartbeat. Like it was alive and feeding off her image.

I was in my zone, desperate to catch the perfect collection of all that encircled her. Around us people moved about, talking, testing light, setting up props. But I ignored it all, falling down to my knees in the cool sand for a shot underneath. She sat on the chair with her legs resting apart, her elbows on her knees. The white threadbare tank top pulled and stretched downward, offering just a peek of her dark mocha areolae. I stood and stepped to the side, snapping shots of the tattoo that had been drawn on her upper arm. I grinned, loving the look, the whole package. This was my doing, the messy, textured hair, the fake tattoo, the tank top and tight men's boxer briefs. All of it. She grinned in return, liking my approval, turning her head oh so slightly as if she were flirting in a cool butch fashion.

"Yes, perfect."

I stumbled backward a bit, my camera glued to my face. My bare feet sank down into the soft mounds of sand, securing me, making me feel right at home there on the beach. And as I continued to capture the magic, I felt it. Felt *her*. I knew without turning that warm amber eyes were sprinkling their heated sweetness all over my skin. It was a feeling that was becoming all too familiar. She had arrived and was watching me.

My heart kicked alive at the realization, ignoring any ounce of reason my brain tried to summon. I took another step backward, trying my damndest to keep focused on my work. My feet kept on, unsure but determined, until they came upon something firm. I reached out, trying to gain my balance as the object beneath me moved suddenly. A strong hand gripped my forearm, steadying me. I lowered my camera and turned, searching for the source. Cal stood glaring at me, raising his feet to brush off the expensive shoes I had stumbled upon. The hand that had steadied me didn't belong to him, however. It belonged to the woman who stood at his side. The woman whose eyes had recently begun to haunt me. She stared intensely into me and I nearly lost my balance again. Alex, though, remained stoic, obviously not nearly as affected by my presence as I was by hers.

"Sorry," she offered, just as calm and collected as her gaze. "Normally I wouldn't interrupt your session, but we need to talk."

I wished I knew her well enough to venture guesses as to what was going on in her mind. But I didn't. All I knew was that her presence moved me, caused my body to react in ways I understood but did not necessarily approve of.

Alex's gaze wandered over to the model, who sat patiently waiting for me to continue, and I searched desperately for a sign of raw attraction from her but saw none. It was rumored that she was gay and seriously involved, but I didn't know for sure. We never really talked. We just watched one another. I looked to her left hand and found the simple gold band on her ring finger. I felt my face flush and glanced down to my own similarly decorated ring finger. I didn't know what it meant anymore. I knew what I wanted it to mean, but it wasn't totally up to me.

I knew why Alex and Cal were there and readied to defend myself. I gave a nod to my girl on the chair and set down my camera. "Take a break, Danny."

The young model rose hesitantly, her expression one of cautious concern for me as the two executives folded their arms. Alex spoke first.

"What's going on here?"

The color of her eyes fooled me, wanting me to believe that she was warm and passionate. Her tone, however, left me feeling chilled to the bone.

"Cal tells me that you fired Isabelle."

I eased a hand down into one of the numerous pockets of my cargo shorts and let the ocean breeze play with my hair. Even though I was shook up, I had to remain calm. "Cal was mistaken." I glanced over at him and gave him an eat-shit-and-die grin. "I don't have the authority to fire models."

"Then exactly what is it that happened? Where is Isabelle?"

I shrugged, inwardly cursing at the mention of the high-maintenance, snotty model.

"I have no idea where she is."

Of course, in reality, I had a few good ideas of where I wanted her to be. But they weren't nearly polite enough to mention.

"Why isn't she here, Gina?" Alex asked, her voice lowering with frustration at my evasiveness.

I swallowed, strangely aroused at her sultry voice. My body and mind continued to conflict over the effect she had on me. I cleared my throat and forced myself to speak. "Because I refuse to shoot her."

I saw Alex's face lighten a little, glad, it seemed, to be getting an honest answer. Her reaction caused more stirring inside. An elation of sorts. My eyes skimmed over her pressed white polo blouse and khaki shorts as I waited for her to respond.

"Why?"

An eyebrow rose over an amorous eye. She had caught me looking. *Oh shit.*

I answered quickly, trying to sound as strong as I wished I were. "She's not right for this cover."

I heard Cal scoff next to her.

"It's not your call," he spat at me. "We decide who's right—"

I took a step toward him and cut him off, my anger growing. "It *is* my call. I'm the photographer; it's my ass on the line." I was no longer concerned about keeping my cool. "I'm doing what I was told—taking this underwear account and making it appealing to the gay market."

I paused and felt a throbbing in my temple. He stood staring me down and I felt like a pit bull, ready and raring to fight but chained back just out of reach.

"What's your point, Gina?" Alex asked.

"As a gay woman, I know what's hot. And Isabelle isn't it."

"She's the hottest model in the country!" Cal let out as if I were unbelievably stupid.

"I don't care who she is," I shot back. "She looks like a fucking skeleton and her attitude sucks." I crossed my arms over my chest. "She doesn't look gay."

Alex watched me carefully while Cal threw up his hands and began to pace. "Show me what you've done."

I opened my mouth, expecting to have to explain myself, but then snapped it shut in surprise. Instead, I moved to the monitor that rested on the table behind me. I touched the screen and brought up the recent photos. First were the ones of Tony, the lean-looking Italian with a strong jaw and body. He was beautiful and more than enough to get the gay men drooling. Next were the few photos I had taken of Isabelle just before she and I both exploded into temper tantrums. I grimaced at her pale body and Easter egg–colored clothing and eagerly brought up the photos of Danny, the athletic-looking young model I had personally called in to replace Isabelle.

Alex studied the photos in silence. Cal came to stand directly beside me and began making more dramatic noises as he looked over the shots.

"These, they look, she looks…"

"Gay?" I questioned, this time with a tone that left *him* sounding completely stupid.

"Yes!" he cried out, before he could stop himself. I laughed at him and his face became livid with anger. "She's wearing men's underwear, for God's sake! This isn't what I wanted!"

I narrowed my eyes and shouted, "Lesbians aren't what straight men and the media want them to be. We aren't all skinny, we aren't all femmes. Isabelle isn't right for this shoot, and I refuse to waste my time with her."

Since Alex had no response, I began to pack up my equipment. The asshole corporate suits would once again get their way, and I wasn't about to go through it again. Too many times, too many shoots, I had rolled over and obeyed against my art. I was fed up, sick and tired of the way gay women in America were being represented on television and in magazines.

Alex spoke as I worked, ignoring the fact that I was taking apart my camera. "I like what you've done. I'll show all of the photos at the meeting with the client. It'll be up to them." She eyed me matter-of-factly, then left with Cal nipping at her heels.

I finished the shoot in a daze, thankful that at least for the time being, I still had a job. I covered my lenses when the sun went down and dragged myself back to my hotel, ready for a long hot shower and a good meal. Reverberating throughout the lobby were the unmistakable sounds of steel drums and Caribbean song. I let the music soothe my mind as I waited for the elevator. The doors opened, I stepped in and pushed the button for the fifth floor. I was alone, but just as the doors began to slide shut, Alex slipped in. She stood next to me, offering me a slight smile. The elevator rose and hummed, and we stood and stared at the ground. Inwardly, my heart increased to a maddening pace. I caught her scent, which I unconsciously compared to her eyes. Warm and fiery.

"You did great work today," she said, startling me.

I raised my eyes to find hers resting on me. My skin tingled at the softness of their caress. The sun had kissed her cheeks and arms and there appeared to be sparks in her eyes. Golden sparks. She smiled again. Easy and relaxed, a bit crooked.

"Thanks." I fought off the stutters and, strangely nervous, kept talking. "The whole Isabelle thing…"

She raised a hand and cut me off. "No need to explain. I couldn't agree with you more."

Shocked, I felt my jaw fall open. "Really?"

"Yes." The elevator stopped and the doors opened. "This your floor?"

"Yes."

She motioned with her hand, allowing me to exit first. Surprisingly, she walked next to me and continued to talk as we made our way down the hall.

"I really like what you did. I think every lesbian who sees those ads will agree. They're hot."

"You think the head honchos will go for them?"

She gave me another easy grin. "I know what they'll choose because it's my job to know. Your work is hot, tempting, edgy. They would be crazy not to run those photos of Danny in every gay magazine and newspaper there is."

I felt my face flush in response to her praise. The fact that she was older than me and was my boss only seemed to heighten my attraction to her.

She stopped and pulled out her key card. Her room was right next to mine. Again, heat rushed to my skin as that realization settled in my mind.

"Thanks," I managed, reaching in my back pocket for my own room key.

"Don't mention it. Keep up the good work."

She left me with another smile and a lingering look that skimmed over my mouth before returning to my eyes. Her door closed, and I was alone and breathless with her fading scent. I stared after her for what felt like an eternity, feeling like a fool with a mad crush—tempted to tell her but wanting to run from her.

When I finally went in, my room was dark and cool, the steady drone of the air conditioner the only sound. I made my way to my bed and sank down. Resisting the urge to let sleep wash away all my thoughts, I switched on the bedside lamp and reached for the phone. I kicked off my sandals and rested one foot over the other. I could still feel some remnants of sand, grains that were like the shards in my mind, still sticking to me, rough reminders.

I dreaded the phone call to her and hated myself for dreading it. I had lost more than just weight the past couple of months. I had lost faith and knew deep down that I had lost her. Her line rang five times before she picked up. And when she did, she sounded like she had the day before. And the day before that.

Beaten, sad, distant.

"Hello." She knew it was me. I could tell by her tone. I could also tell that she had been drinking. Had it been anyone else on the line, she would've sounded more her usual self. She always seemed to play it up for me.

"Hi." I spoke softly and lightly, already on guard and wary of her state of mind.

"Hello," she repeated, this time in a sullen greeting.

"How are you?"

"Fine." Her voice raised a pitch as she slurred.

"You don't sound fine."

Silence.

I hated this. Hated this goddamned game she always seemed to want to play.

"I miss you," I confessed, hoping it would help to open her up a bit.

"No, you don't, but that's okay."

I clenched the receiver tightly, frustrated. *Here we go again.* She was going to tell me how it was that I felt.

"I do miss you. More than you know." I missed us. The way we used to be.

She laughed. "It's okay; you don't have to do this. I know you don't miss me."

God damn it. I wanted to hurl the phone across the room. I was so sick and tired of this. "Don't tell me how I feel."

She paused a moment, sighing. "Look, you need to just forget about me. Just stop thinking about me."

"Baby, listen to me, please. I love you. Can't you just accept that?" My voice quaked with emotion. She was killing me inside. Slowly and surely.

"I don't disbelieve that you think that you love me."

That was it. That was her response.

Oh God. I collapsed against the bed, the phone clutched to my chest. My body shook with quiet sobs. I couldn't do this anymore. I just couldn't. I heard her continuing on from the receiver, oblivious that I wasn't listening. I didn't know what to do. How to feel. I only knew that I could no longer bang my head against the wall just to convince her that I loved her. Not when she wasn't willing to accept it. It was useless.

I rose up and tentatively placed the phone to my ear. She seemed to hear my shaky breaths, the hitching in my throat.

"I don't know what to do," I confessed.

"Yes, you do."

She didn't slur those last few words; in fact, she sounded assured and calm. I hung up. It hurt. Hurt so badly. I stood and hastily wiped the wetness from my face, angry and torn. It was the first time I had allowed these feelings to manifest. I was finally ready to let them out after weeks of pushing them down, trying desperately to convince her.

I walked into the bathroom and stripped off my clothes. I turned the water on as hot as I could stand it. I stepped in and let it assault my skin, punishing the sand and sun from my body but doing little to erase her words, her final surrender. It beat down on me, just like her mood, steady and hard and painful. And I let it. Let it until it turned icy and cold.

When I emerged I grabbed a towel and patted my tender skin dry, eyeing myself in the mirror. The woman there appeared wounded, her eyes deep and lost. My throat tightened and I knew I had to get out of there. I couldn't stand to look at her.

I dressed quickly, jeans and a tank top. I said fuck it to the bra and headed out with my nipples hard little stones under the tight cotton. The air outside felt cool and fresh and I welcomed it as I hailed a cab. I rode in silence and paid the driver extra for allowing me to. The sea breeze kicked up as I made my way to the door. I could already hear the music, loud, thumping, wild. Several laughing men lingered around the entrance and they openly eyed me as I went inside. The bartender glanced at me and then did a double take as he poured a shot of whiskey for someone else. Sensing but ignoring the questions in his eyes, I ordered.

"Give me two of those."

Slowly he retrieved two more shot glasses and turned them right side up. "You know where you are?"

"Yes."

My answer wasn't good enough, though. After handing another patron and me our drinks, he motioned with his hands.

"These are all men here."

I downed the burning liquid. "You're very observant."

He wasn't impressed. "There's no women here, honey."

I downed the other shot, squeezed my eyes shut at its strength, and said, "There is now."

I left him and his gender problem behind and walked right onto the crowded dance floor. I stood and stared up into the searching lights, allowing the warm, muggy air to lull me. Slowly, I began to move. The bass shook me to my bones and the thump rattled in my chest. It moved me. In every way possible. And then, like a miracle, I began to feel free.

I melted into the music and into those around me. We were all one, a slave to the beat, pulsing and gyrating, hips brushing hips, breath kissing breath. I raised my arms and felt strong hands on my waist. A man moved in front of me, facing me with a grin. He was smaller than me and shirtless, with a playfulness in his eyes.

"I spy something different."

Then the hands from behind gave way and another voice, this one in my ear, said, "Something with tits."

I felt him move and watched as he rounded me to join his shirtless companion, tossing an arm around him.

"You are hot, though," he continued, stroking his chin as he looked me up and down. "Okay, you can stay!"

The song changed, mixing slowly but surely into a new rhythm. The guys continued to dance around me and we moved together, like a well-oiled machine. They touched me and I touched them. It wasn't sexual. It was the beast of the beat. Our bodies glistened and pumped. I felt connected, I felt wanted, I felt good. My eyes drifted closed as my arms raised over my head. I felt hands on my torso, inching up under my tank top but stopping below my breasts. I was sexy, yet I was safe.

It was wonderful. I opened my eyes and focused through the thick haze of grinding, pulsing bodies. I blinked. Once, then twice.

I stopped moving. My breath hissed from my chest. Alex. She was there. Standing along the back wall. Watching me. My body tensed at her stare, my heart pounded with sudden need. Oh God. I wanted her, wanted her not only to watch, but to touch, to put her mouth on me. I swallowed hard and did the only thing I could do. I danced.

With my eyes fastened to hers, I slithered and pulsed, lacing my hands over my partner's as he glided his over my exposed torso. I pretended he was her and I showed her what it would be like if he were. I tilted my head back in pleasure and writhed beneath his touch. I saw her jaw clench with intent and, wanting more of that from her, I reached out and pulled the small man in front of me closer. I ran my hands deliberately over his moist chest and abdomen, stroking him as if he were her. They moved into me, one from behind, one in front. We rubbed and touched and breathed. I watched her watching me. I saw her eyes flash with a molten amber desire. She was turned on. Dangerously so.

She pushed off from the wall and strode closer, skirting the dance floor. She stalked slowly, like a deliberate predator, watching me as she moved, a sleek black huntress in dark jeans and black sleeveless shirt. She circled us from a distance and I followed her, turning, drawn to her eyes, drawn to her desire. She neared the waving chain wall that led to another room. She stood staring at me. Waiting for me.

Hypnotized, I left my partners and headed for her. I made my way through scores of dancers, my sights trained firmly ahead, holding her to me like the force field of a magnet. People around us parted ways, the music grew foggy and distant, time seemed to slow. I reached for her as I drew closer. I cupped her fiercely warm face and slid into her. My mouth found hers with a hunger I had never experienced before. I plunged into her, over and over, claiming all that she gave me. She felt hot and slick and hungry. Her fingers tangled in my hair, holding me to her. Her tongue swirled around mine aggressively and I heard her groan with an insatiable desire. Her body rubbed up against mine and she tugged my head back. When our lips parted, mine tingled, full with excited blood.

"This way," she breathed, her eyes flashing with yearning.

She pulled me along after her, her free arm shoving back the dangling chains. We hurried, passing numerous shadowy figures, all of them locked in various shapes of embrace. We reached the far wall and she turned, yanking me to her. Immediately, I grabbed her hands and pressed them up against the wall. I kissed her just as aggressively, hard and fast, long and wet. She groaned again as I pressed into her, holding her captive. Desperate for more of her, I tore my mouth from hers and attacked her neck. I felt her flinch under my teeth and she whispered raggedly in my ear.

"Don't leave any marks."

The fire inside me flared dangerously. The fact that she belonged to another only heightened my desire. The rage and hurt from my own relationship pounded through me, turning me into a hungry, ravenous being. I needed her, needed this. I kissed her again, determined and driven to have her. She kissed me back, battling for dominance. I was stronger and hell-bent on getting my way. I craved her skin and assaulted her neck like a thirsty creature of the night. She squirmed beneath me and freed her hands from mine. She pulled on my head, breathing again about marks. But I refused to hear her and kept on, again sucking her.

She tasted so good. Hot and sweet. I ran my hands up under her shirt and squeezed the warm weight of her breasts. She arched into me, still tugging on my hair. I found her nipples and pinched. She cried out and then clenched her teeth just before she jerked me in for another heated kiss. As our tongues dueled, I reached down to her jeans and quickly unbuttoned the fly. She stole her mouth from mine as I shoved the denim down over her hips.

"Hurry. Oh God, hurry." Her breath tickled my neck.

Other voices and soft cries floated to us, encouraging. She began to buck in their rhythm, desperate for the pleasures they felt. With her pants pulled halfway down and her demands in my ear, I reached out and cupped her layered flesh through her panties, rubbing the heel of my hand against her shaft. She tensed powerfully and bit into my shoulder. I felt her wet heat and felt my own crotch flood with excitement. She was so incredibly hot, and alive, and ready. I had to have more. Had to feel more. She wanted it too.

I tore down her underwear and slammed her back harder against the wall. She looked into my eyes like a desperate, dying creature.

"Make me come," she insisted. "Now."

She leaned forward slightly and teased my lower lip with her teeth as she spoke. "Hurry, Gina."

A low moan came from within me. I kissed her forcefully as my hand found her slick, hot core. She shuddered and cried into my mouth as my fingers edged her blood-filled clitoris, stroking up and down the sides, playing it just right. She turned her head, desperate for the breaths that weren't coming. I moved my hand lower, gathered the warm silk pooled at her hole and spread it over and around her growing cleft.

I rubbed and stroked her, forcing the pleasure to build. She quivered at the direct contact and I knew she couldn't take much more. With my fingers adequately lubricated with her desire, I stopped the sensual assault and pushed up into her, nearly lifting her off her feet. Her eyes flew open, wide with intense pleasure. A hoarse gasp escaped her as I braced myself to take her weight. She hugged my shoulders tightly as I lifted and supported her left leg, holding her open to me. Her body bore down on me, encasing my fingers, swallowing them up inside. I pumped her slowly at first, long and deep, loving the feel of her all wet and tight. She made low, throaty noises and continued to close her eyes tightly and then open them in surprise as each wave of ecstasy washed through her. Tiny beads of sweat formed on her upper lip, the pleasure I was milking coming to the surface.

"Please," she managed to say. "Fuck me."

Her eyes held mine and I saw the erotic haze cloud her pupils. My insides burned brighter with white-hot heat and I pumped her shorter, harder, faster. She tossed her head back and strained her neck.

"Mmm. Mmm."

She couldn't speak, but I didn't need her to. My fingers fed her, filled her, fucked her. I pushed my thumb forward and found her twitching clit. Her body tightened as my hand performed its incredible magic.

I kissed her and found that she was barely able to kiss me back. I looked into her face and wanted to get lost in her. I wanted to crawl back down inside her with every inhalation she took, wanted to curl up in the warm confines of her soul. She seemed to sense this and focused on me. We spoke. We shared. We welcomed.

And then she came.

Her soul bled into mine and we swam there in that warm tide of raw existence for what felt like an eternity. Her body tensed and then shook, her eyes clenched and then devoured, her mouth moved and then silenced. Eventually she let out a long sigh and fell limp against me. I moved cautiously and slid my fingers out of her tight, pulsing crevice. I stood back and watched as she dressed herself. My hand felt heavy and stiff and I opened and closed it, feeling the sticky wet of her against my skin. She buttoned her fly and gazed at me. I expected her to speak but was surprised and startled when she grabbed my neck and pulled me to her for a kiss.

It was softer than before, but more deliberate. Her full lips sucked mine, her tongue rimming them, teasing them. And then, in an instant, she turned my body and shoved me up against the wall. Her hands pressed into my chest, ensuring I wouldn't escape. She slowly licked her lips and lowered her hands. I reached for her wrists, not sure I was ready for what was in her hungry eyes. It would be a huge exposure on my part. And the final blow to my already sinking relationship.

She seemed to sense this, sensed how close I was to the edge. She fought me gently, encouraging me, and tugged open my jeans with a mischievous laugh.

She dropped to her knees and held me firm by my pants. Inch by inch they went, exposing the heated skin of my thighs. Her breath sent shock waves of lust up my spine, causing me to gasp and grab hold of her head. I held her back, unable to take it and unsure of my desire. Fucking her was one thing, but letting her fuck me was another. My head swam in a sea of confusion, lust, and betrayal. Her fiery eyes looked up into me, slowly baking into my conscience, sweetening it, warming it, seducing it with pleasurable promises.

My hand fell to my side, useless. My other remained in her hair as she leaned closer to my center. I watched her lower her gaze and extend her tongue. She worked her way up my thighs to my panties and I nearly collapsed as my knees buckled from the warm, velvety caress. She braced my hips with her hands and moaned as she licked her way to the soaking cotton that held my flesh. Her tongue flattened against the fabric of the panties, stroking me up and down with just enough pressure to make me buck. My hand tightened in her hair. Suddenly I didn't think I could continue. I heard someone climax not far from where we were. It sounded wild and low, like a howling animal.

"I...I can't," I rasped. This wasn't what I really wanted. This wasn't where I wanted to be. And she, she wasn't who I wanted.

She looked up at me. "Yes, you can. I'll make sure you can."

She started to pull my panties down but I stopped her, thinking somehow that if they remained, I would be okay, things would be okay.

She studied me a moment, as if trying to understand. Then she moved into me again, this time rimming her tongue under the seams of my panties. I swallowed hard and tilted my head as the pleasure raced up through me. She teased my clit by stretching her tongue to lightly skim it and then pulled away back to the edge. I shivered as she traced all around me, over and over, shooting for my clit in quick, torturous movements. Unknowingly, I rocked my hips into her, my body growing desperate for more.

She conceded and pressed her face into me, her mouth and tongue alive and feeding, sucking me through my panties. I cried out and held her head to me. The pleasure was great but not nearly enough. It was killing me, and suddenly I was reminded of the desperate look in her eyes just moments ago. I was now feeling the intensity she had felt. She sucked me harder, groaning into me. I groaned back, panting, dying. It wasn't enough, dear God it wasn't enough. And I had to have it.

Hastily and nearly trembling, I moved my hand from her hair and tugged at the side of my underwear, exposing my craving, starving flesh. She stopped long enough to let me and then refastened onto me. She fed my aching flesh its pleasure and then fed herself with the reward of my nectar. My mouth fell open and sounds escaped me as the pleasure intensified. I shoved into her, loving it, loving every last bit of it.

I looked down at her head and watched it bob back and forth, my meat held firm between her powerful lips. I came as I watched her work me. My legs stiffened and I pushed myself into her forcefully, insisting she take all of me. She held me in her mouth for ages, swirling her tongue around the captured flesh. I clung to her head and shuddered, my breath coming out in short groaning grunts.

"Fuck," I managed, my eyes closed.

"Mmm," she moaned.

I stilled as the last bolt of satisfaction shot through me, electrifying every cell. My legs trembled and my heart pounded in my ears. I felt her release me and then lick me long and hard with her flattened tongue. I twitched and groaned and nearly fell, unable to take any more. I heard her laugh, but it was faded and distant. My limp body leaned against the wall as my mind began to settle. When I opened my eyes she was standing before me, that sexy crooked grin on her face, my come glistening on her chin. She reached down and gently grasped my jeans and brought them up. My hands came to life and I managed to button them without assistance.

She was watching me curiously, seeming to enjoy the way I was trying to pull myself together.

"That was hot," she said, leaning into me, nipping at my ear.

"Yes," I agreed, feeling a strange, lethargic calm come over me. "Yes, it was."

We left right after that and shared a silent cab ride back to the hotel. She took my face in her hands and kissed me long and tender in the elevator. It lasted the whole way up. We said good night in front of our separate rooms. I let myself in. I didn't bother with the lights. I just threw myself down on the bed and fell fast asleep.

When I woke in the morning I didn't know where I was. I had been dreaming I was at home and in her arms and everything was okay. Just like it used to be. I sat up and turned on the bedside lamp and let my heavy head fall into my hands. I felt guilt, cold and heavy. It stabbed me, plunged into my heart sharply. I wanted her, wanted us. Eventually I sat down and lifted the phone. I dialed her number but she didn't answer. I left her messages pleading with her to talk to me, insisting that we could work it out somehow, but got no response. I paced. Then I called our voice mail and typed in our code. There were no messages to retrieve. She had heard them all.

I dropped the receiver and let it hang itself an inch from the floor. I sat there for hours, staring at the sunlight that was desperate and bright around the pulled-tight curtains. I finally rose and stood like a zombie in a shower that was cold but that I couldn't manage to feel.

And that's what brings me to the here and now. This is why I'm smoking the cigarettes that I don't want, wishing for rain when there isn't a cloud in the sky. I'm in pain and wanting, *needing* for everything around me to reflect that. But it doesn't. The world keeps on turning, mocking my pain, knowing but not caring.

I shared my story because I had hoped it would help, but now I just feel worse. Now I am all alone and torn and hurt. And exposed. Do you care? I doubt it. We all have problems and you're probably saying that I deserve this pain. I betrayed myself and my love.

I agree. Maybe I do deserve this.

A soft knock calls from my door. I rise and walk slowly to it. The peephole shows me it's Alex. I breathe deep, my insides still in painful turmoil. I open the door and lean forward to peek out.

"Hi." She's grinning at me and she looks fresh and alive and alluring. Her scent sends my beaten heart racing.

"Hi." I'm unable to smile back and my face feels like stone.

She reaches up and brushes my cheek and instantly I feel hot blood surge some life back into it.

Now for those of you who already dislike me, this won't come as a surprise. But for those of you who have yet to make up your mind or are holding out hope for me, this will seal the deal. Because despite my raging turmoil, devastating guilt, and inner determination to get back what I lost, I find myself pushing the door open the rest of the way. I stand still and watch in silence as she enters, her hand trailing down my chest as she walks past me. She turns then in front of the bed and raises her hands to her neck.

"There aren't any marks, are there?"

I shove the door closed behind me and walk with singular intent up to her.

"No, there aren't any marks," I reassure her, my breath quickening in response to my need.

But there will be this time.

KNOCKING BOOTS
EVECHO

```
One Day Only
"Butchin' Back"
B/Bs and Friends
UNCENSORED
Come as you are
```

Boon nervously wiped her nose, scratched her eyebrow, then dragged her fingers through her spiky hair and on down to play over the soft fuzz at the back of her neck. Her hairline was neat and freshly shorn that morning, something she loved to touch or have someone pet, usually someone like the cute femme sitting across from her who was devouring a falafel salad and sipping on a mango smoothie.

Her leg started bouncing faster in an effort to bleed off the butterflies building up in her stomach. She smiled tightly at her date but her mind was preoccupied with nervousness and impatience. Boon swapped the vibrant wagging to her other leg, slower this time.

It seemed the lunch dragged interminably, but when Boon picked up the bill, her watch showed that it was only three p.m. *Much too early, isn't it?*

She pulled out her battered wallet, which was linked to her belt loop by a thin chain. Inside was a card that announced the party she had been waiting for, the one slated for one day only—today. It was a closed-door affair for butches at the new bathhouse, and Boon had screwed up her courage to go. She stared unseeing at the card lying squashed among scraps of paper and phone numbers in her wallet. For the first time since she came out, Boon was about to admit to liking another kind of woman.

"Yeah, later, babe," she said, winking at the girl who had scored a free meal from her. As soon as they parted, Boon began walking to her destination. Her feet stomped on the pavement, past the adult and record shops, and past the urbanwear stores where she bought half her clothes. She looked at the women headed in the same direction, wondering if she would meet them there.

Naked! I'm going to a bathhouse for a naked butch party! she thought giddily. Immediately, she stopped to inspect her attire of ragged denim shorts, dykey-T and boots, reflected in a shop window. *Will they let me in?* She knew that she appeared underage, what with her androgynous boi looks, but so did most of the club scene. Except that this wasn't a dance club. Boon trembled at the possibilities of what might happen today.

I have to know. No one else could come with her. She had picked up the flyer and hidden it in her pocket because she wasn't confident that her mates would understand. They were all young, and although raucously open about their sexuality, Boon didn't think they would be that open with her if they knew about her secret fantasy.

The venue's frontage appeared like a closed shop. It was discreetly painted dark brown with the lot number stenciled in white on a side panel. There were a few women milling outside, smoking and chatting. Boon eyed a few of the obvious patrons; one had white crew-cut hair and a sleeveless denim jacket that showed her thick arms and big chest, and another, dressed in a leather body suit, was parking her bike. Boon walked straight through the loose crowd, keeping her eyes forward even as she felt theirs checking her out. Her skin prickled and she was very aware of her street hip clothes—her legs were bare from mid-knee to ankle and her top felt very thin. Her denim shorts were suddenly rough and scratchy, and her boots clompy. Boon felt as nervous as an imposter, or a virgin.

The bouncer at the door exchanged her ticket for a white wristband before letting her enter. Inside, the foyer was comfortably lit for business. Boon got into the queue so she could nonchalantly peruse the room without being too obvious. There were at least twenty hot women in the lobby distracting her. For one day a month, the whole building was women's space, but today was a special-themed event. Boon was aware that by standing in view, she was putting herself on display.

When it was her turn at the counter, she was given a transparent

packet containing information and safe sex kits. After a quick laser scan
of her wristlet, a locker key was provided. When asked, Boon nodded
and paid $10 for two towels and shower gel.

"There's information and a map of the venue inside this bag. Lube
and rubbers are available on every floor and in the play areas. If you're
not sure what to do or what to use, ask the guides who will be patrolling
the venue. They're the ones in the fluoro green shirts you can see in
the dark." Boon's head was reeling from the instructions. The woman
stopped talking when she saw the lost look on Boon's face. Gently, she
smiled and asked, "First time at a play party?"

Boon nodded, she was so embarrassed. The brown-haired butch
with the happy eyes was being so kind. She swallowed. "Yes."

"You'll be fine." A locker key was looped into Boon's wristband.
"You can come out anytime to the chill-out area on the first floor where
nothing happens. There, you can rest and eat, or watch the movies and
sports on the big screen."

The greeter then pressed on Boon's hand and assured her, "You
can always say no. Just be sure where you're at." She winked. "Rules
are posted everywhere and the guides are happy to help, just don't try
to get them frisky—they have a job to do."

Boon smiled at that, feeling slightly better. Then they went over
the map together before Boon headed through the turnstile for the
lockers. The glass tunnel to the showers and lockers afforded a view
of the gym. There were quite a few women there, mainly around the
free weights. Boon wondered if the Spandex-clad muscular women
would be interested in her small, slim self. One of the rules was "no
sex in the gym," as it was unsafe. Looking at the sweat running down
bulging limbs, Boon could imagine that other fluids on the equipment
and benches might cause injury.

Rows of lockers and benches in the changing room were set out
for utility, but the choice of a closed or open shower was for pleasure
as well as cleanliness. Boon was suddenly thrown into nude company,
although not all the women were naked—most were partially clothed.
The ruling attire seemed to be towels, sport bras, singlets, or shorts.
Boon tried not to stare but she gloried in the variety of women there for
a single purpose.

She found her locker and started putting her stuff away, but
hesitated at her clothes. She hadn't brought any spare—she wasn't even

wearing underwear! Taking a deep breath, Boon looked around and saw short-haired women dressing and undressing, one had her ass slapped as she was slipping on a harness, and a couple of bois walked around boldly wearing only tight Jockey shorts. Swiftly, before she could think about it, Boon yanked off her top and chucked it into her locker before slamming the door shut, only to open it again to grab a safe sex kit. Then she strolled casually around the back to the showers.

By the time she left the area, her nipples were tightly raised and she was slightly wet from watching women washing themselves, a few deliberately alone and others making out under the open showers. She had been surprised to see some naked couples kissing and fondling each other gently while others were more intent; the prison shower scene she had expected from watching bad porn was not there at all.

Exiting the bright section, Boon turned a corner and saw a couple kissing. A stout brunette butch was holding a lean blonde, possessively running her hands up and down her sides as they kissed hungrily. They were both wearing jeans and polo shirts with the bathhouse's logo, but the blonde had one hand inside the other's fly. Boon was surprised, until the brunette opened a door marked "Manager" and they both stumbled inside.

Turned on now, Boon wandered up a floor. She knew from the map that there were play areas, saunas, a pool, and private rooms where she could see more of what she wanted, or participate. Her nervousness was all but gone, replaced by a low-level flame in her gut. Her breathing was becoming steadily heavier as she caught glimpses and heard unmistakable sounds from the rooms she passed.

The farther inside she went, the darker it got, until she came to a curtained area that separated an almost pitch black section from the rest of the floor. The guide nodded to her as she slipped past the curtain— into darkness filled with slurping, sucking sighs, and moans that gave away the purpose of the room. It was the sex space for anonymous encounters known as the Back Room.

No sooner had Boon walked in when she felt hands on her bare torso. One pair was joined by another; a body rubbed against her back, and lips descended on her shoulders and neck. Her breasts were covered and played with, the hands switching and flowing all over her body, front and back. Boon was drowning in the acute awareness of sensation that blindness brings. She felt a tug and her shorts being unbuttoned even as a large hand covered her wet crotch and squeezed her through the denim. Reaching back, Boon grabbed long hair, and it suddenly confused her.

"No," Boon gasped. She stopped the hands at her waist. *Why did I stop them? Long hair, what's wrong with long hair?* It reminded Boon of femmes, and that struck her wrong somehow.

"No?" a deep voice rumbled into her ear. "You sure?"

The woman behind ground her bulge into Boon's ass and that confused her even more. Boon hadn't been prepared for a packing femme.

The hands lifted off and she felt the coolness of two departing bodies. Alive in the darkness, she could see wristbands floating eerily in motion. The intrusive light of the exit signs barely touched the occupants of the room, but she could hear them and feel the heat. She could smell the arousal in the room, and she almost fell on her knees to search for a source. Instead, she turned around, saw the slit in the curtain, and rushed out into cool air that washed over her sweating body.

Hurrying to the nearby washrooms, she quickly chose the first stall inside. The short swinging doors didn't have locks, but Boon didn't notice. She sat on the toilet, cradling her head. She hadn't been prepared for the sexual overload of the Back Room, but the effect it had had on her was apparent. The coldness of the tiles slithered up her bare back as she leaned backward and slipped her hand into her unbuttoned shorts. She was slick wet. Boon closed her eyes and touched herself to the memory of the room she had just left.

The creak of door hinges didn't break her concentration until she felt the presence of another. Boon opened her heavy-lidded eyes to see an Amazon inside her cubicle. The woman was massively buff, square-jawed, and had long blond hair in a ponytail trailing on her collarbone. She was also palming the cock that was poking out of her boxers as she stared hungrily at Boon. They were both naked from the waist up.

Long hair! Boon fell to her knees when she realized who it was she had felt in the Back Room. Thank God.

The muscular woman moved two steps forward and offered Boon her cock. Faced with the object of her fantasies, Boon parted her lips in anticipation. She rubbed herself harder, almost delirious for her first taste of girlcock. The blonde pumped her tool in her fist slowly, teasingly, watching Boon tremble, fixated on her hand movements. Boon's eyes glazed over with desperation as the cock slapped her face lightly but was kept just out of reach of her chasing mouth. She seized the pale shaft in a light grip and stretched out her tongue to taste it. The silicone toy was smooth but for its molded ridges. The Amazon held the cock still at the base, dipped a finger inside herself, and smeared her wetness on the head just before Boon engulfed it in her mouth. Boon tasted the slight saltiness, and she relaxed her throat muscles to let the cock plunge in, slowly breathing through her nose and suppressing her gag reflex. Now she could smell the heady muskiness when her nose touched the blonde's groin. Boon sucked cock like it was the best thing she ever ate.

To the groans of the butch, she took the light thrusts in her mouth, one hand dropping to touch herself. The standing woman gently rubbed Boon's hair, even the fuzz at her nape, while Boon acquainted herself with the girth and length of her tool. Eventually the butch drew it out and helped Boon stand up. Boon's face was red and saliva glistened on her cheek. They kissed greedily. Boon almost swooned at the feel of the hard body and strong arms enfolding her, an aggressive tongue already plunging in and curling in her mouth. This time, she didn't resist when her shorts were dropped. Big hands covered her buttocks and squeezed, spreading the cheeks for thick fingers to snake in.

Boon was dizzy with desire as she was turned to face the stall wall. The big butch took Boon's hands and placed them at the top of the short partition, covering them there with her own. She kissed and placed nips all over Boon's arms, shoulders, and upper back. Her hips were mock thrusting, sliding the dildo between Boon's buttocks. Boon whimpered with need, knowingly preparing herself for what she wanted. Her ass was humping back but she couldn't move much as the blonde had her trapped tight against the wall.

She failed to notice the glory hole at crotch level until she felt a light touch on her pussy. Someone on the other side of the wall spread her cuntlips and latched onto her clit. The hot mouth sucking her clit into range of a flicking tongue was a new distraction, and Boon moaned loudly. The hard body immobilizing her against the wall, but making her accessible to an anonymous licker, was a restraint on her movements but not her rising response. The cock slid into her easily from behind, and it continued to slide in and out effortlessly. The controlled movements of the woman fucking her and her own juices were easing the dildo's passage. Boon moaned and writhed, trying to have more of both—fucked from the back and eaten out in front. But if she moved as she wanted, she would lose one or the other, so she remained in place, pinned as much by her desire as by the conspiring actions of her lovers.

Then, notching up a gear, the butch started banging her harder, hard enough to shake the stall wall, and the person eating her out changed her tongue swipes. They kept up the rhythm even when Boon cried out, coming again and again, not stopping until they were satisfied. Multiple orgasms later, Boon slumped back totally on the butch behind her, who lightly strummed her erect nipples and nuzzled her ear. Boon's legs were shaking.

"Yes?" the Amazon chuckled.

Boon nodded, her mouth too dry for speech. Her clit was still pulsing and her inner thighs warm.

The butch kissed her and said quietly, "Thanks." Then she gently sat Boon down on the toilet and left.

Boon didn't know how long she stayed in the stall, but an insistent sound from outside seeped into her attention. She leaned forward and peered through the glory hole to see two women fucking on a sink. One of them was balanced on the basin, her knees held up until her booted feet were almost at ear height. She was spread open for the tall woman fisting her. The sight of the red vulva receiving the hand sunk up to the forearm, two bald women in boots fucking each other's brains out, almost made Boon groan out loud as her clit throbbed to life. She cupped herself as if to contain the flowing abundance the view caused. Boon watched the coupling and stroked herself. The one receiving the hand was chanting, "Yeah, yeah, fuck, yeah," while the other woman's reflection in the mirror revealed her delight. Suddenly, the one on the sink shrieked her orgasm and both women grimaced at the clutch of vaginal muscles. They stopped moving to kiss and touch each other's faces tenderly. Then Boon saw the tall woman's arm slowly rotate and pump slightly and her other hand fall on her lover's clit. Their murmurs started up, but Boon stepped into her shorts and quickly slipped out of the washroom to leave them some privacy.

As Boon descended the back stairs, the smell of chlorine rose up to let her know she was nearing the indoor pool. She followed the sounds of splashing and echoing voices to the largest play area in the house. Under the cooperative natural light, it was full on with butches and bois engaged in fucking, licking, jacking, watching, and playing in the water. Swimming wasn't a prescribed activity.

Boon shed her shorts and boots and walked the length of the pool. She had left her inhibitions with her clothes and now she openly prowled for any takers.

She made eyes with a thin boi who was watching her. With an incline of her head, she followed the boi to a shallow alcove within sight and sound of the whole area. Boon pushed aside towels and shoes before sitting open-legged on the stone bench. The boi immediately knelt between her ankles. Boon could not take her eyes from the orgy around her. She was so turned on by the unbridled display of butch love that she could feel her juices seeping out of her crumpled pussy lips.

The boi lifted Boon's left foot and cleaned it with her tongue, then moved up to perform cunnilingus between Boon's toes. Boon watched, fascinated. Experimentally, she moved her other foot under the boi and rubbed the distended clit with her big toe. The boi's thighs spread farther apart, inviting Boon inside. Boon poked her lower digits into the moist crevice but brought them out to pedal the boi's clit when it became clear that she was jacking off on Boon's foot. The boi's squatting position opened her up easily, and she held onto Boon's leg as she skewered herself on Boon's foot. Boon couldn't believe that she was fucking someone with her foot.

The boi was moving energetically, faster and faster she bounced until she shuddered and creamed Boon's foot completely. Sighing with a small smile, she dropped to the floor and proceeded to lick the appendage clean.

A naked woman, who had apparently been watching, came up and quietly spoke to the boi. As if reprimanded, the boi moved off with her eyes lowered. The woman, Boon thought in awe, was a perfectly sculpted female David, right up to her thick curly hair. She wasn't lean or chunky or as buff as the Amazon earlier, but her abs were tight and her athletic upper body vee-d to a slim waist. Boon had never seen a more beautiful butch. There were muscles showing in all the right places on this woman's body, and when she placed an arm on the bench, Boon had a ridiculous urge to worship it.

The butch woman smiled and sat next to Boon, watching Boon drool over her body. She shifted to lie half propped against one side of the alcove and opened her legs, placing one on the floor and the other on the bench. She ran her hand over her pussy, spreading it open in invitation. Two fingers pressed downward to raise her stiff clit.

Boon didn't wait. Her mouth was already watering at the sight of the Adona and to be able to taste her pleasure sent her own clit swelling up.

Boon took the opportunity to slide her hands over the tense abs bunched in position. Her fingers bumped over cakes of muscle, soft and hard impressions that mesmerized her, making her senses scream for more contact with the incredible body.

A hand to the back of her head firmly guided Boon's face to the butch's pussy. She wasted no time diving in, eager to please and hungry for a taste. The woman placed one arm behind her own head and watched Boon eat her out. Her lips parted as her tongue hung out and her breath turned into excited pants. She kept her hand on Boon's head, stroking her hair at first, then using it to direct the pressure. The pleased smile on her face flickered with each lick and suck at the right spot.

Boon used every technique she knew to raise the clit higher into her mouth without making the woman come. She was getting off on servicing the butch and having the gorgeous woman naked in her face. When someone rubbed her ass and stroked her back, Boon tried to twist round to see who was behind her, but the hand on her head gripped her firmly in place. Someone strong lifted her ass and one of her legs onto the bench. Boon whimpered when a thick cock was pushed into her cunt. The butch in front of her suddenly captured her wrists in one big hand and pushed her face back to the job she had abandoned when the cock took her by surprise. The hands roaming her ass were now clasped to her hips and leveraging the cock plowing into her.

Boon tried to concentrate on the erect clit in her mouth, but the woman behind her really knew how to fuck. All three started moving to an urgent rhythm, their grunts and labored breaths catching the attention of the other women in the hall. The thrusts into Boon were short and rapid now. Sensing that the choreographed coming would be dependent on her as the link, Boon sucked hard on the clit and mercilessly tongue-lashed it. She wanted both butches to come in or on her. The reclining woman held Boon's head tight as she roared at her looming orgasm and humped her pussy into Boon's mouth. Fingers found Boon's clit and jacked her off just as the woman behind her drove her cock harder into Boon, coming and jerking with loud groans.

When the threesome finally stopped moving, whistles and applause pierced the pool room. Boon was trembling from the experience, but the grin never left her face. Exhausted, she turned on her side, barely aware when someone covered her with a warm towel, and fell asleep happy.

CONTRIBUTORS

KIM BALDWIN has published three novels with Bold Strokes Books: *Hunter's Pursuit*, a finalist for a Golden Crown Literary Society Award in 2005, *Force of Nature*, and the new romance *Whitewater Rendezvous*. A former journalist, Kim lives with her partner in Michigan. She is currently at work on her fourth novel, *Flight Risk*

ASHLEY BARTLETT is a young writer obsessed with literature from the womb. Although she has tried, Ashley could not escape literary pursuits if she wanted; her constant imagination often steals reality and begs to be written. She lives in Sacramento, CA with the love of her life, Megan.

RONICA BLACK, author of *In Too Deep*, lives in the desert Southwest where she enjoys writing, drawing and photography. She lives to create but also cherishes the time spent with family and friends as well as hiking with her dogs and caring for animals. Her second book, *Wild Abandon*, is now available from Bold Strokes Books.

CHEYENNE BLUE (www.cheyenneblue.com) combines her two passions in life and writes travel guides and erotica. Her works appear in *Best Women's Erotica*, *Playgirl*, *Mammoth Best New Erotica*, *Best Lesbian Erotica*, and *Best Lesbian Love Stories*, and her travel guides have been jammed into many glove boxes underneath the chocolate wrappers.

GUN BROOKE resides in the countryside in Sweden with her family, which includes the newest member, Jarmo the Dog. She writes romance, science fiction, and short stories full time, and feels like she's living her dream. Life with family and friends, watching movies, reading, listening to music and radio, and the concept of cooking/eating/talking are the gold nuggets that inspire her work.

RACHEL KRAMER BUSSEL (www.rachelkramerbussel.com) is senior editor at *Penthouse Variations* and a contributing editor at *Penthouse*, where she writes the Girl Talk column. She writes the Lusty Lady column for *The Village Voice* and conducts interviews for Gothamist. com and Mediabistro.com. She's the co-editor of Lambda Literary

Award nominee *Up All Night: Adventures in Lesbian Sex*, and editor of *Glamour Girls: Femme/Femme Erotica, First-Timers: True Stories of Lesbian Sex*, and *Naughty Spanking Stories from A to Z* 1 and 2. Her erotica has been published in over 70 anthologies, including *Best American Erotica 2004* and *2006*, and *Best Lesbian Erotica 2001*, 2004 and *2005*, and she has written for *Bust, Curve, Diva, Gay City News, Girlfriends, New York Blade, The New York Post, On Our Backs, Punk Planet, The San Francisco Chronicle, Time Out New York, Velvetpark*, and other publications.

JC CHEN is a film and television writer-producer based in New York City. Her first feature film—the award-winning indie *Red Doors*—appeared in theaters and on DVD in Spring/Summer 2006. More information can be found at www.reddoorsthemovie.com.

CRIN CLAXTON (www.crinclaxton.com) writes novels, short stories, and the occasional poem. Her first novel, *Scarlet Thirst*, was published by Red Hot Diva Books. She has had short stories published in *Girls Next Door* (Women's Press) and *Va Va Voom* (Diva Books), and in *Diva* and *Curve* magazines. Her poetry has appeared in *Naming the Waves, La Pluma*, and *A Class of Their Own*.

FIONA COOPER has published a short story collection, *I Believe in Angels*, and nine novels including *Rotary Spokes, Jay Loves Lucy, The Empress of the Seven Oceans*, and most recently, *As You Desire Me*. She works as a medium, soul regression therapist, and psychic artist and runs workshops as well as doing various one-woman shows.

CHERI CRYSTAL lives and loves in New York where she enjoys reading, writing, dancing, long walks, water sports, and sex. Her profession is as a consultant dietitian but her passion is raising her family and writing erotica. Cheri loves chatting and can be contacted at cherilynn@optonline.net.

AMIE M. EVANS is a creative nonfiction and literary erotica writer, experienced workshop provider, and a burlesque and high-femme drag performer. She graduated *magna cum laude* from the University of Pittsburgh with a BA in literature and is currently working on her

MLA at Harvard. Her works have appeared in the 2005 Lambda Literary Award–winning anthology *I Do/I Don't: Queers on Marriage*; *Best of The Best of Lesbian Erotica*; *Harrington Lesbian Fiction Quarterly*; *Call of the Dark*; *Rode Hard and Put Away Wet*; *Ultimate Lesbian Erotica 2006*, and *Show and Tell*. She also writes gay male erotica under a pen name. Evans firmly believes queer liberation cannot happen through mainstreaming that demands the fringe elements of our community be isolated and marginalized and that sacrificing our queer sexuality in order to achieve a false sense of equality is not a valid option.

EVECHO enjoys erotica—reading it, writing it, and playing with it—because it's a great way to excite readers (and herself) while celebrating lesbian sexuality in all its forms. She currently resides in Sydney, NSW, Australia, with her partner. Her other works can be found at www.thesandbox101.com.

LISA FIGUEROA is a Chicana writer from the Los Angeles area who received an MA in English/creative writing in 2001 from CSUN. Her writing has appeared in *Lesbian News* and *Harrington Lesbian Fiction Quarterly*, with an upcoming story this year in *Sinister Wisdom*.

LYNNE JAMNECK is the author of the Samantha Skellar Mystery series as well as several decidedly naughty stories featured in a host of anthologies. Her fiction has also been featured in speculative markets such as *H.P. Lovecraft's Magazine of Horror* and *Lullaby Hearse*. A red-blooded South African, Lynne currently lives in New Zealand with her partner Heidi and the prerequisite cat and dog. Check for updates on Lynne's blog: http://publishedwork1lynne.blogspot.com/

LC JORDAN is a thirty-eight-year-old Midwestern woman with a lifelong passion for reading. Recently LC began penning the stories that kept floating just below the surface of her mind. The search for that perfect alchemy of words is still in the Bunsen-burner stage.

KARIN KALLMAKER is best known for more than twenty lesbian romance novels, from *In Every Port* to the award-winning *Sugar*.

She recently plunged into the world of erotica with *All the Wrong Places* and numerous short stories. In addition, she has a half dozen science fiction, fantasy, and supernatural lesbian novels (e.g. *Seeds of Fire*, *Christabel*) under the pen name Laura Adams. Karin and her partner will celebrate their twenty-ninth anniversary in 2006, and are Mom and Moogie to two children. She is descended from Lady Godiva, a fact that pleases her and seems to surprise no one.

ANDREA MILLER has selections in both internet and print anthologies including *Lipstick on Her Collar and Other Tales of Lesbian Lust*, *Best Women's Erotica 2005*, *Velvet Heat*, *Hot and Bothered 4: Short Short Fiction on Lesbian Desire*, and three editions of the Best Lesbian Erotica series.

NYRDGYRL has lived in the Rockies with her lovely for the past nineteen years. For eighteen of those years she has worked in emergency services as a firefighter. This is her first published work.

MEGHAN O'BRIEN is a twenty-seven-year-old software developer newly transplanted to Northern California. Her novels include *Infinite Loop* and *The Three*. Visit her website at http://www.meghanobrien.com and her Yahoo group at http://groups.yahoo.com/group/meghanobrien.

KAREN L. PERRY is an avid reader of lesbian romance novels. After rereading her library many, many times, she decided to take a shot at writing her own. Her first full-length manuscript is in the hands of a publisher, awaiting the final word. She can be reached by email at Karen_L_Perry@yahoo.com.

VK POWELL, a thirty-year veteran of a midsized police department in North Carolina, was a police officer by necessity (it paid the bills) and a writer by desire (it didn't). Her career spanned numerous positions including beat officer, homicide detective, vice/narcotics lieutenant and assistant chief of police. Now she devotes her time to writing, rewriting, more rewriting, traveling and volunteer work.

RADCLYFFE is the author of over twenty lesbian romances, the Erotic Interlude series (*Change of Pace*, *Stolen Moments*, and *Lessons in Love* ed. with Stacia Seaman) and selections in multiple anthologies including *Call of the Dark* and *The Perfect Valentine* (Bella Books), *Best Lesbian Erotica 2006* and *After Midnight* (Cleis), *First-Timers and Ultimate Undies: Erotic Stories About Lingerie and Underwear* (Alyson), and *Naughty Spanking Stories 2* (Pretty Things Press). She is the recipient of the 2003 and 2004 Alice B. Readers' award, a 2005 Golden Crown Literary Society Award winner in both the romance category (*Fated Love*) and the mystery/intrigue/action category (*Justice in the Shadows*), and a 2006 Lammy finalist in the romance (*Distant Shores, Silent Thunder*), mystery (*Justice Served*), and erotica categories (*Erotic Interludes 2: Stolen Moments* ed. with Stacia Seaman). Her latest novels include *Turn Back Time* and *Promising Hearts* (2006). She is also the president of Bold Strokes Books, a lesbian publishing company.

CYNTHIA RAYNE has been telling stories as long as she can remember. She won an honorable mention in Desdmona's Shivering Short Story Contest (www.desdmona.com). Her story, "Incubus," was published in *Who's Your Daddy?*, an anthology of alpha male stories. Her work can also be seen at www.kinkygurl.com.

REMITTANCE GIRL lives in Ho Chi Minh City, Vietnam, where she worships orchids and writes things. Her stories have appeared in *Garden of the Perverse: Twisted Fairy Tales for Adults* and on the ERWA website.

ROUGE lives in Florida where she writes mystery novels, masquerading by day as an IT consultant. During the summer when the women wear very little, it is difficult to focus on mysteries when so much has already been revealed, hence, the erotic diversion.

NELL STARK lives in Madison, WI, with her partner and two cats. When not writing or working as a graduate student of medieval English literature, she enjoys reading, sailing, soccer, cooking, and beating everyone she knows at Dance Dance Revolution. She thanks her partner for her continued love, support, and superb editing skills, and her beta-reader Ruta for her wonderful comments and encouragement.

RENÉE STRIDER lives with her partner and dog on the shores of an inland sea in Canada. Being anywhere near it, whether in a boat or sitting on a rock beside it, makes her happy. So does writing lesbian short stories, one of which was published in BSB's previous erotica anthology.

THERESE SZYMANSKI is an award-winning playwright who uses copywriting and designing to keep herself apartmented. She's the Lammy finalist author of the Brett Higgins Motor City Thrillers (seven of them), editor of *Back to Basics: A Butch/Femme Anthology*, *Call of the Dark: Erotic Lesbian Tales of the Supernatural*, and *A Perfect Valentine: Erotic Valentine's Day Lesbian Love Stories*; part of the four-person team that created *Once Upon a Dyke: New Exploits of Fairy Tale Lesbians* and *Bell, Book and Dyke: New Exploits of Magical Lesbians*, and contributor to a few dozen anthologies. You can e-mail Reese at tsszymanski@worldnet.att.net.

KI THOMPSON has learned so much in so little time. Thank you Rad for your lessons in writing, and thanks to Kathi, as always.

EVA VANDETUIN is a religious studies graduate student. She sees sex and spirituality as being closely intertwined, and the relationship between the two inspires much of her fiction. You can find more of her work in the web archives of Clean Sheets and KinkyGurl.com.

SASKIA WALKER (www.saskiawalker.co.uk) is a British author who lives on the wild, windswept Yorkshire moors, where inspiration is everywhere. Her work appears in *Best Women's Erotica 2006*, *The Mammoth Book of Best New Erotica Volume 5*, *Naughty Stories from A to Z*, 3 and 4, and *Stirring up a Storm*.

Books Available From Bold Strokes Books

Whitewater Rendezvous by Kim Baldwin. Two women on a wilderness kayak adventure—Chaz Herrick, a laid-back outdoorswoman, and Megan Maxwell, a workaholic news executive—discover that true love may be nothing at all like they imagined. (1-933110-38-4)

Erotic Interludes 3: Lessons in Love ed. by Radclyffe and Stacia Seaman. Sign on for a class in love…the best lesbian erotica writers take us to "school." (1-9331100-39-2)

Punk Like Me by JD Glass. Twenty-one-year-old Nina writes lyrics and plays guitar in the rock band Adam's Rib, and she doesn't always play by the rules. And oh yeah—she has a way with the girls. (1-933110-40-6)

Coffee Sonata by Gun Brooke. Four women whose lives unexpectedly intersect in a small town by the sea share one thing in common—they all have secrets. (1-933110-41-4)

The Clinic: Tristaine Book One by Cate Culpepper. Brenna, a prison medic, finds herself deeply conflicted by her growing feelings for her patient, Jesstin, a wild and rebellious warrior reputed to be descended from ancient Amazons. (1-933110-42-2)

Forever Found by JLee Meyer. Can time, tragedy, and shattered trust destroy a love that seemed destined? When chance reunites two childhood friends separated by tragedy, the past resurfaces to determine the shape of their future. (1-933110-37-6)

Sword of the Guardian by Merry Shannon. Princess Shasta's bold new bodyguard has a secret that could change both of their lives. *He* is actually a *she*. A passionate romance filled with courtly intrigue, chivalry, and devotion. (1-933110-36-8)

Wild Abandon by Ronica Black. From their first tumultuous meeting, Dr. Chandler Brogan and Officer Sarah Monroe are drawn together by their common obsessions—sex, speed, and danger. (1-933110-35-X)

Turn Back Time by Radclyffe. Pearce Rifkin and Wynter Thompson have nothing in common but a shared passion for surgery. They clash at every opportunity, especially when matters of the heart are suddenly at stake. (1-933110-34-1)

Chance by Grace Lennox. At twenty-six, Chance Delaney decides her life isn't working so she swaps it for a different one. What follows is the sexy, funny, touching story of two women who, in finding themselves, also find one another. (1-933110-31-7)

The Exile and the Sorcerer by Jane Fletcher. First in the Lyremouth Chronicles. Tevi, wounded and adrift, arrives in the courtyard of a shy young sorcerer. Together they face monsters, magic, and the challenge of loving despite their differences. (1-933110-32-5)

A Matter of Trust by Radclyffe. JT Sloan is a cybersleuth who doesn't like attachments. Michael Lassiter is leaving her husband, and she needs Sloan's expertise to safeguard her company. It should just be business—but it turns into much more. (1-933110-33-3)

Sweet Creek by Lee Lynch. A celebration of the enduring nature of love, friendship, and community in the quirky, heart-warming lesbian community of Waterfall Falls. (1-933110-29-5)

The Devil Inside by Ali Vali. Derby Cain Casey, head of a New Orleans crime organization, runs the family business with guts and grit, and no one crosses her. No one, that is, until Emma Verde claims her heart and turns her world upside down. (1-933110-30-9)

Grave Silence by Rose Beecham. Detective Jude Devine's investigation of a series of ritual murders is complicated by her torrid affair with the golden girl of Southwestern forensic pathology, Dr. Mercy Westmoreland. (1-933110-25-2)

Honor Reclaimed by Radclyffe. In the aftermath of 9/11, Secret Service Agent Cameron Roberts and Blair Powell close ranks with a trusted few to find the would-be assassins who nearly claimed Blair's life. (1-933110-18-X)

Honor Bound by Radclyffe. Secret Service Agent Cameron Roberts and Blair Powell face political intrigue, a clandestine threat to Blair's safety, and the seemingly irreconcilable personal differences that force them ever farther apart. (1-933110-20-1)

Protector of the Realm: Supreme Constellations Book One by Gun Brooke. A space adventure filled with suspense and a daring intergalactic romance featuring Commodore Rae Jacelon and the stunning, but decidedly lethal, Kellen O'Dal. (1-933110-26-0)

Innocent Hearts by Radclyffe. In a wild and unforgiving land, two women learn about love, passion, and the wonders of the heart. (1-933110-21-X)

The Temple at Landfall by Jane Fletcher. An imprinter, one of Celaeno's most revered servants of the Goddess, is also a prisoner to the faith—until a Ranger frees her by claiming her heart. The Celaeno series. (1-933110-27-9)

Force of Nature by Kim Baldwin. From tornados to forest fires, the forces of nature conspire to bring Gable McCoy and Erin Richardsclose to danger, and closer to each other. (1-933110-23-6)

In Too Deep by Ronica Black. Undercover homicide cop Erin McKenzie tracks a femme fatale who just might be a real killer…with love and danger hot on her heels. (1-933110-17-1)

Course of Action by Gun Brooke. Actress Carolyn Black desperately wants the starring role in an upcoming film produced by Annelie Peterson. Just how far will she go for the dream part of a lifetime? (1-933110-22-8)

Rangers at Roadsend by Jane Fletcher. Sergeant Chip Coppelli has learned to spot trouble coming, and that is exactly what she sees in her new recruit, Katryn Nagata. The Celaeno series. (1-933110-28-7)

Justice Served by Radclyffe. Lieutenant Rebecca Frye and her lover, Dr. Catherine Rawlings, embark on a deadly game of hide-and-seek with an underworld kingpin who traffics in human souls. (1-933110-15-5)

Distant Shores, Silent Thunder by Radclyffe. Dr. Tory King—along with the women who love her—is forced to examine the boundaries of love, friendship, and the ties that transcend time. (1-933110-08-2)

Hunter's Pursuit by Kim Baldwin. A raging blizzard, a mountain hideaway, and a killer-for-hire set a scene for disaster—or desire—when Katarzyna Demetrious rescues a beautiful stranger. (1-933110-09-0)

The Walls of Westernfort by Jane Fletcher. All Temple Guard Natasha Ionadis wants is to serve the Goddess—until she falls in love with one of the rebels she is sworn to destroy. The Celaeno series. (1-933110-24-4)

Change Of Pace: *Erotic Interludes* by Radclyffe. Twenty-five hot-wired encounters guaranteed to spark more than just your imagination. Erotica as you've always dreamed of it. (1-933110-07-4)

Honor Guards by Radclyffe. In a wild flight for their lives, the president's daughter and those who are sworn to protect her wage a desperate struggle for survival. (1-933110-01-5)

Fated Love by Radclyffe. Amidst the chaos and drama of a busy emergency room, two women must contend not only with the fragile nature of life, but also with the irresistible forces of fate. (1-933110-05-8)

Justice in the Shadows by Radclyffe. In a shadow world of secrets and lies, Detective Sergeant Rebecca Frye and her lover, Dr. Catherine Rawlings, join forces in the elusive search for justice. (1-933110-03-1)

shadowland by Radclyffe. In a world on the far edge of desire, two women are drawn together by power, passion, and dark pleasures. An erotic romance. (1-933110-11-2)

Love's Masquerade by Radclyffe. Plunged into the indistinguishable realms of fiction, fantasy, and hidden desires, Auden Frost is forced to question all she believes about the nature of love. (1-933110-14-7)

Love & Honor by Radclyffe. The president's daughter and her lover are faced with difficult choices as they battle a tangled web of Washington intrigue for...love and honor. (1-933110-10-4)

Beyond the Breakwater by Radclyffe. One Provincetown summer, three women learn the true meaning of love, friendship, and family. (1-933110-06-6)

Tomorrow's Promise by Radclyffe. One timeless summer, two very different women discover the power of passion to heal and the promise of hope that only love can bestow. (1-933110-12-0)

Love's Tender Warriors by Radclyffe. Two women who have accepted loneliness as a way of life learn that love is worth fighting for and a battle they cannot afford to lose. (1-933110-02-3)

Love's Melody Lost by Radclyffe. A secretive artist with a haunted past and a young woman escaping a life that has proved to be a lie find their destinies entwined. (1-933110-00-7)

Safe Harbor by Radclyffe. A mysterious newcomer, a reclusive doctor, and a troubled gay teenager learn about love, friendship, and trust during one tumultuous summer in Provincetown. (1-933110-13-9)

Above All, Honor by Radclyffe. Secret Service Agent Cameron Roberts fights her desire for the one woman she can't have—Blair Powell, the daughter of the president of the United States. (1-933110-04-X)